Even hot messes need a h

With the quiet help ⟨
"Baz" Acker has successfully kept his painful past at
bay. But as the end of college draws near, his friends—
his buffer zone—are preparing to move on, while his
own life is at a crippling standstill. With loneliness
bearing down on him, Baz hooks up—then opens up—
with Elijah Prince, the guy Baz took a bullet for last
year. The aftershocks of their one-night stand leave
giant cracks in Baz's carefully constructed armor. For
the first time, the prospect isn't terrifying.

Accustomed to escaping his demons by withdrawing into his imagination, Elijah isn't used to having a
happy herd of friends. He's even less comfortable as the
object of a notorious playboy's affections. Yet all signs
seem to indicate this time happiness might be within
his grasp. When Baz's mother runs for a highly sought-
after public office, the media hounds drag Baz's and
Elijah's pasts into the light. In the blinding glare, Baz
and Elijah face the ultimate test: discovering if they're
stronger together...or apart.

Heidi Cullinan, POB 425, Ames, Iowa 50010

Copyright © 2017 by Heidi Cullinan
Print ISBN: 978-1-945116-06-3
Print Edition
Edited by Sasha Knight
Cover by Kanaxa
Proofing by Lillie's Literary Services
Formatting by BB eBooks

First publication 2015
Second publication 2017
www.heidicullinan.com

Lonely Hearts

Heidi Cullinan

For K.A. Mitchell.

Acknowledgments

Many thanks to Elizabeth Perry for alpha reading and letting me bleed off some production nerves during the initial draft, Damon Suede for helping me clean myself up, Sasha Knight for being my favorite editor in the entire universe, Kanaxa for the amazing covers, Dan Cullinan for doing all the dishes, laundry, and general cleanup, Anna for eating weird things out of cans instead of actual meals while I holed up in my office, and Pastor Larry Trachte for being the best campus pastor there ever was. Thanks also to Sandy C for some excellent eagle-eye notes, and as always huge, huge love to Lillie for combing through this series on the second edition and helping me make it a bit smoother all around. I am Lillie for *life*.

Thanks as always and especially to my patrons, especially Rosie Moewe, Pamela Bartual, Erin Sharpe, Tiffany Miller, Sarah Plunkett, Sarah M, Sandy C, Chris Klaene, and Marie. I couldn't drive the Tesla without you.

I think we ought to live happily ever after.
—Howl in *Howl's Moving Castle*

Chapter One

AS FAR AS Elijah Prince was concerned, gay weddings could choke on their own cheery goddamned glitter and die.

He sat alone in the back of the overflowing reception hall, framed by floral, ribbon, and balloon garlands aesthetically balanced on the head of the most fabulous of pins. The decor came courtesy of the high-priced wedding planner one of the grooms, Walter, had imported from his native Chicago, because only the best would be procured for his darling Kelly. The chairs and tables, decorated with runners of Italian silk, were Disney-movie themed, because Kelly ate, breathed, and farted Disney.

The grooms had arrived at the reception via a fucking *horse-drawn carriage.* The wedding party's table was bedecked in *Tangled* colors and paraphernalia: little-girl purple and Rapunzel-hair gold weaving between toy figurines and play sets. The space for parents and immediate family sported colors and action figures from *Beauty and the Beast,* a sea of bright blue and a gold which *should* have clashed with the Rapunzel yellow yet somehow didn't.

Elijah was at one of the sections reserved for the

choirs and orchestra. His table's theme was light blue and white, for *Frozen*. It made him want to gag. He was the only social orphan at the music table, possibly at the entire wedding. Giles Mulder, Aaron Seavers, and Mina Stevenson were at the table legitimately. Giles and Mina were in the Saint Timothy orchestra, Aaron choir, and they all three had roles in one form or another in the all-male and all-female a cappella groups from their college.

Aaron had already broken ranks, leaving the wedding party to snuggle at the music table with Giles, but though Elijah attended Saint Timothy too, he was in zero musical groups. No doubt someone, probably Aaron, had pleaded with Walter and Kelly on Elijah's behalf to give him an exemption to sit with the musical people.

It didn't matter how bitter and nasty Elijah was. Giles and Aaron had decided to adopt him, and apparently they intended to never leave him behind. Elijah often loathed the level of their intrusion, except when he was weak enough to admit it was sometimes the only thing keeping him going.

"What are your plans for this summer, Elijah?" Mina asked this as Aaron made his Anna figure flirt with Giles's Kristoff. When Giles had Kristoff respond with bald innuendo, Mina laughed and launched a handful of table confetti at them so it appeared to come from her Elsa doll.

Elijah nudged his plate hard enough to knock his Sven figure onto its side as he slumped deeper into his seat. "Pastor Schulz got me a job at the cafeteria. Doing dishes and taking out the garbage." He felt bad about the note of complaint and cleared his throat. "I'm glad to have it."

"You're still moving into the White House with us this fall, right?"

Elijah nodded without enthusiasm. The White House was the old mansion north of the music building that traditionally provided off-campus housing for music students. Aaron and Giles would be there, as would Mina and her friend Jilly. Elijah was slated to room with Giles's old roommate, Brian, who with Elijah would be the other non-music person. It was all tidily arranged.

Except everyone else would be paying rent, whereas Elijah's portion would be paid out of the pity fund Walter Davidson, née Lucas, had set up for Elijah because he was now officially without parental support. The money in the trust would cover his tuition and any books and supplies his summer job wouldn't.

A familiar chuckle sent a shiver down Elijah's spine, and he let his gaze slip to the tall, smiling young man wearing sunglasses at the other end of their table. Baz Acker would be at the White House too.

Mina caught Elijah's hand discreetly under the table and squeezed. "Let people care for you, okay? You're owed a little kickback from the game of life."

"It feels weird." Elijah buried his Sven figure deeper under his plate and cast a caustic glare Aaron's direction, waiting for him to point out Elijah used to hate how no one would help him.

Aaron fixed his gaze on his plate, his pretty-boy expression taking on shadows. "I know. But it gets easier, I promise."

It should have comforted him, this reminder that yes, Aaron did understand. He'd been a stalwart protector of Elijah since he found out they both had remix variations on shit-tastic parents. But as usual, Elijah exhibited an allergic reaction to kindness. "Maybe I should find an even sorrier sap than me to coach through his hell, since it worked so well for you."

Giles glared at Elijah and punched him in the arm.

"You're going to be fine. It hasn't been long since...everything." Mina put a hand in the center of Elijah's back. "Give yourself space to find your feet. Take comfort in people removing some of your concerns."

"I've helped myself since I was in middle school. I don't like this attention, the owing people."

This comment turned the gentle massage at his back into a pointed nudge. "When you were helping yourself in middle and high school, your parents hadn't attempted to gun you down in the middle of a college campus."

"Yeah, well, they did plenty of shit almost as bad before, but nobody saw."

"I think it's why we want to help you. We know you faced worse, and it upsets us."

"Yes, but these people donating to the damn trust fund don't know me. They only feel sorry for me." Given the burgeoning tally of how much *poor Elijah* money Walter had collected, a whole lot of people felt sorry for him. It weirded him the fuck out.

"They won't feel sorry for you if they talk to you for more than five minutes," Giles drawled. This time Aaron punched *him* in the arm.

Mina ignored them both and kept soothing Elijah. "Maybe some feel sorry. But anyone there that day, any of our parents and families—we understand exactly what kind of hell you were living with. We want to take some of it away from you."

You can't erase hell with a check. Before Elijah could figure out a less caustic way to phrase that, Walter's friend Cara stood up to make a toast, and the conversation came to a blissful end.

The first attendant's speech was cute, but a little too much so. When it ended with someone clinking a spoon against a wineglass, inspiring the grooms to kiss, Elijah slipped a flask of cheap whiskey out of his suit coat pocket and took a heavy pull. When everyone whooped and catcalled because Walter pulled Kelly across his lap and kissed him deeper, Elijah emptied the flask some more.

"Go for the tonsils, Lucas," Baz Acker called.

Elijah tipped his head all the way back, fully intending to drown himself in blissful, drunken oblivion, but before he could, Giles leaned across the table and swiped the flask from Elijah's hand.

"Hey." Elijah glared and tried to retrieve his alcohol.

Giles moved it out of reach. "You're sleeping in the same room as me, and I'm not spending the night listening to you retch into the toilet." He tucked the flask into his jacket pocket and passed over a bottle of water. "Salvo is going up to sing. Mina will want you to watch."

Elijah pasted on a polite expression as Salvo assumed their position on the stage. Though Elijah still didn't want to be here, Giles was right about Mina, and he kept his grouchiness to himself.

They performed an a cappella version of "Something That I Want", which Elijah knew from watching the girls rehearse was a song that played over the credits of *Tangled,* Kelly Davidson's favorite movie of all time. The song was cheesy and this Disney movie shit was totally fucking OTT, but Mina sang wicked lead, and Elijah tapped his toe despite himself. Kelly got up and danced with them, sort of singing but mostly vacillating between blushing and flirting outrageously with his groom, who sat on a chair in front of the stage and ate up the performance with a spoon.

As the song concluded and the audience clapped, Salvo retreated to the wings, and the Ambassadors got up from the table to take their place.

Saying the Ambassadors were hot was like saying water was wet. Each member was either out-and-out gorgeous or exuding so much raw character their rougher mugs only added to their draw. They smelled good as well—this close up, one good deep breath filled Elijah's sinuses with enough man sweat to give him a semi. Aaron was in the Ambassadors, and while he wasn't Elijah's type, he wasn't painful to look at, especially when he was lost in the joy of a song. In the same way Kelly had joined Salvo for their number, Walter became an honorary Ambassador, and his winks and smiles poked through Elijah's natural crankiness and cranked up his libido. Walter was Exhibit A of gay-boy crack: flirty, charming, sexy. It was no accident Walter was the one singing about being a heartbreaker tearing girls apart. *Anyone* with a pulse would go home with Walter.

There was another Ambassador Elijah couldn't stop watching, though while he was even more handsome than Walter, he also came with an overwhelming sense of guilt and shame. Intellectually Elijah knew the limp and occasional hitch as Sebastian Acker danced was from the hush-hush accident in high school that had severely eclipsed his vision and graced him with a partially titanium skeleton. Yet there was no question the harrowing events of the nightmare afternoon with Elijah's parents only a few short months ago had done anything but aggravate those ancient wounds.

How did you say *I'm sorry* when your dad shoots someone in the shoulder? When someone takes a bullet so you and others around you don't have to? What did it mean when said hero had already saved you once before—but then, as now, never had so much as a casual smile for you in the aftermath?

Baz smiled tonight—a dark, delicious leer pulling at Elijah's gut.

Elijah endured the performance in sullen and sadly sober silence. Beside him Giles whooped and applauded when Aaron sang solo. When Walter descended into his adoring audience during the final chorus and the Ambassadors urged everyone to close in on the groom, Giles rose, laughing, to join them.

Unfortunately, at the last second he also grabbed Elijah's hand.

"No." Elijah clamped a hand on his chair to keep himself from being dragged off to the gulag.

Giles tugged Elijah to his feet. "Yes. It's a fucking wedding. You can resume being a caustic asshole tomorrow, but today is Walter and Kelly's happily ever after, and today you're going to dance."

Elijah wanted to argue, to wrestle out of Giles's hold and describe the full detail of how he wasn't dancing at a wedding, *ever*, but Giles was stronger than he seemed for a scrawny geek with big ears. And Elijah might be a caustic asshole, but no, he couldn't make a scene. Not today, not with these people.

It was hell. The whole day had been acid down his back, but this dance, this moment, surrounded by the great music nerd herd, Baz less than six feet away from him as he flirted with Walter and Kelly's friends—this was dancing on knives. Everyone smiling. Everyone happy. Everyone laughing, connected, joyously united for those they loved.

Everyone but Elijah.

He moved woodenly, trying not to stand out. Trying not to look like the short, skinny freak he was. Mina drew him into a circle with her and Jilly. When the song was over, Mina squeezed his hand. He stiffened, thinking she'd haul him off for yet another fucking heart-to-heart/pep talk, but she let him go and went to the stage. There must be another Salvo-Ambassadors number.

Whatever. Elijah wasn't staying for it. He'd done

his time. He'd danced and faked merry. Now he needed to find somewhere to hide until this was over, do his best to forget it ever happened. Retreating to his chair, he scooped up his jacket, made sure his cigarettes were still there, then dug inside Giles's suit coat for his flask.

He'd closed his fingers around it when the music started up. Soft, lyrical strings caught the edge of his heart. Glancing up, he saw Giles, Mina, and a few other orchestra people playing at the edge of the stage. In the center, Aaron and Walter's friend Rose stood at the mic as Salvo and the Ambassadors fanned out around the room.

On the dance floor, Walter and Kelly stood alone, poised and ready to dance.

The song was "I See the Light", another *Tangled* number. Aaron sang the male part of the duet, and Walter's friend Rose did a less-than-Mina soprano, but mostly the music fell away in the brilliant presence of the two young men on the dance floor. Walter glided with suave grace, and Kelly followed with an untutored gait as charming as Walter's practiced moves. Around and around the floor they spun, the soft lighting mimicking the lanterns from the song's source scene in *Tangled*, the whimsically elegant atmosphere amplifying the moment until it resonated like a string.

It shafted Elijah through the heart.

The flask fell from Elijah's hand, as did his jacket. Hypnotized, he watched the two men dance, the song cracking open the rough leather casing he'd wrapped around himself.

Perfection. Happy ending. Walter and Kelly Davidson would end up in a fucking suburb. They'd adopt, or have a surrogate for their kids. Same went for Aaron and Giles—oh, Elijah had seen their faces. They wouldn't go quite this fucking Disney, but they'd be just as goddamned cute. Probably do some big song-and-dance number for the proposal too. They'd have the singers strung out around the perimeter same as this. They'd have an equally exquisite moment for the ceremony itself, one defining and celebrating the two of them. They'd have each other forever, and their union would be witnessed by a thousand friends.

The song ended, and everyone clapped, many also wiping away a tear. Elijah bent to retrieve his things, but his hand trembled, and when he dropped the flask a second time, it skittered away from him into the crowd. He thought about leaving it, but only for a second. He may not get a happily ever after, but he damn well was having his fucking whiskey.

This time when he picked it up, he gripped it tight, clutching it to his chest as he rose. He stood on the edge of the dance floor, which was filling up with the wedding party as the orchestra-chorus began "You've Got a Friend in Me".

Elijah glanced around desperately for an exit. He found one, but not before his gaze once more grazed Baz, and weakened by the hole in his armor, Elijah let his gaze linger as the truth seeped into his heart.

I'm never going to have this. Not this kind of family. Not these kinds of friends. Not with an Aaron or Kelly or Walter or Baz or anyone. No one's ever going to love me this way. I wouldn't know what to do with it, even if they did.

He let himself have one moment of wallowing in misery, and then he packed the pain away, back into the dark corner it had lived in since as early as he could remember. He ducked through the beaming, swaying guests and escaped out the side door, safe in the knowledge nobody was going to miss a scrawny, scowling loser, knowing while he wasn't ever going to get a happily ever after, he could still find a way to get high.

AS THE WEDDING guests applauded, Sebastian Acker tracked Elijah's exit behind the darkened panels of his glasses. That last, naked glance ghosted on his conscience the same way everything about Elijah did. Leaning over to Marius, Baz spoke quietly in his best friend's ear. "Gonna nip outside."

Marius frowned and nodded at Damien, the third leg of their dynamic trio, who was also the Ambassadors' student director. "Don't be long. He said something about doing last call, in case people go to the hotel early."

Last call. The comment sent a jolt of sorrow through Baz, which he did his best to smother from Marius's notice. "Right. I'll keep it quick."

"If you miss it because you were getting high in the Tesla, I'll never forgive you."

"I'll be there."

With a squeeze of Marius's shoulder, Baz wove his

way through the crowd, winking and flirting in an attempt to hide his discomfort. When Baz slipped around the corner of the building, he found Elijah a polite distance away from an amicable group of middle-aged smokers. His shoulders hunched as he sucked on a cancer stick between swigs of alcohol.

Safe and sound.

Reminding himself Elijah was out of the woods, Baz returned to the reception. Howard Prince was in jail, and there was no way he could shoot an Acker and do anything but stay there. Except no matter how Baz reassured himself, the urge to shadow Elijah, to protect him, hadn't faded away after the shooting.

For now, however, Baz had an entirely different dragon to slay.

As Baz returned to the reception, Damien nodded toward the rest of the upperclassmen Ambassadors leaving the banquet hall. "We're going downstairs. Marius found a room we could use, where we can have some privacy. I have everybody but Aaron. You mind fetching him?"

Baz spread his fake smile as wide as it could go. "Not at all."

He was glad for his sunglasses as he approached his friend, who was chatting with Giles and two Salvo members near one of the speakers. When Baz smiled, nobody knew the gesture didn't make it all the way to his eyes.

"Ambassador, you have one final performance of the year." He ruffled Aaron's hair. "Let's go."

Aaron followed Baz out of the room. "Is something

wrong? You look upset."

"Nothing's wrong. Nothing I didn't know was coming, anyway."

"But what—?"

"You learned the Pink Floyd song, right? The one Damien handed out before the graduation ceremony?"

Through the heavy tint of his sunglasses, Baz saw Aaron blink. "Yes, but what—Oh."

Yeah. *Oh.*

The Ambassadors had been Baz's lifeline since he joined as a freshman. They hadn't given a shit he was gay—some, of course, were happy to hear it and had shown him a good time. They didn't care about his senator uncle and crazy political family except to crack a few jokes about where was his Secret Service. They did care about his grim high school history and the reason for his disabilities, but they loved him enough not to bring it up, to help him move away from the past.

The Ambassadors were everything to Baz. But once a year, they had to have this moment, when the graduating seniors sang their last song. This year the remainder of Baz's first-year class would say goodbye—not Baz, because he'd put off reality as long as possible. He'd had an extra year to avoid the inevitable because anyone in music therapy or other five-year program was still with him, but that year was up. He couldn't make time stand still completely.

He couldn't keep *his* Ambassadors around forever.

They wove their way through the crush toward the basement of the marina, passing silent rooms, a small kitchen, a storage area. In the distance, Baz heard the other Ambassadors speaking in hushed voices.

In the center of the room, Damien cleared his throat. "It's been a hell of a year. We got six new amazing members. We gained a sister choir—and don't think for a minute they're not gonna kick your asses in any tournaments you enter together." He squeezed Baz's hand tight. "We had our scares. Our challenges. But we made it through. Every man here is a hero. A brother." He let out a shuddering breath and lowered Baz's hand. "I'm gonna miss each one of you like a fucking arm."

Baz told the tears to fuck off. "You've got a lot of arms, man."

Damien swung Baz's hand, lifting it, a quiet acknowledgment. "Yeah. I do." He pulled out a pitch pipe, blew the note and counted them in.

For the fifth time in his life, Baz sang the graduating Ambassador brothers goodbye.

The group had been singing "Goodbye Cruel World" at their final concert since the early eighties, when pulling a Floyd was current. The arrangement was pretty pedestrian, but it never altered. Maybe the original composers could have done better, but this wasn't a moment for flash. This was sending graduating members home.

Baz didn't let himself dwell on that, not during the song. He pushed Damien up under his solo. He felt Marius beneath him, rumbling the basement floor of the bass section with a resonance no one would ever be able to replicate. Baz swelled with his brothers, with

Aaron and Sid and all sixteen of the Ambassadors. He belted the last chorus with his whole soul, his heart. The final note hovered in the air, held until the last Ambassador ran out of breath. They kept still another four beats after, suspending the moment as long as they could.

Then it was over.

They embraced. They man-patted, they wept, they whispered promises to stay in touch, vows they all knew would be more difficult to keep with each passing day, until they were the old Ambassadors lingering alone in the homecoming crowd, grasping for their ghost of this moment, this time. Aaron and the other first-years had the same stunned look of horrible realization they all did when they were the newbs—comprehension that this was only the first goodbye, and someday it would be them singing their last note.

If Baz could have gotten his shit together, this would have been *his* last call. Someday it would have to be. But the panic this thought instilled in him made his paranoia about Elijah's safety seem a moderate worry in comparison, so he boxed the fear in the mental cell it had crawled out of.

Baz deliberately left embracing Damien and Marius for last. He flirted with Aaron, teasing him about how he'd have to be Baz's choir wingman now. He baited Sid about being the old man in the White House with him. He put off approaching his best friends as absolutely long as he could, but at last they found him, and the bastards hugged him together.

"This isn't goodbye." Damien's voice was gruff.

"We're only moving into the Cities, and I'll be in town a lot until Stevie graduates in December."

Marius's cheeks were already salt-streaked as he spoke in his calm, steady voice, so sexy he could seduce a nun. "I'm not moving out of the White House until the end of the month. And as Damien said, I'm not moving far."

Baz shut his eyes tight. "I know." But Marius would be in med school. How much time for hanging out would he realistically have?

Marius removed Baz's glasses, bringing an uncomfortable wave of brightness that threatened a headache, but Marius had already pulled Baz in low, blocking out the light with his hands. "I'm not leaving you alone. I don't give a fuck how you try and shut me out, you can't. You're my brother, and I've got your back. Damien and I both do. Always."

Marius's and Damien's vows couldn't soothe Baz's soul. They said they weren't leaving, but they were. They were starting their real lives, ones where the three of them didn't share a living room and a daily schedule. Damien was getting married. Marius would be right behind him as soon as a girl hooked him in the mouth. People moved on. Everyone did, eventually.

Everyone but Baz.

Damien clutched Baz's head, kissed him on the cheek, sighed. "Enough. This *isn't* goodbye, and we have a wedding to dance at. And one of us has to stay sober enough to drive to the hotel."

"Well, thank God that's not me," Baz quipped. "Though I suppose I have to audition a new driver soon."

Marius hooked his arm. "You still have a driver."

For now.

Baz punched Marius in the arm, teasing him about how was he going to survive without Baz's sick wheels. He did what he could to distract himself from the heavy truth. No matter what they said, this was the end.

Distraction, however, never came cheap to Baz, and lingering with people he was about to lose did him no favors. He knew he should celebrate this last moment, drink up their companionship one last time, but he couldn't. Every second with them now was a reminder they were almost gone. What he needed was a way to check out. He had a handful of narcotics and a few other pharmaceuticals in his car, which combined with the fifth stashed in the glove box would go a long way to smoothing out the jagged edges the evening had left on him. Sex would be good too—a rush, a release, and a blissful crash. Except everyone at this wedding came with strings.

The memory of Elijah's naked gaze returned, but Baz shoved the thought away the same as he always did. Elijah was off-limits. Baz wasn't able to articulate why. He only knew it was the same kind of instinct as the one urging him to *protect Elijah*. Ignoring those impulses never came with pleasant consequences.

Except tonight, something had changed. Tonight Elijah lingered in Baz's mind like a cancer. Made his feet itch, sent him to the bar for four too many whiskey sours. Made him yearn for the pills and better booze in his car.

Sent him out the door via the patio where he'd last seen Elijah.

This time he didn't tell Marius or Damien where he was going. He was too busy talking up a mental justification for seeking Elijah out a second time, preemptively staunching the panic he'd feel if Elijah wasn't still standing there or somewhere else equally obvious. It kept mingling with the memory of that terrible gaze, sending his anxiety higher.

His breath caught in exhausted relief as he saw Elijah huddled on the deck, staring out at the lake with the same hollow expression.

Emboldened by alcohol, driven by a loneliness scraping the bottom of his soul, Baz sauntered over to Elijah with a rakish smile. "Hey, sailor. Care for a drink?"

Chapter Two

As BAZ GRINNED at him and waited for a reply, Elijah, king of the acid quips and one-liners, could find nothing to say.

Better yet, he completed his village-idiot look by letting his mouth hang open. Was this a joke? Would Marius and Damien pop out of the bushes giggle-snorting at how moronic Elijah was? Would he end up on the stage holding flowers, and they'd laugh as pig's blood splashed on his head?

With a chuckle, Baz plucked the flask from Elijah's hand. "Whatever this is, it must be good, if you're numb already. Mind if I give it a sample?"

Elijah continued his impression of a potted plant. His erection thickened as he watched Baz's Adam's apple work against the whiskey, but this was as animated as Elijah got.

Baz lowered the flask and spat, making a face as he wiped his mouth. "Holy *shit*, it tastes like rancid, hairy ass. What the hell is it, and how in God's name are you swallowing it?"

Elijah's cheeks burned. "It was the cheapest."

Baz's expression remained unreadable behind his glasses as Elijah chastised himself for finding infinite ways to be a tool in front of the one guy he wanted to impress. He tried to crawl into his trick head, the mental fortress allowing him to blow anybody and sleep like a baby after, but he couldn't get there. All he could do was stew in the knowledge that the only thing he was blowing right now was the remotest prayer of Baz ever speaking to him again.

What a fuck of a nightcap to the greatest shitshow on earth.

Except Baz didn't laugh, didn't roll his eyes. He said, "I have an eighteen-year-old bottle of Oban in my glove compartment. It'll ruin you for other stuff forever, but if you're okay with that, I'm more than willing to share."

Baz was looking at Elijah the same way he had the day in the parking lot in March, his glasses knocked away and his shoulder bleeding out onto the snow as he regarded Elijah with the strangest cocktail of hope and relief.

"S-sure," Elijah replied.

"Excellent." Rakish grin in place, Baz held out his arm.

Telling himself he finally understood why Carrie had gone with Tommy to the prom, Elijah tucked his slim hand into the crook of Baz's elbow.

They walked in silence around the marina to the parking lot, where Baz strode with purpose toward the farthest row. For a moment Elijah tried to guess which vehicle was Baz's, then got completely distracted by a sleek red car tucked beside a copse of trees. It looked about two seconds old and slightly space-age. Elijah entertained a delicious image of getting fucked over the hood, imagining the fit the stuck-up middle-aged asshole who owned the thing would have if he knew a scrawny gay kid was thinking about using his midlife crisis as a fucking post.

Except they kept getting closer to the car, until the only conclusion Elijah could reach was that this wet dream of a machine belonged to *Baz*.

Baz grinned at Elijah. "Nice, right? I've wanted a Tesla forever. Got it last week. They were holding off until I got my ass together enough to graduate, but me taking a slug in the shoulder made them soft."

Tentatively, Elijah ran his hands over the frame. The car was sexy as fuck, largely because it was so quiet about it. "It's incredible."

"I tricked out everything I could. I wanted the Model X for the *Back to the Future* doors, but I soured when I realized it's more of an SUV. Plus my ceiling was $100k, and I'd get less bells and whistles with the X."

One hundred thousand dollars. This car costs one hundred thousand dollars. If Elijah had one hundred dollars, he felt dizzily rich. Of course, with his *poor Elijah* fund, he could technically buy this car. And feel guilty as fuck for wasting other people's money. He ran his hand over the trunk, trying and failing to comprehend the gap in economics between the two of them.

Baz beamed like a proud father. "I love the all-glass roof. With the performance package, it smokes down the road. Well—so I hear. Rides pretty great."

"You haven't driven your own car?"

"Can't."

Elijah's body locked up. "You—can't? My dad—?"

"No. I haven't been able to drive since I was six-teen. In fact, I got in one good day and one godawful night before I was done for good. Your dad had nothing to do with this. But even if he did, it would have nothing to do with *you*."

That was a load of shit, but Elijah was so busy be-ing relieved he wasn't responsible for Baz not being able to drive his own car, all he could do was exhale in relief.

Baz punched Elijah lightly in the arm. "You want to molest the outside a little longer, or you ready to sit in the cockpit?"

Everything inside Elijah lit up. "You mean—drive?"

"Not after your cheap whiskey and the good stuff I intend to offer you once we're inside. But we can put it on the agenda for later. Go on. Get in the driver's seat."

They were going to have a later? Elijah cast a side-long glance at Baz, again wondering if he was walking into some kind of a setup. *What the fuck is going on? You've acted as if the sight of me revolted you ever since you discovered we were attending the same college. Except for the time you saved my life.*

He couldn't ask any of those things, though, be-cause as soon as he went to open the driver's door, he paused. "Um—where the fuck are the door handles?"

Baz's grin split his face as he kept walking closer. "They're right there. The silver things."

"Yes—the silver things flush with the side of the car. How am I supposed to—"

He stopped talking as the handles popped out.

"They retract for aerodynamics. Also, because it's bitching cool. Reappear when the keys get close." Baz cracked the door and held it open for Elijah. "Your car, sir."

Elijah slid into the Tesla. The seats were butter. It didn't just smell like a new car—it smelled like *money*. Money and geekery and excellence. He ran his hands over the steering wheel and ghosted his fingers over the huge glass panel on the dashboard between the wheel and the passenger side. It was almost a built-in iPad. It was dark at the moment, and Elijah itched to see it light up and blow his mind.

"That's the dashboard control center." Baz gestured at it as he climbed into the passenger side. "Full touchscreen, controls everything. It has internet too—all but video."

Elijah was about to ask for the keys, but he couldn't see an ignition switch. "How do I turn it on?"

"Put your foot on the brake."

Elijah did. The lights lit, the fan purred softly, but the car itself made no sound.

"Never gets louder than this." Baz gestured to the hood. "There's no engine there. It's in the rear, between the wheels. About as big as a breadbox. So in addition to the hatchback, we have storage at the front end—they call it the frunk—where the combustion engine would be."

Elijah let out a sigh full of arousal. "Holy shit, this is so fucking cool."

"Oh, honey, this dog has so many tricks it needs a circus. You can raise and lower the suspension manually or let it adjust itself according to weight. You can manipulate how the sound comes out, so it's perfectly situated around you as the driver or balanced between us."

Baz whipped through a dizzying array of features, all of them fifty times more decadent than anything Elijah would have ever thought to dream of, let alone expect to actually have in a car. Elijah was still hung up, though, on the first magic trick. "How did you start the car without a key?"

Grinning, Baz pulled a black fob out of his pocket and dangled it between them. "This is the key. Just needs to be in the car. Pretty standard on new vehicles these days, but I like to think the Tesla's is cooler. I don't think many start by a foot on the brake. It turns off when we get out too, and locks itself after thirty seconds, sucking the door handles in."

Elijah had no idea magic keys were standard now. He thought of the 1996 Oldsmobile his parents had occasionally allowed him to drive, wondered briefly what had happened to it. Since his mother was in a mental institution and his dad in prison, neither of them could drive it right now.

Baz opened the glove compartment and withdrew a bottle of golden alcohol. "Care for a drink?"

Yeah, Elijah could handle a little oblivion. He accepted the bottle, and after a glance at Baz to make sure it would be okay, took a hit straight from the fifth. The buttery, smoky scotch played on his tongue, making goose bumps break out across his skin.

"Whoa." The taste kept exploding in his mouth,

long after he'd passed it to Baz. "God, it makes me want a cigarette."

"Go for it." Baz touched the glass screen, slid an image on the panel, and half the car roof peeled away to reveal the increasingly purple sky.

"I can't smoke in your brand-new car."

"Why not? I'm going to." Baz pulled something else out of the glove compartment—a baggie full of small, white, rolled joints. "Unless you have a moral objection to weed." He waggled his eyebrows over the top of his glasses. "They're *medicinal.*"

"I only mind if you don't intend to share."

The grin splitting Baz's lips gave almost as good a buzz as the lit joint he passed to Elijah.

Leaning back, Elijah stared up through the moon-roof as the scotch and marijuana unkinked his brain. The rawness and tension seemed to mist out of his body, rising up toward the jet trails above. "This is nice. The only thing that could make it better would be if I still had the Xanax they gave me in the hospital."

Popping the console between them, Baz withdrew a brown bottle and tossed it into Elijah's lap.

Elijah stared at it. He remembered well the blissful unplugging the drug gave him, and he hadn't been kidding when he'd said it would make the moment perfect: the scotch, weed, and Xanax combined would untether him completely, sending him blissfully into happy land. But he also knew it came at a steep cost.

He gripped the sides of the bottle, running his thumb over the label prescribing the medicine to *Sebastian Percival Acker.* "If I take this, I'm gonna turn into a pile of mush. I'll grin like an idiot, dance like a hooker, and sing like a canary."

"Sounds good to me."

It did to Elijah too…except. "I'll also offer to blow you. A lot. And if you don't let me, I'll wander off and keep trying until someone does."

He glanced to the side to check how that comment was received but mentally cursed as he remembered the glasses rendered that impossible. All he got was Baz settling into the corner between his seat and the door, rolling the bottle of scotch on his upraised knee. "So Xanax makes you horny."

Elijah thought about letting the remark stand, then decided, fuck it. It had been fun to ride the fairy tale of Baz Acker actually giving a shit about him, but he knew firsthand fairy tales were a lot more Grimm brothers and much less Walt Disney. Time to lay his cards on the table. "No. More shuts down the part of me keeping me from wandering around like a fucking idiot. Xanax puts my internal babysitter to sleep. I'll want to have a good time."

With you. Because I've wanted a good time with you for a long, long while.

Baz kept quiet, moving only to retrieve the joint and take a long drag. "It more puts the demons to sleep for me. Though I'm impressed. I don't think I could cut loose enough to want to fuck just *anybody*."

Elijah slugged some scotch before he could bring himself to reply. "Less cutting loose and more…letting out the lonely." He played numb fingers over the steering wheel. "I wouldn't sleep with just anybody."

"But you would sleep with me, because I'm not just anybody? You're gonna give me a big head, Prince."

I want to give you all of the head. But the ribald response got swallowed by another wave of guilt. "You saved my life."

Beside him, Baz went still. "Is that what this is about?"

Elijah frowned, not sure what *this* was. "Why I want to sleep with you? No. That's because you're hot. But the other thing…makes me feel weird. And bad."

Baz didn't respond right away, and Elijah kicked himself for fucking up getting laid. He should have refused the Xanax and ridden the scene out. Except he knew he'd have broken at some point. It was too weird.

It was fucking unfair how he had to go and be rational and cautious right now. Why couldn't he have one good night? One good time? Wasn't he fucking owed one?

Baz cleared his throat. "You still haven't said if you *want* a Xanax, only what will happen if you do."

Say no. Be safe. The thought drifted into Elijah's conscience before being drowned by a slosh of Oban. "Oh, I want one."

Fuck those fucking glasses. "So you were letting me know what I was buying?" He retrieved the pill bottle from Elijah and rolled it around in his hand.

Elijah tracked the movement, all his emotions and fears smashing against the weed and booze in his system. Baz cracked the medicine cap off with one hand and split a pill with the deftness of one who'd done it a lot. After pocketing the bottle, he held up the half-circle.

Elijah stuck out his tongue.

Laughing, Baz put the pill between his teeth and dropped it into Elijah's mouth.

As Elijah swallowed the Xanax with scotch, Baz whispered kisses along his jaw, trailed down the center of his throat, mimicking the medicine's descent. Elijah shut his eyes and slid his hands over Baz's shoulders, into his hair. When Baz pressed the nearly spent joint to his lips, Elijah took a deep hit, holding the smoke inside him as long as he could, wanting to fly as high as possible.

With Baz.

Baz brushed a dry kiss over Elijah's parted lips, catching the lower mound of flesh with his teeth. "I haven't shown you the Tesla's backseat." He ran fingers down Elijah's chest, popping one button, another. "I can still drive there, baby."

Elijah leaned into those exploring fingers, wishing the futuristic Tesla had teleportation capability. Since it didn't, he only let himself shiver under the blistering heat of Baz's touch a moment before he said, "Race you there," and opened the door of the car.

AS ELIJAH STUMBLED out of the front seat, Baz clutched the bottle of Oban and tried to gauge how big of a fuckup he'd initiated. He hadn't meant to let it go this far. The idea of hanging out in his car with Elijah had felt so good, so safe, he couldn't stop himself.

Elijah opened the passenger-side door and glared.

"Fuck. You're having second thoughts, aren't you. I knew it." He pushed away from the car.

Baz grabbed him before he escaped his reach. "Slow down, tiger. You're not going anywhere."

If Baz hadn't held him so tightly, he'd have lost Elijah in the squirming. "The fuck I'm not. I can read *that* expression through those fucking glasses. Take your pity somewhere else."

With a growl, Baz yanked Elijah onto his lap. He winced at the impact on his bad hip, but he swallowed the yelp of pain and focused on the more important issue. Pulling off his glasses, he held Elijah's chin tight.

"I don't pity you. I wouldn't fucking do that to you."

The manhandling and rough tone took some of the wind out of Elijah's sails, but not all. "What *are* you doing? You've been fucking with me ever since we met in Saint Paul. You haul me out of a nightmare, but when I try to thank you, you shove me on a bus to South Dakota with a wad of money like the sight of me revolts you."

Baz winced. "I didn't—"

"I was there. You fucking did. And when you saw me years later in the computer lab at Saint Timothy, you all but vomited on your way out the door. You looked away anytime you saw me on campus—right up until you leapt in front of a fucking bullet for me. But then you ignored me until tonight, when you get me drunk and high and promise me sex, don't follow through, and I catch you *wearing that face*. So fucking figure it out. You want me or not?"

Jesus Christ. Baz opened his mouth to argue, but Elijah shifted and let in a shaft of setting sunlight directly into his eyes. This time he did cry out, a tight gasp of exquisite pain as he slammed his eyes shut and hunched forward to reclaim the shadow.

Swearing under his breath, Elijah pressed Baz's glasses clumsily onto his face. "You shouldn't have taken them off."

No, he shouldn't have, not facing the setting sun with a headache from the wedding already killing him. "You said you couldn't read my face with them on."

"So *that's* what you listen to? You won't fuck me, but you'll blind yourself? What kind of screwed up are you?"

Baz pushed his glasses into place. "I wasn't pitying you. I was trying to decide if I'd fucked up by hunting you down. For once I thought I'd try to see the train wreck coming and stop it. I don't pity you. I worry about you."

"How would you fuck this up by doing me? Do you have some stupid idea I'd get all gooey over you if you put your dick in my ass? My name's not Aaron Seavers, thanks."

"I fuck shit up. I worry about you."

"The name is Prince, bitch, not princess. I can take care of myself." He flicked Baz lightly on the nose. "You're a lot wetter than I thought."

Baz nipped at Elijah's fingers as he pulled them away. "This the Xanax kicking in?"

"Yes. I warned you."

Baz skimmed his hands up Elijah's sides, lingering

on his hipbones. Stared up at that dark hair framing his pale face, angular features. Angry eyes that couldn't hide his arousal. "Still wanting to fuck me, even though I'm wet?"

"You're more damp than wet." Elijah ran his fingers through Baz's hair. "Plus you're one of those assholes who looks hot when you're emo. So, yes."

"Climb into the moonroof and I'll blow you."

To his surprise, Elijah *pouted*. "But I was going to blow *you*."

Baz squeezed his hip. "Climb up there now, hooker, or I won't put my finger in your ass."

Elijah skimmed his body over Baz's on his way to the roof, pausing to suck briefly on Baz's bottom lip. "Crying shame. I'd be the best you ever had."

Baz pinched his nipple. "Up. Roof. Now."

Elijah's wink tipped Baz's erection from semi to full-on painful wood. "Yes, sir."

His foot slammed into Baz's hip a second time. Biting his tongue, Baz moved it to the console and arranged Elijah's knees against the seat, putting his groin level with Baz's mouth.

"Whoa." Elijah's torso undulated as Baz undid his dress pants and tugged the waistband down. "Hard to keep my balance. This moonroof is huge. Nothing to hold on to."

"My hair." Baz skimmed the trousers to Elijah's thighs and let the mound of tiny ass fill his hands. Before him, Elijah's long, red cock swayed in front of his face.

A pinch of Elijah's ass sent those hands onto either

side of Baz's head. "I'll end up pulling it."

"Good." Baz sucked on the patch of skin above the dark nest of Elijah's groin, rubbing his chin in the wiry hair. He smiled as Elijah's abdomen quivered, going concave as his cock teased Baz's throat. Baz buried his nose in the thatch, drinking in the sweat and smell of dick. It did more to erase the shadows from his brain than a bottle of scotch, a bale of weed, and a basket of Xanax ever could.

"Fuck, suck it already." Elijah didn't pull Baz's hair, but he buried his fingers deep. "And where's the finger in my ass?"

Baz licked Elijah's belly and slapped his butt. "Bratty."

"I haven't gotten laid since...before."

Empathy washed Baz out. He stroked Elijah's ass, his thighs. Baz licked the underside of Elijah's shaft. "Then let me make it good."

"I don't want it good, I—" He gasped, tugging Baz's hair as Baz sucked on his balls and teased one finger at Elijah's asshole.

As one hand kept up insistent pressure, Baz reached the other into the console for the vial of lube. When he found it, he switched his mouth to the other sac and greased his finger.

Elijah cried out in falsetto when the finger breached his ass, and he thrust his cock into Baz's face. "*Ohgod. Please. Please.*"

"I won't leave you hanging, baby." Baz sucked on the creases of Elijah's thighs, moving counterpoint to the finger gently fucking from behind.

"It feels so good." Elijah ripped at Baz's hair now, desperate, crazed. "Everything feels so good."

"Let me make it last." He whispered the words over Elijah's skin, pausing to slide his tongue up the dick brushing his cheek. "Let me make it better."

"People might come—*ah*." He panted as Baz added a second finger inside him. "I'm sticking out the roof of your car. It's pretty obvious what we're doing."

Baz sucked on the tip of Elijah's cock, digging his tongue in the slit before pulling away to speak. "Stick your head out the roof and enjoy your blow job." Baz reached for the dashboard controls with his free hand. "We need music, though. Who's your favorite artist?"

"RuPaul, but that's not good make-out music. Try Hi Fashion. *Unghf.* Oh my God, your fingers are long."

Baz hadn't heard of the band, but Spotify had— except as soon as he keyed them up, Elijah jerked out of euphoria.

"*No.* Not the 70s shit. Hi Fashion. H-I Fashion, not H-I-G-H Fashion. 'Amazing' and 'Lighthouse' and 'I'm Not Madonna'."

Baz tried again, and sure enough, there were all the songs Elijah had rattled off. He hit random play, and as a bass backbeat thumped through the Tesla, he pushed deep into the sweet ass and took Elijah's cock into his mouth.

Elijah was right—everything felt so good. His car, sexy and sleek and keeping them safe. The music, which was kind of distilled Scissor Sisters. The sweet abandon of Elijah's body as Baz made love to it, fucked it, sucked it down. The tug of Elijah's grip on Baz's hair. The buzz of drugs and alcohol—it all swirled around them, erasing the pain and darkness, leaving them with nothing but light.

Baz wanted to make it last forever.

"I want you to fuck me." Elijah thrust deep into Baz's mouth, whimpering as a third finger speared his ass. "I need you to fuck me."

Baz couldn't answer, mouth too full of dick, but he didn't have to reply as sensation quickly overwhelmed Elijah's ability to speak, leaving Baz to focus on the feast. Elijah was a perfect handful, perfect mouthful. If they moved to the backseat, Baz could sit in the center, have Elijah straddle him backward or forward—or both—and as the song they listened too suggested, park and ride.

Except the two jabs to his hip and the flash of sun in his eyes had exacted their toll. Sometimes the right kind of bang could make all his metal insides light up, and they did now, a nice complement to the spiderweb cracks of pain across his skull. He needed topical analgesic for his hip, two oxycodone and twenty minutes for it to kick in before he could entertain any action. His flagging erection was testament. Pain could be an aphrodisiac, yes—but not this kind.

So he drove Elijah to a punishing climax, making him howl into the marina parking lot. He swallowed the spray hitting the back of his throat in three thick gulps, teasing deep into Elijah's ass to milk him as much as possible. Spent, Elijah went limp, and Baz lowered him to his lap, carefully arranging him away from the angry hip.

Elijah collapsed on Baz's shoulder, breathing rough against his neck as he returned to earth. Baz shut his eyes and cradled him close, aching at the way he fit. The song playing now was sweet, and it wrapped the moment in safety and softness.

I don't want this to end.

The thought sent an electric thrill of terror through Baz. It had to be a side effect of the drug cocktail—projected yearning from last call, watching a high school friend get married and chase down a life Baz knew he couldn't have anymore. Yearning to keep Elijah close couldn't be real, because Baz Acker was the dictionary definition of dissatisfaction and distraction.

Yet he couldn't shake wanting this moment with Elijah to stay. When Elijah pressed a drugged, open-mouthed kiss on Baz's neck, Baz shut his eyes and sank into a well of safety he would have sworn ten seconds ago didn't exist.

This was worse than wandering around agitated and lonely. This was what had led him chasing after Aaron last year and eventually breaking his friend's heart. He couldn't hurt Elijah. He couldn't let anyone hurt Elijah. He needed to text Marius, have him take Elijah to the hotel, pour him into a bed, and apologize on behalf of his asshole best friend. Again.

Elijah lifted his head. Baz touched his smooth cheeks, grazing the barest hint of fuzz on his jaw. He stared into those dark, endless eyes and got lost all over again.

"How about you have a cigarette and fill your flask with Oban while I take a few pills, and we go in and dance?" When Elijah's mouth flattened into a thin line of complaint, Baz pulled Elijah's lip into the pout he loved. "Then I'll bring you back here and fuck you."

He expected a protest—not naked yearning. "You'll change your mind."

Baz stroked the open line of Elijah's neck. "No."

"You really want to dance with me? In front of people?"

Baz pressed a reverent kiss on his chin. "Especially in front of people."

Elijah still seemed wary. Baz vowed if he did nothing else tonight, he would wash that doubt away.

Chapter Three

IF DRUGS COULD make Elijah feel the way being with Baz Acker did, he'd have died of an overdose years ago.

Baz kept his hand on Elijah at all times, usually on his ass. When people gave them questioning glances, Baz became more proprietary, all but pissing a circle around Elijah.

They had to linger at Baz's end of the table, where he reassured Damien and Marius he was fine, just *occupied*, which he punctuated with an open grope of Elijah. For his part, Elijah tried to play giddy trick, which wasn't hard, but he came up short when Damien started to lecture Baz.

"Do you think that's appropriate?" A darting glance indicated Elijah.

Setting his teeth in a feral grin, Elijah leaned into Damien. "Oh, sweetie. I'm sorry. Were you jealous?"

A feminine gasp reminded Elijah Damien had a fiancée, but Baz's bright laughter cut through before panic could set in. "Down, Cujo. He's being a nice guy."

"Don't pity me." Elijah mellowed into a simple glare. "You want to fuss over somebody, go to Aaron."

Damien raised his eyebrows at Baz. "Must be like looking in a mirror."

Baz tipped his mouth in a crooked smile that could mean about anything. It faded, though, when Marius put a hand on Baz's arm to pull him aside, the cocky expression replaced by thin-lipped earnestness.

Damien spoke into Elijah's ear. "A word of warning. Talk to Marius the way you did to me, and it'll be Baz who snarls."

A tendril of shame curled through Elijah. "Sorry."

"You're not." Damien didn't seem upset, though. "Don't get stars in your eyes over him. He doesn't mean to, but he'll break your heart. Marius and I have the scars to prove it, and we're only his friends. If you're fool enough to think you're the exception, you're already screwed."

Elijah shrugged, turning away so Damien didn't see the flush on his cheeks. "You can stand down. I'm not looking for a savior."

"He is."

Those words echoed in Elijah as Baz finally extricated himself from Marius and took Elijah to the dance floor. That he was hoping for a savior in Elijah made his skin crawl—but then he remembered the confession from the Tesla.

I worry about you. Not something you said to someone you hoped would save you. That was the other way around.

Elijah frowned at Baz, who was enigmatic once more behind his glasses. "You don't make any fucking sense."

Baz's only response was to quirk an eyebrow and draw Elijah closer. An extended remix of "Get Lucky" played, and Baz was trying to lead them in a dirty dance, but it hadn't escaped Elijah's notice Baz barely moved at all, doing his best to keep his weight off his left hip. Elijah had assumed the handful of pills Baz popped in the car was Baz joining the party. Obviously those drugs truly had been medicinal.

He flicked the center of Baz's chest. "What the fuck are you dancing for, if you hurt?"

"Honey, if I only danced when I didn't hurt, I never would." He drew Elijah closer, bringing his stomach into contact with Baz's groin. "Besides, moving around usually helps."

Sounded like a crock of shit to Elijah, but he was tired of keeping track of Baz's BS. "So you're telling me you hurt all the time? That sucks."

"Beats being dead."

The quip had an edge to it. "What the fuck happened to you in high school, anyway?" Too late, Elijah remembered the Xanax lack of filter. He held up his hands. "Forget it. Ignore me. Or lie. Tell me you fell out of a jet or something."

Baz pushed hair out of Elijah's eyes. "I was bashed outside of a Boystown bar on my sixteenth birthday. I lived. My boyfriend didn't."

Elijah stumbled. He shook as he recovered his balance, staring intently at Baz.

What did Baz find that night you first met in Saint Paul? You, trapped in an alley with a bad trick. Must have been one fuck of a flashback. That's why you freak him out. You're a goddamned ghost. You probably even look the same as the old boyfriend.

Elijah told himself it was fucking stupid for the knowledge to hurt. What, he thought one fucking blow job through a moonroof meant fairy godmothers were real?

Baz's eyebrow arched over the glasses. "No pity, and all Xanaxed up too. I'm impressed."

"I've been to reparative therapy. Some of us get our hell in one whap upside the head, some of us spend ten months on our knees."

You are an asshole, Elijah's rusty conscience screamed at him, but Baz only smiled. "I like you, Elijah Prince."

Elijah tried to throw his walls back up, but he was far too drugged. "Fuck."

Pretty sure that was a wink behind those glasses. "Give me another fifteen minutes to let the oxycodone fully kick in, and you're on."

"Yes, so we can live out Sid and Nancy: This Time They're Gay."

Elijah watched to see if he'd get the reference. It was an admittedly obscure test—how many millennials knew about a codependent, tragic 1970s punk romance glamorized in a mid-eighties movie? But Elijah wanted him to pass. *Come on. Show you're a freak like me.*

Baz neither confirmed nor denied. With a sideways grin, he drew Elijah in close. "Don't try to brush me off. I know how to push your buttons now. I can make you putty in my hands with barely any effort at all."

He skimmed a touch up Elijah's side and a deft

tuck into his crack. Elijah would have had a tough time resisting that sober, but as it was, he all but sat on Baz's index finger in front of a bunch of Minnesota Nice. He groaned when Baz pulled away, but Elijah swatted at him—and missed—when he laughed.

"You'd better be good, is all I can say, you neurotic mess." Elijah rested his cheek against Baz's chest and shut his eyes when Baz enveloped him in a swaying embrace. "And if you say it takes one to know one, I'll bite you."

"Promises, promises."

Everyone around them boogied to Daft Punk, but the two of them downshifted into a slow dance. It was nice, until he saw Baz limp. He pressed his fingers to Baz's ribs, trying to guess which ones were titanium through his skin, which of course he couldn't.

Baz kissed his hair and slid a hand over Elijah's ass. "Oxy's full power. Still up for a tour of the backseat?"

Oh yeah. Elijah was up all right. Nuzzling Baz's shirtfront, he opened a button with his teeth and teased at the hairless chest above the vee of his undershirt. "Bring it on, Sid."

Baz laughed and slipped a hand into Elijah's waistband. "Oh no, you don't. *I* call dibs on Nancy. I'm the one with the drugs, after all."

ON THE WAY to the parking lot, Elijah tried to light up a cigarette, but Baz pulled the pack out of his hand and replaced it with a hard box of some other brand before Elijah could protest.

"Bought them at the bar. They're menthol. Have to be better than whatever the fuck you're gagging on there."

Elijah tapped the cigarettes, peeled off the wrapper and took a whiff. Yummy and expensive, like the scotch. "I'd make a joke about your need to queen out over what I put in my body, but you have such good taste, you make it difficult to argue."

"Money's got to be worth something."

Elijah lit up, enjoying the rush of quality nicotine. "How loaded are you, anyway?"

"Pretty. My parents both work, though not traditionally. Largely what they do is make money breed. My mom is angling for public office, so she's running a lot of charity things as well. Community organizer and all. I think she'd have bitten on the calls for her to run for the House if it weren't for my accident. I told her to use it, make me her goddamn platform, but she says not until I get myself together." He made *gimme* motions for Elijah's cigarette and took a hit before passing it back. "Dad owns half of Chicago. He's one of those buy, rip apart, sell people everybody loves to bitch about. Pays for three houses and a skyline downtown apartment, plus all my fucking around, so no complaining from me. And it'll finance Mom's candidacy if she ever gets off her ass."

"They're still together?"

He shrugged. "I don't think they've fucked each other in years, and I rarely see him unless it's for something official where we need to look like a functional family. But if they have pieces on the side, they're quiet about it. They're more about the whole than the part. Plus it wouldn't be good for Uncle Paul, since they're neck-deep in his campaign."

"Uncle Paul is who, exactly?"

"Senior US Senator representing the great state of Illinois."

Elijah's stomach flipped over. *Holy. Shit.* "Your uncle is Senator Barnett?"

"Yep. His dad was a senator also, and his brothers are all in politics in some fashion or other. We're kind of the Illinois Kennedys on my mom's side. Hated about that much too. Paul's been after Mom to take up the family business for years. She should. Dad would totally dig being a political spouse."

"Is it easier dealing with a shit life with money? Because I could see it going either way."

When Baz held his hand out, this time Elijah passed the whole pack and the lighter, and Baz paused to light up before he answered. "Sometimes. Easier to be distracted. Easier to feel guilty."

"Why guilty? What the fuck did you do?"

Baz shrugged. "Lived. Moved on to other guys. General survivor shit."

Elijah took a drag while he considered. "Makes sense. What a clusterfuck if I'd fallen for somebody along the way. Of course, they'd have had to push past my barbed wire, which nobody's suicidal enough to do." He rolled his eyes and ashed his cig. "Except Aaron, the shithead."

Baz passed over the cigarettes. "Aaron's a good kid. He and Giles are right together."

Yes, and sometimes Elijah hated that. He withdrew his now-Oban-filled flask. "I fucked Giles, you know."

Baz chuckled and blew a stream of smoke. "I fucked Aaron."

Elijah remembered—mostly how upset Aaron had been when it ended. "Is he as sweet and innocent as he looks?"

"Yep."

"Bet he purrs like a kitten."

"Affirmative." He stubbed out his cigarette into the gravel with half of it remaining. "I assume Giles takes a second to get over himself, then fucks with abandon?"

"He's got ninja skills. Total top, though. No switching except maybe for novelty. Surprised the hell out of me."

"Hmm. Too bad I passed him up."

Elijah hit him with the flask, laughing. "Shut up. Really? You want to rearrange?"

"We'll save it for next time." They were at the car now, and Baz pressed Elijah into it. "Somebody got me in a *mood*." Baz sucked lightly at Elijah's neck, inspiring him to tip his head to the side. "We're climbing into the backseat, I'm firing up some Maino, and you're sucking my cock until I decide to put it in you."

That's what they did. Baz leaned over the console from the backseat and fussed for a second, and once the sultry beat of R&B pulsed from the stereo, Baz settled against the door, spread his legs wide and arched an eyebrow over the top of his sunglasses.

Elijah didn't need a second invitation.

He tugged at Baz's fly, palming him through the

expensive fabric to get to the goods. He admired the pretty, cut length of Baz curving to the right—then stuck his ass in the air, nestled into Baz's crotch and sucked him fast and deep into his mouth.

He pulled off quick, mostly wanting to get Baz's attention and make it clear he meant business. Sucking cock was Elijah's greatest skill. He'd worked on Grindr to get a rep as a hot, talented mouth, which meant if he priced fucking higher, he could mostly stick to blow jobs for cash because they were still great and seemed like a bargain. When he actually wanted a guy, his talents got him gratitude and affection.

For Baz he got out the big guns—lots of attention to his balls, sucking them gently, running his tongue around the tender sacs, massaging them as his mouth returned to the shaft. The music wouldn't have been his first choice, but it worked—apparently Maino was a fan of blow jobs, because the beat let Elijah climb on top, bob and weave and lick in time to the rhythm. The car was silent, shutting out the world, keeping them in a sleek, futuristic red bubble. Elijah glanced up, lips spread, figuring by this point Baz's eyes ought to be rolled back in his head.

He shuddered, a moan escaping when he found Baz staring intently at him—as far as he could tell with the shades—completely contained, a small smile on his face. His hand moved down Elijah's back, slipping beneath his waistband, moving insistently south as he pressed Elijah deeper onto his cock with his free hand.

"I should have said…" his fingers tightened on Elijah's hair, "…I like a little desperate on my dick. Let me at your ass."

Elijah fumbled with his own fly, getting his waistband slack in time for Baz to push his dress pants down, his briefs. Baz's fingers teased the sweat of Elijah's crack, but only for a moment. When those same fingers brushed Elijah's jaw, he turned, whimpering, to take them in his mouth.

When they left, he latched on to Baz's cock, took him deep and moaned as Baz pressed at the pucker of his ass.

One stroke was all the warning he got—Elijah sucked in a lungful of sex-tinged air into his nose, opening his throat and helping Baz fuck his face. He tripped out of his head, lost to the metric of cock, air, cock, distracted by the thrust of two of Baz's fingers. It was dirtier than he expected. It was wicked. It was almost more than he could handle. He loved it so hard he wondered if the tears leaking out of his eyes weren't entirely the strain of so much dick.

He gave Baz desperate—he whined, gasped, let Baz muffle the sounds with his cock. Spread his knees as wide as the seat allowed to give Baz plenty of access to his ass. The fingering made him crazy. The facefucking, the drugs—been there done that. But his bare butt aimed at the window in a silent car getting frigged *while* he was held down, his mouth used as a hole, *while* he was tripping on quality chemicals—*fuck, fuck, fuck,* he was going to blow if his cock so much as brushed anything.

Though initially Baz was cool as hell, the whines made him feral. Elijah called up every whorish cell in his body, turned loose and let guttural pleasure burn in his throat.

Just when he thought he was about to be rewarded with a flood of spunk, Baz whipped him off and around, so they were back to front. Shaking, *aching*, Elijah tried to sit on Baz's dick, only to be pushed forward again.

"Gotta suit up."

Oh. Right. *Jesus.* Before he could dwell on the thought, though, Baz hauled him onto his now-condom-coated cock.

Elijah arched and moaned as that curved dick speared him, rubbing him all the right ways.

Baz sucked on his neck as he thrust into Elijah, pinching his nipple, teasing open the front of his half-unbuttoned shirt. "That's right, baby. Give it to me. Open up and take it."

Elijah did. The blow job had been incredible, but his life goal became getting this dick inside him as much as possible. He kept trying to grab himself to jack off, but he was so overstimulated he couldn't make his hands work well enough to get there. When Baz took hold of Elijah's cock for him, he tipped his head back and whimpered.

Baz nuzzled Elijah's chin until he turned. He sealed their mouths together, jerking Elijah until the combined sensation of dick pounding his ass and hand on his cock sent him sailing over the edge into his own personal fireworks. As he twinkled to earth, the last thrust told him Baz had found his own light show.

They kept kissing after the climax—slow, lingering,

neither of them wanting the moment to end. Elijah knew he didn't. Maybe it had simply been too long, but that sure as hell felt like the best fuck he'd ever had. Good banter before too. Dance was pretty decent, even with the hip. The car and expensive booze and cigs were merely frosting, but Elijah did enjoy sugar.

He's going to hurt you. He's a train wreck. You're not a whole lot better. Put this shit down and walk away.

He tangled his fingers in Baz's hair. "You fuck good, Nancy."

Baz nipped and tugged Elijah's ear with his teeth.

Elijah shut his eyes against the tenderness. The walls he usually kept himself safe behind broke free of the Xanax barriers and scraped into place, moving him from unable to leave him to unable to linger.

"I should go. My roommates Moopsie and Cutesy are likely looking for me. You have good odds on a lecture coming from Damien and Marius too."

For a moment he thought Baz would try to get him to stay, and he held his breath, half dreading, half hoping for it. But Baz only kissed his neck and ran a hand across his arm before letting it fall away. "You're probably right."

He was *absolutely* right. But as Elijah sorted out his pants and climbed out of the Tesla, he wished with every fiber of his being he wasn't.

FOR BAZ, THE reception went by in a fuzzy, Elijah-filled blur.

Before they rejoined the others, they dabbed out

come stains on their clothes in the car, laughed at the futility, then lit up cigarettes and sauntered to the marina. Once there they went their separate ways, but Baz kept his gaze on Elijah.

He should be relieved. This was the part that made him crazy, the moment when a guy wanted *more* and Baz knew he couldn't do it. It was refreshing to have somebody on board with him for a change. Elijah was right, they were Sid and Nancy all the way. Terrible idea. Sure, they could fuck occasionally. They'd had a fun night together, bled off some raw from a rough day. End scene.

Except Baz couldn't stop thinking about him. It wasn't simply the sex, either. And of course he wanted to explore finding out if Elijah was as enthusiastic a top as he was a bottom. But it was more that he wanted…well, more. More banter. More side eye. More of Elijah regarding him warily, like he didn't trust Baz at all. Getting all intense and up in Baz's face.

Looking hungry. Aching. Wearing the expression on his face matching the feelings Baz concealed inside.

Baz tried to push Elijah out of his head, or at least into the quiet obsession he'd been previously, but he wouldn't go. That made sense when they were still at the reception. It made no sense when he was at the hotel with Marius.

Okay, a lot of it was Baz couldn't stop wondering if Elijah had gotten out of the reception in one piece—Baz hadn't seen him leave. Giles and Aaron were watching him, right?

He could check. Aaron was rooming with Elijah.

Marius watched Baz pull out his phone as they entered the elevator. "Everything okay?"

"Just checking on something." He tapped open Aaron's contact information.

"If the something is Elijah, he left with Aaron and Giles twenty minutes ago."

Baz paused, registering the censure in Marius's tone, but he still tapped out the text. *Hey, Aaron. Elijah make it to your room okay?*

He let out a breath when the reply appeared on his screen. *Yes. He's already asleep.*

K thx. Baz clicked his phone into sleep mode and tucked it into his pocket. He ignored Marius giving him *a look* and continued toward their room with all the confidence in the world that Marius, the world's biggest mother hen, would launch into Baz in his own time.

Actually, he acknowledged as he opened the door with his keycard, Damien was more hen, the one to get in Baz's face about stupid decisions. Marius did more silent judging. He did his shepherding around the edges. What was weird, though, was neither one of them had lit into him once he'd come to the reception after fucking Elijah. Damien had raised an eyebrow, and Marius was decidedly full of glances with heavy meaning, but nobody had sat him in a chair and said, "Hey, what the hell were you doing with Elijah Prince?"

He wasn't sure what it meant that they hadn't.

Frowning, he stripped out of his clothes and into a pair of boxers. He was tugging the waistband into place as he caught a glance of Marius sprawled on his bed, hands behind his head, an enigmatic expression on his face.

Baz sighed and ran a hand through his hair. "Okay. Fine. Say what you've got to say, and stop making me crazy."

"Get yourself ready for bed first. I got your light out already."

Baz glanced around the room, and sure enough, his portable lamp sat on the desk beside Marius's overnight bag. It was tricked out with a special red bulb which, while not exactly a standard treatment for photophobic vision, helped Baz. The red light made his life look like hell's boudoir or old-time-photography darkroom, but it meant he could take off his goddamned glasses and remove his contacts without the wrong flash of light giving him a five-hour migraine.

"Thanks." He saluted Marius and went to the bathroom.

Getting ready for bed was more than brushing his teeth and maybe scrubbing stray jizz from his face. To start, he had to plug in his light. Once that was done, he removed his glasses and got to work.

There were the pills first—antidepressants, antiseizure meds, a gazillion vitamins, and an assortment of painkillers that had joined his crusade post-bullet. After he sloshed those into his bloodstream, he washed his hands, set up his tray and took out his contacts. In most photophobia cases, they would have been enough to stop the light sensitivity, but not for Baz. Sometimes he could go with just contacts, but not for long and only in certain circumstances. He had a habit of tipping his glasses down to wink, but that almost always meant it felt like someone put an ice pick into his head.

He didn't have simple sensitivity. He had seriously fucked-over retinas, especially his left eye, and by rights he shouldn't have been able to see anymore at all. Vision for Baz had come after a zillion surgeries and a couple experimental treatments his uncle had flown him to Switzerland to receive.

The contacts, in addition to being his first, most important shield from too much light, were also his corrective lenses. Once they were out, he was raw in every way. His actual sight wasn't too bad, just a little blurry with a hint of astigmatism. The light was everything—or rather, a tiny bit of it was way, way too much, because he had no filter. It varied from day to day, his sensitivity, but at his best moments he was still a vampire. The glare from a computer screen could burn like acid. The glow of a bedside lamp could cut into his skull. The flash from a smartphone could make him pass out from pain.

Sometimes, tonight being an example, even the red light stung. He cleaned his contacts—eight hundred dollars a pair—and set them aside to marinate. He washed his face and brushed his teeth, did a few stretches to see if he could unkink his hip. When it didn't work, he dug his TENS unit out of his shaving kit and hooked it up.

He regarded himself in the mirror, taking in the blurry sight of himself without his sunglasses, with electrodes glued to his hip and shoulder. He wished he could make the contacts work alone, because he looked better with his actual eyes, he thought. He remembered Elijah bitching about not being able to see them. A lot of people thought he was a poser to wear shades all the time, and that was fine because they didn't know. Though it meant the only people who ever saw him this way were Marius, and occasionally his mom, if she came into his room at night when he was home. Since he rarely went home, it was mostly Marius.

For another month, anyway. Then it would be nobody.

He wondered if Elijah had liked what he'd seen, in the moment Baz had taken the sunglasses off.

Putting his darkest shades on, he grabbed the battery unit in one hand and unplugged the lamp. "Incoming," he called through the bathroom door.

"Ready to receive," Marius replied.

They'd developed the call-and-answer technique over the years whenever they were on the road together, this ritual of Baz undressing his eyes and Marius preparing the outer chamber with red light. Once Baz had been faster than Marius. They'd both missed a choir performance—the whole reason they'd been out of town in the first place—because Baz lay in bed sobbing from pain, Marius hovering beside him with ice packs and whispered apologies. Ever since, Baz didn't open the bathroom door without his sunglasses on and a shout to make sure he didn't step out into a world of hurt.

The hotel room glowed red from two Marius-replaced bulbs, one on the desk and another by the bedside. Any other lights in the room were unplugged, and light switches were duct taped firmly into the off position. As Baz cracked a bottle of water from the mini bar and collapsed onto the bed, Marius scuttled into the bathroom and applied the same procedure to the switches in there. If one of them needed the john in the middle of the night, they'd do it in the dark or use Baz's portable light. All the tape and red lights would stay in place until Baz had his contacts in again.

Marius returned to the main room and flopped on the bed with Baz. "Okay. De-cloak, then tell me what the hell is going on with you and Elijah Prince."

Now Baz wanted the damn glasses as cover, which was probably why Marius had waited to grill him. With a sigh, Baz folded the shades up and set them on the bedside table and rested the TENS unit on his chest, the regular pulse of the electrodes a soothing backdrop. "Nothing's going on. We hung out. We fucked. End of story."

Marius's response was to raise an eyebrow.

Baz stared up at the ceiling. "Seriously. Move along, nothing to see here."

"I noticed he was extra colorful."

"Yes. We had a little weed, and he had a Xanax. He seemed stressed. Don't worry, he's had both before. Well, I'm assuming about the marijuana because he handled it like a pro. It's not as if I was corrupting him or anything."

"Did I say you corrupted him?"

"You've got your *I'm disappointed in you, Baz* voice on."

Marius grabbed one of Baz's spare pillows and crammed it under his neck as he lay on his side and regarded Baz thoughtfully. "To be honest, I'm more worried about you than disappointed."

Baz blinked. "What? Why?"

"Because you've been obsessed with Elijah for a while, but this is the first time you've engaged with him. And you don't seem to have him out of your system."

"What the hell is that supposed to mean?"

Marius shrugged. The red light erased all the shadows and made his skin seem to glow like a god's. "I don't know. This is new territory. Usually I'm worried about the other guy."

Baz sighed. Turning off the TENS unit, he yanked the electrodes off one at a time, wincing as the adhesive occasionally resisted giving way. "*I* worry about Elijah. Which, when I told him so, pissed him off. Told me he wasn't a princess and could take care of himself."

"*Why* do you worry about him?"

The shadowy memory filtered into Baz's brain. "I met him before Saint Timothy. On one of my benders in Saint Paul—before you started going along as my nanny. I took a cab to this house party, but it was pretty skeevy, so I did a circuit and left. Except on the way to my cab I heard somebody cry out in the alley beside the house."

Marius tensed, half sitting up. "Oh *fuck*. You didn't."

"What was I supposed to do, whistle so I couldn't hear? Of course I went in. Turned out to be a group of losers from the party and the *entertainment* one of them had brought, who wisely refused to go inside when he realized what kind of assholes had hired him."

"Elijah."

"Yes. I threw a hunk of concrete at one of them, called 911. That sent them scattering, since they didn't want to be picked up for solicitation. Of course, the cops tried to hang it on me, but I'd already called my uncle while I waited, and the arresting officers received a pretty high-ranking phone call before they could so much as produce a pair of cuffs. I got Elijah off too. Put him on a bus, gave him all the money I had on me and told him to go the hell home." His nostrils flared, and he shut his eyes. "Which was fucking stupid, obviously, given who I sent him to. I should have...done something else." He didn't know what, but his stomach still turned when he thought about Elijah's parents.

"So you feel guilty because you saved his ass? Wouldn't taking a bullet for him cover at least a little?"

"I don't feel guilty. Well—I do. But that's not why." He sighed. "I don't know. I'm better when I know he's okay. I didn't mean for tonight to get so out of hand."

"He's going to live in the White House with you. Did you fan flames you can't control?"

Baz snorted. "Are you kidding? He blew *me* off after. Fucking danced with anybody *but* me. Didn't so much as look my way." Marius laughed, and Baz threw a pillow at him. "Shut up. It's not funny."

"The fuck it's not. Sebastian Acker, heartbreaker

first class, has been sent home without supper."

"I did so get supper. I got goddamned dessert. Cream-fucking-filled."

"Yes, but no return trip to the buffet for you. I hear there's an informal *I got fucked by Baz* support group. Maybe they'll let you in."

"You're enjoying this *far* too much. You're supposed to be on my side, remember?"

"Oh, I am. I happen to think this is the best thing that's happened to you in a long time. You might build some character out of it."

Baz indicated his naked chest, zigzagged with surgical scars, some of them angry and recent. "I got the goddamned character-building badge, thanks."

Marius's expression didn't dim, not with pity, not with shame. He simply continued to stare patiently at Baz, waiting for him to stop pouting.

This was his best friend.

Baz shut his eyes against the pain that had nothing to do with light and everything to do with the impending first of July and his best friend's removal from his daily life.

Marius's hand fell on Baz's ankle. "I am not. Leaving. You. Stop fucking acting like I'm shipping off to Afghanistan."

"Can you be gay so I could marry you and be done with it?"

"Yes, because my orientation is the only thing standing in the way of our marital bliss."

"True. I shouldn't wish myself on anybody."

Marius's massage of Baz's ankle became a sharp

slap. "Jesus. You want to talk about a goddamned *princess*. Stop pouting."

"Sorry." Baz arranged himself on the bed beside Marius and gently tweaked his nose. "You're a saint, you know?"

Marius tweaked him back. "I do."

"I keep trying to do this on my own. I do want to graduate, eventually. I just…don't know how. To do real life. I don't want to end up in my parents' house forever. But I don't know what else to do. How to be. Only with you and Damien." *And you're leaving.*

"You'll figure it out. We'll help you."

Baz was pretty sure he was beyond hope. The thought depressed him. He teased the stubble on Marius's jaw. "I'd get tits and a pussy for you, if you'd marry me."

Marius slapped him away. "*Stop*. You're so trans insensitive."

"You know I'm good in bed. It's been a few years now, but I bet you still remember the New Year's Eve when you were drunk and—"

With a growl, Marius leapt on Baz, wrestling him as he clamped a hand on Baz's mouth. Baz giggled as they fought, as Marius cursed him out for being an ass—and it was good, right up until Baz's giggles tripped over into hysterical tears.

Marius didn't miss a beat, only shifted from holding him down to simply holding him, cradling him tight and whispering over and over again while he pulled Baz's face into his shoulder, that everything was going to be okay.

Chapter Four

WHEN ELIJAH LIVED on the streets of Saint Paul, he'd have done anything to have a regular job with regular money and a legitimate roof over his head. As little as five months ago, he'd lain in his dorm room with his parents threatening to cut him off or rebaptize him into hell, and he'd bartered with any listening deity for any way out, any way at all.

Now it was the end of June. He had a pristine bedroom in a subdivision. He got a hug from the pastor's wife every morning, a promise he could stay as long as he needed, and cookies each afternoon because she thought he was too thin. He had friends checking in from their home bases. He had a job, as regular as rain, and the only time he had to get on his knees to make money was to open a case of canned tomatoes or pull rogue forks out of the automatic dishwasher.

Elijah was grateful all day long. But sometimes he felt more panicked and stifled than he had the night he'd returned to South Dakota and begged his parents to let him come in, lying about how Jesus had led him home.

He scolded himself when he felt that way. Did he hate being beholden to everyone? Hell, yes. But unless he wanted to sleep under an overpass and wrap himself in righteous indignation and independence, this was his way out. He was safe now. They all told him this, over and over and over. He understood they weren't lying. This wasn't some bait and switch and they'd get angry and threaten him if he didn't do what they wanted. That was his parents' shtick, and they were safely packed away.

So why, he wanted to know, now that he was warm and safe and getting a cookie tummy, did he wake up in cold sweats and sometimes cry himself to sleep?

He never asked anyone the question, but Pastor Schulz, his temporary host and live-in counselor, didn't need an invitation to read Elijah like a book, and he didn't wait long to say what he thought about the latest chapter.

"You're panicking because you're safe now." Pastor crossed his leg over his knee. They were in his study at the house, having an impromptu session after Elijah almost dropped the stack of plates for the table during a panic attack that came out of nowhere. "You've had a rough set of circumstances for a long while, but you're smart and capable, and you knew it wasn't safe for you to react to the horror of your situation in real time."

"I *do* feel safe here." Elijah huddled deeper into the afghan Liz Schulz had tucked around him on the love seat. "I know I'm okay. I'm sorry I can't act like it."

"As I've told you before and will tell you as many times as you need to hear it, Elijah, I have no expecta-tions of your behavior. There are no conditions on your staying here. I know you'll move in with your friends before the end of the summer, but you're welcome here until the moment is right for you. October, December—whenever that is. It is my pleasure, and Liz's, to help you as long as you want our help, and our only motivation in doing so is our desire to show compassion to a child of God who needs extra love right now." His thin white eyebrow raised toward his Friar Tuck-like bald head as he added, "I admit I itch, for selfish reasons, to remind you what your parents and their community advertised as Christian behavior was anything but."

"Trust me. I didn't need a map to figure that one out. Just a Bible with all the bits left in." Elijah worried the corner of his bottom lip in his teeth and stared at the frothy white shag throw rug on the floor between them. "I don't like how I'm freaking out when I'm okay."

"This is the time to be gentle with your vulnerable self, not scold him for perceived bad behavior." Pastor picked up his teacup and frowned absently over the top. "I think sometimes you'd have done well with a small vacation away from Saint Timothy this summer, to let yourself truly unplug."

"Well, Giles and Aaron offered about seventy times. And Mina. And Walter and Kelly. Damien and Marius too. Practically everybody tried to adopt me." *Except Baz. Haven't seen hide nor hair of him since the wedding.* Elijah poked his thumb through one of the crocheted holes in the afghan. "I wanted a job, though. I know people keep chucking money into my fund, but...it makes me feel weird if I'm not contributing too."

"Whatever makes you safe is the right choice for you right now."

Elijah did feel safe with Pastor and Liz. They felt like grandparents—not his real ones, because his fruitcake mom and dad hadn't sprung from the sea— but what grandparents *should* be. They were Mr. and Mrs. Norman Goddamned Rockwell, live and in person. They *were* Christian, yes, but quietly so. Pastor didn't wear his clerical collar unless he was going to campus. The most in-your-face aspect of their faith was how they prayed before meals, but it was a trancelike murmur of *Come, Lord Jesus, be our guest, may these gifts to us be blessed, amen* and nothing more. Sometimes Liz would kiss Elijah's forehead and whisper, "God bless you, child," but it didn't seem like a burden. More of a benediction.

Except the more Elijah thought about what Pastor had said about how he was panicking because he was safe—well, he'd buy that, but there was more to it too. Sometimes, when Elijah was able to peel away the guilt from his reaction, he realized he was also restless and trapped by the tidy bows wrapped around his life. Yes, the cookies and lace-edged linens were wonderful. But not a lot of sex happened when you lived in the campus minister's spare bedroom. He'd had a few offers on his Grindr account, but he couldn't bring himself to sneak away to fuck, so he didn't get laid.

Safe was great—but it was a bit boring. The most risqué thing Liz and Pastor did was watch *Hot in Cleveland*.

Elijah didn't smoke except around his work shifts.

He couldn't bear it if Pastor or Liz caught him, though he knew they wouldn't say anything. Probably wouldn't so much as give him a look of disappointment.

Sometimes the blind acceptance didn't simply make him itch. It made him *nuts*. Which was awful. Sleazy as hell. But it was still the truth. His tenure at Chez Schulz wasn't doing anything for his creative writing, either. That had been flagging since his parents ramped up their censure after Christmas, but he'd thought of little else while he recovered from the shooting.

Mina approved of his trying to write. "You should do more than post on those free fiction sites," she kept telling him when they spoke on the phone. "Your stuff is good. You should get paid."

The idea of getting paid for his work had always been a dream, but *now* it felt like a way out. He didn't know what he could reasonably expect from publishing short stories or a novella, but he found himself dreaming more and more often of declining his poor-me fund because he was able to pay his bills himself. Obviously not right away. But...well, if he wrote a *few* stories...maybe in a year he could be independent?

Maybe two years. Enough money to replace the cafeteria job would be good. That had to be reasonable, right?

Maybe it was, maybe it wasn't—but he did know you didn't get paid if you didn't actually write the goddamn words. Yet every time he attempted to work, he stared for an hour at a blank notebook. Sometimes he got out a random article or gerund phrase, and one weekend he'd written a whole page before he'd ripped it out and shredded it over the trash can.

Sometimes his inability to write bothered him more than anything else. He'd written ever since he could remember. Poetry, short stories, journal entries. He had his fantasy novel too, but he'd decided long ago he shouldn't take it too seriously until he was older. Every time he opened it up and read what he'd written, all he could see was his youth and inexperience.

But online gay erotica? Come on. He was basically masturbating on the page. He'd published on Nifty for *years*. Naughty Nate had five thousand followers on his Archive of Our Own site, and they liked his original stories as well as his fanfic. Downshifting into writing for pay couldn't possibly be too hard.

Except after never suffering so much as ten minutes of writer's block in his life, he was stopped up worse than an oxycodone addict. Elijah didn't know if his authorial constipation was happening because he was trying to write for money, or because he was a hack unless he composed to escape hell.

How sick was he that if it was the latter, he kind of wanted a little hell back.

He didn't actually, but he felt so *empty* not writing, like the guy in *A Clockwork Orange* after the Ludovico technique. Evenings spent escaping into dystopian fantasy or the erotic adventures of idealized college students were fun. Trying not to spill on Liz's furniture and worrying when the next panic attack would creep up on him wasn't any kind of a good time.

So he smoked a lot in the alley one block over from

Liz and Pastor's place, he stared at a blank notebook page, and he worked. Mostly he worked.

At food service, usually Elijah ran the dishwasher. It was a gross job, and it made his hands raw and red. He had to scrape off and rinse other people's half-eaten food into the disposal, which was a real cosmic kick in the nose. He couldn't stop calculating how many kids on the street the scraps would feed, and his average for an eight-hour shift covering two meals—for summer students only—was forty to fifty hungry homeless. The amount of food nibbled at or discarded completely uneaten made him angry.

One day so many fully intact pieces of chicken breast came through he started saving them. At first it was a kind of self-torture, each barely eaten thigh and wing fueling his indignation. When he'd filled a one hundred and five ounce can, however, guilt and panic overcame anger. What was he going to do with all this food?

He decided he'd take it out to the trash bins. He'd seen some stray cats there. He thought about putting it on ice in a cooler with a label *free safe chicken* and seeing if he could figure out where homeless people were staying in the area, but that felt complicated, and he didn't know if anyone would appreciate it. Or how he'd get there. Or if it actually *was* safe, and what if no one found it before salmonella, and he accidentally killed someone? So he hauled the can to the alley.

Lewis Abrahamsen was in the alley.

Technically Elijah had known Lewis existed before they worked together. They were both sophomores, both skinny and awkward über-twinks, and as far as he could tell, they were both gay. He would have sworn he'd seen Lewis's profile on Grindr last year, but not for long and not anymore.

Lewis was…weird. Slightly off, different in a way that made Elijah feel the guy wasn't fully in focus. He always seemed pissed, or moody, or pissed and moody, and he smoked more than Elijah. Several times Elijah had passed him and seen red-rimmed eyes, from crying or drugs, it wasn't clear. Either angle meant more baggage than Louis Vuitton, so Elijah elected to pass. He had a matched set of bullshit all on his own, and his recent disaster with Baz had only driven home the need to stay away from headcases.

The day Elijah went to the alley with his industrial-sized pizza sauce can full of discarded chicken parts, Lewis was there, smoking another cigarette. By rights Elijah should have met him before on that count alone, but the alley was technically off-limits for smoking. The whole campus was. If Elijah wanted to light up, he used the alley near The Shack, because he was all about rules now.

Lewis didn't seem as if he gave a fuck about the rules. He leaned against the wall across from the door to the kitchens, drawing on his cigarette with aggression, tracking Elijah warily as he hauled his can around. He pushed his messy strawberry-blond hair out of his face and frowned. "What do you have in your hands?"

Elijah's cheeks heated, and he vowed the next time he felt like measuring how much food the cafeteria wasted, he'd lie down until the urge passed. "Nothing."

"It looks like a pizza sauce can full of half-eaten chicken."

"Yeah." Elijah set the can beside the Dumpster and kicked it out of the way. "It's...for the cats."

"Great, so there will be *more* of them the next time I come out for a smoke."

Elijah thought about pointing out Lewis shouldn't smoke out here anyway, but he'd sound too much like Aaron. He looked around for something to wipe his hands on and settled for his apron. Watching Lewis smoke reminded him he hadn't had a cig in over twelve hours, and the yearning hit him upside the head. Fuck the rules anyway. "Hey—can I bum off you? I'll pay you back inside. Mine are in my locker."

At first Elijah thought Lewis would say no, but Lewis pulled a pack out of his pocket and passed it over, followed by a lighter. "You're Elijah, right? Elijah Prince?"

The way Lewis said *Elijah Prince* made Elijah pause with the lighter at the tip of his borrowed cigarette. Great. He'd almost forgotten about his unwanted celebrity. He inhaled, shut his eyes while he breathed the smoke out, and nodded. "Yeah."

Lewis ashed his cigarette. "Sorry. I mean—I heard a little about the whole thing with your dad in the parking lot—" He winced and put his cigarette in his mouth. "I'll shut up now."

Elijah shrugged. "My parents are religious nutjobs. I got kicked out when I was sixteen, went home because it was too rough on my own, and faked a conversion. Last year in the middle of second semester, it all caught up with me, and when my dad found out I'd made a fool of him, he came to campus with a gun. Now my mom is in the process of being committed, and my dad is awaiting trial for attempted murder and terrorism."

"Shit." Lewis ground the butt of his cigarette into the dirt and pulled out a new one. "He shot the guy with the sunglasses, right? Baz Acker? The one whose dad is a US senator or something?"

"Uncle. And yeah."

"Damn."

They smoked in silence for a few beats, and Elijah used the time to study Lewis at closer range. He was cuter up close. Nice bone structure. Pouty lips. A little too groomed for Elijah's liking—lots of eyebrow plucking going on. Possibly some makeup. Lewis's clothes were off the usual queer wardrobe as well. His jeans were wrong, to start. Clubwear should be so tight a dance move threatened to split a seam, and everyday attire should have freedom of movement but an emphasis on the package and ass. The ass was fine, but still not right, and either Lewis had nothing to declare, or he'd gone out of his way to disguise his package. Which was odd.

But it wasn't only the jeans. Gay guys wearing Hot Topic *Maleficent* tees wasn't unusual, but this one all but had *hey, this is a girl shirt* stitched on the hem. Same for the shoes: a pair of Keds with flowers on the edges. When Elijah spotted two rhinestone studs in Lewis's ears, he thought, *hmm*.

"You're Lewis, right?" *Not Louise?*

Lewis cocked an eyebrow. "You know me?"

"Of you, more like. Seen you around." He waited for more from Lewis, got nothing. Fine. Small talk. "What's your major?"

Lewis flattened his lips. "I was going to do elementary ed, but...I guess I'll do English."

A huge-assed story hung in the *I guess*, and it promised to be something Elijah didn't want to get involved in. This was why he'd given the guy a wide berth. "I might do English too. Taking some lit courses first semester, and if it goes well, I guess that's what I'll do."

"Who do you have, Ronson or Keil?"

Elijah had no idea. "Is one better?"

"Keil is the best. Get her for anything you can."

"I'll bear it in mind. Thanks."

Elijah would have gone inside, but Lewis passed over another cigarette, and Elijah hated to turn down nicotine.

Lewis pocketed the lighter once more after Elijah finished with it. "You do any of the music groups?"

Elijah shuddered around an inhale. "Fuck, no. A lot of my friends are into it, though."

"Choir or orchestra?"

"Both. My roommate last year was Aaron Seavers."

Lewis lit up. "The tenor? He's *amazing*."

"Yeah, he's all right. His boyfriend is in orchestra. And they both do stuff for Salvo, the girl group. My friend Mina is in it."

Lewis had seemed carefully vague before, but now he dropped all pretense and nearly backed Elijah into the corner in his excitement. "I want to try out. But

I'm not in choir. Salvo, though. And—and the Ambassadors. They're the best."

"Go for it." Elijah did his best to skirt away from Lewis without being obvious. "The Ambassadors are hell to get into, I know."

"Sure." Lewis ran a hand through his hair—hair which was noticeably *not* gaily tousled, just shaggy—and averted his gaze. "Salvo's probably not as bad, right? Since it's only in its second year?"

"Well—yes and no. Mina says there are a zillion girls interested, but they were mostly upperclassmen last year, so they have a lot of spaces. Except they're girls only, you know that, right?"

"Of course. I was only…asking."

Elijah got a weird buzzy feeling from the tone in Lewis's voice, making Elijah feel like he'd stepped on something wriggling and alive and desperate to grab on to his leg. He pulled out his phone to check the time. "I better get back. This wasn't my official break. Thanks for the smokes."

Lewis waved this concern away, and Elijah hustled out of the alley into the relative comfort of other people's discarded food.

BAZ'S BIRTHDAY WAS the last night he was with Damien and Marius in the White House.

Technically their leases were up the night before on June 30, but Aaron and Giles weren't moving in until Friday, Mina until Saturday. Her roommate Jilly would drop off her things but not be fully moved in until

August. Brian, Giles's old roommate, wasn't yet sure exactly when he was coming. Elijah had never been clear about when he'd arrive.

Sid, the only other returning housemate from the year before, was there the night of Baz's birthday too, though he was in and out, helping Karen and Marion with the last of their things from the carriage house apartment. While he was home for the summer, a crew would do some repairs and upgrades to turn the first-floor practice room into a bedroom for Sid, since Baz had elected to turn his room into a single now that Marius was leaving. Sid stopped to have pizza with them when it arrived, and a beer once he'd done all he could for the girls.

"When do you leave in the morning?" Marius asked him as he passed over the bottle opener.

"Five." Sid cracked the cap and sank into his corner of the couch in a fluid motion Baz had seen him do a million times. "It's four hours to Door County, and I told my mom I'd be there by noon to help man the store."

Damien leaned over the coffee table to pick up the opener as Sid discarded it. "I'll be out of here shortly after you. We want to get the Saint Paul apartment scrubbed but good before Stevie comes Saturday."

"When does your job start?" Sid asked.

"The fifteenth." Damien popped his beer open but didn't drink it right away, rolling the sweating brown bottle between his palms instead.

Marius reached around Baz to give Damien a reassuring pat on his thigh. "You'll be great. Stop worrying."

With a grunt, Damien took a deep hit of alcohol. As he set the bottle down, he raised an eyebrow at Marius. "What about you? Med school starts earlier than Saint Timothy, right?"

Marius nodded. "Orientation is the first week in August, classes the second. But I already feel like the whole month of July is going to whiz by me. I have to get organized, plus I wanted to do some of the reading ahead of time because I know it won't be long before I'm trying to catch up with myself."

Marius was the original overachiever. He'd turned his time at Saint Timothy into a five-year pre-med major because he believed there was no such thing as too prepared. The idea that he could be behind on anything, ever, was laughable.

Nobody said this, though, only let Marius fuss as per usual. "Med school will be rough no matter what I do. There's no escaping it. I hope this apartment works out and I can study and sleep at odd hours. I'm trying not to judge my new roommates by you guys, but man."

"Nobody's gonna beat the White House, ever." Sid raised his bottle in a toast.

Damien and Marius raised their bottles too. Baz joined them.

"To the White House," Marius said.

"To the White House," they all echoed, and drank.

The silence got heavy, the inevitable parting hanging before them.

Damien punched Baz lightly in the arm. "So, old

man. Twenty-five."

Baz spun his bottle on his knee. "Guess so."

"Did they call you?" Marius asked, a note of censure in his tone.

He meant Baz's parents. "Actually, yes—one of them, and it was the Y-chromosome, if you can believe it. Sean Acker stopped his golf game, told me he was glad I was alive and announced there was another twenty-five grand in my account to celebrate."

Marius wasn't impressed. "Your mother?"

"She was in meetings all day, but Stephan called to offer her best and let me know the predicted time of arrival of the artisanal malt beverage assortment we're currently enjoying. My uncle's intern sent one of those gold-edged cards and informed me more money went into my trust fund. So you know, everybody represented."

Marius still frowned, but Damien smoothed out the argument before it could start. "You and Sid ready to break in a new house crew?"

Sid smiled wryly. "Fuck, I think they'll break *us* in. This is a pretty tight group. Baz and I will be the grandpas in the corner talking about how things were in our day. Gonna be weird without you two. And Karen and Marion. Man, growing up sucks."

The air got heavy again.

Damien cleared his throat, forcing out a laugh. "Remember the time we locked ourselves out with soup boiling on the stove?"

They played *remember when* for an hour, and it was fun, less weighty than dwelling on the present, but it still pained Baz. This was their last chance to build up *remember whens*, and there wasn't any getting away from it. When the heaviness got to be too much, Baz excused himself, saying he needed a pill, and went up the stairs. He did take a pill—a whole Xanax, and he made a landing pad for it with the last half of a joint.

Marius came upstairs before he was halfway through. He said nothing about Baz's smoking, simply pulled out the chair from his desk like he always did. Except his desk was empty, as was his side of the room. All his belongings would be gone when his parents came in the morning.

Marius would go with them.

He sighed as he slouched in his seat. "I wish you'd have let Sid move in with you."

They'd had this argument a million times, but not often while Baz was on drugs. He shrugged and lay back on his bed. "Less fuss. This way I can fuck who I want. And he has a crazy fall schedule. Would cramp my style."

"I had a crazy schedule too, and we did fine. Also, you haven't had anybody up to the room in months."

"Yeah, well, somebody shot me in the shoulder. I'm off my game."

"They're going to bed soon. Come downstairs. Enjoy the last of the night with us."

Baz took a long toke of the joint, holding it deep in his lungs. *Push it away. Push it all away.* He let the breath out, feeling his mind pixelating away on the drugs. "I don't want to watch the end."

Marius didn't argue, and eventually, with a sigh, he

left.

When the joint was done, Baz removed his contacts and climbed into bed, riding a haze of hipster beer, prescription medication, and the last tokes of the best Chronic he could scare up in Minnesota. He drifted in and out of sleep, watching colors and shapes float above his head.

At some point the shapes took a form. As sleep pulled him under, Baz surrendered to a drug-soaked dream. All his friends from all his years at Saint Timothy danced to silent music around his bedroom. Keeter, Marius, Sid, Damien, Aaron, Giles—everybody was there. They laughed and ground on one another, and Baz watched.

A figure formed at the end of his bed. Dark and slight, naked where the others were clothed. It was Elijah. Everyone else in the dream was soft and hazy, moving through a fog, but Elijah was sharp-edged. His body was angular, pale, his skin networked in ugly red scars. He didn't dance, didn't laugh, only sat on Baz's feet, staring.

It wasn't until Baz drifted into a deeper plane of his subconscious that he realized Elijah's real-life body didn't have any scars. They'd only seemed familiar because he was looking at the mirror image of his own.

Chapter Five

MUCH AS ELIJAH hated to admit it, things got a little better when Aaron, Giles, and Mina moved into the White House. They showed up at Pastor and Liz's place asking him how he was doing, dragged him on trips to the store and walks around campus. They foisted Giles's old laptop on him, as well as a new, much smarter smartphone piggybacked onto Giles's family's plan. They glared at him when he smoked too much, nagged him in text and Snapchat when he didn't come over to the White House enough, and demanded to know when he'd move in. In return, Elijah made snide remarks, complained they drove him crazy…and didn't have any more of those weird panic episodes.

The reason he stayed away from the White House, though, wasn't because he wanted to cement his role as Aaron and Giles's personal Grumpy Cat. That honor went entirely to Baz. He was both the reason Elijah stayed away and the reason why when he did show up, he was so surly Giles swatted him and asked what the hell his problem was.

Which was pretty rich, since Baz made Elijah look like he had a sunny disposition. He spent most of the time in his room, or pacing the kitchen, or sitting in his

Tesla in the garage. He slammed pans around before inevitably ordering takeout, or sat for an hour on the couch channel surfing but never landing on anything.

He never said a single word to Elijah. If he needed someone to drive him over to Marius or Damien in the Cities, he asked Giles or Aaron, or Mina.

Elijah was about ready to trip him to see if *that* would get Baz to acknowledge he existed.

Aaron, damn it all, noticed the weird tension and commented on it.

"Did something happen with you two?" He dug into a bowl of Cheetos and frowned at Elijah as he munched. "I thought you kind of connected or something at Walter and Kelly's wedding, but I guess not?"

Elijah threw a Cheeto at Aaron's head and picked up the remote.

Aaron didn't let it go. "Did you fight or something?"

Elijah set his jaw and fixed his gaze on *RuPaul's Drag Race*. "You'd have to notice someone was alive to fight with them." He winced at how seventh grade the comment sounded. "Have you been composing? I thought I heard the piano earlier."

"Some. Mostly I've arranged songs for Salvo and the Ambassadors for the fall. I think I need more coursework under me before I can compose very well."

Maybe that was Elijah's problem. He should look into writing classes. He needed to pick courses for the fall, straight up. "I have to figure out a major. English, I guess."

"Sounds smart, with all your stories."

"You do know English is reading dead white men, sweetheart, not writing."

"I have to take music history to learn how to write music. This could be the same kind of thing."

Elijah sat with the idea a minute, trying it out. He hadn't thought of English except as something easy. The idea it might give him what he wanted was a little more hope than he knew how to handle.

He was working up the courage to ask Aaron if he'd read any of the Naughty Nate stuff and maybe what he thought about it when a door opened on the second floor. Baz bounded down the stairs, jingling his keys. "Aaron, babe, could you give me a lift into the city? I'll cab home. You can use the Tesla for whatever you want tonight."

Aaron glanced uncertainly between Baz and Elijah. "Um, sure." He patted his jeans. "I gotta go find my wallet, though."

Baz saluted on his way to the kitchen and the garage beyond. "I'll wait in the car."

After Baz disappeared, Aaron glanced awkwardly at Elijah. "You're...*sure* nothing's going on between the two of you?"

Elijah smiled, sharp and brittle to mask his hurt. "Not anything *I* was told about."

Aaron left it at that, disappearing up the stairs to his own room. Elijah stayed on the couch, gripping the remote so tight it almost cracked.

God, but he wanted to storm after Baz and ask him what the fuck his problem was, but he'd die before he gave the bastard the satisfaction of a dramatic performance. All he could think about, though, was this was what it was like when he came over to the White House to visit. By the fall, he was supposed to live with this crap full-time. Elijah didn't know how many more times he could be snubbed by Baz before he'd break.

Swearing under his breath, he fished his cigarettes out of his backpack and headed out the front door. Usually he smoked behind the garage, but he'd go the long way to avoid His Royal Highness.

"Should never have fucked him," he murmured as he cupped a hand around the tip of his cigarette. Pocketing the lighter, he took a deep drag and went around the corner—and ran smack into the center of Baz's chest.

"*Jesus*—" He tried to catch his cigarette, but it tumbled out of his hands and broke in half as it hit the side of the building on the way to the sidewalk. Cheeks burning, pride smarting something fierce, Elijah glared into the fucking sunglasses.

Baz said nothing, only stared back, unreadable as ever.

Elijah's traitorous brain played memories of being touched and teased in the back of the Tesla. Those hurt, but remembering the way Baz had smiled that night slayed him. *Yeah, well, he's not smiling now. And obviously the whole "need to protect you" line was a pile of steaming shit.*

Elijah wanted a killer exit line—seven or eight rose to his tongue, but he couldn't make any pass his lips. *You hurt me* kept threatening to spill out instead.

Baz's lips flattened into a subtle frown. As one eyebrow tipped delicately above the plastic rim of his glasses, he reached for Elijah.

When the front door opened and Aaron came out, Elijah ducked around Baz and made a beeline for the rear of the house. He sat on the bench in the garden, clutching his cigarettes and holding his breath as he kept one eye on the door from the garage. It remained shut, and all he heard was the sound of two car doors slamming before the eerily quiet crunch of wheels over gravel as the Tesla drifted silently away.

Elijah choked down two cigarettes by the time the door did open—but it was Mina who sat beside him, not Baz. She put his head on her shoulder and gently hugged him to her side.

"I hate him," Elijah whispered, in a tone belying the truth that he very much did not.

Mina kissed his hair. "Karen left a half a box of wine in the carriage house apartment's mini-kitchen, I have popcorn, and I can swipe Baz's copy of *Howl's Moving Castle* from his room. Want to stay over tonight?"

Elijah swallowed a stupid, achy feeling over Baz having his favorite movie and nodded. "Yeah. I do." He snuggled in closer to Mina. "Thanks."

"Anytime."

AARON DIDN'T SAY anything about Elijah as he drove the Tesla out of Campustown, but once they were on Interstate 94, he pounced. "What's going on with you and Elijah?" Aaron turned down the music and gave every indication he was settling in for a real answer.

Baz shrugged and averted his gaze out the passenger window. "Nothing."

"You don't ever talk to him. It's like when he's in the room, you pretend you can't see he's there. I think it bothers him."

Oh, Baz knew it bothered Elijah. Even before their encounter just now. He rubbed his thumb over the carbon-fiber pattern of the Tesla's trim.

Aaron wasn't done. "Are you doing to him what you did to me after we hooked up? Because let me assure you as the one who's been on the receiving end of the silent treatment, it sucks."

Baz shut his eyes. "Sorry."

"He's about seventy times tougher than me, but he's more sensitive than he lets anyone know. The more caustic he gets, the closer you are to a raw nerve. If you stand still and wait for that to burn out, you usually get to see what he's hiding, and it'll break you."

Elijah could break Baz without showing him anything. Which was why he'd stayed away. He felt too raw as it was.

Baz scraped his nail over the trim he'd stroked earlier. "You should tell him he's better off. I'm an ass, and I'm a ton of work. I should have asked Marius to give you that speech a year ago."

"He did. Kind of. Walter took care of the rest." Aaron switched lanes to pass a minivan. "The thing is, you aren't actually an asshole. Not all the time. And for the record, I think it's *your* version of Elijah's caustic remarks."

Baz slipped two fingers under the bridge of his glasses and applied gentle pressure to ward off the tension headache. "Trust me, kid. Nobody wants to be around my bullshit right now." He sighed and let his hand fall to his lap. "Which is part of what this command performance is."

"Where *am* I taking you? I mean, I get the hotel address, but why? I figured it was some swanky booty call."

Baz's lips quirked in a half-smile. "No booty. Gloria Barnett Acker has requested the honor of my presence in the Park Suite of the Saint Paul Hotel. Or, in layman's terms, my mom flew here to read me the riot act."

Aaron's grip on the wheel became white-knuckled, and his shoulders hunched in piano-wire-taut tension. "Are you—okay? Do you want me to come along?"

Too late Baz remembered Aaron's intensely negative association with parental summons. "Hey—no. It's cool. My mom doesn't do dramatic scenes. The worst thing she's going to do is make threats about putting conditions on my allowance, which she'll never follow through with. You have to remember these are the people who bought me a one hundred thousand dollar car—which I can't drive—because they were soft after I took a slug in the shoulder."

"Okay. If you're sure."

"Why don't you come up and meet her? She'll probably feed you dinner and vow to buy you an instrument. She likes you."

"I don't need her to buy me anything."

"Yes, but she needs to give gifts. Her assistant has a zipper pouch of assorted gift cards on hand at all times. Usually iPad minis too, though she's been giving Fitbits lately. She shows love by showering people with things."

The last shards of Aaron's tension unkinked, and he settled into the driver's seat. "So your mom's pretty cool."

Baz considered how to answer. "She's unconventional. She absolutely loves me and would do anything for me. She has her moments of magic and wonder, yes, but she never held me on her lap and snuggled me—she's not that kind of mom. Nanny Gail was the cuddler. And she was good at it, so I didn't complain." He traced the seam between the passenger window and the door. "Mom means well. I definitely couldn't function without her as my backup."

"But she's still going to ream you out?"

"Pretty much."

A pause, and the tiniest return of tension. "I can stay. Giles and I were going to go to a movie, but he wouldn't mind if I put it off."

"Tell you what. I'll text you once she's finished the lecture and let you know I'm okay. And if it turns out I'm not, I'll call you and you can come pick me up. But I won't need to call you. This is an old fight. It's about my reluctance to face the future, and the way I've leaned on Marius and Damien instead of letting them move on. Which I've already bowed to before she can yell, asking you for a ride instead of calling one of them."

"You know I'd drive you anywhere, anytime. Same goes for Giles, and Mina."

"I do know. And thanks."

"You could ask Elijah too. In fact, you should. He really is a great guy. And—" Aaron flushed. "I read his online writing. Holy crap."

Baz had found it too. "He's good. Wicked way with words, that one." Wicked mouth and hands as well.

You had to fuck it up with him, didn't you?

Aaron adjusted his grip on the wheel. "What I'm saying is, you shouldn't freeze him out."

Baz held up a hand. "Message received. I'll stop being a dick."

"Well, I wouldn't go that far. It's not a good idea to set yourself up for failure. But being tolerable might not be a bad goal."

Laughing, Baz leaned over and planted a wet kiss on Aaron's cheek. "If you'd flipped me this kind of shade when we were flirting, I'd probably have asked you to marry me."

"I'm glad I didn't, because I'm going to marry Giles." He blushed, looking happy and slightly serene. "Not exactly officially yet. We've sort of agreed we'll get engaged later, but we're not in a hurry. There's nobody else for me but him."

Baz was happy for them. Jealous, but in an abstract way, because he knew this kind of settled happiness was well beyond his reach. It would be nice, but he knew better.

You could have had a hint of it with Elijah.

The GPS led them off the interstate and through

the streets of downtown Saint Paul to the Saint Paul Hotel. They pulled up under the awning, where Baz passed over the key fob and explained the car start and shut-off to the valet, giving them his mother's room number before linking his arm in Aaron's and leading him into the lobby. When Aaron rubbernecked at the opulence, Baz slowed to let his friend get a good look.

"This is pretty swank," Aaron declared.

"Old swank. My mom's favorite kind."

He took them to his mother's suite, where he rang the buzzer. The door was opened by Erika, the intern his mother's assistant was managing at the moment. She was just out of undergrad and hoping for a foot in the door at one of his mother's foundations. Her smile was bright, her expression eager, but Baz could read her terror too. It made him like her. Too many of the interns were overconfident sharks who pissed him off.

Unfortunately, her naiveté meant she was already toast.

He smiled back at her. "Hi, Erika. Is my mother in? Stephan texted me and said this would be a good time, but we can go grab a drink in the lobby if it isn't."

"Oh no—absolutely fine." Her manic evened out as she aimed her beam at Aaron. "Hi. I'm Erika Green, one of Ms. Acker's assistants."

"Aaron Seavers." He stuck his hand out and shook hers. "Baz's friend from school. Pleased to meet you."

Erika ushered them into the parlor part of the suite and gestured to the sofa and chair. "She's on the phone in the other room. I'll let her know you're here. Can I get either of you anything to drink?"

Baz talked over Aaron before he could say he didn't need anything. "Did she wheedle an espresso machine out of them as usual?"

"As a matter of fact, yes." Erika was on firm footing now. "Double shot latte? With a little honey?"

"Well-remembered." Baz nudged Aaron's leg. "What can she get you?"

Aaron had the *I don't want to bother her* look about him. "I'll just have coffee."

"Sure." Erika bustled about with the machine.

"He wants some cream and my mother's caramel syrup too," Baz added, and let Erika do her thing.

Erika *dripped* water from behind her ears, and Baz would lay money on Stephan, his mother's barracuda executive assistant, eating Erika for brunch before the month was out. He was shocked she'd lasted this long. He couldn't save her, but he could give her a few moments of feeling competent.

Stephan breezed through the French doors from the other part of the suite. "Sebastian. So good to see you. I was surprised I didn't receive a call to collect you. But now I see you brought a chauffeur more charming than I could ever hope to muster." Stephan held out a finely manicured hand to Aaron. "Stephan Warner. I'm Ms. Acker's executive assistant."

Aaron blinked under the 800-watt beam from Stephan's polished expression and tentatively accepted his hand. "Aaron Seavers."

"Wonderful to meet you. I trust you're settling into the house well enough?"

Aaron cast a confused glance at Baz, *How does he*

know me? written all over his face.

Baz shut his eyes in a long blink so he could stay the urge to roll them. "He's fine. I brought him up to meet Mom, but he needs to get back. As I understand it, he and his boyfriend have a date."

"Absolutely. Gloria is finishing up a quick conference. Shouldn't be but another few minutes."

"Here's your coffee." Erika placed a delicate cup and saucer in front of Baz and another in front of Aaron, and glanced around hopefully.

"It looks amazing. Thank you," Baz said.

"Yes, thank you." Looking overwhelmed, Aaron picked up the cup—sans saucer—and held it like a shield. Baz wondered if he should maneuver him out the door and let him off the hook. If this was his reaction to Stephan, he probably wasn't ready for Gloria.

"Erika, I haven't received your report yet, and I asked you for it several hours ago."

Erika and Aaron both snapped their spines straighter at the tone in Stephan's voice. Erika cowed as well. "Sorry, sir. I was prepping notes for Ms. Acker's conference call."

"Now that's done, and you're playing barista. If you want to work at Starbucks, this can be arranged."

Erika murmured an apology, Stephan revealed the shallow limits of his soul, and Aaron looked so far beyond uncomfortable Baz was working up an exit strategy, when the French doors opened and Gloria Barnett Acker swept into the room.

Chapter Six

"SEBASTIAN." GLORIA BARNETT Acker opened her arms to embrace her son.

Baz rose and stepped into her hug—it smelled of French perfume and crisp linen, and it felt like home. "Mom. Good to see you."

She turned to Aaron. "Thank you for driving Sebastian. I hope he didn't put you to too much trouble."

"Oh, no. I don't mind at all." Bless him, but he was scrutinizing Gloria, making sure she wasn't about to boot Baz into the street.

Gloria pulled Baz to the couch as she sat beside him. "So the White House is having quite a turnover, as I understand. The girls are getting settled into the carriage house apartment?"

Aaron glanced at Baz before replying. "Mina is. Jilly couldn't come until August."

"Oh, that's right. I remember her parents kept trying to pay for the summer though she couldn't come until later. But you and Giles are settled? What about Sid? Did you get the practice room converted to a single yet, or is he not coming until August? Brian was another late one—but what about Elijah? I know his arrival was never confirmed."

Aaron cast a naked *What the hell is going on here?* look at Baz.

Baz resisted the urge to throttle his mother. First Stephan, now her. He'd told them both he didn't want the new crew to have full disclosure yet, but either they'd forgotten or decided it wasn't convenient.

He answered her questions first before dealing with Aaron. "Giles and Aaron are all set. Brian will be there mid-August. Elijah will be over when he's ready." He turned to Aaron, hating this part. "She knows about all this because the management company who owns the White House is part of the family business."

Aaron's eyes widened. "You...*own* the White House?"

Gloria waved her free hand at him, dismissing the revelation. "I bought it when Sebastian moved in. It made me feel better, knowing it was kept up properly."

"Which is why there's a killer security system on a student rental." Baz tracked Aaron's reaction, relieved it was mostly surprise. He hoped the other residents were as blasé about realizing they were part of the Barnett-Acker family project. "The good news is, if you ever can't quite make rent, I can probably get the landlord to look the other way."

"Oh, I'm going to make my dad pay the full year in advance." Aaron sipped his latte. "That's pretty cool, you owning the White House. I was worried it would get eaten by the development creeping up the hill."

"When Baz is ready to get rid of the property, we'll give it to the college, but until then, it will stay in Acker hands." She patted Baz's knee. "Darling, have you eaten? I haven't ordered dinner yet. Aaron, what about you?"

"I'm fine." Aaron glanced at Baz, one last double-check, and Baz gave him a nod telegraphing *Yep, I'm fine, cut yourself loose.* Aaron nodded in acknowledgment. "I should be going home."

"I'm sorry my phone call delayed you. If I can't buy you dinner, let me treat you. Stephan?"

While Aaron made noises of protest and Stephan retrieved the wallet of cards, Baz had an idea. "Aaron was taken by the beauty of the Saint Paul Hotel. It's too bad there's not time for you to give him the historical tour."

Gloria beamed at Aaron. "Isn't it lovely? We stayed here when I was a girl, and I fell in love at once. I admit I use any excuse to come back." She accepted the wallet from Stephan but set it aside, looking thoughtful. "Tell you what. I'm arranging for the manager to set up a weekend getaway for you and Giles at your convenience. I'll make sure he gives you a tour and sets you up with a few special events."

Aaron blinked. Rapidly. "You don't have to—"

Baz cut him off patiently. "Let her do something for you. Besides, how much do you think Giles would enjoy a romantic getaway?"

"It will be *wonderful*," Gloria promised, clearly warming to the idea. "I'll call Oliver Thompson and have him find a perfect show for you."

Aaron protested a little more, but not long before switching to thanking Gloria, accepting her polite hugs and giving Baz one last double-check before disappearing into the hall.

"Stephan, you'll set everything up for Aaron?" Gloria spoke with the same careful lilt she always did, but there was an edge to her tone this time, one Baz knew meant *It's time for you to leave me alone with my son.*

Stephan inclined his head in a nod. "Absolutely. Shall I arrange a telephone meeting with Mr. Thompson as well?"

"Please. Oh, and tell Erika she can work in her room for the rest of the evening. The same goes for you."

Baz tried not to panic over the DEFCON levels his mom was setting off. Getting rid of the staff? Making it clear she and Baz weren't to be interrupted? Baz began to regret letting his buffer get away. God, he *wished* his mom would threaten to chuck him out penniless as Aaron's parents had. That he could deal with. But she'd never behave so crudely in a million years.

No, Gloria would politick Baz to death.

Once the door to the suite was closed, she threw the deadbolt and crossed to the bar, where she poured herself a glass of cabernet and made Baz a scotch neat. She passed Baz the drink and sat on the other side of the sofa beside him. "Well. Here we are, darling. I hope you've been well?"

Baz set his scotch beside his coffee and glared at her. "Mom, if you're going to yell at me for not graduating, do it already. Don't puff me up first like a goddamned lobbyist."

"I'm not yelling at you for anything." She sighed and put her glass aside as well. "I've been approached about running for political office, and this time I don't think I can do anything but accept."

Relief rolled off Baz in great steaming clouds. "Mom, that's fantastic. Of course I want you to run for office. Haven't I said so for years?"

"Nothing is official, and it's vital you not share this information with anyone. Not even Marius or Damien."

"Of course I won't tell anyone. But you were born for this, Mom. This is your first step toward climbing your way to the top. God, I hope it doesn't take you long to be running for the other US Senate seat beside Uncle Paul."

"That's just it, sweetheart. The US Attorney General will be stepping down by the end of the month. Your uncle is the favored candidate for the soon-to-be-open position. His nomination would be tricky, but we believe the Republicans won't be able to resist the bait of his open seat. Especially when they see what a greenhorn the governor is offering as his replacement."

Baz stared at her as everything clicked, at last, into place. "You. You're the greenhorn. Except you aren't. It's a pretty big leap from no office to US senator, but if anybody could do it, it's you."

"Yes. But not many people know. Which means if we set up the dance correctly, I can capture the flag— giving a plum position to your uncle and setting him up for bigger things, helping the President and the Democratic Party. I can finally have my dream of taking my place in the Barnett political dynasty."

Baz squeezed his mother's hand. "Mom, of course

you have my blessing. This is amazing. You have to say yes. Right now."

She shook her head. "Sweetheart, you don't understand. If I do this, if I say yes, the Beltway press and the Republicans will be all over me. The Democratic party has promised they'll send in a crack team to support us, but no matter what we do, the opposition will dig deep. They'll uncover all the dirt and rattle every skeleton. Of me and my family." She laced their fingers together tightly and stared achingly into Baz's face. "You, sweetheart. They'll come after you."

Baz could see it already. Every nuance of his bashing, of Jordan's death. Any trick he'd ever fucked would be interviewed. He'd be spun out as a playboy, a wastrel, an unstable bomb waiting to go off. After all these years of deliberately avoiding his past, it would be played out on the evening news. Over and over again. It would be hell beyond his worst nightmare.

Yet as he took in the hope and eagerness on his mother's face, he knew the real nightmare would be knowing he was the reason she didn't take this step.

He kissed her hand. "I think I'll talk to Pastor Schulz tomorrow about how many courses I'd have to complete to leave Saint Timothy with a religion major. That ought to throw off their playboy story."

Her eyes glazed with tears she didn't shed. "Oh, Sebastian. Are you sure?"

"It'll be wonderful. I always wanted a senator for a mother."

She embraced him tightly. "Sweetheart—thank you. I suspected this was what you'd say, but I truly would decline if you wanted me to."

No, this wasn't going to be fantastic. But what, she should say no because it might be hard on him? He who didn't know when his graduation date was? "I'm sure. One hundred percent."

"Thank you so much, darling." She stroked his back. "Since you're so certain of your support...I admit, I have a favor to ask of you already."

Baz blinked. "Um—okay?"

"Part of the reason I'm approaching you now is because there's an event this weekend. A house-party fundraiser for Chicago area Democrats. Paul thinks I should be there, and I'd love you to come too. The theory is to beat rumors off at the pass. It doesn't have to be overt, obviously—we'll let them assume."

"Assume what?"

"It would be wonderful if you could attend the gala with someone people would assume is your boyfriend."

Baz recoiled.

She petted him, trying to hook him in the tractor beam of her fixer smile. "Sweetheart, I don't mean you actually have to have one. We can find someone suitable to be your escort. It's foregrounding, in case you need cover later. If the press bother you once the announcements are made, we have the narrative ready to roll out. Or we don't use it at all—but then we have an option." She adjusted her smile to full wattage. "So what do you think? Shall I have Stephan send you some profiles?"

He stifled the urge to protest, having ridden this tiger before. Fighting would entrench him more deeply.

He had no delusion this would be an escort-only situation. She was trying to marry him off. So he had to head her off.

His options were to refuse to go, argue he didn't want a date, or provide his own. Which normally wouldn't be a problem, but he couldn't do this to any of his friends. Damien was obviously out, what with the engagement and all. Marius would do it, but when the shit hit the fan, he'd need to fake gay during his first year of med school. No. Aaron and Giles were out too, because he wasn't messing up that relationship. Sid wouldn't touch this with a ten-foot pole.

One name lingered in his contact list, and suddenly his mother's file of prospective suitors didn't sound so bad.

Except yes, it did. She'd call in favors from people in her network who had gay, bi, or desperate sons. This one event would become four, or five, and if his mother liked the way they looked together—good odds, as she'd pick the guy out—she'd begin campaigning for the pretend relationship to be real. He could already hear the pitch. *It's not as if you have any interest in actually dating someone. And if the two of you come to an agreement, there's no need for you to be exclusive.*

The metaphorical migraine she'd stirred up became a literal one. *What the hell happened to being ready to decline if I said no?* Obviously nothing more than a line. He'd been politicked once again. He'd all but lain down on the track and helped her tie his body to the rails.

One lifeline. You have one available lifeline. And Aa-

ron's blessing to use it.

"Of course I'll come to your party. But I can't let you send me any profiles of prospective faux boyfriends." Baz smiled. "My *actual* boyfriend would get jealous."

The lie wasn't the problem—Baz had delivered avalanche-level snow jobs to Gloria Barnett Acker since 1996. He knew how to adjust the corners of his mouth, dip his head, hunch his shoulders sheepishly to suggest *golly, who'd of thunk it*, but Sebastian Acker was in love. As she bluffed right back, pretending it didn't annoy her to have her careful orchestra disassembled even in this small way, Baz expertly dished out breadcrumbs of fake intel as she demanded *all the details*.

What twisted his gut into knots was the knowledge that to pull off the act, he had to produce this boyfriend, the actual human he'd be roping into the farce. Instinct told him he could summon a goddamned mountain of politicking, and Elijah Prince would simply stand there with his arms folded, calling bullshit. Looking angry and suspicious and hurt, the way he had on the steps of the White House hours before.

When Baz's mother rose to refill her drink so they could have a proper toast, Baz popped the lid off his bottle of oxycodone, chased two with a healthy swallow of scotch, and hoped to hell he hadn't bitten off more than he could chew.

HOWL'S MOVING CASTLE was Elijah's favorite movie, but it always made him sad.

He'd glue his eyeballs shut before he watched any of Kelly Davidson's Disney pap, but Diana Wynne Jones's story was genius and Hayao Miyazaki could right all the wrongs of the world. That the movie happened to have romantic shading was a side effect. That this side effect always got under his skin was an annoyance to be endured. Sometimes enduring was harder than other times, though, and once Mina fell asleep, he got off the couch she'd converted to a bed for him, slipped into her flip-flops and padded down the apartment stairs to have a cigarette.

Naturally, as he lit up at the foot of the stairs, a car pulled into the drive, and Baz stepped out of it.

The headlights cut across him as the sleek black car retreated, so there wasn't any point in trying to hide. Ashing into the bushes, Elijah rested a hip on the wall and stared at Baz, waiting to see what happened next.

Hands in his pockets, Baz leaned on a decorative lamppost beside some lattice fencing. "Hey. How's it going?"

Elijah took a slow, careful drag before blowing the smoke out of the corner of his mouth. "Sorry—were you talking to me?"

"Yeah." Baz shoved his hands deeper and nodded at the main house. "Um—hey. I know we haven't...said much to each other lately. And this is the wrong way to go about it, but...I have to ask you something. A favor."

Normally the broody-male routine would at least give Elijah a cheap thrill, but the one-eighty from complete cold shoulder to *aw-shucks, I'm such an awkward hot mess, please forgive me because I need something* pissed Elijah off. "No worries. People fuck me, act like I'm a syphilitic leper, then ask for a favor all the time. Just keep me abreast of where we are. Maybe we can come up with a signal."

The bastard had the nerve to laugh. "You're right. It would be stupid to ask. I'll figure out something else."

For a moment, snark deserted Elijah, panic and raw loneliness overcoming him as he realized Baz was about to turn him loose after one goddamned exchange. Angling across the sidewalk, Elijah cut Baz off before he could disappear into the garage.

"Oh, no you *fucking don't*. You do *not* ignore me for five weeks, rub your toe in the dirt and say you need something from me, then bail when I bleed off some hurt."

He shut his eyes as he winced at letting the word *hurt* escape his filter.

Setting his jaw, Elijah glared into the depths of Baz's sunglasses and planted his flag. "You're not going anywhere. We're having this out. Right here. Right now."

Baz held up his hands, shoulders sagging in defeat. "Seriously, not tonight. I'm tapped out."

Baz tried for an end run, but Elijah reinserted himself in the way. "Fine. You can go hide in your cave and brood, as soon as you tell me what you were going to ask me."

The weary-moppet act fell away as Baz bared his teeth. "Changed my mind. Not asking you for anything, ever. Back the fuck off."

"Fuck you and your goddamned moods. Fine, ass-hole. I don't want to know what you were going to tell me. Probably that you had a fucking hangnail. Well, suck on it. I'll make it easy to never ask me for any-thing, ever. I'm not spending one more ass-tastic minute in this house so long as you're in it, and I'm sure as fuck not living here. Not for the summer, not the school year, not for the goddamned zombie apoca-lypse. I'll stay with Pastor, and if it doesn't work out, I'll stay at the Kiss My Ass Motel."

It was a line demanding a dramatic exit, but Elijah didn't know where the hell to go. If he went upstairs, he couldn't have another cigarette, plus if Baz followed him, he'd wake Mina. If Baz didn't follow…

Fuck. This. Elijah shoved the cigarette between his lips and stormed down the alley to who the fuck knew where. In his pajama pants.

Baz grabbed Elijah, knocking his cigarette into the gravel. Pushing Elijah against the garage, flattening one arm above his head, Baz used his other hand to pin Elijah's shoulder in place.

Elijah shut his eyes in a slow blink, masking a shiv-er of want before cloaking himself in outrage once more. "What the *hell*—"

"Shut. Up." Baz loosened his grip, but not by much. The dark holes of his glasses bore into Elijah. His jaw was tight, the cords of his neck tense. The *aw-shucks* routine was gone, as was the edge. Now he was merely raw and wrecked. "I'm sorry. I don't have anything to say, except I'm an ass and you deserve better."

It was true. Nobody fucking deserved this. But wrecked Baz was Elijah's kryptonite. "I would have simply put out, you know. You're the one who paraded us in front of everyone we know. They keep making sad eyes at me because I was dumped. Which is fucking cold, because I told you I got it was a one-off. I didn't think we were fucking dating, but I thought we'd at least progressed to eye contact in the hallway."

Baz sagged, body curving around Elijah as he let his forehead hit the siding of the garage. "It's stupid. I fucked up. It was a real asshole move to volunteer you after the way I've treated you. I'm—sorry."

"Volunteer me?"

Baz's body went rigid, lips thinning into a line. "I can't take you yelling at me any more tonight."

Wrecked Baz was fading, which meant so was Elijah's empathy. "Tough. Tell me anyway."

Baz stared at Elijah, expression blank. *Those fucking glasses.* "If I tell you, you'll move into the White House? As soon as possible?"

Yes, because it had been so much bullshit, his defiant insistence he would go off and live anywhere else. Except he wasn't giving in so easily. "I'll think about it."

"No. If I tell you, you're moving in. Tomorrow."

Elijah let go of Baz to fold his arms over his chest. "I'll think about it."

Baz scowled and mimicked Elijah's pose. And said nothing, only stared at Elijah, waiting for him to fold.

Jesus*god*, Elijah wanted to shake the fucker. "Why

the hell do you care if I move in or not?"

"Because I care, all right?" He ran a hand through his hair, and the filtered gold light played over his face, casting shadows, making him seem like a demon emerging from hell to glimpse heaven. "Because you should be here. They want you here. You wanted to be here, until I fucked up. I want you here." When he glared at Elijah, the streetlight glinted on his rims, completing the demonic image. "Snark all you need to, but it's true. So get it over with, then agree you'll move in, and I'll tell you what I was going to ask you. You'll get testy about that too, which is fine. I'll stand here, and you can hurl whatever you want at me. But first you're promising to move in."

The whole thing was so insane Elijah didn't know where to start. He considered giving him the finger and escaping up the stairs, at this point ready to wake up Mina and let her keep his demon at bay.

Except Baz had sunk to wrecked again. Sighing, Elijah pulled out a cigarette and scowled at Baz as he lit it. When Baz motioned for the pack, Elijah arched an eyebrow. "They're GPC menthols."

"I'll buy you a carton of Davidoffs tomorrow, but for now, let me at the damn nicotine."

Elijah had no idea what the fuck a Davidoff was. Probably some rich-person cigarette. Rolling his eyes, he passed over the pack and the lighter. Baz tapped out a cigarette, lit it and took a long, slow drag. He made a slight face as he exhaled, but he gave no commentary on the poor quality of Elijah's tobacco.

"I can't get into the full details, but the short version is my mom is making me haul ass to Chicago this weekend for some fancy fundraiser. She wants me to have a…date. She tried to set me up with someone herself, but I told her no." He ashed the tip of his cigarette. "I kind of…told her I'd bring you."

By the middle of the speech, Elijah had seen this coming, but the admission still left him dizzy. He smoked for almost a minute before replying. "So it's a joke, right? I'm supposed to be the bumpkin you use to—"

"What? No. *No*." Baz frowned at him, annoyed. "Why the fuck—how much of an asshole do you think I am?"

Elijah blew smoke at his face.

Baz held up his hands and grimaced before sucking on his own cigarette with intensity. "Fine. I had that coming. I'm a jerk. And you're going to tell me no. I don't have any idea how to convince you, because you turn me so goddamn inside out I'm not going to try. But fuck this idea I'd make fun of you."

Why did you say you'd bring me? "I don't have the right clothes."

Baz waved this away. "Whatever. I'd buy the clothes."

"I don't know how the forks work and whatnot."

"It's probably not a fork-focused thing, and if it is, learning that takes ten minutes." Baz glanced at Elijah as he drew once more on his cigarette. "These are your only objections? Forks and clothes?"

The night was warm, but Elijah hugged himself as if he were cold. "Why don't you ask Aaron? He'd look good on your arm."

"Giles would deck me."

Giles *would* deck him. Elijah dropped his cigarette on the ground and rubbed it out with his toe. He immediately lit up a new one. "I work this weekend."

"I'll help you find someone to cover."

"I don't know anyone in Chicago. If you abandon me, I have nowhere to go."

"I won't abandon you. But if I were to, you'll be driving my car. You could drive yourself here. If you want backup, I'll toss in a five-hundred-dollar prepaid Visa card."

Elijah's lungs were protesting from too much nicotine, but he kept smoking anyway. "This isn't a joke. You really did ignore me for over a month, then ask me to be your date to the prom."

"Fundraiser. And, yes. Sorry."

This was way too *Carrie* for comfort. Elijah scrambled out of the metaphor. "I can't. Sid never went to a fundraiser with Nancy. It's not in our script. Sorry."

"*Sid and Nancy* is not our script. Neither one of us is very punk rock." He tapped his leg thoughtfully, making the smoke tendril from his cigarette dance. "Can't find a better metaphor. Trying to build something off the fundraiser thing, but all I can get is *The Princess Diaries*."

The streetlight caught Baz's hair, making the brown gleam almost blond. The breeze ruffled it at the same time, sending some cottonwood whorls like magical dust around him.

"Howl," Elijah said before he could stop his mouth.

"You're Howl Pendragon."

Baz grinned. "Ha. Now *that* metaphor I like. With the Tesla as my moving castle? Howl doesn't drive either. And you're Sophie. Refusing to see your own beauty, blocking any attempts to undo your curse."

Elijah glowered. "You expect me to get your heart back for you from a fire demon? Or be your servant while you run around making girls cry?"

"I'll do my own cleaning, and Calcifer can keep my heart in the fireplace. Unless you agree to go with me to Chicago. Then I'll put it in the frunk."

Baz smiled, making the *Howl's Moving Castle* theme soar in Elijah's head. *His* heart was on the ground between them. "Okay," he said.

And that was that.

Chapter Seven

ELIJAH LAY AWAKE until four in the morning, staring at the ceiling of Mina's living room while thoughts ping-ponged around his brain.

He understood, objectively, he'd stood in the alley and let Baz make *Howl's Moving Castle* associations before agreeing to go to some fundraiser thing in Chicago. What he didn't understand was why.

Probably it would all be a moot point because it was only a few days until the weekend, and you had to put in for time off a week in advance in the cafeteria. Besides, what would Pastor say when he heard about this nonsense?

Except Pastor had been all over Elijah getting away. And running off for a Chicago weekend would be exactly the sort of thing Liz would champion.

Whatever. It was one of Baz's stupid larks. If Elijah went down to breakfast, Baz would ignore him as usual, not pull out a map and a set of pushpins. He'd think of someone better to take as his date to the big, fancy shindig.

It would be fun, though. Could be a movie. Get in a car with a hot guy, road trip to Chicago, put on a tux, dance, and…well.

Elijah burrowed deeper into the covers, feeling hollow and foolish. Fuck, why had he said yes?

Because he seemed as if he cared. Because you're such a sad fucking sack, you'd go down for anybody you thought might so much as pretend to notice you.

Gritting his teeth, Elijah closed his pillow around his head and turned his face into the back of the couch, pleading with his brain to shut the fuck off and let him sleep.

Wouldn't you fucking know it, he had another one of his half-nightmare, half-flashbacks of Journey to God, the reparative therapy hellhole his parents made him endure once he gave up living on the streets. As he slept, Elijah knelt in a dream-fuck version of the prayer circle, cold and hungry as he faked redemption—that part had been real, but the swooping, batlike shadows tearing at him were his subconscious's own invention. When he woke, he was drenched in sweat and spiked with adrenaline.

It was six thirty in the morning. He'd slept two and a half whole hours, and though he was groggy and slightly nauseated, Elijah could tell he was done resting for the foreseeable future.

Mina had a coffee maker in her mini-kitchen, but Elijah didn't want to wake her, so he padded downstairs to the main house and started up the pot beside the stove. The White House was silent, all mechanical clicks and whirrs of appliances, and after his dream, he was jumpy. He nipped out to have a cigarette while the coffee brewed, and as he sat on the bench in the garden, he thought about his dream.

He wasn't scarred or anything by the reparative therapy. Well, no more than was standard, he assumed. It might have been different if he'd gone actually thinking he could pray away his gay, but since he went as part of his grand scam, he'd felt more like James Bond than Oliver Twist. Ever since the shooting, though, he'd dreamed of camp, all fucked up and weird. It pissed him off.

The bats were kind of cool, though. Maybe he should write them down. He took a deep toke of his cigarette, letting the nicotine expand his brain. Yeah. For the fantasy story, obviously. He knew just the part where the scene would go. The hero in the cellar, chained to the rock, demon shadows swooping around him to draw out his terror.

Fuck, that would be pretty cool. He smoked an extra cigarette and let the edited scene play out in his mind. He always saw his writing as a movie in his head, and this bit he would pay cash to see on the screen. Normally he'd scold himself for thinking of this, not the porny stuff he *should* be writing, but hey. At least he could write. Too bad he hadn't brought his laptop along.

Maybe he could find some paper and a pen in the kitchen. After depositing his spent cigarette into the tin can he used as an ashtray, Elijah went into the house.

Baz sat at the kitchen table, sipping a cup of coffee as he tapped at an open MacBook Pro.

He didn't say anything, and as far as Elijah could tell he didn't look away from his screen. The careful architecture of the bat-swooping dungeon scene crashed like broken glass on the floor of Elijah's mental head-space, and he scowled as he poured himself a mug of coffee.

Christ. Why did *he* have to be up now? Yes, it was his house too, and he actually paid rent. But seriously, now? And fucking hell, here it was, goddamned silent treatment all over again. If it weren't so early, Elijah would call Pastor and go home. If it weren't so far, he'd walk.

Trip to Chicago. Date to the fundraiser. Whatever. Nothing but a crock of shit.

"So when did you want to leave?"

Elijah almost dropped the carafe. Glancing over his shoulder, he saw Baz in his same position at the computer, but he also noticed a rigidity in his shoulders. Turning around, Elijah fumbled the glass pot into place. "What—what do you mean?"

Baz didn't look up from the computer, or if he did, he hid it behind his glasses. "The fundraiser isn't until Saturday, but it takes six hours to drive, so we should leave tomorrow. Could leave today."

Six hours? "Can't we fly?" *We're actually going?*

Baz shrugged a shoulder. "Could. Planes suck, though."

Elijah hadn't ever been on one, so he wouldn't know. Part of him wanted to pop that cherry, part of him worried he'd have some sort of freakout and get kicked off the plane.

"It's a pretty drive through Wisconsin." Clearing his throat, Baz shifted in his seat as he pushed the laptop away. "If we left today, we'd have more time to shop. Otherwise it'll be crammed into the day we drive or the day of the thing itself."

Shop? Oh. Right. Fancy clothes for the fundraiser. And let's not forget fork lessons. Elijah gripped the handle of his mug, staring into its inky depths. "Probably best to miss as little work as possible."

"We'll find someone to cover. Pastor will help."

The idea of roping Pastor into this—fuck, simply telling him about this—made everything too real. "I don't know. I think maybe this whole thing is a bad idea. I should stay, earn money."

"Forget the money."

Elijah glared at him. "Easy for you to say."

A tic formed in Baz's cheek. He shut the computer and glared right back, or ostensibly he did. Fucking sunglasses. He looked as if he wanted to say something but kept swallowing it.

Elijah gripped the mug so hard he thought he might break it. *If he offers to pay me to be his date at the fundraiser, I'm throwing this coffee at his head.*

Baz threw up his hands. "Fine. If you don't want to go, say so."

God, Elijah hated how this guy could tie him up inside. "I didn't say I didn't want to. I said I shouldn't. I need to make money. Be responsible."

"You have enough money in your fund for school. More than enough."

"Yes, and my fund makes me want to throw up."

"Why?"

"Because it's at two hundred and fifty thousand dollars and still rising. Somebody, *one person*, put twenty-five thousand in just the other day. I could go to school twice with what's in that account. I don't understand where it all came from. Who all these people are. I owe all of them. I don't know *what* I owe them. Just that I do and have no way to ever pay them back."

"You don't need to pay anybody back. You certainly don't owe penance in the school cafeteria."

"What the fuck would you know about it?"

He snorted. "Penance? I know plenty."

Elijah clutched his coffee to his belly, sloshing some on his pajama pants. He stared at the floor, feeling angry, anxious, and hollow. "I don't want it. The money. The help. But I don't have any choice. I have to take it. But I don't know what to do with it." Tears pricked his eyes, and he shut them. Tight.

When he heard the scrape of Baz's chair, his stomach flipped over. He tried to drink his coffee, but his hand shook. Fuck, fuck, *fuck*.

Baz's bare feet appeared in front of his own. Hands took the coffee cup away.

Elijah wrapped his arms around his belly and kept staring at the floor, except now he stared at Baz's groin and feet. "You don't understand."

"The fuck I don't. Ever since that goddamned night when I was sixteen, I've had bubble wrap around me. Yeah, I was a privileged rich kid, but after I was the *tragic* rich kid. My whole family and all my friends live to wipe my ass. *Poor* Sebastian. Don't upset him. But don't let him hurt himself. Don't let anything happen. You want to talk about feeling like you owe somebody?

Every goddamn day they all remind me I'm the boy who lived. Then they want to know why I can't move on."

Baz was so close each breath Elijah drew was Baz-scented. Night sweat and coffee and a whisper of morning breath, lingering detergent and old deodorant not cutting the mustard anymore. How fucked up was he? Baz was baring his soul, and all Elijah wanted to do was lick him.

When Baz put a hand on Elijah's hip, Elijah had to grip the counter to keep from leaning into him. *Talk. Stop being such a fucking mopey tool.* "Why...why do you..." *want me?* "Why...me?"

On Elijah's hip, Baz's thumb made a slow circle. "I don't know." Slower circles. Like a massage. Four inches from Elijah's groin. "I don't know."

Elijah dug his fingernails into the Formica. "You're going to be a jerk again. And then we'll be in the middle of the fucking desert or something."

"No deserts in Illinois."

"Fine. You'll leave me in a cornfield."

"You're the only one who can drive. You can leave *me* in the cornfield."

"Like I would."

"You would, actually. I think... I think that might be why. Why...you."

Elijah's cock was an iron bar in his pajama pants. A glance down revealed it was as obvious as it felt. "Stop it. I can't think when you do that."

Baz's only answer was a quirk of his lips and more kneading.

Elijah let go of the counter and tried to knock Baz's hand away, but snake that he was, Baz shifted his grip to Elijah's aching cock. When Elijah parted his lips on a groan, Baz ducked and caught Elijah's mouth, stealing inside.

Common sense cracked and broke apart as Baz pressed him into the counter, stroking his cock through his pants until he forewent all pretense and slipped his hand past the elastic. Sobriety made one last stab, reminding Elijah these were the pajama pants Liz had bought him. He had work tomorrow morning. Honest work, for humble wages. Tonight he'd watch more Netflix with Liz and Pastor. A good life. What he'd said he wanted. Stability. Honest people.

Sane people, who didn't run hot and cold on him every five fucking minutes.

Except maybe Elijah was as sick as his old man insisted, because in the face of Baz's sensual assault and wicked promises of a clean getaway, it was all he wanted. Even if he did get left in the middle of a cornfield.

No. Don't be stupid. Stay here. Be good. You do owe these people, and you can't repay them by running off like a vapid twink in short shorts following a fat ten-incher.

He'd put his hands on Baz's chest and was going to push him away when voices came from the other room. They both froze as Aaron and Giles giggled and spoke sleepily to one another. Heading toward the kitchen.

Elijah pushed away.

Baz gripped him by the arm and dragged him into the pantry.

Elijah sputtered, shoving and fighting to get free, but Baz crowded him against a shelf full of cans. Outside in the kitchen, Giles and Aaron banged pans, opened the fridge and murmured innuendo between pauses to make out. *Fuck this.* Elijah opened his mouth to complain loudly enough to get their attention.

He stopped as Baz removed his glasses and set them on a shelf.

The pantry was dark, but light shone beneath the door, and in its pale glow, as his eyes adjusted, Elijah could make out Baz's face. All of it, not hidden by sunglasses. Same as in the Tesla, except this time Elijah wasn't buzzing on multiple substances. This time Baz stared nakedly back at him, all his guards down, all his veils aside.

"Please." He caught Elijah's hand, drew it to his lips. "Please."

"Stop." Elijah tried to pull his hand away, but Baz held it fast. They whispered, Giles's and Aaron's carefree chatter a strange background to their desperation. "Stop it. No." Baz kissed his hand again, and Elijah thought he was going to cry. He set his teeth. "*Stop it.* You don't even like me."

In reply, Baz pressed Elijah's hand to his mouth, but didn't kiss it. Only held on to it as if it were the only thing anchoring him to earth.

Fuck.

When Elijah didn't think it could get any worse, Baz spoke, a rough, ragged whisper tearing across his heart.

"I'll help you. Get out of the work study. For the

weekend or for good, whichever you prefer. I'll help you find a way to feel you're paying people back." He shut his eyes, and weirdly, the gesture made him seem even more naked. Every crinkle, every line of tension shone like a beacon in the dark. "Please. Tell me what I have to do to get you to come along."

Elijah felt heady and terrified. "I can't take your weird moods. If you give me the cold shoulder while we're having Baz and Elijah's Excellent Adventure, I'm going to punch you in the face."

Baz's grin, framed by shadows, sent chills down Elijah's spine. And perked up his dick. "There. Now you're getting the hang of it."

Elijah grabbed Baz by the ears, sighing as Baz's hands moved over him. Smells of bacon and eggs and peppers drifted in from the kitchen, along with whispers of Giles and Aaron's plans for the day.

He groaned as Baz dipped into his pants. Elijah thrust into his hand as Baz kissed his way along Elijah's neck. "You're so much fucking work. *So. Much.*"

"Come with me today. Let's pack a bag and leave right now."

"I can't." Elijah whimpered as Baz teased his crack.

"You can. I'll help you. Say yes."

God, he smelled so good. Elijah was ready to let Baz fuck him against the shelf while Aaron and Giles listened in. *Shit.* "Yes. Fine. Yes. We'll go."

Baz brushed a kiss on Elijah's mouth. Elijah opened his eyes and got trapped in Baz's gaze inches from his own.

The door to the pantry door opened wide, and light

streamed in.

Baz's back was to the kitchen, but Elijah yanked him down anyway, pressing those tender eyes into his shoulder. "Shut the fucking door," he called out over Giles's outburst of surprise.

The door shut. Elijah held Baz a moment longer, then let go.

Baz lifted his head again, and they regarded one another.

So naked, so fucking naked without those glasses. So young. So handsome.

So Baz.

Elijah let out a sigh of surrender.

Eyes crinkling and twinkling in the shadows, Baz smiled.

CLEARLY, BAZ ADMITTED as he shampooed his hair in the shower, this trip with Elijah was going to be a roller coaster. Because until Elijah had walked into the kitchen reeking of cigarettes and looking as if he expected Baz to tell him the plan was off—well, this had been exactly what Baz was going to say.

When he was alone, it all seemed so insane. He needed a herd around him to deflect his moodiness, and plenty of time to marinate in his own asshattery. A weekend with Elijah only, surrounded by the home-front chaos with Elijah expecting him to fold, was a recipe for disaster. By the time he got out of the shower, Baz didn't think, he knew he should call it off. Wrapping a towel around his waist, he went to his room ready to get dressed, go downstairs, and do what he had to do.

Elijah was there, surprisingly, pacing the length of Baz's bed, looking ready to explode. "I can't do this, I can't go."

"You can," Baz replied, then dropped the towel and pushed Elijah onto the mattress.

Elijah had changed into jeans and a T-shirt, so when he got stiff, his cock ridged inside the narrow confines of snug denim instead of invitingly tenting his pajama pants. Baz dragged his own rapidly growing chub along it as he made love to Elijah's neck. Elijah pushed weakly at him before sighing in surrender and shoving his fingers into Baz's hair.

"You're such a fucker." Elijah gasped and moaned as Baz tongued his collarbone.

Baz thought about taking him up literally on the suggestion, but now that Elijah was in front of him, he was as determined to go as he had been not to five minutes earlier. Climbing off the bed, he pawed through his dresser, indexing what he wanted to wear and what he should pack.

Elijah sat up on the bed, hugging his knees to his chest. "How can you see? Are you Batman or something? It's so dark."

Baz had his red light on, so they were in full hellscape mode. He shrugged. "Used to it, I guess."

"Can you see better this way than if you had regular light in here?"

"It's not about better." Baz tossed a pile of underwear and socks into his suitcase beside his jeans before switching to his closet for shirts. "My sight sucks no matter how you slice it. But it's nice to lose the glasses at home."

"The red lights are cool. Weird, a little creepy, but cool." Elijah's voice had a tremulous quality, like he was trying not to be nervous and failing.

"My dad's sister thought it up. She's an engineer. Came here and rigged several rooms." After tucking a wad of T-shirts and a hoodie into the last space in the bag, Baz dragged his travel toiletry and light kits out. He opened it beside Elijah on the bed, checking fluid levels on the shampoo and contact lens cleaner, indexing the supplies he'd need from his bathroom.

"What's all this electrical stuff? And the tape, and clips?"

Baz blinked at his kit, imagining how it must look to someone who didn't know what it was. "A portable red lamp. My aunt made it. There are extra bulbs in there too, so I can swap out ones in a hotel room. The tape and clips are for keeping curtains shut and light switches stationary if need be."

"Damn. That's…organized."

"Gotta be."

"I seriously would never have pegged you for being this anal retentive," Elijah remarked as Baz finally zipped up the last case and stacked them into the neat triple nesting set which turned the bags into a single unit.

"Choir tour. Had to get good at living off a little and packing up fast."

Longing flickered briefly on Elijah's face. "You guys

go all over, stay in people's houses, right?"

"Sometimes." Baz hoisted the suitcase as he slipped sunglasses on and nodded at the door. "You ready?"

Elijah didn't look ready, but he followed Baz down the stairs all the same.

Mina, Aaron, and Giles sat in the living room half-watching *The Big Bang Theory* with the remains of their breakfast littered around them. Aaron had his head in Giles's lap, but he focused on Mina, smiling as she waved her hands in punctuation to a story featuring a high amount of outrage. She wound to a pause as Elijah and Baz approached.

Elijah hunched his shoulders and looked like he wanted a fifth and a cigarette. Mina, Aaron, and Giles took on a remix of concerned expressions.

Baz leapt into the breach. "So. We're gonna take off."

Mina's and Giles's eyebrows went up, but Aaron zeroed in on Elijah. "Where are you going?"

Baz rubbed his neck. "Thing came up, and I have to go home for the weekend. I need a driver and a date for a gig, and Elijah volunteered."

Elijah moved his gaze to the ceiling and said nothing as the rest of them exploded into various objections and expressions of disbelief.

Baz slipped into full Acker charm offensive, complete with comforting smile, hand gestures, and *I got this* body language. "It's no big. A weekend fundraiser thing, in and out." He shifted his bag on his shoulder and nodded at the door. "We're gonna go over to Pastor Schulz's place, get Elijah packed up, and head out from there. If anything goes wrong with the house, call the management number over the phone."

"But what about your job?" Giles said this to Elijah.

Elijah had red splotches on his cheeks. He looked ready to bolt or attack but couldn't decide which. "I don't... I need to go talk to the manager." He aimed a sharp glance at Baz. "And if it doesn't work out—"

"It'll work out." Baz could hear the threat in there, that Elijah would stay if the manager was so much as mildly disappointed. So not happening. If Baz had to call his mom and beg her to send an intern to fill the space, he would.

Giles seemed bewildered mostly, and while Aaron studied Baz carefully, in the end he must have decided he liked what he saw, because he only hugged them both and told them to keep in touch. Mina, though, was some work. "How long will you be gone? Where are you staying?"

"Long weekend, essentially. Staying at our Barrington Hills place because the fundraiser is at some country-estate thing by Mirror Lake."

He would have fielded her inquisition all day long, but she was wily, Ms. Mina. She turned to Elijah and said, "Can I see you outside for a minute?"

"I'll put my stuff in the frunk and meet you at the Tesla." Baz managed to pull off breezy, but in reality he was pretty damn panicked.

Aaron followed him to the garage. "Baz, what's going on?"

"Mom's having a fundraiser. Gotta represent." He popped the frunk, stowed his bag, unplugged the Tesla.

"Yes, but with Elijah?"

"You did point out we were a good match."

Aaron studied Baz a moment, then shook his head. "Be careful, okay?"

Baz tossed him a salute. "Will do."

Aaron left, but Elijah didn't reappear, so Baz did some more housekeeping. He phoned Stephan and let him know the vague game plan for departure, promising to keep him abreast as the adventure unfurled. He warned him, too, about the possible need for massaging of Elijah's employer. Stephan told him to consider the matter resolved.

One call down. Baz hovered over his top contacts, thumb wavering until at last he selected Marius and waited for the phone to ring.

"Hey there." Marius's voice rumbled in Baz's ear. "What's up?"

"Wanted to let you know I'll be out of town for a bit. Hitting the home front for the weekend."

"You're going to Chicago? Why?"

"Fundraiser thing of Mom's. She tried to set me up, but I told her I'd bring my own date." He let a beat pass, then finished it off. "Taking Elijah."

Marius said nothing at first, but eventually sighed. "Shit."

It would have been easier if he'd yelled. The silence weighed on Baz, and he felt compelled to fill it. "Don't make a mountain out of it. It's all for show." Except of course he'd led his mother to believe he actually did have a boyfriend.

"You know I would have gone with you. Even

LONELY HEARTS   121

faked being your date."

"You have shit to do. Med-school prep."

"Do you think taking Elijah to Chicago is a good idea?"

Probably not. "Absolutely. Talk about somebody who could use an airing."

"Baz, don't fuck with his head. I'm serious. It's one thing to let your hair down with him at a wedding, but Elijah doesn't need your bullshit."

Baz exhaled and ran a hand through his hair.

"I'm not saying you can't go." Marius's tone gentled. "I'm saying keep your head in the game. The one with hair."

Baz had wandered into the drive, but he peered around the corner of the house to make sure Elijah and Mina weren't coming his way. "I don't mean to fuck with him. I'm not that big of a dick."

"You're not a dick at all. But your moods can be rough to weather. Plus you get pissy when you bump up against a limitation when you're trying to impress somebody. Look—I can get away for a bit. Why don't the three of us go?"

"No. You can't actually get away, and you know it. And—" He stopped, realizing the truth of what he was about to say. Huh. "I won't be a jerk. If I need to queen out, I'll call you. I won't take it out on him."

"Damien's gonna shit a brick."

"Yeah, well, he's good at that. Pass the news on to him, please." Baz spied Elijah coming around the front of the house, and his heart kicked into his throat. "Hey. I gotta go. I'll keep you informed."

"You'd damn well better."

Tucking his phone into his pocket, Baz faced Elijah. He did his best to play it cool, to act as if nothing mattered, but this fucking mattered. He wanted to demand to know if Mina had talked him out of it, to know what she'd said so he could undo it, but he bit his tongue and waited. Trying not to hold his breath. Trying not to admit it felt like everything in the world hinged on whatever the hell Elijah said next.

Elijah didn't say a damn thing. He stared at Baz as if he didn't trust him farther than he could throw him. Even from ten feet away, the sooty, lingering gaggy smell of cigarette smoke hung in the air.

With a sigh, Elijah held up a cord. "You forgot your phone charger."

Baz accepted it carefully. "You ready to go?" *Say yes. Come on. Say you'll go.*

Elijah shoved his hands in his pockets. "I have to talk to Pastor first. But if he says it's okay, then…yes."

Baz grinned, feeling like he'd saddled a mythical beast. "Awesome." Because he knew he could get Schulz to say yes.

ELIJAH WOULD HAVE figured he'd drive to Pastor and Liz's house in a daze of half disbelief, half hysteria over what he was about to do, but the Tesla's regenerative braking kept wigging him out. It was supposed to be some energy-saving thing, but all Elijah knew was every time he took his foot off the gas, the car started slowing down before he pressed the brake. When Elijah's foot did depress the pedal, the car jerked to an abrupt near-halt.

"Sorry," he said for the umpteenth time.

Baz waved this objection away as he had all the others. He lounged in the passenger seat with his long body splayed through all available space. "Marius still takes a minute to figure it out whenever he drives."

Elijah was taking far longer than a minute. Part of his problem was he'd never driven anything even a third as cool as this car. Not a brand-new car. Not a nearly new car. *Never* a fucking Tesla. What if he wrecked it?

How the hell was he supposed to make it *all the way to Chicago* without wrecking it?

When he pulled into the Schulzes' drive, he let out a sigh of relief. It was short-lived, however, as he fumbled for a means to turn off the car.

"It'll shut itself off once we leave with the keys." Baz cracked his door and climbed out. "Come on."

Despite Baz's assurances, Elijah still lingered at the Tesla. It was weird to not turn off the car.

He was distracted from his conundrum when the door to the house opened. "Elijah—oh, and Baz too!" Liz pulled Baz into a hug Elijah knew from experience would smell like vanilla and feel the way a fresh-baked cookie tasted. She bussed one cheek and playfully slapped the other when she was finished. "Come on in, both of you. You have perfect timing. I just took sugar cookies out of the oven."

Liz, as Elijah's expanding waistline bore witness, ran a bakery out of her kitchen. She had a license or whatever official thing she needed to sell her baked goods at the campus coffee shop, several Campustown establishments and a few boutiques in Saint Paul. The markup was steep, but everybody paid because they knew one hundred percent of the profits went to anti-trafficking charities. Theoretically the costs for supplies were taken out of the total before it was passed on, but Elijah knew the truth. More often than not Liz paid for things herself.

In addition to the promised sugar cookies, she had Rice Krispies bars laced with caramel sauce and choco-late chips, and mint brownies. Liz ushered them into places at the table, plunked milk and cookies in front of them, and continued to bustle about the room as she spoke. "I'm in a flurry because tomorrow I have to go to Viv's place and help her with the gluten free items. You have to have a special kitchen for them because of contamination. She was willing to get the license, though, so now we have more options. But that means I have to bake double today."

Elijah opened his mouth to offer his help, which he'd given before, then remembered he was supposed to tell her he was leaving. Oh, and could someone tell food service he was bailing? He cut a gaze to Baz, his change of heart probably written all over his face.

Before he could get over his queasiness, let alone move on to calling things off for real this time, Baz spoke. "You know, you should get an intern. Someone not only to help with the baking, but the distribution and marketing. They'd get to put it on their resume, and you'd get extra hands."

"I can help her." Elijah glared at Baz. "I help her a lot, actually. I can help right now."

He got up to wash his hands and put on an apron, but Liz pushed him into his chair. "As if I'd let you interrupt your visit. Though the internship is a fine idea." She pulled a tray of cookies out of the oven and put in a waiting pan of brownies. "What are you two up to today? I hope, Sebastian, you're taking Elijah out to have some fun."

"How funny you should ask." Baz draped an arm over Elijah's shoulders. "I'm trying to convince him to go on a weekend getaway with me."

"Why, how *wonderful*." Liz tossed her potholder on the counter and plunked across from them at the table. Her eyes danced with gentle Liz mischief. "Where are you going?"

"I'm not sure I should go." Elijah shrugged out from under Baz's arm.

This put Baz's hand on his back, and said hand immediately trailed to Elijah's hip. "Mom's having a fundraiser and asked I come with a date. Everyone else is too busy to come."

Elijah scooted forward on his seat, away from Baz's hand. "I have to work. I have to earn my keep."

Too late, he realized it had been the wrong thing to say. Liz got *that look* in her eye, right about the same time Baz settled his hand on Elijah's ass.

"Elijah, you owe us nothing. You're more than covered for school as far as finances go. You *should* get away. A trip to Chicago would be terribly exciting."

Elijah made one last-ditch effort. "The cafeteria is

counting on me."

"Robert will be happy to deal with it for you." Liz reached across the table and tapped Elijah playfully on the nose. "You should go. You could use an adventure."

"What am I taking care of?" Pastor Schulz came into the kitchen, making a beeline for the brownies.

Baz gave his pretty speech about the fundraiser, Liz effused about what a wonderful idea it was, Pastor agreed and insisted it wouldn't be any trouble to get Elijah out of the cafeteria job, and somehow it was all decided despite Elijah trying, multiple times, to object. In fact, when Baz admitted he wanted to take off by noon, Liz herded Elijah upstairs to help him pack.

Elijah couldn't make any headway in his protest, even one-on-one.

"You and Sebastian both need this. The pair of you are overdue for some relaxation, and you're good together." Liz sighed as she tucked Elijah's underwear into the side pocket of a carry-on bag. "I know he can come off the wrong way, but..." She paused with a roll of socks in her hand. "His stories are his own to tell. All I can say is when he came to campus with Gloria to see if it was a fit, Robert brought them here for dinner. He was polite, charming—and so lonely. He broke my heart."

How Baz could be lonely with his eight-million choir-member posse and herd of willing conquests, Elijah couldn't guess. "It doesn't look right, me running off with him."

Liz *pished* over her shoulder as she pulled T-shirts and jeans from Elijah's drawers. "For heaven's sake, this isn't a Jane Austen novel. Don't start about the money, either. People didn't give you money so you'd work like a dog and live like a monk. He's not going to let you spend anything anyway." When Elijah tried to protest, she held up a hand. "Do you know what you've yet to say to me? *Liz, I don't want to go.* Nothing here or downstairs has been anything but why other people think you shouldn't go. If you *don't* want to go, say so. But don't you dare say no for anyone but you."

"I can't leave *today.*"

"Why not? If you're worried about the cafeteria, we'll find the manager before you go. If I know Robert, though, he's already called and squared things away." She set aside the clothes and took Elijah's hands. "Sweetheart. Do you *want* to go?"

It was the grandmother look. Elijah was toast. He moved his gaze to the floor, but it was too late. "I'm worried I'm going to make an idiot of myself. That he'll be sorry he asked me."

"Sweetheart." Cupping his cheeks, she lifted his face to be level with hers. "He won't be sorry. Don't you know he's sweet on you?"

Only Liz could use the phrase *sweet on you* and make Elijah melt, not roll his eyes. "He runs so hot and cold. I don't know if I want him sweet on me."

"Yes, you do." She winked, released him with a kiss on his forehead and resumed packing. "Pack up your laptop. Maybe you'll get some writing done."

Elijah meant to protest, but somehow he didn't. Somehow he ended up helping Liz put together a suitcase, which did include his laptop. Despite his protestations, she pressed five twenty-dollar bills into his hand. They couldn't leave, though, until she packed them a barrage of snacks. She sent them out to put Elijah's things into the Tesla while Robert fetched the perfect cooler from the basement.

Baz tried to carry Elijah's suitcase, which Elijah shut down immediately, clutching the bag to his chest as he went to the car. He waited at the frunk for Baz to open it, but he didn't. Baz sat on the hood instead, his mouth set in a grim line.

"If you truly don't want to go, tell me. If you don't trust me, or it's too much, or you aren't into it—say it."

Elijah dropped the suitcase on the driveway, catching it at the last second to soften the impact as he remembered the laptop. It softened his fury too, because he'd been ready to deck Baz. "You just spent an hour making sure I *couldn't* get out of it."

Baz's lips thinned. "Yeah. I…realized. Which is why I'm apologizing. Sorry. If you don't want to go, we won't."

Elijah still wanted to hit him. He also wanted to press his face into Baz's chest and hope for arms to wrap around him. For Baz to chuckle darkly and make some kind of innuendo. Because those touches on his shoulder, hip, and back continued to burn. And his mouth ached for more kisses like the one in Baz's room.

With the sun's angle, Elijah could see Baz's eyes behind the lenses. The outline, anyway. They crinkled slightly, despite the glasses, despite the house and huge leafy maple casting full shadow over them.

Elijah tightened his arms against his midsection. Yes, he wanted an adventure with Baz. He wanted it so much he had to work not to drool. Which was why he was so terrified. What happened if something he wanted this much turned to ash in his hands?

He lifted his face to Baz's gaze. "Why me?"

Baz hesitated. Eventually he sighed, and Elijah could practically see the walls coming down. "Because you don't look at me the way anyone else does. You act as if I'm a real person." His lips quirked, like he was going to smile but gave up. "I want to have that to myself for a while."

Elijah's heart tried to turn over, but he wouldn't let it.

Baz smiled. A real smile, soft and almost shy.

There wasn't any stopping Elijah's heart now. It rolled over, stuck out its tongue, and showed its belly. Elijah gave in—to his heart, to Baz, and to the urge to sag against him.

He didn't drool when Baz put his arms around him. But he did melt as surely as if he were a block of ice being embraced by the sun.

Chapter Eight

THE FIRST HOUR was weird.

Baz felt naked after the not-really-but-sort-of throwdown in the driveway, which didn't combine well with the realization he'd propelled himself to this point mostly on being textbook oppositional defiant. Except for the last part where he said the truth. A truth Elijah had responded to, which should have made him happy but mostly left him feeling like somebody'd peeled him to his titanium skeleton and hooked it up to his TENS unit.

His instinct was to deflect with some ribbing, but Elijah was already driving the Tesla like a nervous granny. Rocking the boat probably wasn't the best course of action. Plus his conversation topics were severely limited. Teasing was out, and so was *Tell me about your childhood.* Fuck, pretty much everything but the last few months was too grim for entry chatter. What was left? *How's your talk therapy going? What's the prognosis on your fucked-up parents?*

In shifting to give his hip some relief, he spied the cooler and wicker hamper in the backseat, and he relaxed. *Bingo.*

"Which of Liz's treats is your favorite?"

Elijah flicked his gaze from the road. "Sugar cookies." He slid his right hand lower on the wheel, relaxing his grip slightly.

"Mmm. Good choice. Speaking personally, my heart belongs to her red velvet cupcakes."

The tiniest quirk of a smile. "They're good, but the sugar cookies will always be my favorite." His hand tightened again, not much, but enough to make Baz notice. "She made them the first night. When they brought me home from the hospital after...my parents."

Oh, okay. They were gonna go there. "They're good people. Pretty much walked me through my first year. I wasn't in the White House right off, and if I needed some space, Pastor would pick me up any hour of the day or night, or Liz, if he was unavailable. Marius was my roommate, and he was great from word go, but it still took me a while to ease into things."

"It blows my mind how different I feel from last summer." He let one hand fall off the wheel, but it remained poised and ready to leap into action. "More put together, like I know the dance moves of how to go to school. But it's weird. Not having parents around. Not fighting them. I don't miss it, obviously, but sometimes it seems as if somebody took away all my body armor and cranked the lighting."

Baz leaned against the headrest. "Yeah. Wish I could tell you it went away."

The pause went on too long, and Baz was about to say something benign, such as was the music okay, when Elijah started talking once more.

"Pastor told me it's kind of PTSD." His lips thinned, and he swallowed as if he had something nasty in his throat. "I keep getting panic attacks. Not all the time. For no fucking reason, either, usually. Pisses me off."

"I never went in for panic attacks as a rule. I was more random fits of rage." Baz tried to step on the rest, but Sia sang sweetly about how big girls cry, and the gently winding road through beautiful valleys said, *Come on. Get it out, it'll feel good.* "I've figured out how to manage those, but I can't quite quit pushing people away when they get too close. The nicer they are, the more right they seem, the more I want them gone. Doesn't make any fucking sense, but there it is."

Elijah huffed a bitter laugh through his nose. "Yes it does."

Baz raised his eyebrows. "Okay, tell me."

"Because if you let them in, you have to feel." His jaw tightened. "If they fuck you over, it hurts ten times worse than if you'd kept them out. And it's not as if you don't have other shit to manage. There are only so many wounds you can take, and at some point you have to cut your losses and circle the wagons."

Baz stared out the windshield. "Fucking lonely way to be."

"Yes."

They went quiet, but this time it wasn't weird or awkward. They watched things go by, commenting on random bits of scenery, rolling their eyes together at the massive yellow JESUS billboard outside a small town near the Minneapolis-Wisconsin border, laughing when

Baz pointed out it looked like a giant cuss, as if the town had fucking had it and was letting the highway know. When Elijah remarked he wished he had a coffee, Baz poured some from the giant thermos Liz had stowed in the back. He distributed some baked goods too, a brownie for himself and a liberal pile of sugar cookies for Elijah.

"How do we charge on the road?" Elijah glanced at the dash.

"There are PlugShare stations all over the place. You practically trip over them. And if we didn't have one, we'd pay somebody to use a regular plug. This thing costs nothing at all to run. But as it happens, we'll be stopping at the Supercharger station in Wisconsin. Either Mauston or Madison."

"Is one better than the other?"

"Not really. We push it to get to Madison, but from the readout, your mileage stats say it won't be a problem. Conversely, it's a harder push to get to Barrington Hills from Mauston, but again—not going to be an issue. Also, I'm serious, the PlugShares are everywhere."

"Why go to the super-thing then?"

"Because it's free and fast. Thirty minutes, and we'll be good to go for another two hundred miles, give or take. Free of charge. Pun intended."

"Thirty minutes." Elijah had both hands on the wheel, but they flexed this time in a way that made Baz's focus narrow, especially with the tone of voice he used to finish his thought. "That's…a nice break."

Yes. Yes it was.

This silence was charged, thoughts of those upcoming thirty minutes better than any Supercharger. Baz used the transit time to search for a hotel close to the charging spots, and since Mauston had one just off the road from the charging place, he declared it the winner.

Elijah lost some of his sexual tension as he ogled the Supercharger while Baz set up the charge, but when Baz took his hand and indicated the hotel across the road, Elijah was back in the game.

"I hope they have a room." He double-timed with Baz along the grassy bank.

"I booked ahead."

Elijah's index finger slipped onto Baz's wrist. "Excellent."

They didn't say a word from the front desk to the door, but as soon as Baz threw the lock, they were on each other. Hot mouths in the foyer, trembling hands fighting to get clothing out of the way. Once Elijah got Baz's shirt off, he licked his collarbone, whimpering when Baz's finger breached his crack.

"*Ungh.*" Elijah set his teeth on Baz's shoulder, digging fingernails into his back. Hobbled by jeans at his knees, he spread his legs as best he could, pushing into Baz's burrowing fingers.

Baz ran his tongue down Elijah's ear as he breached the rim of Elijah's hole. "What do you want, baby?"

He tensed as Baz pressed the tip of his finger in dry. "Dirty. I want it fucking dirty."

"Mmm." Baz nipped Elijah's lobe, kneaded a handful of ass, then slapped it. "On the bed, head at the bottom."

He helped Elijah out of his clothes and indulged in a moment's admiration as his lover lay naked and sprawled on the comforter. He took off his jeans and boxers but left on his shirt before jacking himself slowly, anticipating what was coming. Elijah stared up at him, quivering, his expression needy.

Digging into his jeans, Baz tossed the lube he'd swiped from his toiletry bag onto the bed by Elijah's ass before kneeling over Elijah's face, presenting his ass inches from Elijah's mouth.

"Oh fuck," Elijah whispered, and went in.

Baz did too. He allowed himself a second to trip out from the joy of Elijah's tongue in his ass, lapping at his crack, and then he greased his fingers and went in. Balls, taint, nudging around the hole. Groaning and rocking back as Elijah whimpered and chased his finger as he licked deep into Baz's ass. When Baz finally gave it to him, Elijah moaned and started nipping and sucking.

Baz drew hard enough on Elijah's thigh to leave a mark. *I'll give you dirty, honey.*

They kept it at that, rimming and fingering and raking fingernail marks over each other until Elijah whispered he was close. Baz had intended to stay on top, but his hip was hella pissed now, so he flopped on his back, handed Elijah the lube and told him to knock himself out.

Now Elijah straddled Baz's hips. Slicking his long cock as he ground his balls against Baz's, Elijah stared at him like he wanted to eat him raw. Which, technically, he just had. Baz ran a hand down Elijah's chest, tracing his sternum before tugging at each of his nipples.

Elijah greased them both and closed their cocks tight in his fist. Bracing his other arm beside Baz's head, he licked into Baz's mouth and started to fuck.

Their kiss became a war, a bruising, biting battle for control as they ground their pelvises together and Elijah jacked their cocks. When Elijah began to shake and whimper, Baz dug his fingers in, nipped at Elijah's chin and neck and murmured dirty encouragement.

"Come for me. Let everybody in the hotel hear us fucking." He slipped a hand to Elijah's ass. "You're so dirty, baby. So. Fucking. Dirty."

He watched Elijah's face as he came, spurting over his hand and the hem of Baz's shirt. He held out as long as he could, taking in the sight of Elijah Prince letting go until Baz had no choice but to follow.

They left the room forty minutes after they'd entered it, sated and loose hipped, arms around each other as they wove their way to the Supercharger. Once in the car, their hands kept brushing over the console, and Baz couldn't help noticing Elijah laughed more often, more easily. He felt pretty smug, because what had begun as a selfish enterprise clearly *was* good for Elijah.

Except as they approached the northwestern burbs of Chicago, a thought occurred to Baz, and some of his proud glow receded.

"Oh—hey. I forgot to mention something."

Elijah, who was back in granny mode with heavier city traffic, didn't seem to realize he'd spoken. "I've never driven in a city before."

"Stay in your lane and leave just less than a car length in the space ahead of you."

"Why *less* than?"

"If you leave a full space, someone will fill it."

Grumbling, Elijah hunched over the wheel. "I don't like driving in cities."

They were less than twenty minutes from the house. Baz had to tell him now. He thought about calling for a Starbucks break, but it occurred to him he had better cover when Elijah was fighting traffic. "I have something I need to explain."

Elijah flipped the bird at someone who proved Baz's point about too much space between cars. "So explain."

"When I told my mom I was bringing my own date, I had to sell it. She clearly had *plans* for getting me the perfect Ken doll. So I had to make it clear it wasn't an option, and there was only one way to do that."

Elijah's hands tightened on the wheel. "How?"

"I told her you were my boyfriend."

The Tesla swerved and slowed abruptly before Elijah put his foot on the accelerator. He gripped the wheel tightly as he turned his head long enough to glare at Baz. "You want to kill us? Keep making stupid jokes while I'm driving."

"I'm not joking."

No swerve this time, but Baz decided he was glad he'd done this here, not in a coffee shop where Elijah's fit would have witnesses. "Why the hell would you tell her that?" An angry tic formed in his cheek. "I'd demand to know why you didn't tell me when you lured me into this, but it's obvious. And despicable, by the way."

Baz shifted his gaze out the passenger-side window. "I wanted you to come. And it's not a big deal."

"It's a pretty damn big deal, and I'd have told you no if I'd known."

Lovely thought, that being Baz's boyfriend was a deal breaker. He traced his finger along the window seam. "I'll book you a flight home."

"Don't pout. We're here, practically. Explain what playing your boyfriend entails. Do I get to be me, or am I some kind of Ivy League playboy? Because if it's the latter, I'll need more than fork lessons."

"Yourself, obviously. Honestly, it's not a big deal. She was determined to set me up with someone random of *her* choosing, so who I chose had to not be random. Ergo, I had to have a boyfriend."

"What does she expect of your boyfriend?"

Baz considered lying, but the truth couldn't remain hidden long, and further deception wouldn't work in his favor. "Hard to say. I haven't had one for almost a decade."

Elijah swore under his breath. Setting his lips in a thin line, he punched his index finger at the touchscreen until he shifted the music to RuPaul's *Born Naked* and went straight for "Sissy That Walk". As the synth and bass beat began to pump through the car, he cranked the volume until the music reverberated in Baz's chest. Then he called up the moonroof, dragged his fingers over the touchscreen and pulled the glass top open. He put the windows down too as he glanced over his shoulder and switched to the far lane, where he pushed the gas pedal not quite to the floor, but enough that they were definitely ticket bait.

Baz decided if they did get pulled over, it would be worth it. He wasn't going to point it out at the moment, but Elijah this pissed off was pretty hot. Driving too fast, wind whipping his hair, glaring at the road as if he wanted to grind it into dust. The mousy, cautious gargoyle look was gone. All he needed were sunglasses and a cigarette, and he'd be a slightly shorter version of Baz's longstanding wet dream.

So Baz fished his indoor glasses out of his bag, passed them over, lit a cigarette and handed it to Elijah as well. Elijah looked as hot angrily sucking on the cigarette while wearing sunglasses as Baz's imagination had said he would.

The song ended, and Elijah pushed past "Geronimo" to land on "Dance With U". After adjusting the music to a more reasonable level, he ashed out the window and shook his head. "You seriously are a son of a bitch."

Baz considered his mother. "It's true. But I wouldn't tell her so in those words exactly."

He gave a mental fist bump when a smile quirked over Elijah's lips.

Baz nodded at the radio. "So. RuPaul really is your favorite artist."

Elijah shrugged. "Hangover from when I was younger. Found a copy of his Christmas album at

Target and stole it. For whatever reason that got him under my skin, and when shit got too real, he became a kind of lighthouse. I can't tell you why, because I'm not trans, and I have no desire to do drag. There's something transportive about listening to him. Watching YouTube videos. Now I watch *Drag Race*. Probably something about authenticity. Or maybe hiding in plain sight. I don't know. Also, I guess, an escape I could squirrel onto an mp3 player."

"I was more movies and TV shows, and manga."

Elijah ashed out the window again. "Manga. Is that why you have *Howl's Moving Castle*?"

"There are a lot of reasons I have the movie. So much better than the book, to start."

"I like the book."

Baz shrugged. "It's okay." It wasn't, but he didn't want to fight. Which was why he hadn't corrected him that Miyazaki's *Howl's Moving Castle* was anime, not manga. "I can't tell you why manga is my escape either. There's some seriously fun and fucked-up stuff there, though. Also it's a nice reminder that other cultures make contemporary art, and often better."

Elijah shifted lanes in deference to the navigation system's direction in preparation for their exit into Barrington Hills. "So tell me what the storyline is. For this boyfriend bullshit."

"No story. She thinks you are, and that's about it."

"Yes, but how do I say we met? When did we get together?"

"She knows how we met—well, the Saint Timothy part. We got together at the wedding. Don't you remember?"

"That was a hook-up, not a meet cute."

"Pretend it was, and you're all set."

Elijah pushed his cigarette butt out the window and fumbled for a new one as he exited the freeway. "So we started dating in early June, and then you didn't talk to me until yesterday."

"Fine. Insert some outings for dinner and a movie." Baz anchored his elbow in the window. "You're thinking she's Liz, wanting all the details. She's not. She'll smile, ask you some benign questions, then shoo us away to go play. You'll hardly see her all weekend."

"What, she won't be at the house?"

"It's a big house."

Elijah sighed and held up his hands as they settled in at a stoplight. "Fine."

The music shifted, the dashboard readout telling Baz it was "Fly Tonight". He cranked the music up, lit his own cigarette, and swam in the indulgence of blaring a drag queen's album through the streets of his uptight hometown.

ELIJAH HAD HIMSELF believing he could pull the weekend off until he saw Baz's house.

For one thing, *house* seemed a ridiculous word to apply to the epic beast perched like a jewel at the end of a long, curved driveway. Trees and shrubs dotted the quaintly bricked ribbon leading the Tesla to an imposing front facade. This was also brick, a kind of limestone, and stucco around a gentle circle of flowers.

And a fountain. A big-ass one, gently spurting artful *glubs* of water over three stone tiers. To the right of the wide *Are you sure you belong here?* imposing front door stood a clock. The kind you'd find in an old-fashioned town square, standing about fifteen feet high, proclaiming the time to be five past seven. A pair of bronze figures, boy and girl, sat demurely on a mini bench beneath it, sunning their metal selves as the female read a book and the male stared pensively across the lawn.

"Park in the circle." Baz gestured to the far side, away from the clock. "Leave your stuff. Someone will bring it in later and park the car."

Someone. "So you have servants?"

"Not…exactly. There's a housekeeper who comes in every day, and a gardening service comes three times a week, and a cleaning service. Mostly there's staff. My mother's staff is usually in residence in her wing on the first floor, and the blue bedroom is practically Stephan's at this point. My dad sends interns out to fetch things for his downtown apartment or the office. If Mom has an event, she hires catering."

Sounded like servants to Elijah.

If he'd thought the outside of the house was imposing, it was nothing on what waited for him inside. They entered a huge foyer with almost nothing in it, a few chairs and urns of flowers along the edges, but mostly it was entryways, a balcony around the perimeter of the second floor, and stairs. Huge-ass *Mommie Dearest* showplace stairs, the kind that went halfway up then split in two to finish the rest of the way. They were double-sided too, so you could stand on the landing at the top and could go toward the front door or to the other living-room thing in the other direction.

Great room. The term drifted into Elijah's brain, spoken in the affected tones of the older gentleman who'd plucked him from the street for a night of fun and taken him to a McMansion in the Minneapolis burbs. Before they'd fucked, the guy gave Elijah an unnecessary tour of his house, with particular emphasis on the great room, which as far as Elijah could tell was a living room with high ceilings. Baz's great room could fit about four of the pompous trick's, and it didn't look like a glorified living room. It could be part of a mansion in England. Not only vaulted ceilings but *beamed* vaulted ceilings, in front of a wall of window, with a huge fireplace on one wall and a stately hutch on the other. More plants, less statuary and a lot of paintings decorated these walls, and in front of the fireplace some tasteful yet elegant sofas and chairs suggested it was possible to sit, so long as you were polite about it. In front of the window was a baby grand piano that made Fred, the much-loved instrument at the White House, seem like something somebody dragged out of a barn.

Baz led Elijah into this room, but before they got far a woman Elijah vaguely remembered as Mrs. Acker appeared from an archway, beaming as she gave Baz a kind of half-embrace and an air kiss.

"Darling." She released Baz and regarded Elijah with a knowing but polite smile. "And Elijah. Welcome to our home."

Elijah wasn't sure if he should bow or offer his

hand or what. He did a kind of awkward lean and inclined his head. "Thank you, Mrs. Acker."

She grinned a Baz grin and swatted her son's shoulder gently. "Listen to him. Do you deserve someone with such good manners?" She came forward and treated Elijah to the same embrace she'd given Baz. "Call me Gloria, please."

"Yes, ma'am," Elijah replied.

She laughed. "Why don't the two of you relax downstairs while I finish up? I'll join you for a cocktail in about a half hour. I arranged for a light dinner in the solarium around eight thirty. Does that work with your plans?"

"It'll be fine," Baz assured her.

Elijah, who'd had nothing but cookies and nuts all day, wished they'd stopped for a meal.

Gloria called over her shoulder as she retreated through the archway. "I think it's lobster bisque and those delicious herbed popovers. But if you have any allergies, Elijah, let Baz know, and we'll send out for something else."

Baz took Elijah's arm with a genteel gesture and led him to a side of the double stairs, where *more* double stairs led down into a full-on lower level too fancy to call a basement. The room they entered was slightly friendlier, its sectional sofa less imposing but not by much, its television still dwarfed by a fireplace which could have housed a small boar on a spit. Across from the hearth was a bar, a full-on *bar* with a zillion bottles and glasses and a long countertop with eight chairs lined along it.

It was here Baz led Elijah, pulling out a stool and plunking him into it before slipping behind the bar and collecting a pair of glasses. He poured a healthy amount of Oban and pushed it toward Elijah. Elijah didn't toss the scotch straight down, but he did take a few healthy gulps before settling into a more refined sipping pattern. He'd looked it up after Walter and Kelly's wedding. The stuff cost anywhere from sixty to five hundred dollars a bottle.

He was pretty sure he was the cheapest thing in the whole goddamned house.

Baz crouched below the bar for a minute, rooted around, and emerged with a gourmet bag of nuts and two of chips, one with cinnamon and nutmeg and another with some kind of salt scraped from the tears of a nun or something equally whack. Elijah resisted the urge to pour them into his mouth like a heathen, but he did pretty much dive in as soon as Baz had them cracked open.

"So." Baz leaned against the bar as he sipped his scotch. "How pissed at me are you? Because Mom will probably put us in the best guestroom, but I can ask to be in the suite instead so we have two beds."

"You leave me alone in this house for more than ten minutes and you're a dead man," Elijah said around a mouthful of chips. He started to brush the sugar off his palm, then stopped and reached for a napkin—thick, cream with gilded edging—from a wooden stand. "You seriously grew up here. In this house."

"Yep. Lost my virginity right over there by the fireplace to a pair of varsity lacrosse players."

Elijah couldn't imagine sex anywhere in this house without a plastic tarp laid out first. "Why aren't we staying in your room?"

"Don't have one anymore. She redecorated five years ago, and it became the guest suite. Some of my stuff is in storage behind the garage, and one closet has spare clothes, but most of it is at the White House."

It seemed weird, to have a house this big and erase your college-aged son's space because it didn't fit the pattern you wanted. Elijah didn't make this comment aloud, however, only downed more scotch.

Baz kept watching him. "You want a tour?"

How about a map? "Sure. Why not."

Baz started with the lower level, which had a family room—what they were in, with the bar—a sunroom, a billiards room, and an exercise room bigger than anything Baz would guess a single family needed. There was a wine room, whatever that was, and a second kitchen. There was a theater too—an honest-to-God theater, with fat recliners and studio seating. They took service stairs to the main kitchen, which was huge. A cheerful woman with some kind of European accent greeted them from the stove then went dutifully back to her work. A breakfast nook, big enough to be a formal dining room, stood off to one side, and yet another fireplace decorated the wall. Baz opened a door to the five-car garage, which had three luxury cars in it plus the Tesla. Down a hall from the kitchen was the formal dining room, which Elijah was so goddamned glad they weren't eating in. Crossing the foyer, Baz showed Elijah the living room, which while slightly cozier than the great room didn't seem much more inviting.

They skipped the area where Gloria had retreated, but Baz explained as they went up the stairs that it featured two offices, a bedroom, sitting room, and a large bath complete with steam room and sauna. Up the stairs there were two wings, the west and the east. The west was a suite of two bedrooms and a shared bath. This had been Baz's suite growing up—one room was his bedroom, the other his lounge.

Lounge. Elijah tried to wrap his mind around the idea of having a lounge off his bedroom, then gave up.

The east wing of the second floor housed two smaller bedrooms with their own baths, and the main guest bedroom, which was huge. It had a fireplace, which wasn't remarkable at this point because most of the rooms did. This one was large, though, like the ones downstairs, and the bathroom—bigger than Liz's living room—had a fireplace too. The bathroom had a huge glass-walled shower with five heads and a tub standing in the center of the room on a dais.

Their suitcases had been magicked into the main room of the suite, parked discreetly by the closet door. Elijah hovered in the corner beside them as Baz wrapped up the tour.

Baz, standing by the four-poster bed, frowned at Elijah. "Why are you so wigged out? Is it the boyfriend thing still?"

Elijah would have gladly decked him, but he couldn't risk losing his only guide in this clusterfuck. "Are you shitting me? No. It's not the boyfriend thing, though that's fucking funny now." He gestured angrily at the room. "I can't believe you're for real with this. If your mom hadn't walked out of her room—*suite*, whatever the fuck—I'd have thought this was some kind of joke, that you arranged to have us walk through this fancy joint as if it were yours so you could laugh. But no, this is really your goddamned house."

"Yes, it's my house. Why is it a problem? Why is it a joke?"

"Because *I'm* a joke here. This is so beyond a god-damned fork. I couldn't get a job as part of your staff."

Baz pursed his lips and waved this away. "You're making too much of this. Yes, it's fancy, but Mom entertains. A lot. And now she—well, she'll be enter-taining more, so yeah. It's got a bit of spit-shine. Plus she's here on her own mostly, so it's fussier than when I was growing up. Realize the only part of the house truly lived in is her suite, unless she's having guests."

Guests who were nothing like Elijah. But it was clear this wouldn't permeate Baz's consciousness anytime soon, so he rolled his eyes and turned away, hugging his arms tighter to his belly.

Baz sighed. "We need to go to the family room and wait for her. Unless you want to stay here? You can say you're tired, and I'll send a pizza up."

"No," Elijah bit off. "I'm staying with you."

Baz looked as if he wanted to push on that, the *Why are you afraid to be alone?* all but written on his face even with the glasses, but he only held out his arm and led Elijah down the hall, the stairs, and back to the bar.

Much as Elijah wanted to pour the bottle of Oban into his gullet, he switched to mineral water so that when Gloria Barnett Acker joined them, he wasn't so wasted he embarrassed himself. When it was time for dinner, he let Baz lead him into the sunroom, which was somehow on the same floor as the family room and which had been magically set up with dinnerware while they were on the house tour. As they took their places around the glass table, the housekeeper from the kitchen appeared from a side alcove with a cart. As Gloria tucked a napkin on her lap and asked them about their drive, the housekeeper ladled soup into the china and placed a small plate with a fragrant bread-cheese roll beside the single fork.

"Thank you," Elijah told her as she poured his wine. Nerves, a desperation to not seem like a doof, kept him talking. "The food looks great."

He could tell by her slightly startled and mur-mured, "Thank you, sir," he hadn't been meant to engage with her, a suspicion confirmed when Baz and his mother barely registered her presence, not so much as making eye contact as they vague-gestured a kind of *yes, I see you filling my glass, how nice* move. Which Elijah thought was kind of crass, because Christ, the food *did* look amazing. They couldn't tell her so? No, they chatted about traffic, about Marius and Damien, and even Aaron and Giles.

He waited until they began eating before he picked up a spoon, but he didn't have his soup out of the bowl before Gloria began addressing him directly. "So, Elijah. Have you moved into the White House yet, or are you still with Robert and Liz?"

He put his spoon down. "I haven't moved in yet." He stifled a glance at Baz as he added, "I will once we get back, though."

"Wonderful. And are you still in the room with—who was it again? Brian? Or will you be rooming with Sebastian?"

Obviously he was rooming with Brian, but what was he supposed to say? Where would Gloria expect Baz's boyfriend to live? Baz, however, was fixated on his dinner. "Um, I...don't know?" Elijah hedged.

"Wherever you want," Baz said, before filling his mouth with soup.

"Look at you two. Goodness, Elijah, I can tell you're someone special. It's not just anyone who can make my Sebastian shy." Gloria dabbed at her smile daintily with a peach-colored cloth napkin. "What will the two of you do tomorrow?"

"Shopping." Baz cut into his popover with a knife and fork. "Which reminds me. I'll need a car service because I want to take him to Zeglio's. Is this event black tie?"

"Oh, goodness no. A house party up by Mirror Lake. Cocktails, dinner. Anything from Zeglio's will be more than appropriate. If they don't have anything suitable on the rack, mention a rush custom job will be a favor to Uncle Paul."

They got into a discussion about types of dinner jackets, which Elijah decided was permission enough to eat. The soup was amazing, and so were the popovers. Normally he didn't go in for fish, but if all lobster bisque tasted like this, sign him up. As far as the cheese rolls were concerned, it was all he could do not to lick the plate. He would have eaten more, but none were offered, so he polished off his wine.

When the housekeeper returned and asked them how their meal was, *then* Baz and his mother effused in tones both controlled and sincere. Elijah echoed them, quietly. After a nod of acknowledgment, the house-keeper brought out dessert. Elijah missed the name of it, but it was basically some kind of custard thing in a dish with a stem as long as a wineglass. There were bits of cake in the custard, and cinnamon whipped cream on top, and when consumed with the decadent Italian espresso offered, it was probably the most amazing thing Elijah had ever eaten.

Gloria excused herself before Baz had finished, pleading a "mountain of work," encouraging the boys to send out for anything they might need. She wouldn't see them tomorrow, as she had a full schedule. When she rose, Baz did too, leaning over to kiss her cheek and accept one in return. Elijah wasn't sure if he should stand up too or not, so he tried to split the difference, rising as if maybe he meant to anyway. Once she left and Baz sat, however, Elijah remained standing, rubbing his arms as he wandered hesitantly around the perimeter of the room.

"We can go out on the patio, if you want a ciga-rette," Baz suggested.

Elijah wanted one of Baz's medicinal cigarettes, but he wasn't going to ask for them. "Sure. Except I left them in the room."

"No worries." Baz pulled out his phone, tapped out a text, and resumed eating his custard thing. As he scraped the side of his dish, a thirtyish man with a fake-bake tan breezed into the room, wearing a plastic smile.

"The items you requested." He passed over a small paper bag to Baz and nodded politely at Elijah. Then he disappeared out of the room again.

Baz pushed away from the table, scooping the sack up as he rose. "Wait here. I'm going to grab the Oban, and we'll sneak out."

Elijah would have protested Baz wasn't leaving him anywhere, but since he could hover in the hallway and pretty much watch him except for the ten seconds he was behind the bar, he let it slide.

The patio was a magical expanse of tile and potted urn things at the top of a stone staircase leading to a gleaming blue swimming pool and an expansive backyard which was probably not called a yard at all, but *grounds*. Elijah sank into a swanky fabric lawn chair and stared out across the *grounds* as Baz passed him the paper bag. Inside was a package of cigarettes Elijah hadn't ever heard of before. Dunhill, they said. He didn't think that was the brand Baz had mentioned earlier, but whatever they were, they smelled nice. He lit one and decided they tasted even better.

There was more in the bag, though. A prescription pill bottle of Xanax—in Elijah's name. There were also three joints politely tucked into the corner, sealed inside a mini baggie.

Elijah stared into the bag. "Where the hell did all this come from?"

"Stephan. My mom's Guy Friday." Baz fished the joints out of the bag. "If you don't want the Xanax, you can flush it. I thought...since you seemed on edge. Would have given them to you earlier, but they just showed up."

Elijah wouldn't have had one then, because hell would freeze over before he'd play this circus high, but now that the show was over, he cracked the lid on the bottle and fished out a pill. He couldn't split it with his cigarette and the bag, but Baz relieved him of it as soon as he began to struggle and did it for him, popping it into Elijah's mouth after.

"Are you still pissed?" His mouth thinned as he asked, like he was stressed and annoyed and confused.

Elijah sloshed the pill into his system with some Oban instead of answering. "What's this shopping thing? Why do we need a car service to do it?"

"You need a suit. So do I, frankly. The car service is because the shop is in the heart of downtown Chicago, and as nervous as you got on the interstate coming in here, I didn't figure we should leap right into graduate-level traffic." He lit a joint. "So you *are* still pissed."

Elijah wasn't so much pissed as confused and terrified. He motioned for the joint, not giving a shit he had a lit cigarette in his other hand. Once the weed joined his chemical symphony, he cracked the lid on the freakout he'd been banking ever since he'd pulled into the drive. "I didn't think you were this guy, is all."

Baz took the joint back. "What do you mean, *this guy*? What the hell is that?"

"The guy with *staff*. A house with a courtyard

clock. *Suites.* Somebody who can magic me up a prescription."

"Why is that bad?"

Elijah swigged Oban. It wasn't *bad.* It was...fucking insane. Elijah felt as if he were on the set of gay *Dallas* or *Dynasty.* "It's weird. It makes me uncomfortable." He put his cigarette to his lips and murmured around it. "Feel like an idiot, pretending to be your boyfriend. Jesus, they must all be laughing."

He startled as Baz abruptly straddled the chair and loomed over him. He didn't remove his sunglasses, but he pulled them down enough to glare. "Will you fucking stop? You could so be my boyfriend, and to hell with anybody who laughed. Quit pretending you're a leper."

Nostrils flaring, Elijah flicked the center of Baz's chest. "You should have fucking let her set you up. You should have laid this out so I could have seen how awkward I'd feel and say no. If you were so against walking out with her choice of fake boyfriend, you should have gone on Grindr and picked a boy toy for the weekend. You shouldn't have put that on me. This is the most fucked-up trick I've ever done, and I'm not even getting paid."

Oh, how he hated himself, the way his body yielded and dick got hard when Baz threw the joint on the ground, sat on his thighs, cupped his chin and leaned in dangerously close. "This isn't a trick, goddamn it."

It was—the other kind. The nasty kind. The one he played on himself. Elijah's throat got thick. "I hate how stupid you make me. Feel me up in a cupboard, pout, and here I am. I guess at least the food was good."

For a horrible second he feared his barb had hit its mark. The hand on his chin almost fell away. But at the last moment, Baz caught a headwind. "I asked you—fine, tricked you—because I wanted *you*. Stupid's an open market, baby. I don't know why, but nobody undoes me like you. You want to know why I ran from you for a month? *That*. That right there." He traced the tip of his nose along Elijah's. "I'm done running."

Elijah didn't need Xanax for the confession to peel his heart open, but the drugs didn't do him any favors. "I don't know how to behave here. I don't know how to play this game, how to be safe. Don't tell me I'm safe, because it's a crock of shit. There are a million ways for me to look foolish and be laughed at. And that's *here*. I'm scared to death of this house party."

Baz's expression softened. "Anyone laughs at you, I'll tear them apart." He stroked Elijah's cheek and drew a circle around his lips. "Hush, Sophie. You're beautiful."

It was, mostly, a quote from the movie, and it finished Elijah off. Shutting his eyes, he leaned into Baz's touch. "Don't eat my heart, Howl."

"Never," Baz vowed, sealing the promise with a kiss.

Chapter Nine

ELIJAH DIDN'T EXACTLY forget the rest of his first night at Baz's house, but he had to admit it was hazy.

He had shards, here and there. Baz trying to fuck him on the patio, Elijah objecting, Baz plying him with booze and weed and finally the second half of the Xanax. After that things became distinctly gray. Did getting a blow job count as sex? If so, he had to cede the patio to Baz. Something had happened in the shower—he was pretty sure he *tried* to get Baz to fuck him, but if he got any action there, it was a hand job. Or…something.

Either he'd bent over the tub dais and been in the rimming Olympics, or he'd dreamed that part.

He knew Baz poured a metric fuckton of water into him, and the cheesy bread things magically appeared at some point. Cigarettes and another blow job on a narrow balcony off their room. He knew he'd swayed on the same balcony after, Baz wrapped around him while Elijah slurred sappy shit he was willfully not remembering.

Now, however, it was morning. Full, horrible morning, steeped in hangover and hell, and Baz with a tray of breakfast beside the bed, patiently explaining they had less than an hour before the car arrived to take them shopping.

"I can't leave this bed," Elijah wheezed, seconds before Baz hauled him out of it.

This shower was solo and filled with the horror of possibly retching all over it. The antacid Baz left on the bathroom counter helped keep that at bay, as did the dry toast and green tea. He didn't feel human enough to get dressed until the Vicodin Baz offered him kicked in. He only got one leg in his jeans, though, before he had to sag into Baz. "Why did you let me get so drunk?"

"You actually didn't have much more than the night of the wedding. The only thing different was the Xanax." Baz nuzzled, licking Elijah's ear. "Sucks it makes you this hung over. Because, baby, when you cut loose…"

Elijah's blush burned him head to toe. "I guess it's good you got the car thing. No way I could drive."

Baz pressed a kiss on his temple. "If you get dressed, you can work in a cigarette before they get here."

Elijah did get his cigarette, and half of a second one before a sedate black car pulled into the circle by the clock. The inside was leather and lush, complete with a privacy-screen thing Baz slid electronically into place as soon as he'd given directions to the driver. Elijah worried Baz would want to make out or something, jostling his still-unsteady tummy, but Baz only tucked Elijah into his side and indicated points of interest as they drifted past.

There were a lot of points of interest, because it was a long-ass drive into the heart of downtown. Which, thank Christ Baz had arranged for someone else to drive, because Elijah wanted to piss himself *riding* in this traffic. He'd never bitch about Minneapolis congestion again.

He tried not to rubberneck when they got out of the car and approached a not-exactly-well-marked storefront in a rather nondescript building. There was no marquee declaring the store's name, only some lettering on the window in a font blending in more than it stood out. Kind of dumb for a business. How in the world would anyone find the place?

They walked through the door, the crisp, sharp scent of expensive fabric blooming like roses around them, and Elijah realized this wasn't a place you found. This was a place you knew about.

He cowered when a man in a smart suit emerged with a smile and an expression saying *Can I help you?* in a manner indicating he doubted this was possible—but the second the guy clocked Baz, the wall fell away and the salesman all but drew him into an embrace. "Mr. Acker. What a delightful surprise. How can I be of service?"

Baz told the story of the last-minute event, so sorry to bother but it would be such a help to Uncle Paul— the performance had Elijah feeling queasy in a way unrelated to his hangover, so he drifted around the room, looking without touching. No price tags, which couldn't be good. There wasn't actually much stuff displayed in the small, heavily mahogany space. Bolts of fabric on the wall were clearly more for show or example than actual construction. Some shoes. Ties. Cufflinks and tie tacks. Shirts—there were some of those, and some suits on hangers, but like the fabric bolts, these seemed more for decoration than options for purchase.

He startled when Baz touched his waist. "What?" He bit back, *I didn't touch anything.*

"They have my measurements on file, but not yours."

Measurements. Elijah knew this gig from the suit Pastor had bought him for the wedding. He was glad he hadn't brought that now. It had been the nicest thing he'd ever owned, but it was off the rack at Nordstrom. The greatest adjustment they'd made to it was to hem the pants. After he was measured, he modeled a pair of wool trousers whose fabric was so soft and rich he shivered as it passed over his skin. The pale peach shirt was crisp, weighty, yet somehow also light. Aside from needing to be hemmed, he thought the clothes fit him pretty well—except Baz and the tailor pointed out what should be tucked and let out. The same treatment was given to a suit coat, and while Elijah's clothes were pinned and marked with white pencil, Baz held up cufflinks and ties and socks and shoes.

Elijah gave him a cutting glare he hoped made it clear Baz should continue dressing him and not invite him to fuck up the Cinderella routine.

Baz's fitting went a lot faster, and soon they were

out the door, to have lunch and "wander a bit" until their suits were ready for a final fitting.

"Where do you want to go?" Baz asked as they climbed into the car.

Home to Saint Timothy. Elijah leaned against the window. "Wherever."

"Have you been to Chicago before?"

"No."

"Well, what do you want to see?"

Elijah refused to turn away from the window. "I don't know. You pick."

Eventually Baz leaned into the partition window and said, "Take us to Navy Pier."

A gigantic Ferris wheel loomed over the place where the driver dropped them off. Also a large building full of shops, a long boardwalk, and a host of ferries boasting the best views of the city for a gaggle of eager tourists.

This, actually, wasn't bad—well, it was horribly tourist, but Elijah felt at home in this crowd, and he let Baz lead him around by the hand. They mocked the souvenirs, ate hot dogs from a cart, and shared a lemonade. They rode the Ferris wheel, which was incredibly boring and lame, and the giant swings, which gave Elijah an adrenaline rush and left him grinning like a fool for fifteen minutes after. They took a boat ride, snuggled together on the top deck. A chirpy woman told them the condensed version of Chicago history while Baz nuzzled Elijah's ear.

"When we get to the house, I'll give you fork lessons. Answer any question you have about tomorrow night." His hand trailed down Elijah's arm. "We can leave from the party, if you want. Get a hotel room somewhere quiet out of town. Or we can leave early Sunday morning. Whatever you want."

"Hotel...would be good." Elijah sagged into him. "Sorry."

Baz kissed his hair. "Don't be. I owe you a lot for this. An early escape and modest hotel room is the least I can do."

What happens after the escape? What happens when we're at the White House? Elijah couldn't begin to guess. "Chicago is pretty, from a distance."

"Yes. I prefer it best viewed from the Twin Cities."

They said nothing after that, sitting together quietly for the rest of the ride.

The second fitting was quick. Elijah's suit fit like a glove, though the tailor fussed and promised to make a few more minor alterations to his suit and Baz's before sending them to the house. Baz took Elijah to pizza on the way home, the deep-dish kind the city was famous for, so thick and huge Elijah was able to only choke down a single piece. He and Baz lingered in their booth for an hour after finishing, though, sipping at beer, teasing each other, laughing. Relaxing. Being normal, almost as if they were boyfriends out for a night on the town.

Unfortunately when they returned to the house, Elijah once again felt acutely out of place. Baz brushed this aside, leading him into the dining room—the big, formal, scary one. After sitting Elijah in one of the huge fabric chairs, he pulled china, stemware, and silverware out of a hutch and began his instruction.

"The rule of thumb is to work your way in from the outside. You might see a little fork and spoon above your main plate, possibly on their own small dish. Those are dessert utensils. You'll have at least two glasses, one for water, one for wine, possibly a second for another wine. The glasses are easy. You won't do the pouring, and they'll only give you the wine appropriate to the current course. Spoons are also simple: soup and teaspoon. That leaves us with…" he retreated to the wall of china, and when he turned around, he had a fan of knives in one hand and forks in the other and a wicked grin between them, "…the artillery."

He lay the forks out on the left, the knives on the right, giving them all names. Salad fork. Fish fork. Dinner fork. Dinner knife. Fish knife. Salad knife.

Jesus, who the fuck needed this much silverware?

Baz touched the plate between his nest of utensils. "This is the place plate. You won't eat a damn thing off it. They'll remove it and present you with each course." He pointed at the tiny plate with a mini knife laid across it to the place plate's ten o'clock. "That's the bread and butter plate and butter knife. You'll also have your own salt and pepper shaker set, and a fancy menu card telling you what you'll be eating. Your napkin will be on your place plate, folded into some complicated shape. Your place card will be either tucked into it or lying in front of it, telling you where to sit. The hostess will help you out, leading you to your place."

They had assigned seats? What was this, the fifth-grade lunch room? And he'd thought the wedding was bad, where they had assigned tables. "I'll be by you though, right?"

"Yes, well. Maybe. Hopefully." When Elijah turned on him, ready to melt down, Baz put a hand on his shoulder. "It'll be fine. Sometimes they move people around, break up couples, or try to have even men and women. I'll talk to Stephan, ask to make sure we're next to each other."

Elijah wanted to press this issue, to make it absolutely clear this was the only acceptable possibility, but he swallowed his neurosis and nodded at the place setting. "Do it again, please."

Baz went over the layout three more times. He also taught Elijah how to hold his glasses, took him to the bar and showed him how to hold a cocktail glass. Gave him pointers on how to survive a boring or rude conversation. Taught him how to mingle.

"If you don't like a conversation you're having, wait for a beat and apologize because you see me or somebody gesturing to you from the other side of the room. Or simply excuse yourself and say you'll be right back, and then never return. Pace your drinks too. If you get nervous, linger with the bartender. The waitstaff won't want to be chatty, but the bartenders have to be. And once you know where the designated smoking area is, you have another escape."

"You act as if you won't be with me."

"I'll be with you. But it's easy to get drawn away for a moment or two, and I don't want you to feel like you're floundering. If you panic, ask where I am. Remember, we're supposed to be dating. They'll think it's cute if we can't be parted for more than a few heartbeats."

"What about my past?"

"Half-truths and brevity. You don't get along with your parents. Yes, it's the gay thing. So tragic when people are shortsighted. And if they did hear about the shooting, it's a gauche subject, and they can't address it too much directly. *Nasty business* and so on, you pulling a sober face and nodding agreement, nothing more. The truth is, they don't want what you're afraid of. If you start weeping and talking about how it felt to watch me bleed on the snow, *they'll* be seeing someone on the other side of the room."

Nausea swelled with the memory Baz conjured. "Don't even talk about that."

"Exactly my point. Nobody wants to go there. It's small talk. Stupid, inane small talk. *Look, see us all being semi-human.* Oh, the drink tray. Moving on." When Elijah sighed and sagged in his chair, Baz ruffled his hair. "Come on. One more cigarette, a bubble bath, and bed. We have a big day tomorrow."

Elijah almost fell asleep in the bathtub, and though he meant to stay awake long enough to give Baz a thanks-for-the-nice-day blow job, somehow it was morning, Baz emerging from the bathroom wearing only a towel and a wry smile. And sunglasses.

He hoped for a little morning loving, but they had breakfast in the kitchen and a morning at…well, the spa. Elijah got a haircut he didn't want to know the price of, as well as a manicure and a massage. At the house they had a light lunch, a few cigarettes on the patio, a dry hump in the bedroom, and then it was time to get ready for the main event.

They looked good together in their custom suits. Elijah didn't feel like a kid playing dress-up for once, and Baz was basically a walking boner machine. They drove the Tesla, which had been magically packed with all their bags. Moonroof open, RuPaul crooning, they cruised through the winding roads to the estate where the party would be held.

"I have a hotel booked I think you'll like." Baz stole Elijah's cigarette for a hit. "Just over the Wisconsin border. Moose features heavily in the theme."

Elijah could give a shit about moose. He wanted to ask what would happen when they got to the White House, but he couldn't figure out how, so he smoked and tapped his finger against the wheel to the music.

As he turned down the driveway Baz indicated, he steeled himself for more opulence. He wasn't disappointed: the house was bigger than Baz's place, a gleaming diamond with another circular driveway. A tiny turret on the top of the main wing made the place almost look like a church. It had no clock, no urns of flowers. Didn't need them. It said *money* with simplicity and stately lines.

Young men in tailcoats and white gloves greeted them at the apex of the circle, opening their doors and handing Elijah a valet ticket before whisking the Tesla away. They didn't need to be told how to start or stop it, either. Elijah clung to Baz's arm as they drifted up the sidewalk to the front door, where another man in tails and white gloves admitted them with obeisance and ushered them toward a middle-aged woman with upswept hair and a silvery suit dress, and a man who had to be her husband beside her. They greeted Baz and Elijah warmly, graciously, and urged them to move through to the patio to join the rest of the guests.

Basically it was Baz's house dialed up a few notches. Grander foyer. Bigger patio, larger grounds. A service bar had been set up on either end of the building, but no shortage of waitstaff drifted past with trays of champagne. Clusters of guests littered the estate, most of them older, though some of them were distinctly youthful. Everyone had on plastic smiles and custom suits.

Gloria appeared, making a great show of welcoming Baz and Elijah before dragging them to pods of guests, introducing them, hinting at their backstory. It quickly became clear queer was their greatest selling point. All the guests were liberal to the bone, falling over themselves to show gay was okay. Everyone seemed enchanted by the idea of "little Sebastian" finally falling in love. A few women said they wanted to be invited to the wedding. Elijah worried this would flip Baz out, but he only winked and assured them *naturally* they'd be on the list.

Basically, that's all it was. Elijah didn't have to say much of anything at all. He clung to Baz's arm, looked embarrassed when people made a fuss, and parroted all the small-talk stuff Baz had coached him through. It wasn't fun, but it wasn't awful. The only bad moment was when he'd let go of Baz to steady a glass of champagne he'd tried to place on a tray, and in the half second he was distracted, Gloria dragged Baz off, leaving Elijah alone with the large-eyed tipsy woman who wanted his advice on how to redecorate her library. The game of *so sorry, I'll be right back* worked like a charm, and after that he simply never let go of his faux-boyfriend for anything at all.

"You're doing great," Baz assured him when they were alone in the bathroom. "We only have the dinner left, and the speeches. Then we can do one circuit around the room and beat it out of here."

"You told the guy, right? To make sure we sit together?"

"Yes. It'll be fine. Don't worry."

Elijah didn't, much. He trusted his fancy clothes and Baz's warm arm and easy social grace, and he almost enjoyed the party. He pretended he actually belonged. That Baz truly was his boyfriend and the silly women would in fact be coming to their wedding. He wasn't sure he ever wanted to be the kind of person who shopped in hidden suit shops, but once in a while? Maybe okay.

They were herded toward the dining room, where the hostess stood like a shepherd. Telling Baz he was seated three chairs down from his mother on the east end of the table—

—and Elijah was on the other end, twenty people away.

"Thank you," Baz said when Elijah's mouth opened in automatic protest. He herded them toward Elijah's end of the monstrous table, pulling out his chair, bending to whisper in his ear as he eased a rigid Elijah into his seat.

"Baz," Elijah whimpered, clutching at his arm as discreetly as he could.

"You'll be fine." Baz twined their fingers together, gripping his shoulder as he spoke quietly into his ear. "I don't know what happened, but I swear to you, I had this fixed."

"Can't you move over here?" He was whining, he knew, but he couldn't help it.

"I'll try. But if I can't, *you can do this.* You hear me, Elijah? Fuck the forks. You're amazing and brilliant and strong as steel. You could do a dinner party in your sleep."

They were such pretty lies, but that's all they were: lies. Because Elijah knew he couldn't do this. When Baz moved away, disappearing into the sea of other guests taking their seats, the fragile soap bubble of confidence that had buoyed Elijah through the evening popped. The eccentric, puffed-up people shifted from humorous to horrible. Their smiles stopped being silly, lacquered instead with judgment and censure. The mountain of silverware and china were things to knock over, to drop, to break.

He *would* fuck this up, and they would laugh, or worse, stare. He would reveal himself unworthy, awkward, and wrong. It wasn't a matter of if. It was simply a question of when.

Maybe Baz will be back. The last dregs of his stupid happiness made one more rally, scrambling to make everything be okay again, to allow him a way to belong. *Maybe he'll get it sorted out and sit beside you, and you can laugh later about what a hot mess you were when left on your own.*

The worst part was he fell for it. He really thought Baz would rescue him. That somehow all the other times Baz had swept in, bedazzled his life, and then vanished had been the aberrations, and now, magically, things would be different. For ten full, painful minutes he got himself through by believing everything would be okay because Baz promised it would be.

The waitstaff began pouring the water, asking him to please remove his napkin so they could set the soup course. Elijah realized the horrible, hollow truth about himself. No matter how many times this happened, he'd keep following Baz into the deep water, a dumb puppy eager to show off his dog paddle.

Every goddamned time, Baz would vanish, leaving Elijah to flounder and ache alone.

BAZ COULDN'T FIND his mother. She wasn't anywhere in the dining room, or the foyer, or the patio. It didn't help that with his vision he was the worst one to hunt someone down across a crowded room. She'd worn the same color blue as three other blondes, and he'd approached two of them accidentally before conceding he'd missed her entrance to the dining room while he searched elsewhere. By the time he re-entered, nearly everyone was seated and the waitstaff had begun clearing the place plates for the first course. Heart sinking, he started for Elijah to apologize and give him one more pep talk, but he didn't get three steps before his mother appeared, capturing his arm and leading him away.

"Darling, where have you been? This is the part where I need you—I asked Helen to seat us next to Moira Arend."

Baz swallowed a groan. Moira Arend, the eccentric heiress. Eccentric *lesbian* heiress. *This* was the desperate reason she'd dragged him to Chicago? "Mom, she's not going to give two shits about me. I need to solve the seating arrangement. Didn't Stephan tell you I needed to be by Elijah? This whole thing is freaking him out, and now I'm on the other end of the earth."

"Helen was insistent couples be broken up. Besides, I called in all my favors getting you next to me."

Baz stuttered to a stop and stared at her, incredulous. "*Mom.* He's upset. He's not built for this bullshit."

"Then you should have let me find you a date."

"You finding me a date wasn't an option. I told you. He's my boyfriend."

It wasn't until the words were out of his mouth that he realized they weren't a line anymore. Or rather, he didn't *want* them to be a line. He'd loved this weekend with Elijah. He hadn't felt restless or lonely. He'd woke both mornings eager to spend the day with Elijah. The realization was a thin ray of sun breaching an otherwise dim and dusty room. A ray of sun which wouldn't blind him.

Gloria pursed her lips. "I'm sorry this has been hard for him, and I wish I could help. But perhaps it's best he receive this trial by fire. If he can't handle a simple dinner party, he'd never last long-term anyway."

Baz blinked at her, no idea where to begin object-ing to that callous line of garbage, but before he could so much as sputter, the hostess appeared at their side, urging them with polite firmness to take their seats so the meal could begin. Baz didn't have a chance to deliver so much as an apology to Elijah before he was escorted to his seat.

He could see Elijah from his end of the table, but only barely, and the setting sun streaming in through the picture window was enough to keep him from too many overt checks. He kept trying to think of an excuse to go there, but there wasn't one. At best in a few courses he could excuse himself for the restroom, but that would piss off his mother. Which, part of him thought, would be only appropriate, since he wanted to throttle her.

Moira Arend was indeed seated across from them, and Gloria bent herself into a pretzel trying to capture her in conversation. As promised, Baz featured heavily in her effort, as did Elijah. She turned their separation into a lure. "You must forgive Sebastian. He's distract-ed because his date is at the other end of the table, and they're in that stage where they can't fathom parting for more than a sigh."

Moira set down her wineglass, her polite mask melting away as she gave Baz a look of utter empathy. "You be distracted all you want. I feel the same way, and Deirdre and I have been together six years." She fixed her gaze on Elijah's end of the table, her gaze softening further. "Hopefully our partners have each other. What's your boyfriend's name?"

"Elijah Prince."

Moira smiled. "Yes, that's right. Deirdre and I were talking about how besotted you were. I'm afraid we were ogling the two of you a bit. How long have you been dating?"

They *looked* besotted? Baz surprised himself by blushing and made it worse by averting his gaze. "Not…not long."

"You poor dears. A new relationship, and you have to parade through this circus. Take him somewhere nice afterward."

Baz rubbed his cheek, flustered by his own shyness. "I…have this hotel. On the way out of town. He wanted to go home tonight, so I dug up this quirky place decked out like a cabin in southern Wisconsin."

Moira nodded in approval. "Wonderful. Give him my best, and tell him Deirdre still hates these things. She gets three days at a spa every time she attends. You'll have to ask him what penance he requires."

Baz nodded, still abashed, and his mother took the moment to swoop in and collect the networking bounty she'd dragged Baz into this for. It was clear whenever Moira met Gloria Barnett Acker, she'd largely see her sweet gay besotted son.

In the end he didn't use the restroom ruse to check on Elijah. He worried a check-in would make things worse and focused instead on locating the earliest point of extrication. Though his mother had wanted him to stay through the cocktail hour and the speeches, Baz decided he'd more than done his part. When they were dismissed to retire to the lower-level lounge, Baz beelined to Elijah, ready to get on his knees to apologize and whisk him away.

He didn't find a fragile Elijah, however, or even a furious one. The date he collected was wooden, dismissive. He largely brushed aside Baz's mea culpa, and flatly rejected the suggestion of immediate departure.

"I need another hour to make sure I'm sober enough to drive," was all he would say. When Baz offered to go with him outside to the smoking area, Elijah refused, saying he could go by himself. "I could use a moment alone."

A moment alone from the guy who'd refused to so much as go to the toilet by himself was not a good sign. "Elijah, I swear to God, I did everything I could to get down there. Did something happen? How can I fix this?"

"I won't be gone long. I'll be right back, in fact."

"Elijah," Baz protested, but his date slipped away, and the only way to re-engage him was to create a scene.

Baz seriously considered it, would have if he'd thought that wouldn't have pissed Elijah off more. Instead he followed quietly to the smoking area, keeping a reasonable distance. As they returned to the party, Elijah didn't speak except to give a polite thank you when Baz procured him a tall glass of sparkling water.

"I'm sorry," he said over and over. They wove through the lounge, or rather Elijah kept walking away from Baz and he kept following. When Elijah spoke again, it was to tell Baz he was ready to leave.

"Great. I'll give the ticket to the valet, and we'll bust out of here."

"We have to say thank you to the hostess first." Elijah's lips quirked into a nasty grimace. "Even I know that much."

Baz could give two shits about the hostess right now, but he followed Elijah anyway, made pretty with the Helen who had fucked up his evening. When they emerged to the main level and gave their ticket to the valet, he felt as if he were taking his first breath of air.

The second they were inside the Tesla, Baz began to babble, trying to explain how his mom didn't move them because there was a donor, and he would have pressed for it anyway but he found her too late. He tried to explain about Moira, how that had been the one good part because she understood, but Elijah turned on the radio and jacked up the volume to drown him out.

Heart sinking, Baz stopped mid-sentence. After a mile or so, Elijah fumbled with the map, swearing when his efforts made him swerve over the line and get honked at.

Baz took over. "Let me put in the coordinates for the hotel."

"Put in Saint Timothy."

Fuck. Baz didn't argue, didn't point out driving that far would take them until five in the morning when they factored in a stop to charge. He figured his job was to put up and shut up. And pray to God he hadn't fucked up so much they were ruined.

The music sucked. It was some random local station playing canned crap, but Elijah didn't change it, and Baz wasn't touching the dashboard for any money right now. He didn't light Elijah's cigarettes for him, didn't take one for himself. He checked his phone as they got close to the border, thinking probably he should cancel the hotel, then decided to eat the charge.

He considered answering one of Marius's or Damien's zillion *how's it going?* texts, but he couldn't work out how to ask for help on this. He wasn't sure he should. Maybe his mom was right. Maybe this was too fucked up. Not like he wanted the Barnett-Acker circus, but he couldn't exactly ditch it. Maybe this had been a dumb lark. Maybe better to get out now.

The radio played a slow, sad song, a bright tenor apologizing for being too late, begging his lover to say something, anything, acknowledging he didn't want to give up but it was probably over all the same. It cut into Baz, highlighting his emotions and pouring salt in his wounds. As the song swelled to its apex, Baz scrambled for new words, another apology, a plea, anything to fix this. He turned toward Elijah, ready to spill his guts, say anything to make them okay.

He stopped as he got a good look at his faux-boyfriend. Elijah seemed tense—nervous, not pissed. Skittish, the same as he'd been in heavier traffic. Except there was nobody on the road here, just a few cars and semis. Baz wanted to ask if Elijah was okay, except it was a stupid question because obviously he wasn't. He abandoned his apologies and tried instead to work out what was wrong and how he could fix it.

Elijah punched the dashboard screen with his finger, switching the radio off.

"I can't."

Elijah's knuckles went white, his arms shaking. He stared at the road ahead as if it might suck him in.

Baz sat up straighter. "Elijah? Are you okay?"

"I can't. *I can't.*" His breathing got short and fast, his hairline peppered with sweat—and he took his foot off the gas. The car behind them swerved, honking as it sped around the rapidly slowing Tesla. Elijah paid it no attention, shaking his head as he locked his arms and kept his feet off the pedals. "I can't. *I can't do it.*"

Holy fuck. Baz glanced at the lane behind them—the few other cars were moving over, but at some point they'd slow too much and get hit. He put a tentative hand on Elijah's shoulder. "It's okay."

"I can't do this. I can't."

"You don't have to do anything you don't want to, baby. Except right now I need you to give the car some acceleration so we don't get rear-ended and die."

A snort-sob escaped, but Elijah didn't shed a tear. His whole body trembling, he halfheartedly depressed the gas pedal, bringing them up to fifty miles an hour.

That would do.

Baz scanned ahead and saw an overpass, and an exit. "There. Pull off up there, and we'll sort it out. Okay?"

"No. I don't want to talk. I want to go..." for a moment his face broke into misery, "...to Liz and Pastor."

Baz ached for him, long, hollow columns of grief

down his neck and into his gut. "I'll get you there. I promise. Make the car go for me, get us to the off-ramp, and we'll make a new plan. You can have a cigarette. Or five."

The car sped up slowly, despite the fact it could get to sixty-five miles an hour in four point two seconds. Elijah wiped furiously at his eyes, but Baz still saw no sign of tears. "I don't want to get off here in the middle of nowhere. But I think I need to sleep. Have...have a Xanax."

Yes, even with his shit vision Baz could see a panic attack threatening. "The hotel isn't far. The one I'd already booked." The words *I'll get my own room* formed on his lips but wouldn't pass through.

Elijah nodded stiffly. "Fine. As long as it's close."

It was. Fifteen minutes and a cigarette for each of them later, they pulled into the parking lot of the Stoney Inn. It was decorated like an overgrown cabin, all rock and wooden beams and prints of moose and fir trees. As he'd booked it, Baz had thought it was funny, but in that moment its quirkiness was a balm. It was a PlugShare stop, and the business of pulling in backward to the particular spot and dragging out the charging cord gave them some cover from the awkward. So did the cheesy, moose-and-pine-filled lobby and the cheery female receptionist who handed them their keycards. Baz worried all the way up the elevator that maybe he shouldn't have booked the Premier Suite, too much of a reminder of his family's bullshit which had started all of this, but no. The Stoney Inn's best room was still pretty tacky and lowbrow. Thank fucking God.

As the door to the room shut behind him, Baz clutched the handle of his suitcase, tracking Elijah as he moved around the room. He wracked his brain for the right thing to say. To do. To offer. Everything ran out of his head. He needed to see Elijah's face. Close enough to read it, to see if he was as walled off as he'd been at the party. To find out if the mini breakdown on the interstate was his last gasp before he sealed himself off forever, or if Elijah had experienced the same cracking apart as Baz.

When Elijah turned around, Baz held his breath, the sad pop song's chorus ringing in his ears. He blinked against the glare from the room lamps, squinted through the dim of his sunglasses. Saw the tic in Elijah's cheek, the hurt, the fury in his gaze. Let the breath out in a rush, riding out a shiver.

Open. Not closed off anymore. There was still hope.

Chapter Ten

ELIJAH COULD STILL taste the fear in his mouth.

It didn't make any more sense now than it had in the car, but it was there, hovering like a hellbeast on the edge of his vision. Something about the dotted line on the map indicating the shift between Illinois and Wisconsin had undone him. As if, when he crossed it, darkness would fall. The more he'd told himself the thought was ridiculous, the worse it got, until the metallic, bitter tang of panic overcame him.

If it hadn't been for Baz talking him through, he wasn't sure what would have happened.

That pissed him off, Baz rescuing him again. It had felt so good to brush him off, knowing Baz was ready to get on his knees to grovel. Elijah had reveled in the power. He hadn't figured out how he was going to leverage it at school, but he'd worked up this great mental proposal about getting in the dorms and fucking the White House entirely...and then the goddamned dotted line had done him in.

Now here they were, in Baz's moose hotel. Baz had passed him a bottle of water and a pill, but otherwise they were standing exactly where they'd been since they walked in the door. Elijah in the middle of the room,

Baz off to the side. Baz poised and ready to slay drag-
ons, Elijah weak enough to let him. His arguments
about a dorm evaporated as Xanax bled into his
bloodstream. Fuck getting out of the White House. It
would be a miracle if Elijah could talk himself out of
letting Baz take him to bed.

"I hate you," he whispered, clutching the strap to
his bag he hadn't been willing to relinquish, as if
holding on to it meant he still might leave.

He waited for Baz to argue, and when Baz remained quiet, Elijah gave in to the fury he'd been
sandbagging since the removal of his place plate.

He dropped the bag and marched forward. "I seriously fucking hate you. I can't believe I keep letting you
do this to me."

Baz said nothing, didn't move.

A dim voice dragged out logic, pointing out it had
only been a dinner, and Baz was right, nothing bad had
happened. This fact, combined with Baz's willingness
to accept his shunning, only fueled Elijah all the more.
"You always abandon me. You always *will* abandon me.
God, your friends fucking told me you would, and I
said I knew, *and then I did this.* Well, I'm done. Fuck
you. Our fake relationship is over. Thanks for getting a
suite. I'm sleeping on the couch. Tomorrow we'll go to
Saint Timothy, and—"

"It wasn't fake to me. And I don't want it to be
over."

Elijah faltered, opening and shutting his mouth a
few times before he could reply. "Excuse me?"

Baz let go of his suitcase. "It was real for me. It still

is. I spent the whole dinner worrying about you, trying to figure out a way to get to you. Mom was using me to butter up some rich lesbian, and it worked because Moira loved how I was fussing. Which I hated, because I wanted to be buttering *you* up. To show *you* off, then laugh about what a joke the party was while we listened to RuPaul on the way here."

It was sweet, and it sounded genuine, and it brought back panic in a choking fog. "What, you were going to give me your ring and ask me to go steady?"

"Maybe. I hadn't thought that far ahead. Maybe I needed to be freaked out about not being with you to realize."

"Maybe you had too much to drink and need to lie down, sleep this attack of boyfriend off."

The voice of reason reared its head again, scolding Elijah for being too harsh, but he couldn't help it. This was too close to things he didn't dare let himself admit he wanted—and anyway, it didn't seem to matter how much shade he chucked at Baz. It all bounced off his titanium skeleton.

"I'll sleep on the couch. But when I wake up, I'll feel the same way."

Elijah began to scramble, reaching blindly for any buffer he could find. "We don't know how to boy-friend. We can barely friend."

The distance between them now was basically an arm's length, meaning Elijah could smell Baz now. Spicy and sweet, bare hints of tobacco and sweat. "We did boyfriend all weekend just fine, when we were pretending it was fake."

Mayday. Man all battle stations. "It's only Saturday night. The weekend is barely half over." When Baz's sideways smile made him dizzy, Elijah shut his eyes. "Stop it. You can't nip off a few good lines, grab my dick, and we're fine. We can't date. Maybe we could fuck occasionally. But that's it. Anything else is ridiculous."

A shiver ran through him as Baz's body brushed his, hands skating over his arms. "Let's be ridiculous."

Elijah didn't wrap his arms around Baz, but he did turn his face up to be kissed. Except the kiss didn't happen. Baz ran his nose along Elijah's eyebrow instead.

"You make a good point. We should slow down. No grabbing anything. Work on a friendship, let the physical yearnings fuel the fire."

Now Elijah grabbed him. "The hell I went through all this and you're not putting out."

A kiss, featherlight, on his forehead. "I thought you were sleeping on the couch."

Fuck him for dragging logic into this. "After. I'll go to the couch after. Or do me on the couch. I'm not particular."

"If I do you, you sure as shit won't have the energy to crawl to the other side of the bed, let alone the next room."

Elijah thought, seriously, about telling him to fuck himself, but going to sleep alone while his freakout still echoed in his head wasn't something he could handle. And he wanted to get done. By Baz. Needed it, almost. But he was still sore about losing all the power he'd found during the dinner. It had been cold and awful, but it felt safer than this. He wanted some cover back. "You can fuck me, but only if you don't wear your glasses."

Baz paused. Elijah held his breath. *Maybe I went too far.*

Then Baz's hands slid up Elijah's sides, and he nodded as he kissed Elijah's cheek, the corner of his mouth. "Sure thing. But you have to let me do some maintenance first."

He let go of Elijah, hauled his suitcase onto the table in the mini-kitchen and started unzipping. Seeing the red lights, remembering what Baz had said about his light kit and why he traveled with it, Elijah felt like a bag of limp dicks. "Never mind. Keep them on."

"I have to do it eventually. Might as well get it over with now." He began flipping off lights, switching out bulbs, taping switches into the off position. "I'll keep my contacts in until right before we go to sleep because it's too much of a risk otherwise. But yes. I'd appreciate looking at you without my personal dimmer switch."

Elijah wrapped his arms around himself, trying to be angry as his control slipped away. "Did you do this at your mom's house too?"

"The bedroom has a few Baz-centric things worked in, since it's the one I use when I stay. But yeah, I taped things down and swapped bulbs, usually while you were sleeping. This is a little more intensive here, since I'm starting from scratch."

The more Elijah watched him work, the more he felt like a douche for his demand. "I'm sorry. I shouldn't have said anything."

In the middle of pinning a curtain, Baz glanced over his shoulder at him. His smile was weary, not dazzling. "It's okay."

Elijah could not stop his fucking mouth. "I'm sorry for being a diva. I'm just pissed. Scared. I don't know why."

"It caught up with you. I get it. It's no big deal."

It *was* a big deal, and Elijah couldn't shut up about it. "I flipped out over the stupid state line on the map. It wasn't about you, or the stupid dinner or your too-fancy house. It was dotted lines. I'm a fucking mess. You don't want to date this."

That was too much confession, and it combined with the memory threatened to bring it all up, until Baz put aside the clips and faced Elijah. No pity, no judgment, only calm as he leaned against the window.

"When I first came home from the hospital, I was still pretty banged up. My eyes were healing from the surgeries, and I wasn't used to the way my body was different. I felt like a helpless alien. One day I was in the kitchen with my mom. She was making me a smoothie in her Vitamix—a culinary-grade high-powered blender I swear could puree a tin can. She'd decided a blueberry smoothie was going to boost my immune system or some shit. So I sat there while she made it. Or rather, I sat there until she turned the fucking machine on."

His mouth thinned briefly into a line of self-depreciation. "I couldn't see well, only shapes and shadows, the dark glasses making things weirder, and she kept yammering on over the top of the noise about antioxidants. I snapped. Fucking screamed, swore, and shoved the blender off the counter. Blueberry everywhere. Six hundred dollar blender, dead. Knocked my glasses off, stepped into a sunbeam and gave myself one fuck of a migraine. Over a fucking blender. To this day I can't stand to be in the same room as those machines when they're running. Nobody beat me with a blender, but I can't handle them." His hand on Elijah's tightened. "I get it. You don't have to apologize. And you're not a mess. Or, I guess…we're the same kind of mess. And yes. I do want to date it."

Elijah closed his eyes. "What if it doesn't work out and we're stuck in the same house?"

Baz put the last clip in place on the curtains and moved into the bedroom, where he applied the same treatment to the curtains, lights, and switches. "If it doesn't work out, we're adults. We can be civil to one another. Except it's going to work out."

Elijah sat on the edge of the bed, watching Baz finish light-proofing the room. It didn't take long, and then he was done. After taping off the last switch, he stood in the red glow of the bedroom. He walked up to Elijah, loomed over him.

Took off his glasses and set them beside the bed.

They stared at one another, bathed in crimson, and though they were both still clothed and all that happened was Baz removed his glasses, Elijah couldn't help thinking they were both more naked than they'd ever been. He'd glimpsed Baz's eyes several times now, but never like this.

Unable to take it, Elijah averted his gaze and started to undress. He'd feel better once they were fucking, he thought, but as Baz pulled off his shirt, Elijah couldn't help giving himself a good look, because they'd never undressed in the light before, red or otherwise. And honestly every time they'd fucked Baz had remained at least partly clothed. This wasn't a frenzy, and Elijah had time to indulge.

The network of scars across Baz's skin shouldn't have surprised Elijah, but it did. Chest, back, and hip—most of them were old, though of course the ones on his shoulder were still raw and fresh. When Baz caught Elijah inspecting them, his lips flattened briefly. "Sorry. Little bit Frankenstein."

His gaze settled on the angry red pucker of skin where the bullet had gone in. "The new scar makes me upset, is all. It's my fault."

Baz sat on the bed beside him. "The fuck it is. That is entirely on your dad. You aren't responsible for anything he did. You said no. You walked away. They chased you."

"Yes, but I tricked them. I acted like I was converted for two years. I got a year of college out of them."

"You did what you had to do to survive. That's not your fault."

He shut his eyes. "I wanted retribution. I knew how much it would piss my dad off, which was why I did it. I wanted to poke the bear. When I did, he swiped at you."

"No. He swiped at you, and I got in the way. On purpose." Baz tipped Elijah's chin up with a finger.

"You want to blame yourself for his shit, you have to get through me. I'm the one who took the bullet."

Elijah let out a shaky breath. "Why did you do that?"

Baz didn't answer. He stroked Elijah's cheek and ran a hand along his shoulder, over Elijah's back, lingering on the waistband of his jeans. Nudged Elijah to his feet, helped him out of the last of his clothes, lured him gently into the bed, under the covers.

They didn't kiss, barely embraced, only lying beside each other on their individual pillows, neither able to bridge the space between them.

Elijah focused on Baz's body, visible from the waist up above the sheet. Except for the scars, his skin was smooth. Un-landscaped. He had tufts of hair on his chest. In the red light, the scars stood out. He was pale, skinny, too tall and defeated. He didn't look like the man who kept scrambling Elijah's circuits.

This wasn't the flirty man-whore who had pulled his hair in the back of the Tesla. This was somebody else. Not Baz. This was the guy on the pill bottle. Sebastian Percival Acker.

Elijah crawled closer. Moving in concert, Baz turned over so Elijah could put his head on Baz's chest. He teased the patch of hair between Baz's nipples. "I still don't think it's a good idea for us to date. Not for real."

"We can call it whatever you want. All I know is I don't want to stop being with you once we go back." Baz rested a hand on Elijah's hair and threaded his fingers hesitantly. "I get tired of being alone. I think you do too. We could be alone together, instead."

Yes, that was a pretty thing to say. It made Elijah's body hurt with want. He pushed the yearning away. "We're too messed up. You know how Sid and Nancy ended."

"I thought we were Howl and Sophie now."

Elijah broke. "Baz," he whispered, curling his fingers against Baz's chest.

The hand in his hair slid to his neck, massaging lightly. "I won't hurt you."

"Yes, you will."

"But I won't mean to." Baz brushed a kiss on Elijah's hair. "I don't care what you want to call it. I want to keep being with you. Sex. Talking. You yelling at me. Touching me."

Elijah wanted to tell him no. Because it would end badly. Sid and Nancy were real life. Howl and Sophie were fictional. But really, what would change? He already ached for Baz, had since forever. Now he could ache with memories of having had him.

He kissed Baz's chest. Opened his mouth over his skin, sucking gently. He shivered as he realized it was scar tissue under his lip, and he subtly shifted closer to Baz's neck.

Elijah tipped his head back and stroked Baz's face. "What color are your eyes? Everything is red in this light."

Baz's lips quirked. "Brown. I'll show you in the morning."

Elijah kissed him. A kiss on his chin, licking lightly at his stubble. Sucking in his bottom lip, opening for his tongue. Humming quietly and spreading his knees apart when Baz's fingers found his crack.

Gasping and tensing when, after Baz leaned over to fumble at the nightstand, those fingers became slick with lube.

Baz bit Elijah's bottom lip as he teased his hole, but when Elijah mewed and pushed against his finger, helping him inside, Baz opened his mouth over Elijah's and kissed him deeper. He pushed into Elijah's mouth as he worked into his ass. Gripping the bedspread, Elijah bore down, sliding into the rush of sex.

"You're so hot." Baz fucked his mouth and ass languidly, deliberately not enough in either place. "I could fuck you all damn day and still want you. And you haven't shown me the flip side."

Elijah shifted on the bed, straddling Baz so he could sit on those fingers. "Tomorrow. I'll show you tomorrow."

Baz bit out a groan as Elijah clenched his ass. "Fuck, baby."

Elijah arched his back, shivering as Baz nipped at his throat.

Baz pulled his fingers out of Elijah and tried to roll toward the nightstand, but Elijah stopped him. Trapping Baz with his knees, he sat up, aimed himself over his groin, grabbed his cock from behind and held it still as he came down on it.

The tip went inside. Baz's hand clamped on Elijah's arm, staying him.

Elijah tensed, keeping tight hold of Baz's cock. Baz's hand skittered to Elijah's wrist. He didn't let go, and he stared at Elijah.

Naked, naked, naked.

Elijah caught Baz's hand. "I always used condoms with tricks."

"I didn't."

"You have something you need to tell me? Something you know? Something you don't?"

Baz's eyes closed for a second, then opened, vulnerable and soft. "You telling me I'm not a trick?"

"You said you didn't want to be."

"And I want to know what I am."

Heart, breaking open. "Not a trick."

Baz let go. His gaze didn't leave Elijah's.

He pushed up.

Elijah had gone bare before. Kids at camp. The one guy after conversion therapy. But someone he knew online had contracted AIDS, with his boyfriend, because they rushed the window period. On the streets, the guy he used to crash with behind the trash bins ended up in the clinic for syphilis. Condoms started to sound like a good plan, though every trick balked. Which he'd always thought was dumb. He was the fucking hole trading around. But maybe they figured he was the bottom, so he didn't matter.

Tonight, he mattered. It still felt dangerous to trust this idea, but going bare helped for some reason. He knew there was a risk, that this was stupid, but fuck that anyway. This felt like power. Giving fate the finger. No halfway. Both of them naked in every sense. Together or not at all.

When Baz flipped him onto his back, tucked his

knees up and fucked in hard, Elijah let go. Put his arms above his head, shut his eyes, and let Baz ride him. Baz inside him. Baz fucking him slow and deep, hitting the spot that made his teeth buzz over and over.

He came before Baz—short, abrupt, spurting over his belly. Baz paused midstroke, but Elijah dug his fingernails into his arms, hissing slightly as he worked Baz's cock with his own ass. Elijah wrapped his arms around Baz's back. "Come inside me."

He did. He began slowly, still fussing about the way Elijah hissed and winced, until Elijah slapped his ass and met his thrusts with the intensity he wanted. Needed. Tears ran out of Elijah's eyes as he thrashed his head from side to side, electrified by the twinges of pleasure-pain, riding a mini sparkler as Baz tensed, bucked, and buried deep as he came.

They lay joined for a long time, Baz on top, draped on Elijah. At some point he pulled out, rolled over, and they half-dozed on top of the comforter until Baz got up and went into the bathroom for what seemed like a long time. When he came out, he had his glasses on once more, until he got into the bed, dragging Elijah under the covers with him. Once there, he put his glasses on the bedside table.

"No lights on but the red." He kissed Elijah's shoulder on his way to his pillow. "Contacts out. My eyes are bare now. Even a little regular light will hurt them."

Elijah snuggled against his chest. "No light."

They tangled as they slept, sometimes kissing sleepily, sometimes cuddling, sometimes simply touching. When Elijah woke, he felt heavy but sated, not weary.

Baz kneaded his hip, reaching around for his cock.

Elijah fucked gently into his hand, but his ass sent out warning signals. "I can't party in the back right now. Somebody loved my ass too much last night."

"Good." Baz stroked Elijah with intent. "Because my ass is all kinds of lonely."

Elijah shivered. For a moment, he closed his eyes and rode the sensation of Baz touching him. Then, tossing aside the covers, Elijah straddled Baz and pinned him to the bed.

A HUFF OF air left Baz's lungs, a sizzle of thrill running through him as Elijah trapped him between his knees and gazed at him. The dark intensity usually cutting him a withering glance now pierced Baz with lustful intent instead.

Let go, let Elijah take you on a ride.

He fully intended to. But first, unfortunately, there were ground rules.

Baz ran his hands up Elijah's arms. "Left hip is a bitch. If you want to push my knees up, which I would recommend, there's a fine line between *feels great* and *narcotics needed*. It's not the height of sexy, but a well-placed pillow is my friend."

The lustful gaze didn't vanish, but it sharpened with focus, Elijah taking notes. His fingers tickled Baz's forearms. "Noted. Any other hot tips?"

"Shoulder is okay, unless you try to do pushups on

it or something." He slow blinked, hating this next part. "Don't get focused on getting me off. It's possible we might get a free pass because this is super hot, but my cocktail of drugs hasn't worn off yet. If my joystick doesn't work, leave it. It's not you. It's drugs."

He watched Elijah's face, feeling hollow and queasy. He'd never told anybody he'd slept with about that before. Well, Marius, but telling him didn't count. That night had been them drunk and goofy, Marius giving in to curiosity, Baz excising an old crush. Baz still didn't know what this was with Elijah, but it wasn't either of those things.

Elijah let go of Baz's arm and teased the whorls of hair around his belly button. "Please tell me the guys who beat you up had their toenails pulled out. And shoved under their eyelids. With acid on them."

Vengeful Elijah, it turned out, was highly arousing. "Nobody got the death penalty, but anybody who had our DNA under their fingernails got multiple life sentences. Uncle Paul hired some lawyer friend who ate them for breakfast, lunch, and dinner. Possibly there's more I don't know about, honestly. A lot of shit happens in prison, and my uncle had an axe to grind. He was and still is wrecked over it."

Elijah frowned. "Why is he wrecked?"

"Because it wasn't a random attack. They were religious crazies, ginned up by their fuckjob church, out to take out the gay-loving senator's fag nephew. They were pissed because he was LGBT positive at a time when you didn't get away with it. The wingnuts wanted to make an example of him, through me.

Except the church swore on the witness stand they never told anybody to attack. Uncle Paul couldn't nail them for assault, but he found other, subtler ways of getting them. Couldn't bring back Jordan, though." Swallowing bile, he finished it. "I hadn't learned how to jump in front of bullets yet, and they didn't have any anyway. A bat swinging at you is fucking scary. You don't realize you've ducked until you've done it."

Elijah's face lost all its edges, tipping into horror and...ache. "Oh shit, *Baz.*"

Baz shut his eyes and swallowed several times. "Sorry. Talk about a mood killer."

Elijah rolled forward, flattening himself to Baz's chest. Trembling fingers tightened weakly in his hair and gripped his shoulder as Elijah buried his face in Baz's neck. He breathed out several times, shaky, his abdomen going concave against Baz's now-flaccid cock. He rested his forehead on Baz's collarbone, his lips brushing across Baz's skin, breath tickling the hair at his solar plexus as he spoke. "That's why. With my dad. Taking the bullet."

Baz didn't have it in him to work up a lie. "Yeah." He put his hand on the slope of Elijah's ass. "Sorry."

"Not sorry." Elijah lifted his head enough to kiss Baz's collarbone. "In the moment I felt the most scared and alone, helpless because there was no escape—there you were. Literally saving my life. Not because you wanted something from me or because we were friends. After years of being told I wasn't worthy to be saved by the people who were supposed to love everyone uncondi- tionally, the coolest guy on campus rescued me because it was the right thing to do."

Baz scrambled for a rebuttal, because holy fucking shit, he was no goddamned Christ figure—and then Elijah loomed over him, intensity fully online, inviting, almost demanding Baz go under. The fingers in Baz's hair tightened, pinning him to the pillow. "We're going to Saint Timothy today."

Baz tried to nod, but he couldn't. *Hello, erection.* "Okay."

"I'm moving into the White House."

Big erection. "Sounds great." He stared up into the lovely sight of Elijah with the reins firmly in his hand.

Elijah kissed him, slow and easy, sliding his hips so their cocks ground together. It didn't escape Baz's attention how Elijah kept his weight to the right. He eased in, fucking into Baz's mouth until Baz's jaw went slack, like he was waiting for a cock. Elijah's hands stroked, kneaded, wringing things out of him he didn't know he held back. When Elijah broke their kiss and trailed down Baz's chin and neck, Baz arched to give him better access.

He gasped, quavering when Elijah played with his nipples, one with fingers, one with his mouth, then switched. A current of electricity ran through him, endorphins flooding through his bloodstream, doing what no prescription or bag of party drugs could ever do. He realized he hadn't ever let go this far. He wanted to slide all the way under, to shut utterly off— and the realization he'd gone there without so much as a thought made him abruptly tense.

Elijah massaged his shoulders, murmuring and kissing him into compliance. "Shh. I've got you, baby. Let go."

Baz shuddered, shutting his eyes. For a moment there was darkness, fear at how vulnerable he'd become with Elijah, sludges of sorrow from the story he tried not to think about. Elijah kept whispering, promising, leading him by a velvet rope into the pink-edged place where letting go wasn't an act, it was a state of mind.

When Elijah's mouth closed over him, his eyes rolled into his head and his shoulders unhooked their metaphorical bungee cord and sank into the mattress. He got lost on the sensation of hot mouth on his cock, tongue laving his balls, teeth grazing his thigh. When hands pushed his knees up, he shut those muscles down. His heart caught when his left thigh met the resistance of a pillow, and he shattered when he realized his right one had one too.

He didn't have to hold his legs open—Elijah took care of that while he licked Baz's taint, easing the long-untried muscles of his ass open. Baz wasn't sure how Elijah managed to brace his legs *and* get a fingertip inside him—with lube—but he didn't question. If Elijah had somehow developed a third arm, Baz welcomed his alien lover with legs spread.

When Elijah breached him, Baz forced his eyes open because he wanted to see. There Elijah, towering over him, glowing red like a beautiful demon. He might be slight, but at that moment he filled more than Baz's ass. He was his world.

Elijah bent forward, still fucking, urging Baz up, doubling his pillow so he could fuck his tongue into

Baz's mouth as he rolled stroke by stroke into his ass. Baz opened for him everywhere, and when the pillows became a liability, he tugged them out and wrapped his legs around Elijah's back.

"I'm okay," he murmured when Elijah paused mid-thrust to check on him. *So much more than okay.*

Elijah kissed the corner of his mouth, a deliciously wild and possessive look on his face. "I'm close. You coming with me to my party?"

Baz shook his head and sucked on Elijah's bottom lip. "I'm good. You go on. I'll watch the show."

He did watch. As Elijah fucked harder, faster, riding the wave, Baz didn't come, but he surfed something great. A rush of warmth, possibility, and the glittering foam of contentment. As Elijah collapsed, shaking, against him, Baz wrapped his arms around his lover, shut his eyes and let the velvet rope Elijah had used to lead him here settle comfortably around his heart.

Chapter Eleven

WHILE BAZ SHOWERED and put his contacts back in, Elijah smoked on the suite's balcony, doing his best to convince himself he was Baz Acker's boyfriend.

The conversation from the night before felt surreal. Elijah wanted to convince himself it had been a show or an act, except there was no reason for that kind of a performance. Unless Baz simply wanted to be a manipulative asshole.

Probably, Elijah decided as they poked at their waffles from the complimentary breakfast, this was Baz's oppositional-defiant thing again. If Elijah suddenly embraced their relationship, Baz would back out of it. The easiest way to protect himself, following this logic, was to pretend to be excited about dating. To maybe suggest something slightly insane and watch Baz flip his shit. So as they resumed their travels homeward, he said, "Since we're dating now, maybe we should go all in and room together."

"Works for me."

Elijah shot him a glare across the Tesla. "For crying out loud. I was kidding. That was supposed to freak you out."

"Doesn't freak me out at all. It's more practical. You don't have much in the way of stuff, and I'll coerce you into my bed every night anyway. I was going to suggest it, but I figured you'd get mad."

"Nobody moves in together when they're first dating."

"Nobody starts dating for real after fake dating. Yet here we are."

"We're not actually going to date. You're going to change your mind. This is just some lark, and you'll get bored of me next week."

"We'll have to see next week, won't we?"

Elijah grumbled under his breath, which made Baz laugh, so Elijah smoked angrily until it was time to stop at the Supercharger. He was ready with his defiant retort for when Baz would suggest another sex break, but Baz didn't, which pissed Elijah off all over again.

"You make me insane," Elijah told him when they got in the car.

Baz blew him a kiss, which went straight to his dick.

When they got to Pastor and Liz's house, Elijah considered reneging and putting off moving into the White House mostly as a chess move, but he couldn't bring himself to do it. It was good to see Liz and Pastor, but…damn it, he'd feel weird leaving Baz after so many days in his constant company. Plus as soon as Baz announced the move was happening, Pastor and Liz got excited and helped him pack. Since Baz was right and all his belongings fit in the Tesla's hatchback, by the time Elijah had himself organized to maybe try objecting, he was already moved out.

He *wanted* to move out. To be able to shuffle in socks up to Mina's room. To roll his eyes at Aaron and Giles in person. To have a mob of people around all the time.

And yes, he wanted to be with Baz. He wasn't moving into Baz's room, though. That he was firm on.

Reception at the White House was warm, especially when they saw Elijah was finally moving in. "You should have texted us," Giles scolded him. "We have to clear out the room you and Brian will be in because all Sid's things are in there from the remodel. We would have had it all ready."

"It won't take us long to move the stuff if we work together." Aaron leaned around Giles to address Baz. "Can we put it in the ballroom, or should we crowd it in the practice room with Fred?"

Baz, leaning against the counter, shrugged. "There's no rush to move it. Elijah's moving into my room."

Everyone in the kitchen turned to Elijah.

Elijah blushed at the ceiling. *Never try to bluff Baz.* "No, I'm not."

Baz grabbed Elijah's hand and tugged him toward the living room stairs.

Elijah would have fought him, but if he escaped, he'd have to deal with the *oh no you didn't* on his friends' faces. So he let Baz drag him past Aaron and Giles's room and the one he'd been meant to share with Brian, down the long hall to the big bedroom with its own bathroom. Baz's room.

He gave it a quick scan, noting how very Baz the

place was, overflowing with odd knickknacks and unique design—brick-red walls, goldenrod trim. Here were all the things he'd expected to find in Baz's nonexistent bedroom in Chicago. Pictures, photos, mirrors—everything on the walls and surfaces glittered, odd tchotchkes only a trust-fund baby could collect.

Unlike his mother's house, there was no overarching theme of *money*, more *this delighted me and I took it home*. There were bits of funky china, a brass penis statue, several framed photos of Baz, Marius, and Damien in goofy poses, one of the three of them in drag. A black feather boa draped across a shelf full of figurines. Elijah didn't recognize most of them, but he did spy a Pazu catching Sheeta figure from *Castle in the Sky* and an absolutely stunning sculpture of Howl in half-bird form gently touching the chin of a gray-haired Sophie. There was some Japanese hot guy in a tuxedo with tails biting on the edge of his glove and basically inviting the people watching him to undress and start masturbating, but Elijah didn't know who the figure was meant to be.

The shelves were almost all figures and carefully arranged mementoes, but *stuff* was everywhere: electronics, hats, Mardi Gras masks, several tiaras. The walls were filled with framed posters for anime movies and shows, foreign art films, choir tours.

There was a fire escape visible through the window too—Elijah knew it was functional because he'd stared at it while he chain-smoked out back. It was one of those where the stairs descended as you walked down them, with a small drop ladder at the end. He considered, quite seriously, making a run to it.

Before he could, Baz closed the door and pressed Elijah against it. He tipped his glasses to the top of his head, letting Elijah see how annoyed he was.

"Don't hurt your eyes," Elijah said, wishing for the shield back.

"I'll worry about my eyes. *You* tell me why you won't move in with me."

Elijah tried to get mad, but it was difficult with Baz glaring at him. "I already told you. It's dumb. Nobody moves in together this fast."

"We're not most people."

What lovely bullshit. "What happens if I want a break from you?"

It was a legitimate question. A rational question. The hurt in Baz's gaze, however, still made Elijah feel guilty. "It's a big house."

Elijah refused to cower. It was hard, because Baz's eyes were pretty. Lots of streaks in the iris. "What if I want a break to sleep by myself?"

"You tell me, and I sleep on the couch."

Like Baz would ever meekly leave without wheedling first. "You can't be the one to leave. You have the light thing."

"I'll rig up the living room. Or camp out in the practice room. Just stay here. Please."

"*Why*, Baz? I moved into the house. I'll be down the hall."

"I want you *here*."

With all your other things. Elijah opened his mouth to point out he was human, not *objet d'art*, but then

Baz touched his chin with his index finger, and everything went still.

There was no way Baz was consciously mimicking the pose of the *Howl's Moving Castle* figurine, yet this was exactly what he was doing. Elijah's imagination completed the shadows into dark wings, but otherwise it was the same: shorter, hesitant Elijah standing before the taller, hunched, aching Baz, tentatively trying to capture his attention.

On a shelf the pose was charming, but to live it out, Elijah discovered, was more than simply intense. It was a lens. A moment of clarity—or, perhaps, a delusion of clarity. With the single finger holding him more firmly than any direct grip, Elijah was convinced Baz did not mean him to be a thing. The Tesla might move, but this was Baz's castle. This room was his home, his safe space.

It didn't matter that everyone had told him Baz wasn't serious. That was a smokescreen. He didn't want to take risks, but he was now. He wanted Elijah. Not as a trophy. As company.

Please be in my home with me.

Elijah shut his eyes. "Tell me again this isn't you bored. Because it will *hurt me* if you're only fucking around."

"I've told you several times now. I've *shown* you."

He had. Elijah couldn't argue with this, but he couldn't open his eyes, either. "I don't owe you this. And agreeing isn't some contract. I get to leave if I'm not happy. Even if that makes you *un*happy."

"No, you don't owe me anything. I owe *you* for

Chicago." His nose nuzzled Elijah's timidly. "Please don't demand your own room. I'll do everything I can to keep you happy."

With a sigh, Elijah nodded. "Okay."

The finger at his chin trailed along his jaw as Baz's hips closed in on Elijah's and his mouth moved down Elijah's cheek. "Thank you."

Elijah pushed his hands up Baz's chest to loop them behind his neck as he settled in for a kiss. What began as a sensual sealing of an understanding soon became making out. Elijah let go of the last of his resistance, yielding to Baz's groping hands. He wanted to hook his leg over Baz's hip, but he could obviously only do the one, and he worried if even that would be too much. So when Baz peeled him off the door, Elijah did the pivot toward the bed for them.

When Baz caught the knob on the way and cracked the door open, however, Elijah balked. "What are you—?"

Baz swallowed the objection and pushed Elijah the rest of the way to the bed. Leaving the door ajar.

Elijah fought to object, but Baz pinned him to the mattress, stole his breath, torturing him so when he was able to make sounds, they were only groans and gasps. Through it all, Elijah stole glances at the door, certain Aaron or Giles would be standing there, mouth hanging open. His brain wouldn't let him imagine Mina.

Baz chuckled. "You can pretend all day long you don't like knowing they can hear. I was with you on the patio and balcony when you got off on being done in the open."

Baz teased first one nipple, then the other, until Elijah arched and thrashed against the bed. "But not...*these* people."

"Yes, these people. That's the biggest thrill of all."

As Elijah protested weakly, Baz made exaggerated *mwahahaha* sounds along Elijah's sternum. He climbed off Elijah's legs to get to his cock, and Elijah opened his knees, not wanting to get in anybody's way. He couldn't stop watching the door, though, so he missed everything Baz was doing—until a cold, slick finger pushed into him at the same time a hot mouth engulfed his cock.

He cried out—way too loud, and as the finger turned, pushing deeper to find X marks the spot, Elijah's cry became a dirty moan.

Downstairs, everything went quiet.

"Oh God, they heard," Elijah whispered. In Baz's mouth, his cock got a little harder.

Baz hummed around it before pulling off, staring up at Elijah with a wicked grin. "Absolutely they did. Let them hear some more."

Elijah tried to resist him, but Baz had become adept at wringing noises out of Elijah, and it didn't take much. The sensation was plenty, but the *fucking open door*. That got him in the gut.

What were they saying? What did they think? Elijah moaned on the downstroke, high on the dark thrill of being bad.

Baz blew his brains out, finger fucked him until he burned, turned him over to fuck him. Elijah lifted his hips for the pillow, spread his knees and got hot all over in the hope-terror someone might finally come upstairs to see what was going on. He gave Baz everything he asked for, his body, his obedience, and his porn-dubbed cries and grunts.

But, he reminded himself, this was simply Baz showing off. Marking territory. It didn't mean they were going to have Walter and Kelly's Disney wedding or compose songs together like Giles and Aaron. It meant Baz had successfully identified and executed Elijah's exhibitionist kink and was attached to the idea of having him around for a while. And for now, Elijah was attached to that idea too.

He cried out as he came on the sheets and Baz came inside his ass. He collapsed on the mattress and went obediently into the baby spoon after Baz shut the door, took off his glasses and climbed behind Elijah.

When they finally went downstairs half an hour later, they wore different clothes, their hair was disheveled, and Elijah's neck was full of hickeys. Mina had gone to her room, and Aaron and Giles sat together on the sofa, appearing somewhat ruffled. In fact, Aaron's shirt was on inside out. Aaron bit the corner of his lip, an abashed *I know you know I know* sort of look in his eye. No doubt at some point it was hard to tell who was hollering, Elijah or Aaron.

Elijah felt vaguely anxious and unsettled despite the proof that as long as he was with Baz, he'd clearly be getting the best sex of his life. He ended up writing for three hours solid that evening, zoning out into a personal time warp on the floor in the corner of the ballroom, until Mina put a plate of spaghetti next to him. He blinked at it, as if he'd forgotten what food was, but his stomach remembered well enough.

He glanced up at her, wanting to say thanks, but he felt woozy, his head still half in his manuscript. She was probably going to yell.

She didn't, though. Crouching beside him, she kissed his cheek and glanced at his screen with a smile. "Oh, the fantasy one. Interesting."

Usually Elijah hissed at anyone who tried to read his work in progress. It still made him lurch inside when Mina saw, but she truly was an exception. "I wrote a short too. The start of one, anyway. Crazy kinky."

She smoothed hair away from his face, her expression thoughtful. "I have to say, I was dubious about the two of you, but if it's getting you writing again, I'm fully on board."

Elijah wanted to deny the Lifetime original movie *Adventures With Baz* was the reason he'd uncorked, but he was pretty sure she was right. "He'll get bored of it any second."

"Maybe he'll get bored. Maybe not." She nodded at the screen as she rose. "Until you find out, ride the wave. Get some story out of the stress, and enjoy the sex. Just be safe, okay? Baz has been around the block."

Elijah focused on stuffing spaghetti in his mouth, hoping marinara would hide his guilty expression.

Chapter Twelve

IF BAZ HAD known Marius was going to stare at him all through lunch like he'd grown an extra head, he'd have stayed at the White House.

Three days after returning to Saint Timothy after his weekend with Elijah, he'd taken Uber to the U of M campus. Baz read up on first-year medical school on the way in—MS-1, he now knew, was the lingo—and he was ready to commiserate about gross anatomy, pathology, and biochem. That's not what happened, though. Marius demanded all the details about Chicago, so Baz told him, and now Marius looked as if Baz had announced his return from Mars.

Probably this was because he'd casually slipped in there that he and Elijah were dating. And rooming together.

"You're dating. Actually dating."

Baz poked a fry into ketchup and glared at Marius. "Is it so impossible to believe I might be in a relationship?"

"Yes."

Baz tossed down the fry. "Fine. I'll admit it's not my usual."

"I'm not saying it's bad. I'm saying I'm surprised."

Marius slouched in his booth seat, still studying Baz as if he were part of an experiment. "I guess I shouldn't be. You don't do anything halfway. Why court him cautiously, when you could move in together?"

"Did you fake your freakout so you could interrogate me?"

"No." Marius's stunned amusement evaporated. "Oh my God, Baz. It's going to be insane. So crazy bad. The schedule is unreal, and the *workload*." He ran a shaking hand through his hair. "I have no idea how I'm going to do it all. I mean, I will never do laundry again. Or cook a meal. Which means my budget is all off. And my idea I could pick up some weekend job is out."

Fucking money. Baz wished he could give Marius a grand or two, but he'd never take it. "What about your roommates? Can you work out some kind of communal thing for laundry and so on?"

"That's funny. Really fucking funny. They're so loud and insane. I'm going to have to study at the library. So I'm going to pay through the nose to only sleep there, and with earplugs."

Now *Baz* was stressed. "Come back to the White House."

"I can't do a half-hour commute. In addition to gas and paying to park, I'd lose all that time. If I could use it to study, it'd be fine."

"You need a med-student roommate. Or someone else who has as intense a schedule as you. Or people who aren't assholes."

Marius sloshed his beer in circles before downing

the dregs and pouring himself a new glass. "Trust me, I'm looking. I don't know that I'll find anything, though. And if I do, I've still got to break my lease."

The problem plagued Baz through the rest of their meal, and once they'd said their goodbyes, he wandered campus a bit instead of calling Uber for a ride home. There had to be another way for Marius. In fact, he felt like he almost had it, and if he limped one more time around the block, he'd find it.

It took two blocks, and he'd blown out his hip, but he'd figured it out. After snagging a Starbucks, he settled into its sidewalk seating and pulled up his contacts on his phone. Walter Davidson answered on the second ring.

"Hey, Sebastian. I mean—Baz."

"This a good time?"

"Perfect. I'm walking out of the library, trying to figure out how to kill the hours until Kelly's done with his summer class. What's up?"

Baz glanced around, searching for something to ID where he was. "Well, I'm at the Starbucks in the Radisson on campus. You want some coffee?"

"Absolutely. I'll pop over on the train. Give me ten minutes, and your next latte's on me."

Baz took some ibuprofen and an oxycodone while he waited. By the time Walter hopped off the commuter rail in front of the cafe, Baz was still feeling pain, but he didn't care so much.

He rose as Walter came up to him, and they did the gay-boy kissy thing before getting in line. Once they had their drinks, Walter adding a sandwich, they settled into a table. While Walter ate, Baz calculated his best point of entry.

"So you guys still live near campus, right? Aaron says you moved in June."

Walter nodded as he wiped his mouth and finished chewing. "Yeah. We moved to this two-bedroom in Seward. It's nothing great, but it's close to campus, the train, and it comes with a washer and dryer. There's a Pizza Lucé two blocks away, so I'm going to be fat as fuck, but I'll die happy."

Two bedroom. Baz did a mental fist pump. "Seward's pretty expensive, right? That's the big liberal district, and close to campus, everything must be at a premium."

Walter grimaced. "No shit. I had us upgrade, so we have a study in mild grime for the pleasure of fifteen hundred dollars instead of a nightmare of rat semen for an even grand. It means Kelly has to find a second job and I have to beg my old man for an allowance increase, but you do what you have to, I guess."

Baz didn't have to lift a finger. This was setting itself up. "Would you guys be open to a roommate?"

"Theoretically, yes, that was the plan in taking the two-bedroom, but we got cold feet. Who wants to room with a newlywed gay couple?"

"What if it was someone who came pre-vetted? Someone I could promise is so LGBT friendly he chews me out over my PC faux pas? He would basically be there to pay rent, sleep, be friendly over coffee on his way out the door, and occasionally forget his laundry in the washer."

Walter put down his sandwich. "Where is this unicorn?"

Smiling, Baz sipped his latte, nibbled on his cookie, and fixed everybody's problems.

By the time Kelly texted Walter to find out where he was, Marius was on his way over, and soon Kelly was too. Another round of lattes had the three potential roommates forming a more perfect union, and as they arranged a meeting at the apartment, Baz acknowledged his work here was done. Because he could get Stephan to discover a sub-leaser without Marius knowing it had happened.

As he pulled up the Uber app, though, he felt an unexpected pang of...something, and he closed it again. He opened the text client instead.

You busy, babe?

He didn't realize how tense he'd become waiting for a reply from Elijah until it arrived. *I was writing, but mostly in circles at this point. What's up?*

Through his glasses, Baz glanced up at Kelly's and Walter's smiling faces. Kelly had moved his chair so close to his husband he was practically in his lap. It made Baz ache.

I'm on the U of M campus, saving the world. NBD. He hesitated before plowing ahead. *I was gonna ask if you could give me a lift, but I don't want to bug you if you're working.*

A total lie. He really wanted a ride. The thought of sitting in the back seat of a stranger's car for a half hour hollowed him out.

If there's dinner in it for me, I could be persuaded.

Baz had to bite the corner of his lip as joy expanded inside him. "Hey, Lucas. I mean—Davidson. What was the pizza place you said was making you fat?"

"Pizza Lucé on Franklin."

"Thanks. Elijah's bringing the Tesla in so I don't have to Uber."

Kelly beamed. "Sounds wonderful. We could all go, unless you'd rather be alone."

"Company's good." He ignored the subtle smile from Marius and replied to Elijah. *I have good pizza on standby.*

Excellent. Where am I meeting you, exactly?

"Is it okay if I tag along to your apartment while I wait for my ride?"

Walter glanced at his husband before nodding. "Of course. We can all go together right now, if that works for you, Marius."

As they rose from their chairs, Baz texted Elijah Walter and Kelly's address, and the emptiness faded to a dull roar, a hollow filled with the shape of a saucy, dark-haired boyfriend.

IT WEIRDED ELIJAH out to drive the Tesla on his own. What if he wrecked it? Baz's reply was always "Insurance much?" Except Elijah didn't believe for a second the loss of the car would be anything but huge for Baz.

So Elijah drove into the Cities like a grandpa, keeping just under the speed limit, obsessively checking his blind spot before lane changes. He followed the Tesla's navigation instructions as if they led to Heaven. He switched from Hi Fashion to RuPaul because he needed the confidence boost and "Champion" gave him focus. Before long, he pulled into the parking lot of a rather sad-looking apartment complex, at which point he had to call Baz.

"I can't figure out where to park. Everything has a number on it."

"Hold on." Baz's voice went muffled for a second. "Coming outside with Walter. He says it has to be on the street, but it's tricky."

Walter and Baz appeared shortly thereafter, and Elijah immediately got out of the car. "You drive," he said to Walter. "I don't want to think about parking this somewhere *tricky*."

Walter's gaze was carnal as he accepted the fob and rounded the hood, bending to run his fingers over the fender. "Fuck, this is a sweet set of wheels."

Baz brushed a kiss on Elijah's ear, a slightly awkward gesture. "I'm going with him. You want to come along, or go inside?"

Elijah felt dumb getting in only to park a car, but he didn't want to go inside, either. "I'll wait here and have a cigarette."

He lit up as they drove off, watching Walter discover the head-fuckery of regenerative braking. He switched to taking in the neighborhood once they disappeared around the corner. It wasn't a bad area, but it wasn't textbook-pretty, either. A fence bordered the edge of the parking lot, and beyond lay the tracks for the public transit system. Farther still was the highway which had brought Elijah here from Saint Timothy.

Another apartment building lay to the west, and more parking and a tall office/apartment complex on the other side.

There was a realness here unable to permeate in Timothy. A homeless man shuffled with a shopping cart at the far edge of the lot. The cars in front of Elijah had more of a mixed metaphor—plenty of beaters in college parking, but some of the ones here had car seats. The city of Minneapolis swelled around him, noisy and smelly and unforgiving. It made Elijah remember the days when *he* was the homeless man. Except he'd been a kid, wide-eyed and terrified and reeling from the revelation that the world was a seriously awful place to exist.

He couldn't articulate it in his sessions with Pastor, but as he lit up a second cigarette in Walter and Kelly's parking lot, Elijah acknowledged it was the homeless memory more than his parents or even the shooting bringing on his panic attacks. Being so alone and helpless, realizing in a way no sixteen-year-old should there would never be anyone there to help him but himself.

Which didn't explain why he was here, now, waiting for Baz and Mr. Fabulous.

Baz and Walter appeared in the distance, around the same bend where the Tesla had vanished. They both had their hands in their pockets, walking close together but not touching. Elijah got the idea they were having a fairly serious conversation. But when they got close to Elijah, Baz smiled and reached up to tip his glasses down so he could wink.

The gesture scrambled Elijah's circuits, but when Baz took his arm, Elijah punched him lightly in the chest. "You shouldn't expose your eyes."

"It only hurts for a second, unless I'm already having a migraine. Besides, you were so sour. I had to lighten you up."

Walter had gone ahead, but Elijah still kept his voice low. "This is weird, being here. They're the perfect people, and I'm the rat at the picnic."

"You're not a rat. You're perfect." Baz pulled him close, copping a generous feel of Elijah's ass. "I'm trying to set up Marius with Walter and Kelly. His roommate situation sucks, and they need someone to share rent. It could be a perfect arrangement."

The apartment was small but cute. It had about zero character, compared to the old-world charm of the White House, but Walter and Kelly had filled it with their things, giving it a touch of home. A Disney-esque but decidedly hot framed print of a cartoon naked man seated on a rail beside cute little animals hung over a slightly worn armchair. A couch full of pillows and afghans opposed a flat-screen television, and a desk sat beneath a window overlooking the parking lot. The kitchen had canisters on the counter, dishes in the sink, and two backpacks spilled open on the small IKEA kitchen table.

With everyone else occupied with chatting, Elijah snuck into the hallway and gave himself the rest of the tour. The bathroom was pretty standard, though he liked the deep blue shower curtain and matching accessories. The first bedroom had to be the spare, mostly holding half-empty moving boxes and a rather sad futon, but the other one was obviously Walter and Kelly's. Two dressers overflowed with personal items, and a laundry basket of unfolded clothes sat on a neat bed with a thick, inviting comforter. The walls were decorated with David Kawena Disney heroes and Tom of Finland prints—over the bed was a framed Flynn Rider, looking pretty goddamned fine.

Done with his tour, Elijah felt awkward and unsure of himself and so wandered to the kitchen and watched the others interact. Kelly Davidson paused his earnest hallway conversation with Marius to accept a drive-by embrace and kiss on the cheek from Walter, who scooted behind him to open a folding door and change a load of laundry. Marius asked about utilities, and Kelly explained the rates.

Elijah, who had somehow ended up with Baz's arm around him, turned to look up. "I don't know who to pay rent to and when for the White House. What about the utilities? Who do I talk to?"

"There's a lockbox in the kitchen. They post the breakdowns to whatever email of yours they have on file because it's prorated depending on what room you have."

"Well, I didn't give anybody my email, and I'm not in the room I was supposed to be in."

Baz stroked his hair in a *calm down* gesture. "It's not a big deal. We'll sort it out."

"I don't want to be kicked out."

"You won't be kicked out."

Before Elijah could press on this point, Walter reappeared, arm around Kelly, Marius in their wake. "We've got a new roommate. I owe you big time, Acker. Can I repay you with dinner?"

"As long as it's this pizza place you were telling me about."

They walked around the corner to Pizza Lucé together. The hostess who seated them knew Walter and Kelly by name and seated them at a table near the window, and they chatted while they waited for their order. Walter told stories about law school, Kelly the hell of retail management. Marius was apparently about to start medical school and was clearly terrified at the prospect. Elijah could see, though, how the three of them would be a good unit.

It was nice to see Baz's best friend doing well, and the pizza was pretty fantastic. Kelly had some kind of homemade vegan cheese on his, which looked weird to Elijah but Kelly practically had an orgasm over it. They turned gigantic cans of crushed tomatoes and rings of peppers into pizza stands, which was quirky and fun.

As they wound up and Marius said he needed to get back to his place, it struck Elijah who the odd man out in the scenario was, and for once it wasn't him. It was Baz.

Baz was Walter's age. The two had been a grade apart at their shared private high school, and they'd both had interrupted school experiences. But Walter was in law school, whereas Baz was a sixth-year undergrad. Marius was twenty-two, and Kelly was Elijah's age, though Kelly was about to enter his senior year because he hadn't had to go to reparative therapy. The thing was, even Elijah seemed to be part of a wave of forward momentum.

Baz? Sitting there with the rest of them, it was clear he was on some kind of indefinite pause. The revelation wouldn't lie down once discovered, and after they dropped off Marius and started for Saint Timothy, Elijah decided to call him on it.

"Are you going to graduate this year?"

Baz shrugged and kept his gaze on the road. "Probably, I guess."

"Do you have a major?"

"I've had seven or eight. Could finish about anything in a semester or so. Was thinking about religion."

Elijah's laugh was quiet, a bit bitter. "Figures. I'm about to drop it. Not like we'd have the same classes or anything."

Silence expanded around them, except for RuPaul telling them they better work, because Baz hadn't changed the radio. Elijah kept thinking about Walter and Kelly's apartment. Everything just so. Two lives unfolding quietly, together. So normal and boring it made him ache with want.

It wasn't normal, or boring, to be driving his sort-of boyfriend's expensive futuristic sports car down a Minnesota highway, listening to a drag queen sing old songs, thinking about when he'd have to get up to go to work at food service in the morning, planning to have leftover pizza for breakfast. It felt good, though.

Maybe it was a little bit cute to reach over and tentatively take Baz's hand, to hold it while he drove. But Baz let him anyway.

Chapter Thirteen

THIS WASN'T THE first summer Baz had nothing to do while other people whizzed around him in a flurry, but it was the first time he felt a completely utterly useless tit about it, and July in particular crawled by. His mom called a few times to check in on him, but the last time he'd called her, some new woman named Giselle answered. "Ms. Barnett Acker is unavailable right now. How can I help you?"

"This is her son. Sebastian. Can you have her call me when she gets a chance?"

"She's in meetings all day, but I'll certainly pass the message along."

Either Giselle had lied, or his mom was really fucking busy, because two days later, Baz still hadn't had so much as a text.

His mom had fluttered off in a whirlwind before, but never when Baz was already at loose ends. Marius and Damien texted him plenty, but they were swamped with their post-graduate lives. Aaron and Giles were usually at the music building, and so was Mina. Baz was okay when Elijah didn't have work study, because they'd watch TV or fuck or fight about something ridiculous, and sometimes he could talk Elijah into a ride in the Tesla. Elijah also doused the house in RuPaul, to the point the music infected Aaron and Giles. Often they spontaneously burst out, "Now *sissy* that walk!" and sashayed their way across the kitchen. Life wasn't boring, not by a long shot. But it didn't stop Baz from feeling restless.

Normally when he felt this way he got high and got laid, but it was weird to get high in the house alone, and the thought of Elijah finding out he'd engaged in a nameless hookup made him distinctively queasy. Though he'd promised exclusivity, Elijah seemed to expect Baz to cheat on him. Frankly he acted as if Baz would kick him out of the house full stop at any given second. It wasn't uncommon for Baz to come into their bedroom to find Elijah sitting on the bed looking guilty for having used the shower. Though Baz had cleared drawer and closet space for him, Elijah lived out of his borrowed suitcase from Liz until Baz unpacked his roommate himself. He half-worried Elijah would object, but he'd said nothing, only started putting his clothes away there after being laundered. Laundry Baz usually did, for lack of anything else to do.

Elijah frequently went to his job at food service. It was grim work, and Baz itched to rescue him from the banality of it, but it seemed to weirdly center Elijah. The idea of manual labor as a sustaining mental force wasn't entirely foreign to Baz, but he'd assumed it was one of those pieces of bullshit people who never had to work those jobs liked to spout. Elijah's reaction gave him serious pause. By mid-July, he'd decided maybe Elijah was on to something. Stocking up on pain pills, he walked over to Liz and Pastor's house and asked Pastor to help him find a job.

"You want a job? Interesting." Pastor settled into his chair on the back porch, where Liz had served them iced tea and was promising to supplement with a tray of cookies. "Have you ever actually worked before, out of curiosity?"

No, Baz hadn't. He squirmed. "I was thinking more volunteer. I don't know if my mother would approve of the optics of me collecting a wage. But surely somebody could use a pair of hands, even ones as worthless as mine."

"Your hands aren't worthless." This came from Liz as she set down a plate brimming with sugary goodness. "I'll take your help anytime you want to give it."

Baz eyed her as he selected a sugar cookie still warm from the oven. "What would you have me do?"

"Any number of things. Baking. Spreadsheets. Packaging and labeling the product. Helping me deliver it. On days you didn't feel one hundred percent, you could sit with people at the senior center. Most of them simply want someone to talk to."

It wasn't exactly what Baz had in mind, but if pressed, he couldn't exactly name what he *had* expected. "How often would you want me?"

"As often as you had time."

Baz had time every single day, but he figured he should start small in case this blew up in his face.

The next morning at nine, he got a ride to Liz and Pastor's place from Aaron before he went in for his shift with the strings camp.

"Why didn't you ask Elijah for a ride?" Aaron asked as they covered the short distance to Pastor's subdivision.

Baz shrugged. "Didn't want to bother him."

It was a weak excuse, but Aaron let it slide. "You two seem to be doing okay."

It was heartening to hear they looked okay from the outside. Baz didn't care to expand on that point, though, so he turned the mirror back. "You and Mulder seem fine too."

"Yeah." Aaron smiled and shifted his grip on the wheel. "We have a good time working together. He likes working with the high school kids more than me, but I get to direct some, so it's okay. They all seem so young. Hard to believe some of them could be in choir with us in a few years."

Aaron continued to babble about the camp until they arrived at Pastor's place, at which point Baz was eager to escape.

Liz welcomed him with a hug and ushered him inside. She brushed off his uncertainty, hanging an apron around his neck and putting him in charge of a mixer once he'd washed his hands. "You'll be my sous chef for the morning," she told him as she pulled ingredients out of the cupboard. "But tell me if you need a break, dear, because there's no time clock on our operation. You're going to put me ahead of my production schedule simply by showing up, and you know I never say no to a cup of coffee."

Normally Baz would bristle at his disabilities being discussed so cavalierly, but they were a fact of life, and it was ridiculous to play affronted when Liz had helped autograph his school modifications when in his freshman year he couldn't keep up with the rest of his class. She'd dusted the fuss off his shoulders too, when being so different upset him.

Today was a good day, so he was able to work for almost an hour before his hip made it clear he'd be sitting soon or having oxycodone for lunch. Liz poured him a cup of coffee and sat with him, gazing at the counter full of baked and ready-to-bake trays with satisfaction. "Usually I'm not this far by this time of the day, and my back is killing me. Anytime you want to help, please don't stop yourself."

Baz blushed around his coffee cup rim. "It feels good to do something. Drives me crazy doing nothing."

"Yes, I agree. Which is how I ended up doing this. Everyone thinks they want to sit around and watch television, until they do it. Humans need occupations. I admit, I enjoy volunteering far more than I did working. I think there's something about choosing to give your time. Knowing you're doing it because you want to, because good things need doing—that's better than a paycheck."

"Before the accident, I assumed I'd go to Yale like Dad. I worried what would happen being an out gay executive, but that was kind of the fun part, thinking how I'd knock down walls." Baz had replaced his mug on the table, and he ran his index finger thoughtfully around the rim. "Yale never crossed my mind when I was finally looking for colleges, and any place at the family firm would be figurehead only. I wasn't even sure I wanted to go to school, but everyone seemed convinced I should go *somewhere*. Then Nussy came and did the workshop with our choir, and I thought, I'm following that guy. Such intense energy, such power, so much good feeling. And yes, it's been wonderful. Except…it's as if I stayed at the bar past last call. There's nobody pushing me to do something. Or rather, they're pushing me do to *something*. But I don't know what my something should be."

Liz plucked the carafe off the trivet between them and refreshed their cups. "In my day, school didn't happen for everyone. I had to fight to go, especially once I met Robert. I remember my mother telling me it was a sinful waste of money to keep on going to school when everyone knew I was going to end up a pastor's wife." She *hmphfed* as she replaced the carafe. "Woman went to her grave scandalized because I got my doctorate and worked outside the home. I'd come home with commendations from the governor for my work with public service agencies, but all she could talk about was how terrible it must be for Robert to have to eat so much takeout. It hurt so much to hear her dismiss me. But you know, sometimes I'm glad. Not that I wouldn't have preferred a loving mother. But sometimes her antagonism, her doubt, fueled me to prove her wrong."

"That's just it. Nobody has any expectations of me." He gripped the handle of his mug for courage to get the rest of the thought out. "It's as if I died with Jordan, except he went to sleep, but I keep shambling on. I don't know what I'm supposed to do with this life he died for."

Her wrinkled hand covered his on the table. "Honey, he didn't die for you. He was killed."

Baz swallowed a hard lump. "It's easier to think the other way, so it means something."

"I disagree, if the burden of survival has you so tied up in knots." She turned his palm over so she could knit their fingers together. "Life is often terribly grim. Plenty of people are monsters, and most of them justify those monstrosities away. But seeing that doesn't have to change how you chart your path. It wasn't wrong of you to assume you'd have a good, privileged life. It doesn't mean you have to do something differently now. Surviving when Jordan didn't doesn't mean you must be a martyr to make his loss worthwhile. You can't put such a burden on yourself. You're still Sebastian Acker. Maybe your limitations and definitions of success have shifted. But you don't owe anyone. Only yourself."

"I want to owe *someone*, though." Baz paused, not sure how to articulate the emotions swirling inside him. Liz's absolution felt good, but impatience rushed in its wake. "I don't want a corner office buying and selling companies or playing pawn in a political chess set. I want…" His brain raced, tripping over itself as he glimpsed the edges of something he'd searched six years to find. "I want…to help." God, did that sound lame. He shut his eyes, tried to focus.

He saw a parking lot frozen with snow, Elijah facing a man with a gun. Felt the world rushing in his ears as he leapt forward. Heard the gunshot, felt it pierce him. Felt the pain of it, the warmth of Elijah's body against his as they rolled. The sense of victory, of saving someone from a horrible fate. Eating the pain for himself, grinning madly at the paramedics as they assured him he'd be okay. Of course he'd be okay. This was fucking nothing. He'd taken a bat to the head without asking for it. Getting shot on purpose had been easy. He could suck up bullets all damn day.

He opened his eyes, meeting Liz's gaze with fire in his belly. "I want to help. I want to help people in pain. I want to take pain away. I know I can't, not really. But I want to. Because surviving has to be worth something."

Liz leaned closer to touch his face. She regarded him with eyes both younger and older than her age, her gaze arresting him. "Surviving is worth whatever you wish it to be. It's not a burden to navigate. It's a laurel to wear. You've seen the darkness, and you survived it. You overcame it."

"But I don't know what to *do* with it," Baz whispered.

"Whatever you want. That's what you do."

"What if I don't know what I want?"

"Start with what feels good. What seems right. What fits the bill today?"

Baz glanced around the kitchen helplessly. His gaze rested on the stacks of mini banana bread loaves. "Baking with you. Being productive instead of sitting around."

"Excellent." Liz pushed to her feet and took his hand to lift him up too. "Let's stop sitting around."

A FEW WEEKS into rooming with Baz, or shacking up with him or whatever the hell they were doing, Elijah reluctantly conceded he probably should stop assuming he'd be chucked on the street any second. Some of this came from his own acknowledgment of logic and facts, but it didn't settle in until one of his weekly sessions with Pastor.

In the past they'd always sat together in the living room or his home study, but now that Elijah had moved out, he went to Pastor's office, which was in a kind of octagon turret at the top of a set of nearly circular stairs in the campus chapel. Every wall space was shelving, and each shelf overflowed with books and papers. High windows let in soft light, filtering it in streams across Pastor's desk and the wingback armchair strategically placed to the side of it.

Elijah sat in the chair, hunkered against the padded flare of one of the wings, sweating through the Herculean task of admitting what he was afraid of so Pastor could help him exorcise false demons. Which today was addressing his fear of losing his new housing.

"I don't actually think I would get kicked out on the street. I mean, I paid for a space in the house. Or rather, Walter's fund thing did. Even if Baz hated me, it's nothing to do with him." He bit his bottom lip. "Well, except his family seems to buy out all his problems. So probably that's not as safe as I think. Except…I don't actually have any reason to think Baz will chuck me out of his life on a whim. Though of course it's what people keep telling me he will do."

"Is it Baz you worry about abandoning you specifically, or is he simply playing out more loudly your general fear people will not be there for you?" Pastor uncrossed and re-crossed his legs at his desk chair. "Do you believe Liz and I will turn on you too?"

"I believe I might disappoint you."

"Ah. So we'll change our minds about liking you, but it won't be because we're bad people. We'll realize you aren't worthy. Is that the script in your head?"

Elijah blushed crimson and stared at the pattern in the carpet. "Yes, but it sounds stupid when you say it out loud."

"Good. Let's say it out loud often."

Elijah rubbed his arms self-consciously as he stared at the rug. "They told me everything was my fault, every day. Everything bad that happened was because I existed."

"You know it *wasn't* your fault, Elijah. None of it."

Elijah cocked an eyebrow at him. "I wasn't a saint, Pastor."

"You were a child." He paused, then added carefully, "You were grieving."

Elijah averted his gaze again and gripped his arms, hugging them to his body.

They'd never talked about Mark before, Elijah's brother who had been killed in action in Afghanistan. A minute ago Elijah would have declared he didn't want to talk about Mark. He wasn't sure he wanted to now, but he did anyway.

"They told me it was my fault he died."

Elijah felt like he'd been electrified, admitting that. Hot, cold, naked, sick. The way Pastor's body language became tense and angry didn't help, even though intellectually he knew Schulz was about to get angry on Elijah's behalf.

"Elijah." Pastor's voice was tight, tense, like he was trying to be neutral but couldn't quite make it. "Elijah, there's absolutely no way that's true. It was utterly cruel and abusive of your parents to say such things to you. It would be at any age, but at *ten*, it's criminal."

They hadn't said it when Elijah was ten. They'd said it later, when he came out. But then, he supposed they *had* blamed him indirectly when Mark was killed. They blamed the gays for everything starting from that moment. And at that moment, Elijah had known he was gay.

It was all abruptly too much, and Elijah shook his head as he shrank into the chair. "I don't want to talk about this anymore."

"That's perfectly fine. If I may, though, I'd like to keep pressing you on the issue of feeling unworthy. Do you feel that way with Sebastian?"

"Sort of. He confuses me. I mean, I know I push people away, hurting them first so they can't hurt me. I'm trying not to do that with most people, but I can't stop with him. I want—" He stopped, shut his eyes and swallowed before he could continue. "I want…him. A lot. I maybe get a few good tries at not preemptively attacking him, and I fail…but he actually gets *more* aggressive then. The more I try to run, the more he wants me. I feel like he's led me way out into the deep water where I can't swim, and any second he'll leave me to drown."

"What in the deep water makes you so scared?"

It was a raging sea of terrible darkness in his mind. Huge, black, stormy. The emotion shafted him like cold light. "Loneliness. The water is full of loneliness."

"And yet you keep telling me you deliberately keep yourself lonely so people can't hurt you. You say you fear being alone, but the practical effect of Baz leaving you, given what you admit to doing to people close to you, is that he would only make your heart aware of a state you actively court."

Pastor's observation rang in Elijah's brain all the rest of the day. He'd grown accustomed to feeling like a peeled grape after therapy, but this time was particularly bad. He'd cried at the end of his appointment, and Pastor had encouraged him to call in to work. He'd dropped heavy hints Liz would be happy to accept his help with the baking and would feed him dinner. Elijah refused, not because he didn't want to snuggle on Liz's oh-so-comfortable shoulder, but because he wasn't calling in sick because *sad pants*. He did chain-smoke up and down the block past the campus no-smoking zone, in the hour between his appointment and the start of his shift. When he came in the service door to the cafeteria, he smelled like a stale bar and had to drink three glasses of water to repair his throat.

Lewis, punching into the time clock ahead of him, gave Elijah a small smile and a wave.

He'd gotten to know Lewis a little bit more after the chicken-can day. They weren't exactly besties or anything, but they'd come to a comfortable companionship at work. Smoking together, helping each other when they got stuck with a shit job. A few times Elijah had considered asking him if he wanted to do something after their shift, but he'd always chickened out.

That day they ended up both assigned to the front end, which Elijah thought was a lovely kick in the ass from the gods. He and Lewis were both runners, in charge of making sure the servers had adequate stock and the salad bars and do-it-yourself stir-fry had sufficient ingredients. This meant bobbing and weaving around chatting sorority sisters and head-butting *bros* from the football team, and from the latter especially, occasional under-breath murmurs about his orientation. Elijah had long practice ignoring this flavor of bullshit, staving most of it off with his not simply resting but *fucking active* bitch face.

What he had no defenses for was what happened when that commentary was directed at Lewis.

It would *help* if Lewis didn't hang a sign around his neck. Elijah hadn't figured out yet if it was legit gender dysphoria or part of a fucked-over attention/martyr complex, but whatever Lewis was working, it came with a spotlight. Today it was a *Kiki's Delivery Service* "I Can Fly On My Own" raglan tee, which was feminine enough, but then Lewis had sewed goddamned lace around the neckline. Why the hell he was wearing lace to work in food service was anybody's guess, but that's the choice he'd made when getting dressed today. Probably he'd felt the pink polka-dotted hair bow and girls Hello Kitty shoes needed company. Oh, and pink lipstick and magenta eyeliner. Let's not forget that.

Elijah didn't give a shit what Lewis wanted to wear, but the guy might as well have put himself on a golf tee and handed the *bros* a bag of clubs. He dressed so no one would ignore him, and so nobody did. He didn't simply parade his fabulous, either. Twice Elijah had caught him deliberately lingering over a tray of olives, crossing his ankles and sliding a shoe up his shin. It was half ballet, half Lolita, and it fucking worked. *Elijah* tripped at the genderfuck. Whatever game Lewis was playing, he was bringing it.

The rest of the dining hall felt otherwise. Girls at best exchanged knowing looks or giggled at Elijah, but for Lewis, they'd turn on the bitch and be cruel. The guys all but got their dicks out to piss on him. *Faggot* got tossed a few times, but it was clear they felt this dagger wasn't enough. They quickly shifted to *fucking freak* instead. It got to the point Elijah was queasy every time he went out to the salad bar because the atmosphere was electrically charged. It might or might not have been a real risk, but it *felt* as if the dining hall patrons were ready and willing to riot.

In hindsight, Elijah should have seen it coming. It was right out of an 80s teen flick, after all. But Elijah didn't realize what the blunt-nosed football player intended to do with the tray of pickled beets until the dick hefted it out of the salad bar, and even if he'd stood next to Lewis instead of behind the serving counter, at best Elijah could have taken the hit with him. He could only watch the fuchsia-tinted water and sand-dollar-sized slices of purple vegetable rain over Lewis's head.

The hair bow bent and sagged to the side. His carefully arranged hair went flat and covered his face. The robin's-egg-blue shirt and ivory lace dripped hot pink, and Elijah's brain helpfully supplied a memory of helping his mother can beets, running upstairs to change his shirt after she scolded him, saying the shirt was new, and she wasn't having him wreck it with a stain.

Beet juice never comes out.

Lewis's clothes were ruined. But the stain Elijah knew he'd never wash out of his own brain was the laughter. The *applause*. The whole fucking cafeteria—patrons, serving staff, the *goddamned student manager*—standing in a ring around bedraggled, humiliated Lewis.

Elijah's heartbeat pulsed in his ears. Or maybe it wasn't his heart. Maybe *he* pulsed like a nuclear sub, about to explode. His therapy appointment tickled the edge of his consciousness again, and he imagined Lewis dog-paddling in his own black water, fearing not only loneliness but *sharks*. Standing in a circle, watching him bleed out, in no hurry to move in for the kill.

The pulse in Elijah's head broke, spraying no innocent beet juice but *blood-red rage* over him.

Fuck this. Fuck this in the fucking face.

Tearing off his apron, he chucked it at the student manager. He shoved his way past the serving station, put an arm around Lewis and aimed him hard and fast for the exit.

"Bye, faggots," somebody called.

Without turning around, Elijah aimed a middle finger in the general direction of the cafeteria as he slammed open the door to the outside patio with his shoulder.

Chapter Fourteen

E LIJAH GOT ABOUT five steps before he discovered the fatal flaw in his impulsive act to rescue Lewis. Now that he'd tossed a buoy to a drowning victim, he needed to get them both to shore.

Lewis's hazel eyes brimmed with tears, but not one of them fell. The cords in his neck throbbed with tension, and the veins of his arms bulged as if the beet bucket had been laced with steroids. Below a trim, pert nose stained with splotches of hot pink, Lewis's nostrils flared, then contracted. His hands clenched into fists. His jaw trembled, a tremulous fault set to blow. But Lewis held the line, all the way around the union to the street leading away from campus.

Elijah didn't know where to take him. What to ask. What to do. What to fucking *say*.

Since waiting for Lewis to initiate something was clearly not an option, and everywhere Elijah looked was a possible land mine, he decided he'd call in reinforcements. Except when he pulled out his phone and opened the texting app, he had no idea who to aim the bat signal at. He'd call Mina, but she'd gone last-minute shopping with her parents. Aaron and Giles were doing music camp.

Elijah's options dwindled to one.

His finger hovered over Baz's name, but he couldn't press the touchscreen. Putting the phone away, he rationalized his cold feet. Baz couldn't come pick them up anyway. Elijah would walk Lewis to the White House, and if Baz happened to be there…

Stomach lurching, he fumbled for his cigarettes which, as had become his new rule-breaking habit, he'd "forgotten" to take out of his pocket and leave in his locker. Lighting two, he passed one over to Lewis.

Lewis accepted it. The juice on his arms had faded to pink streaks. His jaw trembled as he started to smoke, but it gentled slightly as he took a second hit.

Elijah smoked beside him in silence for half a block. He felt like a cat in a room full of rocking chairs, both for the situation he'd saddled himself with and for the Baz-bomb waiting for him at the White House. He wasn't sure what he thought about God, but in that moment he prayed mostly there was someone, *something* up there willing to help.

Please. He shut his eyes as long as he dared without tripping over the uneven sidewalk. *Please, please tell me what to do. Help me figure out what to say. How to help. How to help him feel less alone.*

Maybe there really was a god or goddess listening— or Elijah was a hell of a lot smarter than he knew. He didn't plan the words. They formed in his mind, accompanied by a great white wave of peace and certainty. Because every time he thought *him* in reference to Lewis, it felt wrong. Lewis as a name felt wrong. The person performing gender *fuck-you* wasn't making a social statement. The bow and the lace and the pink were as personal as the can of beets that had ruined them. Those feminine movements hadn't been taunts. They'd been tentative steps. Territory staked and claimed.

The last whispers of doubt died as Elijah pieced together what he'd grown to know, what he'd witnessed, what he'd observed. "What's your name? Your real name?"

It wasn't the question he'd planned to ask, but it worked. It made Lewis pause, almost tripping on the sidewalk. He took a long, slow drag as he recovered, staring straight ahead as a few tears escaped. "I was…thinking…Layla."

Elijah tried it out. *Lay-la.* "It's a good one."

"I'd spell it L-E-J-L-A. The Bosnian version. Inspired by the supermodel Andreja Pejic. She's Serbian, but it's close enough it feels right." A glance, a sigh, some of the tension cracking away to reveal tenderness. "Because I'm trans. Like she is."

Elijah thanked whatever deity was guiding him for also inspiring Mina to have left a pile of GLAAD pamphlets on the kitchen table. "What pronoun should I use for you?"

More tears, and a quivering lip. But fucking hell, Lewis or Lejla or whoever this was—they were strong. "I…I don't know. Sh—she, but not…" Steel returned with a jerked thumb toward the dining hall. "I want to be out. But I think I suck at it."

Funny. In the cafeteria, Elijah would have agreed. But walking here, now, he couldn't. How the fuck *did* somebody come out as trans, anyway? It wasn't about who you flirted with on the dance floor or walked down the aisle with. It was about who you fucking *were*. It wasn't putting on drag. It was God putting it on *you* without your consent. Elijah had never understood being trans, had frankly been glad to keep his distance because he had his own shit.

But he'd never wash out those beets.

When Lewis/Lejla ground out a butt into the sidewalk, Elijah passed over the pack and the lighter. The White House loomed a few blocks away, but Elijah could see the roof, the window of his own room. Was Baz there? What would he do? How should Elijah explain this?

He motioned for the cigarettes.

They both finished their second one as they crossed the street, but as Elijah aimed his charge at the front door, he met resistance. "What—? The *White House*? Why are you taking me here?"

"I thought you'd like to clean up. This is my—I live here."

Elijah might as well have asked his guest to strip naked and go back to the cafeteria. "I can't go in *there*!"

Help. Mina. Aaron. Giles. Anybody. "Why not? Nobody's home." Except maybe Baz.

"Are you fucking insane? The cool kids live in the White House. You want them to see me like this?"

Cool kids? Elijah stood there, mouth opening and closing as Lewis/Lejla backed into a bush, ready to run. Elijah covered the sidewalk, trying to cut off the path to campus, but that left the way past the garage and into a

depressed housing development wide open. Elijah tried
to think of something reassuring to say, but he had
nothing. All he could do was watch as his friend broke
away from the shrubbery and bolted the other direction.

But the gods were still with Elijah because a new
figure stepped onto the path. As Baz cried out, "Whoa,
there," and steadied the escapee, speaking calmly and
soothingly, Elijah felt foolish for thinking Baz would
ever have done anything but.

BAZ DIDN'T KNOW what was going on, but he knew
he was determined to make whatever had upset Elijah
go away.

"Hey—slow down. It's okay. Everything's going to
be okay." Whoever had run into him was shaking,
almost crying. To Elijah, Baz asked, "What's going
on?" *Please toss me a bone here, baby.*

Elijah wrapped his arms around himself. "This is
Lejla. She—"

"*Lewis.*" The individual in Baz's grip tensed like a
cork ready to pop before glancing away, face burning
with shame. "Not…here."

Elijah recoiled as if slapped, and he tossed Baz a
begging glance.

Okay. So they were both out of their depth.

"Let's go inside. Get you cleaned up." *And while
you're in the shower, I'm getting an earful from Elijah.*

Eyes sealing shut, Lejla/Lewis shuddered. "I just
want to go home."

"Where's home, sugar?"

"Titus. Third floor." Nostrils flared. "Fuck, I can't go there like this. They've probably heard. They'll all laugh."

"Come inside and clean up first. Take a long shower. We'll find you some new clothes."

For reasons unknown, Lejla/Lewis did *not* want to go into the White House, but once Elijah played wingman, the two of them got their guest into the house, up the stairs and into the shower, with Baz's robe hanging on the wall to wear after until they sorted out the clothes thing. As soon as the water began running, Baz caught Elijah's elbow and pulled him into the hall. He didn't have to prompt Elijah for a thing, because as soon as he closed the door, his lover sang like a canary.

"Oh my *fucking God*, Baz, I didn't—" Elijah wore a wild, injured-pissed look as he gestured toward campus. "They dumped *fucking beets on his head.*" He stopped, faltering. "I mean—*her* head." He wilted. "I don't know what to call him. Her. Them. He was always Lewis, but today he came all girled up, more than usual, and I had this weird religious thing on the way here, and I asked his name, and he said Lejla, and I asked what pronoun, and…" He sagged down the wall. "I don't know. I probably fucked up."

Baz crouched in front of Elijah, taking his hand. "Baby, *who* dumped beets on Lejla?"

Elijah stared off in the distance, gaze going hard. "Asshole in the cafeteria. Football fuckwad. Everybody laughed. *Everybody.*"

"Not you."

Elijah slumped forward. "I had to help. But I don't know what to do. I don't know. I suck."

"You're doing fine. More than fine." He cupped Elijah's shoulder and ran a hand down his back. "You did good."

"I didn't do anything."

"Something tells me Lejla would argue otherwise."

Elijah tensed. "Baz, *what do I call her?*"

"Your friend." Baz kissed his forehead. "Come on. Let's find some clothes."

Elijah resumed his freakout because he didn't know what clothes to find, girl or guy clothes. Baz wanted to hug him and point out *that* kind of detail orientation *was doing something*. He'd figured out praising Elijah wasn't calming him down, though, so he redirected to the task.

"Let's start with something unisex, like sweats and a T-shirt."

"But what about underwear? *What about under-wear?*"

Baz ducked into the room long enough to scoop his key ring off his dresser and tossed it at Elijah. "Go to Target. Buy guy's underwear size medium. Girl's underwear size..." He paused, shrugged. "Get something that would fit you if you were a bit taller, with some room to eat a big lunch. Lean on sweats and yoga pants." He passed over a fifty from his wallet, added another couple more for good measure.

Elijah stared at the money for several seconds, still half-crazed. Then he let the air out of his lungs in a rush, took the money, and wrapped his arms around Baz.

Baz returned the embrace hesitantly. It was, despite living together and fucking at least twice a day, possibly their most intimate moment yet. Elijah's most honest, vulnerable offering of affection.

So why did Baz feel awkward about it?

He accepted the kiss a lot more easily, moving past the hump of awkward into wanting to linger and enjoy the feeling of holding his boyfriend more. But Elijah murmured "I better go" against his cheek, and Baz had to relinquish him so he could disappear down the stairs.

Alone in his bedroom, Baz lounged on the bed, browsing social media without reading it, perking up only when Elijah arrived at the store and began lobbing questions at him. Long after the shower stopped, the bathroom door stayed closed. Baz passed the time fielding panicked Elijah texts and photos about what shirt was better and how girly should the underwear be. When the bathroom door creaked open, Baz turned to see his guest framed by the doorway to his bedroom.

While Baz wasn't exactly awash in trans acquaintances, he knew enough people who identified as other than their birth sex to understand there was no look or identifying feminine or masculine tendency making somebody obvious. Gender identity was way too personal. That said, he'd be damned if Lewis-Lejla wasn't the most androgynous figure he'd seen in some time, especially sporting shower-slick hair. Even the Adam's apple wasn't much of anything to write home about. Passing wouldn't be terribly difficult, with the right accessories. The eyebrows could use some shaping. Longer hair would go a long way toward increasing a feminine appearance. The shoulders would always be broad. But overall? He could see Lejla. Maybe it was the suggestion, maybe it was her projecting through.

The question was, what did the person inside that body see?

Baz tried to strike the balance between overeager and disinterested. He saluted instead of shook hands, not wanting to crowd. "Baz Acker. Nice to meet you."

The Adam's apple shifted on a hard swallow. "I—I'm...Lewis." Lewis made a brief face, as if tasting something bad. "I...I don't know what Elijah told you, but I'm...Lewis. At least to the outside. What I told him, about Lejla...he took me off-guard."

"I'm fine either way, for the record. Fine with one identity in one place, a different one in another." When red-rimmed eyes teared up, Baz winced and held up a hand. "Or not. Lewis is fine, if that's what you want."

Lewis put a hand in his hair, face turned away in mortification. "I can't believe this is happening. I walk by and wish I were cool enough to live here, and now I'm standing in your bathrobe wondering if I got all the beet juice out of my hair."

"For the record, the dickwad who gave you the beet bath would be happy to do the same to me. I get out of it because people know I have a closet full of lawyers and the money to pay them." He pulled out a chair and gestured to it as he perched on the footboard of the bed. "Sit. Tell me your story. Or, if you'd rather rest, I'll bug out of here."

"You can…stay." The chair was accepted, hesitant-ly. Legs were tucked up, revealing them to be clean-shaven. "I don't have a story. I'm a girl, but I have a dick. I know I'm trans, but…" Lip in teeth, gaze averted. "I've never come out to anyone before Elijah. I feel weird. I'm happy and sick at the same time."

"You can be out or in. You can bob and weave. I don't think there are any rules except for what you make them."

His guest said nothing, and Baz let the silence build, unconcerned. It took another full minute, almost, but eventually Lewis/Lejla spoke. "There *are* rules, because I'm always breaking them. Everybody laughs at the way I dress, unless I dress boring or like a guy. *Then* guys tease me for being a fag. Which sucks, because I'm not gay. But it's a double slap, because first I have to wear things that feel wrong, and I have to be teased for being what I'm not at the same time."

Yeah, what a nice bite in the ass. "What keeps you from living as female?"

"People who dump beets on me. I've figured out how much I can wear without getting too much teasing, but it makes me crazy. Sometimes I don't realize how much I've girled-out until I'm a mile out the door. Lejla is subversive. She changes how I dress when I'm not looking, and if I deliberately hold her back, I end up sobbing in a toilet stall."

"Have you seen a doctor? Have you been diagnosed with gender dysphoria?"

"My parents don't know, and I'm not ready to tell them." Tears were wiped away. "I mean—they're not like Elijah's. But they wouldn't understand. They're nervous enough thinking I'm gay."

What a lovely dead end. Baz ran a hand through his hair. "Well—shit. I'm no psychologist, but I'm pretty sure you've thrown up some red flags. Subconsciously dressing as the gender you feel you are being the biggest one."

More silence. It was making Baz crazy not knowing what name or pronoun to assign. Why the hell it mattered, he didn't know. It *didn't* matter. Was he going to treat the person in front of him any different as a Lewis instead of a Lejla, or vice versa? No, but—well, that was the thing, wasn't it? It didn't matter, except it really fucking did.

Gender was such a fuckjob. What made Elijah attractive to Baz? Why was Mina not on the menu? He refused to believe it was her tits. It must be something else. Pheromones. Or maybe it was all genderfuck. *Born naked, and the rest is drag*, like RuPaul said. Maybe they were all warped by details. Maybe orientation and gender and even attraction were a thousandfold more complicated than anybody wanted to admit.

What about the underwear, indeed.

Baz cleared his throat. "There's got to be a support group in the Cities."

"I don't have a car. I barely have enough money to go to a movie. The college fund my parents saved for me crashed right before they had to start cashing out, which is why I stayed on campus to work. So unless the support group comes with free bus service—"

"I have a car, and a—boyfriend who can drive it."

He hated how he still tripped over the word *boyfriend*.

His companion frowned. "You can't drive your own car?"

"I have severe retinal damage and photophobia. I was legal to drive for about twelve hours." He paused, tasting the rest of it before he spit it out. "I got beat up, and my sight and some chronic pain are the casualties."

Shock, horror, sorrow—but thank fuck, no pity. Empathy, maybe. A little fear. Made sense. Talk about *it could happen to you.* "I'm so sorry. That's why—the glasses. I had no idea."

"It is what it is." He rubbed his neck, sighed and held out his hand. "Look. We don't really know each other yet. But you strike me as somebody who could use some backup. What I'm saying is, I'm offering. Elijah too. If you stay for dinner, I'm pretty sure you'll have more people in your posse."

He ached at the way this offer of friendship made his guest nervous, not reassured. "Why would you do that? Why would anyone do that?"

Because Elijah brought you home. "Because getting beets dumped on your head for wearing a *Kiki's Delivery Service* shirt and a bow in your hair sucks."

Tension, quick and tight as a whip. "So you're helping because you feel sorry for me?"

"No. Never." He paused to attempt a rephrase. "I can't exactly explain myself, but it's sure as hell not because I pity you. You're Elijah's friend, to start. That comes with certain perks. This is one of them."

"But I barely know him. We smoke together at work, is all. I was never sure he liked me much."

Noise on the stairs stopped them both, and seconds later Elijah appeared, fists full of Target bags. He deposited them in a small sea of red and white around the chair before withdrawing, wrapping his arms over his stomach. "I got some things. Different kinds. You can keep whatever you want."

He set Baz's keys and a wad of fifties on the dresser. Baz raised an eyebrow.

Elijah lifted his chin defiantly and started for the door. "We'll leave you to get dressed."

Baz followed, but on the way out he couldn't resist whispering to Lewis, "I think he likes you."

Once Baz closed the door, Elijah dragged him into the communal bathroom. "I used my money. The stuff from the fund." Elijah leaned on the sink, but when Baz caught his hand, he sort of melted against Baz's body. "It was the first time it didn't make me queasy to spend it. I went a little crazy."

Baz faced the mirror, which presented a full-on view of himself: too tall, slumped from a day of head-aches and hip pain, eyes hidden behind his shades, Elijah's dark-haired, wiry body wrapped around him. Elijah hugging him. Holding himself close. Baz holding him right back.

The sight hit him in the gut. He flipped the lock to the door, threw the switches so the main light went out and the bathroom swelled with red glow. Then took off his glasses and set them on the counter.

Elijah opened his mouth to say more, but Baz qui-eted him with a nuzzle against the side of his head. "Shh. I want to look at us for a second. Without the fucking glasses."

Wordlessly, Elijah complied, but when Baz caught him trying to peek, he shifted his good hip to let him have a better view. They stood a long time that way, silent, holding each other, staring into the mirror.

"I like your eyes." Elijah stroked Baz's arm, meeting his gaze in the mirror. "I see them as brown even with the shades, in my mind. I love the fragmented colors in your iris."

Ungh. Baz cleared his suddenly thick throat. "Th-thanks."

They didn't say anything else. They didn't kiss, not so much a brush of the lips. And yet while he stood there, like the hug in the bedroom, Baz knew this strange, crystalline moment would ring in his head light years longer than any blow job. Even being topped beautifully in a freaky moose hotel. This was...tender. Aching. Perfect.

Mind-bendingly dangerous.

As they left the bathroom and went to talk to Aaron and Giles as they heard them arrive—well past the half-life of the tenderness—Baz had no urge to run. He didn't panic.

Okay, he panicked a little. But not because it freaked him out to be close. Because he'd found a new terror—the acknowledgment he wanted something to stay.

Chapter Fifteen

ELIJAH HAD BEEN prepared for a wide palate of Lewis/Lejlas to come down the stairs, but it still surprised him to see his friend so butched up Elijah felt a bit femmy. Male sweats, hoodie, no makeup, the gender neutral white faux Keds Elijah had thrown in at the last minute, not the faintly glittery flip-flops.

Lewis hung out on the stairs in the shadows. Mina and Aaron and Giles sat with Baz, eager for an introduction and chance to show their support after hearing the story, but Elijah didn't give one yet, meeting Lewis on the landing in hopes of an explanation.

Lewis averted his gaze. "I need to get to my dorm. Didn't feel like any additional attention." Shifted a tightly packed pair of Target bags, glanced at Elijah. "You said…it was okay to keep some of the clothes?"

"Keep all of them, if you want. You don't have to go right away, either. You could have worn what you wanted and changed. We ordered subs. They should be here any second. Will you stay and meet everyone?"

Lewis leaned into the wall, looking pale and tired, eyes red and puffy from crying. "I don't have it in me right now. Sorry."

"Let us give you a ride at least." When Lewis

balked, Elijah crowded a little, hating how he felt like the flip side of when Aaron had badgered *him* into accepting help. "You've got all this stuff to carry. And Baz is going to be all managing mother bear, wanting to make sure you're okay."

Lewis sighed. "I just…need to be alone tonight. It's nothing personal."

Alone for the night Elijah could live with. But he wasn't relinquishing his new friend without getting some digits first.

He did get them, in the loading zone of Titus while Baz retrieved the bags out of the frunk. The three of them went up the stairs together, Baz and Elijah ignoring Lewis's protests that an escort was unnecessary. They got a lot of stares, but half of them were for the Tesla and most of the others went to Baz.

"Ah, Titus." Baz swung one of the Target bags over his shoulder and tipped his head back to take in the building as they approached the side door. "How I haven't missed thee."

"You lived here too?" Elijah glanced around the familiar stairwell, flashing to last year when he roomed with Aaron. And dodged the Campus Crusaders, and hoped to hell his parents didn't find out what he was up to.

"Yep. First floor, room to the right of the showers. Shacked up with Marius until we moved to the White House at semester. Thought I won the roommate lottery, but it turns out my mother had her assistant comb through every freshman until he found the one *most suitable.*"

Lewis stepped aside to let someone pass on the stairway. "I'm in Silas again for the school year, but Titus is the only male dorm open for the summer. So it's mostly me and the football team and four international students."

The full impact of what this truth meant for a second-year student struggling with gender identity hit Elijah as they opened the door to Lewis's floor to a cacophony of male shouts and laughter. Wide-shouldered football players passed casually between rooms, though through one pair of doors simply a football made the journey back and forth. Cries of *dude* and *what the fuck, man?* and *you dumb shit* bounced around as comfortable camaraderie. The men weren't all large, but they were the kind of bark-chewing, back-slapping *bros* only a college locker room could germinate. Young men alone in close environment, playing out the politics and pressures of their team in fifty-year-old buildings composed of concrete blocks and linoleum floors. First years terrified to be away from home, but desperate not to let anyone know how afraid they were. Sophomores eager to stake a place of dominance, juniors and newly minted seniors defending roles previously carved.

The barking calls and whoops put all of Elijah's senses on alert. Lewis took a different approach, pulling the hoodie fully forward, rounding shoulders and economizing movements, as if becoming invisible were an option. Lewis wove through the obstacle course of traditional masculinity like a wraith, hugging the wall, favoring shadows and falling behind Baz and Elijah to use them as human shields.

Baz was Baz. He used every inch of his height and pushed his sunglasses higher on his nose with a practiced air. Each of the guys loitering in the halls noticed him, as they were meant to, and by and large they parted the sea for him. Most shuffled into their rooms, the rest making themselves less conspicuous, leaning over to murmur to a *bro* who was too new to have gotten the memo. A few bruisers held their own, arms folded and quietly making it known they'd throw down if challenged, but nothing more. Baz didn't challenge, so nothing happened except the hallway got quiet and he walked without encumbrance, all the way until Lewis tugged Elijah's sleeve and murmured they'd reached their destination.

Elijah didn't ask if he could come in. He almost pushed Lewis out of the way to make it inside, collapsing into the corner by the closet as he stared, wide-eyed, at Lewis. When the door *snicked* closed behind Baz, Elijah erupted. "Holy fucking shit, *this* is what you're living with?"

Shrugging, Lewis hunkered into the hoodie. "It's not as bad as it looks. They call me names, mostly. Maybe a shove if I don't watch where I walk, and I have to be mindful when I go to the bathroom. I shower when they're at practice though. It's only for another month, until I'm back in Silas."

"Who's your roommate?" This came from Baz, who toured the room idly, scanning the walls. They were mostly bare, though he paused at a bulletin-board collage.

"None now. Don't know who for the fall." Lewis shrugged. "Some freshman, probably. The guy I had last year found somebody else."

But Lewis hadn't, of course.

Baz hadn't moved from the bulletin board. "You're a serious disciple of Studio Ghibli, I see. Favorite film?"

Lewis straightened, body posture calming as the two of them stood before the carefully cut out and arranged anime display. "Everything Miyazaki does is brilliant. I love all of them for different reasons. But probably...*Spirited Away* and *Nausicaä*. And *Princess Mononoke*. Well—and *My Neighbor Totoro*, because you have to start with the foundation. But I don't want you to think I disrespect *From Up on Poppy Hill* or *The Wind Rises*. They're all different shades of perfection, really."

"Favorite character?"

This time Lewis didn't hesitate. "Nausicaä. Though I will always hold a seat for Ponyo too."

Baz traced the image of a gray-haired boy inside the tail of a white dragon. "I'm pretty much team Haku, but you're right about Ponyo. Have you seen the Japanese versions, or only the English dubs?"

"A few in Japanese. My public library had some of the discs, and I got *Spirited Away*, *Howl's Moving Castle*, and *Nausicaä* as gifts, but I've watched most on torrents."

"I have all of them, including the Japanese release of *Spirited Away* on Blu-ray. Next time you're bored, let me know, and we'll have a marathon."

Lewis blushed. "That would be awesome. Thanks."

Uncapping a dry erase marker, Baz wrote his name and cell on the whiteboard above the desk. "We'll leave you alone like you asked, but you'll call us, right, if you need anything? Or if you simply change your mind and want company? Doesn't matter how late. Elijah never turns down an excuse to drive the Tesla."

Elijah resented this portrait of himself, but he stifled his objection when he saw how the comment made Lewis quietly hopeful. "Okay. Thanks."

Baz deposited the bags he carried on the bed. "Tell Lejla she did you proud, okay? And have her tell you the same thing."

Lewis said nothing, but it was clear Baz had found exactly the right thing to say. This left Elijah not knowing how to follow up, so he fumbled a quick kiss on his friend's cheek, hoping the gesture wasn't stupid as fuck, and murmured "Take care of yourself" as he followed Baz into the hall.

The troglodyte who'd dumped beets on Lejla's head stood in the middle of the path to the exit.

It was possible to get past him, but not without standing sideways and essentially executing a kind of shuffling genuflect around his elbows. His bent arms framed bulked-out abs straining a Saint Timothy Trojans green-and-white jersey with the factory folds still in place. He glared at Baz with beady eyes from beneath a buzz cut, an iron stare declaring no slicked-up guy in sunglasses was intimidating *him*.

Elijah tried not to panic, but he stepped closer to Baz, glancing up at him in an attempt to communicate a silent *that's the beet asshole*, but Baz didn't so much as slow his stride. The other residents of the hall shuffled to the periphery, uninterested in taking a side but eager to see how it played out. Some of the guys seemed uneasy, some confused and some pissed, like they'd never battle Baz personally but wouldn't mind seeing him knocked down a peg or three.

Elijah's choices were duck around the asshole his fingers still urged to pull apart or take point beside Baz and hope bullies bounced off Baz as well as bullets. He chose the latter option and pasted on bored, discourage-the-trick face.

Baz slowed as he approached the roadblock, regarding the man-mountain with the same disinterest he would a mannequin display. He was *very* careful not to so much as let his breath brush the freshman—but he angled his head to the side and raked his gaze up and down, going so far as to tip his glasses so it was abundantly clear he was inspecting a piece of meat. "Passable, I suppose, but bulk's never done much for me."

Someone murmured *shit* as the thug's beady eyes opened as wide as they'd go. Mr. Bulk tensed, elbows coming down as fists formed over his midsection. "What the fuck?"

Tension swelled in the corridor, but Baz ignored it, straightening and laying his right palm in a rather affected gesture over his heart. "Dear me. How embarrassing. I must have misinterpreted. My *apologies*. Usually when a man goes to this much trouble to get my attention, he...well, wants my attention, if you know what I mean."

The freshman flushed with confused, dangerous rage. His right fist rose automatically, but the panicked murmurs around him gave him pause. Elijah could see the thoughts forming on his face. *Why aren't the others joining in? Why aren't we beating up this faggot together?*

Baz remained where he was, but his demeanor became concentrated, his casual comments laced with quiet steel. "The creases in your jersey tell me you're new here. So before you say or, worse, *do* things you'll regret, I suggest you do a little homework. But don't think this is a threat, *exactly*. Just because I'm from Chicago doesn't mean I'm with the mob or anything." He laughed, and the sound managed to make even Elijah wonder if maybe, somehow, Baz *was* connected to some kind of revenge-thirsty organized-crime outfit.

The thug didn't lower his fist, but he held still, regarding Baz as if he were a viper ready to go for the throat at any second.

"Tell you what." Baz tucked his elbows into his side and held out his hands, an arrogant CEO declaring to his nest of peons *we're all equals here*. "I remember what it's like to be new, to need to impress the guys and make new friends. So you're going to be *my* friend. You're going to help me take care of one of my friends." He indicated Lewis's closed door with a nod. "Lewis has a difficult time fitting in, same as you. I hear there was a *terrible* run-in today with some pencil-dicked asshole who thinks it's fun to laugh at someone else's expense. Do me a favor and watch out for Lewis. Because people who upset my friends are always sorry."

The freshman blinked at Baz, his expression still

confused but now carefully blank.

Baz nodded, as if to say *yes, it's all settled now, everybody move on.* He resumed his stride, patting the meathead absently on the shoulder as he blithely nudged him out of the way and led Elijah down the hall. "Looking great, guys. First pregame meal's on me."

Silence enveloped them until the stairwell door closed behind them, but before Elijah could let out his breath on a *What the fucking fuck?* Baz caught his elbow and led him with purpose to the exit.

"Game face stays on, no stopping or slowing." He kept his breezy CEO smile in place as they passed a group of football players on the stairs, then covered the distance between the building entrance and the Tesla. The cluster of guys broke away as Baz approached and the door handles popped out, but Baz didn't break character as he pulled his seat belt into place and fumbled with the dashboard controls. "No big deal, simply start the car and pull out like you do this every day."

Elijah wanted to protest he thought he was going to throw up, but Baz had the moonroof open and Maino blasting "Here Comes Trouble", so Elijah swallowed his freakout and did as he was told.

It was cool, he'd admit, the way people watched them as they peeled silently away, Maino's rap a perfect soundtrack to their badass exit. As soon as they were clear of the dorm, though, Elijah pulled onto a side street, parked the car under the canopy of an oak tree, and melted into his seat.

"*What the hell.*" He aimed a glare at Baz, but he was so overwhelmed all he could do was collapse against the wheel. "You fucking lunatic. I thought we were going to be smears on bathroom tile."

Baz snorted, pinching the bridge of his nose as he leaned back in his seat. "Never. Only four guys didn't know who I was, and the lead asshole didn't have any friends. The only cache he has was from providing their lunchtime entertainment, which I now turned into a big fat streak of trouble. He was never going to hit me, not without encouragement. So I didn't give him any."

Elijah made a mental note to never play poker with Baz. Christ. "What was with all the veiled threats?"

He shrugged. "There are a million wild stories about my family. They toss around a lot of money, and my mother is overprotective and managing. Somehow this has become the myth that if anyone fucks with me, their family will find themselves in financial trouble or guys in suits will meet offenders in dark alleys. None of it is true, exactly—though if Precious had decked me, our lawyers would have him ruined within a business day. And it's true, my family's given so much money to Saint Timothy that if they asked for pretty much anything, they'd get it. You have to be careful how you use leverage—but nobody ever thinks it through. Frankly I suspect they get off on the idea I could own a school the way they think I do. So every now and then, when it suits me, I use the song and dance to my advantage."

Elijah's adrenaline remained in spike, and he couldn't stop replaying the image of Baz blithely taking down the guy who had humiliated Lejla. "How did you know he was the guy?"

"The way you flinched when you saw him. That and he was clearly the biggest tool in the room."

Elijah let out a breath, but it was rough. They were okay, he kept trying to tell himself.

Fingers threaded through his hair, a gentle, grounding touch. The belied fear rolled over and became banked lust. Shutting his eyes, Elijah leaned into Baz's hand.

Baz kept kneading. "Let's head to the house. I have something I want to show you in our room."

Elijah just bet he did. He tried to laugh, but all his cells were realigning to getting laid, so instead he turned his face to nuzzle Baz's palm, lingering to place a long lick up the pulse of his wrist. "You're pretty badass, Howl."

Baz closed the distance between them, giving Elijah a kiss half carnal, half bite. "Only when you're with me, Sophie. Only when you're with me."

BAZ'S MIGRAINE HAD started before they returned to the White House, but it was mild enough he could pass it off without Elijah knowing. It helped that Elijah was seriously horny, a state Baz maintained by tickling his ear and then openly groping him once the Tesla was safely in the garage. He would have laid his boyfriend out on the kitchen table, but Mina and Jilly were at the counter making cookies. At first it was fun to let them stall with small talk because he knew Elijah was going crazy with the rain delay, but when he realized how badly he needed a pain pill, he excused them and herded his boyfriend the rest of the way up the stairs.

"Brian's moving in tonight," Mina called into the living room as they hustled up the stairs. "Where should I tell him to put Sid's stuff and the spare junk in his room?"

"Ballroom," Baz called out, shut the door behind them and got to work.

He still got a crazy contact high from the way Elijah came undone for him, how pushing him into a wall or a door or basically restricting him in any way made him go pliant and writhing at once. Baz indulged a moment—against the dresser this time, Elijah mewling and panting as Baz pinched his nipple and undid his pants. But the headache kept increasing, and finally Baz had to break the kiss to lean around Elijah and fish for a prescription bottle.

"Head?" Elijah rasped the question into Baz's chest as he undid his buttons.

"Yeah." Baz popped the pills into his mouth and dry-swallowed them, resting his cheek on his arm. "Gotta give this a few minutes to kick in."

Elijah kissed his way down Baz's sternum, occasionally pausing to lick. "Mmm. You smell like vanilla. Helping Liz bake?"

Baz's head pinched, and he stroked Elijah's hair instead of answering.

Elijah undid Baz's fly with a deft hand. Kneeling on the floor, he stroked Baz's flaccid cock, swirling his tongue around the glans until it was clear the soldier wasn't reporting for duty. Undaunted, Elijah shifted focus to Baz's balls, alternating between licks and sucks.

"That was so hot." He stroked Baz's ass cheek and paused his speech to swallow both balls and bury his nose in Baz's taint. "The most fucking badass thing I've ever seen."

It had felt pretty badass at the time, like he was conducting an intricate social symphony. He wanted to quip something about how good Elijah looked on his knees, or how bad Elijah could be on Baz's ass, but instead he had to bite his arm as his head split in two. What Elijah was doing felt great, but as the pain exploded, he acknowledged fucking or even lying still and being sucked wasn't on his personal menu right now.

Elijah already knew how to read those cards and stopped his assault to instead rise, finish peeling Baz out of his clothes and lead him to the bed. The gesture was nice, but it bummed Baz out he was already a nursing-home patient.

Elijah tucked him naked into bed, sat half-dressed beside him and stroked his hair. "I'm going to switch the lights to red. Do you want me to get you a joint?"

Keeping his eyes closed, Baz nodded with as much economy of movement as possible. His brain felt bruised, especially behind his right eyeball. But when Elijah started to rise, he caught his arm, held it weakly. He smacked a dry mouth before he could get to words. "Smoke with me?"

"Anytime."

Once he buttoned up the curtains and flipped the

switches, Elijah lit the joint for them, kneeling naked over Baz's midsection as he pressed the paper to Baz's lips. Were it not for the blanket, their groins would've met flesh to flesh, but as it was he was glad, because the space between Elijah's heavy erection and Baz's pain-soaked libido could be measured in light years. Elijah didn't seem to care, though, his touches shifting to gentle strokes as he smoked.

"Sorry," Baz croaked. He couldn't keep his eyes open, even in the red.

Elijah kept stroking, occasionally stopping to apply the joint to Baz's lips. "Is this something from the hallway?"

Shaking his head was killer. "No. Does this sometimes. Humid day, maybe, but mostly just because. Sorry."

"Stop apologizing." Elijah held the joint away as he trailed kisses between Baz's nipples. "I know it's a front because you want to make me crazy. Spend the afternoon hot and bothered, thinking about you pissing a circle around a dumb jock. God, I want to lick your feet whenever I think of it." He teased one of Baz's nipples in his teeth. "You do that to me, you know. I've played sub a million times, but when I lay it down for you... It scares me, but I want to do it with you so bad. Whatever you say. Even if it's not what I want. Maybe especially then."

Dizzy with want and need, Baz fumbled at Elijah's hair, gave up and took the joint from his fingers. "Sure, tell me when I'm weak as a kitten and can't do anything about it."

"Why do you think I told you now?"

Baz passed the joint over when Elijah asked for it, but he forced his eyes open and touched Elijah's face. "Same. Feel…the same."

Elijah's expression went soft, slightly scared. He traced the butt of the joint around Baz's lips, unable to meet his gaze. "Sure you're not tired of this scrawny, frowny little rat hanging around?"

Baz didn't dignify the comment with an answer.

He got groggy after that, sludged out on pain meds and weed. Time went fuzzy, expanding and contracting. He sat up at one point, reached for water, stumbled to the bathroom, but he went to bed after. A warm body slipped in beside him, and in his mind he got a lubed finger up Elijah's ass and fingered him good before fucking him into the mattress, but in reality he drooled on the pillow beside Elijah's hair.

Just after midnight he woke in a full sweat, headache gone, stomach growling like crazy. He stumbled into pajama pants as quietly as he could and considered climbing out the window to sit on the fire escape. He thought better of it and padded down the stairs, blinking against contacts several hours overdue to be taken out. He winced at the bright light in the kitchen and groped to shift the lights before trying to open them. An unfamiliar young man stood at the counter assembling a sandwich, and he smiled and waved as he saw Baz. "Oh, hey. Sorry about the lights. Didn't know you were up."

Brian, Baz's groggy brain helpfully supplied. Baz saluted and sank into a chair. "You get moved in okay?"

"Yeah. I left Sid's stuff in there even though Min said I could move it. I never planned to have a single, so it's not like I have enough stuff to fill the place." He gestured to the sandwich mountain. "Hungry?"

"Fucking starving," Baz admitted.

Brian slid a heap onto a plate and brought it over. "I made enough for two out of habit. My dad stays up late programming same as me, and it's kind of our thing, midnight sandwiches. He warns me that's how he got his spare tire, but it's not as if I'm going to find a girl who wants this deep of geek anyway." He pulled a couple KZ sodas out of the fridge and brought them over by their necks as he settled in with his own plate. "Heard you had a headache. Sleep help any?"

Baz shrugged as he scooped up the sandwich. "Hard to say how much of it is needing food at this point."

"Well, hopefully this finishes your misery off."

They ate in silence for a few minutes, but Brian was perky and Baz suspected hyped up on caffeine. His gaze blipped around the room, tracking the red lights. "I love the setup. I'll admit I peeked at the rigging, but I promise I didn't break anything. It's kind of awesome. You have it in every room?"

"Only the kitchen and my suite. And the common bathroom at the top of the stairs."

"Makes sense. Living room has all those windows, and the wiring is probably wonk, old as the house is. You'd have to tear up the walls. Or run a parallel system along the baseboards. Which wouldn't have to be ugly." He laughed self-consciously. "Sorry, I'm wired. Just finished a three-hour Halo marathon. You have a sick gaming setup."

Baz took a swig of his soda and eased into his chair. "You're up late a lot? We'll probably meet like this again."

"Great. You'll have to make sure I stock your favorite sandwich fixings."

They sat together awhile, Baz mostly listening while Brian babbled, but he enjoyed it. It felt less that the world had ended and more like things had rearranged. No, this wasn't sitting up with Marius or Damien or Sid. But it was good. Different, but good.

When he finally went up the stairs, it was three in the morning. He entered the room as quietly as he could, but Elijah sat up anyway, bleary but focused on Baz as he went into the bathroom. "Feeling better?"

"Yeah." Baz kept the door cracked while he pissed in the darkness, washed his hands and flipped on the red lights to take out his contacts and swallow his drugs. "Sat up with Brian. Shot the shit, had a sandwich."

"Good to hear."

Baz cleaned his contacts, put in some eyedrops, washed his face. When he finished in the bathroom, he padded to the bed, not wanting to disturb Elijah, who he'd assumed had gone back to sleep. Except when he slipped beneath the sheets, ready to spoon his boyfriend, Elijah drew Baz into his arms. Kissed his cheek. Nipped at his chin.

Slid his hands into Baz's pajama pants, palmed his ass.

"Shh." Elijah sucked briefly on Baz's lip before trailing tender kisses down Baz's neck. "Lay back and enjoy the ride."

Baz's fingers threaded into Elijah's hair despite his attempts to stay them. "I...I'm better, but I can't—"

Elijah lifted his head to stop Baz's mouth with his own. "I know, baby. But if you tell me it still doesn't feel good, I'm going to call you a liar."

It did feel good. Elijah's mouth and hands, yes—God, yes—but the *way* Elijah touched him was what felt best of all. The way he didn't seem to care, even a little, that Baz's dick never got more than semi-soft. The way he managed to keep the sensual spell going when Baz had to say no, he couldn't bend his hip that way tonight. Elijah continued to kiss him, massage him, as he turned Baz onto his side, propped a mountain of pillows under his knee and fucked him that way instead.

Baz didn't cry, exactly. Mostly he let go. Went limp as Elijah moved inside him, an expert now on how to make it good even when taking so much care. He swam in the quiet sea of safety Elijah made for him, knowing him so well he fucked him instead of asked if he wanted to talk.

It was too much, was all, and when Baz sighed in his quiet, mental version of an orgasm, some tears fell out. Exhausted, relieved, happy tears.

Wiping a particularly fat one away, Elijah kissed Baz's ear with aching softness and curled up wordlessly behind him.

Shutting his eyes, Baz reached over his head, fumbling to take weak hold of a fistful of Elijah's hair. Held on to it, lightly, until his muscles went slack and he drifted into a deep, safe sleep.

Chapter Sixteen

AFTER LEAVING IN the middle of his shift, Elijah assumed he was fired. That turned out to not be the case, because on Friday morning the head of food service himself showed up at the White House to apologize and assure him "disciplinary measures have been taken." The student manager and other staff had been spoken to, and Elijah's job waited for him. He wondered if this was part of the myth of association with Baz, this kid-glove handling, or if this was part of his *own* special-snowflake package.

Elijah leaned on the doorframe and crossed his arms over his chest. "What about Lewis?"

"He has his job too, of course. Provided he sticks to the dress code from now on."

Elijah dug his fingers into his arms. "*Dress code?*"

"Well—yes." His gaze skittered away. "Ahem—appropriate work attire."

Fucker. "Which is what, exactly?"

"It's stated in the manual. No inappropriate slogans. No distracting clothing."

Yes, because *I Can Fly By Myself* put people off their all-you-can-eat pizza buffet. Elijah pulled his smile as wide as it went. "Thank you so much for stopping by.

You can take your goddamned job, and your manual, and your appropriate attire, and shove it all up your clenched little asshole."

After slamming the door in the man's face, he pressed his forehead against it and blew his breath out in a hiss so he didn't scream. He relaxed significantly when familiar arms went around him and Baz's breath warmed his ear.

"You make me hard when you get feisty, Sophie."

"I wanted to *punch him in the face.*" Elijah clenched his fists, then sagged. "Now I don't have a job."

"You don't actually need one."

"Yes, but Lewis does. And now he's there by himself." Fuck. Elijah should have thought things through. He was pretty sure he'd burned the food-service bridge and kicked the smoldering remains into the ravine.

"Talk to Pastor. He can help Lewis find a new job. This shit is his bread and butter. He loves pulling rank."

"It's going to be the same shit, different department, though. Either that or Lewis will get stuck in the library archives or something heinous. He needs something where he can get out. Preferably where he could actually be she, but let's not—" He cut himself off while the idea bloomed in his head, then turned around, grabbed Baz's cheeks and tongued him hard. "*Fuck yes.* It could be *Lejla* at the internship with the home bakery."

Baz rubbed his jaw, embarrassed. "Ah. About that. I meant to tell you—I'm...working with Liz. Baking with her, for more than simply afternoon fun. Volunteering, nothing official."

Elijah blinked. "Cool, but why didn't you tell me?"

He shrugged, averting his gaze. "Just trying it out, didn't want everybody excited I'd maybe found something to do with myself and then bail again. But I like it. I want to keep doing it. Anyway—I'm sure she'd welcome more help. So we could be there together, is my point. Unless she doesn't want to."

Elijah wanted to make a big deal of Baz working with Liz, to tell him how awesome he thought it was, but he could tell he should hold off for a bit. *Focus on Lejla.* "Well, she'd have to set it up as work study, and I don't know how that shakes out. But maybe there's somewhere she could work where it could be like a fresh start. In Lejla outfits, as Lejla. Do you think Pastor would have any info?"

"Possible." Baz kissed his way down Elijah's neck. "Better send Pastor a text."

Elijah got out his phone. "I'll call, it's faster—*Oh.*"

He dropped the phone as Baz reached into his pajama pants and palmed his cock.

Elijah pushed him away. "Baz! Giles said Brian came in last ni—" Baz's mouth closed over him, and he shut his eyes and tipped his head against the door.

Without so much as stuttering the blow job, Baz handed him the phone.

Elijah accepted it with a shaking hand. His other went into Baz's hair. "I can't...text a pastor while—*Oh fuck, Baz.*"

Baz hummed around Elijah's cock before releasing it. "Oh, now *there's* an idea." Rising, he took Elijah's hand and led his shaking legs to the stairs. "Yes, you should fuck Baz. Right now. Then you can go save the world. I'll have dinner waiting when you get home."

That was, sort of, how it went. Elijah fucking Baz was practically a permanently inked portion of his daily morning schedule, though this was the first time Baz had lured him into it with a living room blow job first. As had been the case last night, it was only Elijah who came. In fact, this time Baz fell asleep after, as if he'd come his brains out.

Elijah padded back downstairs and called Pastor, but his secretary said he was in a meeting. When he tried Liz, she texted him to say she was at a thing, and would it be okay if she called him later? Elijah told her yes, but he wasn't sure what to do with himself. He texted Lewis.

Hey. How's it going?

Lewis responded within a minute. *Fine.* There was a pause. *You?*

Food service dickhead came by.

Yeah. Here too. Another pause. *Basically told me it was my fault.*

Asshole. I told him to fuck himself with his appropriate attire.

Wish I could.

Well…I have an idea. But I'm still working out kinks. I want you to talk to Pastor Schulz. But first, you want to come over for dinner tonight?

Can't. Mom's coming. School shopping.

Tomorrow then.

Don't think it's a good idea. I don't want to meet with

anybody right now or rock any boats.

Oh. Before Elijah could think of what to say to that, Lewis texted again.

What did you two do in the hallway? I couldn't hear what Baz said through the door, and now everyone is weird, especially Trace.

Trace was the beet bully, Elijah assumed. *Baz pissed a circle around you, basically. Told people to leave you alone.*

I wish he hadn't. They'll be worse now.

Elijah liked the alternate reality where the throwdown magically fixed everything. It had certainly felt as if it should have. He texted a reply. *Maybe this time it will be different.*

Maybe you've been watching too much Disney.

That comment smacked right across the face, of course, and Elijah stopped texting.

It was nine in the morning. He'd called all the people on his list, Baz was still asleep, and Brian hadn't woken up yet. Mina was busy with Jilly.

Elijah had a cigarette. Then he had another one. Finally, when he acknowledged nobody was going to call him back, including Lewis, he made a pot of coffee, poured a big-assed cup, and took his laptop into the piano practice room to write.

It was slow going. The silence drove him nuts, and the entirety of Spotify felt wrong. Even RuPaul failed him, which never happened. On a weird lark, he tested samples of the *Kiki's Delivery Service* soundtrack, and ended up buying it.

He wrote six thousand words about a freshman getting diddled by his senior student piano instructor over a baby grand to music sounding like it belonged on a cute little Japanese merry-go-round. It was so gloriously fucked up he couldn't stop. He didn't, either, not until he wrote *the end*.

Normally he thought it was gauche to type the words, but this time he did it, because for the first time in a million years, he'd finished something. He'd probably get arrested if anybody found out what he wrote it to, and it was horrible to have spent his poor-me money on music, but he was so glad to have broken through his block, he didn't care.

During a third read-through, the door opened and Baz came in with new coffee and a bowl of something smelling meaty-stewy, making Elijah's stomach yowl. He accepted it with a guttural noise of appreciation and scarfed it.

While Elijah ate, Baz turned his laptop around and peeked at the document. Elijah considered swiping it away, but he was so hungry he couldn't bring himself to stop him.

That, and he wanted to know if it was as good as he felt it was.

It was a circle of hell, watching someone read your work. The only thing keeping Elijah from blurting out, *What did you read? What made you make that face?* was the food he was stuffing in his mouth, which was why when he ran out, he went to the kitchen to refill his bowl and grab a glass of water. He tripped when he saw the time—how the hell was it eight o'clock? What happened to lunch? Why had nobody called him?

A glance at his phone told him people *had* called him. He must have had his headphones on and missed every ring. Liz, Pastor, even Walter. And Baz, and Aaron.

He frowned at Baz as he returned to the practice room. "Why didn't anybody tell me my phone—?"

Baz held up a hand and didn't look away from the screen.

Sullen, Elijah ate, or tried to. He was more full than he thought, so he drank his water and paced behind Baz. He should call Pastor and Liz at least. Except…he wanted to hear what Baz thought of his story. He was terrified, but in a can't-turn-from-the-wreck way. If Baz hated it, Elijah would probably never write another word.

If he thought it was good…he might not write another word either, because what if those were the only words Baz liked?

When Elijah had himself riding the vortex of a well-constructed doubt spiral, Baz closed the laptop and lay on the rug. Grabbing Elijah's ankles, he tugged him over and kissed him on the mouth.

"Baby." Baz sucked under his chin, undid his fly and dove inside. "Fuck, but you have a beautifully dirty mind."

Really? Elijah wanted to ask what specifically had been good, but Baz had claimed his mouth again and put him on his back.

Baz kissed Elijah's body as he peeled his clothes away. "I'd take you…on the piano…" he paused to fuck his tongue in and out of Elijah's belly button,

"…but Aaron would kill me if I broke Fred. I like this story better than the one set in the science lab."

Elijah lifted his hips so Baz could remove his jeans. And then his underwear. "You did?" Wait. "You've read *more* of my stuff?"

"I've read *all* of your stuff."

Elijah wanted to ask about that, but Baz had wandered to his mouth as he jacked their cocks together. By the time Elijah's lips were free, he was breathing hard and begging as he rolled to his stomach, spread his knees and tipped his ass in the air. "Fuck me. *Now.*"

Baz licked up his crack before standing and divesting himself of the rest of his clothes. "We're lucky Aaron and Giles like to fuck in here. There's four different lubes on the bottom shelf of the bookcase."

Aaron. Giles. *Roommates.* Elijah glanced over his shoulder. "The door—"

Baz knelt behind him, pressing a lube-slick finger into Elijah. "Don't worry, baby. I cracked it open."

SATURDAY MORNING BAZ was due to go on delivery rounds with Liz, but even after a hot shower and a bowl of oatmeal, he felt sluggish and achy. He tried to hide it from her when she picked him up, but they didn't make it out of the driveway before she frowned at him. "You're hurting, sweetheart. Why don't you take the day off?"

Baz grimaced around the rim of the Starbucks she'd brought him. "If I took the day off every time I ached, I'd live on my couch."

"Fair enough, but you seem to be having a harder time shaking it today. Can you get in for a massage?"

"Had one yesterday." Baz adjusted the pressure on his hip. "I need to resume hydrotherapy. They had me in it after the shooting, but I quit for the wedding and never restarted." He sighed and rubbed his temple. "I hate going. It's all the way into Saint Paul, and it kills two hours minimum of my day."

Liz tapped her finger on the steering wheel. "I keep meaning to give hydrotherapy a try. A friend of mine was telling me how anyone can use the punch cards, and a therapist gives you a custom plan. She said it's done wonders for her knee. Maybe the two of us could go together. Use the buddy system."

Baz had figured it was idle musing, but it turned out Liz was completely serious. Before they finished for the day, she got him to cough up his therapist's number and asked for permission to schedule them at the same time.

"Sure, but I don't need a therapist." He rubbed his neck. "I have an exercise program on file. I just need to show up and use it."

"Do you have a time you need me to work around?"

Baz didn't. And on Monday morning Liz called to tell him she was picking him up at three and they were going that very day.

He was weirdly nervous about it, so he puttered around the house, looking for something to occupy himself. He thought about seducing Elijah, but his boyfriend was holed up in the corner of the practice room, writing up a storm. Over the weekend Mina had helped him upload a few shorts to online vendors, which had sent Elijah into something of a nervous tailspin. He alternated between chain-smoking out back and huddled over his laptop with Aaron's noise-canceling headphones, endlessly scrolling online sale sites. When asked why he did this, Elijah would say, with excessive consonants and a bulging vein in his forehead, Amazon rank meant nothing, nobody knew what it meant and there was no point in paying attention to it. Yet he refreshed the Gay Erotica page every five minutes, and when Giles unhooked the router to help Brian set up some fancy new hub, Elijah bit their heads off.

Monday he was in a quieter phase, still checking his stats obsessively but with a new document open on the side. Brian had soothed the savage beast by introducing him to a program called Scrivener which apparently did magical book things. At first Elijah complained it was too complicated and he'd stick to MS Word, but Brian had brushed past the bristles and forced Elijah through a few tutorials, and now Elijah looked as if he wanted to weep with joy. He'd murmured something about this being exactly what his fantasy novel needed, then disappeared inside his now-extensive Joe Hisaishi soundtrack collection.

Unwilling to disturb the fragile peace, Baz stayed away.

The rest of the house bustled now—everyone was moved in but Sid, who was staying home to help until just before school started at the end of August. Jilly had a thing for making cookies, and Giles had a thing for eating them. Baz had learned to amuse himself by sitting in the kitchen to watch his housemates weave in and out. Jilly and Mina were thick as thieves, moving like a unit through household chores and huddling together to speak in half-finished sentences as they mocked out possible Salvo songs for the fall. When Giles and Aaron were around, the girls' dynamic changed. They included the boys, but the color of their tone subtly altered. Sometimes, Baz noted, Aaron and Giles got a bit too self-involved and missed cues from their female housemates.

It wasn't anything, though, on how things shifted when Brian was in the room, or rather, how Brian behaved when Mina and Jilly were present. He'd joke with Aaron or Giles, and after their sandwich bonding he was completely easy with Baz, but put one set of XX chromosomes in the room with him, and he turned into a mouse. He wasn't so bad with Mina, but if Jilly came into his space, he either left or became absorbed in something so deeply he might as well have been invisible. Baz didn't think it was conscious—something about *girl* made Brian lose his shit and run. Something about *girl Jilly* had him melting down.

Baz still felt slightly outside the others, and he hoped to hell the sensation eased when Sid returned. For now, however, he had his current status quo and his therapy date with Liz.

The hydrotherapy pool was at Regions Hospital in Saint Paul. Liz parked in the ramp, and they walked together over the crosswalk to get to the therapy unit, where they segregated into their respective locker rooms. Baz undressed and climbed into his swim trunks without excitement, hesitating over donning a T-shirt to hide the worst of his scars. The pool would be full of little old ladies who would want to chat him up, and he wasn't in the mood to navigate around their queries. Remembering his mother's impending public-relations nightmare, he decided he might as well keep practicing and left the shirt in his bag.

He rinsed off in the shower in an effort to keep some of the pool's chlorine from seeping into his skin. When he re-emerged, he was surprised to see a man only about a decade or so older than him at a locker beside his own.

The man met Baz's gaze and smiled. "Hey."

The gaze lingered a moment, taking in Baz's glasses, his scars, but also his damp abs and package outlined by wet trunks. The cruising ended there, but it had happened.

"Hey." Baz returned the favor, and he took his time. The guy wasn't sculpted, but he clearly worked out, and he wasn't difficult to look at. Bulky, but in a way Baz appreciated. Dark hair, roguish face, eyes promising a good time Baz would have considered teasing out, pre-Elijah. The man came with a gold wedding band on his left ring finger, though.

Also a pretty nasty scar on his neck. An old one, but it hinted at the kind of fuckery requiring one to pay occasional visits to a warm water therapy pool.

The man tossed his towel over his shoulder and turned to stick out a hand. "Ed Maurer. You a new patient?"

Baz enjoyed the firm handshake and added a brief daddy fantasy. "Baz Acker. No, just a bad one. Tired of fighting my hip and shoulder."

Ed nodded and rubbed his neck with a grimace. "Yeah, I've tried skipping, and I'm always sorry. Are you a student at the U of M?"

"Saint Timothy." Baz snagged his towel and walked with Ed down the tiled hall to the pool entrance.

"The one to the east, right? What's your major?"

Baz waved vaguely at the air in front of him. "College."

Ed laughed. "I was business management, but I wasn't terribly good at it. Can't work full-time anymore anyway."

Baz glanced at Ed's neck. "What happened?"

"Semi-pro football. Lucky I didn't die or end up paralyzed for life. Weird thing is, I'm better the more I move, so long as it's careful movement. It's a desk that'll kill me." He nodded at Baz's patchwork chest. "You look like you have a better story than a wide receiver's cleat to the shoulder."

"I'm a combo platter. Wrong end of a few assholes with baseball bats several years ago, lunatic religious fanatic with a gun this past March."

Ed's eyes were wide, and he blinked. "Shit—you're *that* kid. I read about you online. Jesus. I'm so sorry. The story made me ill. Please tell me the asshole is in jail."

Gallows humor took over. Baz raised an eyebrow. "Which one?"

"Christ. You old enough for me to buy you a drink after the pool?" When Baz's gaze shifted to Ed's ring, the man laughed and held up his hands. "Not that kind of drink. I got plenty of man at home, no offense."

They were in the pool area now. Liz was already in the water with her therapist, chatting amiably. Baz waded in via the stairs, pleased Ed followed. It would be nice to have a Y-chromosome to talk to. "I could probably work you in for a drink date, but I need to talk with my ride." He nodded to Liz.

"You do that. If not today, I'll catch you next time."

They kept pace with each other as they walked laps in the shallow end. Ed, it turned out, was married to some ballet dancer who used to be famous but now taught dance to underprivileged kids in the Saint Paul area. "I help him and work at the Halcyon Center part-time. Working with kids, mostly, though every now and again Laurie makes me put on a suit and shake hands with people with money."

"Sounds a lot better than sitting behind a desk."

"It is. Wish it paid better, but guess you can't have it all." Ed shifted the float weights he was pushing and frowned at Baz. "Is it okay to ask you about the shooting thing? I don't want to pry."

"I'd rather talk about the shooting thing than the baseball-bat thing, so yeah, knock yourself out."

"How did it happen? I never understood from the articles. He was after his own kid, right? But you got in the way?"

Baz shrugged and focused on moving his plastic

paddles through the water. "The Princes are pretty grim people. Wanted to correct the wrongs of America through torturing their son. He outwitted them, and when they found out, they were pissed. Nobody quite saw the gun coming, though."

"Except you did. You jumped in front of it."

Baz tried to remember the moment, but it was as hot and jumbled as it always was. "Maybe I did on some level. It felt...familiar. I'd seen that kind of rage on someone's face before. The determination to destroy. I guess I've always been a bit more ready to believe in things jumping out of bushes since the...first time."

"Is the kid okay?"

Baz thought about Elijah safe in the White House, huddled over his laptop, swearing at Amazon stats. "Yeah. He's fine."

They switched to lighter topics. Ed told Baz about his former football career and confessed affection for Britney Spears. He apparently also had a passion for ballroom dancing, something he enjoyed doing with his husband. Baz told Ed about being in the Ambassadors, and he talked about Liz's baked-goods charity business and how much he enjoyed working with her. "I like doing something I know is actually bringing about some good. I mean, I get delivering cookies for resale isn't directly stopping human trafficking or anything."

"It counts plenty because in addition to raising awareness you're bringing in cash. Trust me, I know firsthand how vital funding is to charitable organizations. Halcyon Center is always a breath away from closing unless we wring out all the grants and show up at every grand gala ball to beg money off the rich people. Of course, I spend the whole time calculating how much more they could have donated without the catering bill, but my husband tells me to hush and enjoy my rubber chicken."

"The thing is, my family has a lot of money. I don't need to get a degree to get a job. I could make myself the spokesperson of about any cause, but I don't know where to put my passion. I enjoy working with human trafficking because of Liz. But I don't want to pick something at random because I'm bored. I don't want to be *that* rich asshole."

"Having rubbed elbows with great herds of rich assholes, I'm pretty confident you're not one. And to get it out of the way—yeah, I want to recruit you into *my* charity because it would suit my purposes. But the thing is, you're right. You need to have a passion for it because volunteering can be pretty grisly work. It eats at weird corners of your soul. So my question is, what makes your blood pump? If you could develop a superpower, what evil in the world would you try to right?"

It was the kind of question Baz had posed to himself a thousand times after his conversations with Liz, but something about the way Ed delivered it flattened the usual mental obstacles. The conversation about the shooting rang in his head, the showdown with Lejla's lunchroom bully echoed around it, and the whole business was laced with the memory of how sometimes Baz saw Elijah out of the corner of his eye, and his boyfriend looked just like he did that night in the alley, hard and terrified and alone.

"LGBT kids." He clicked the edges of his plastic paddles together, letting the frustration spill out of him. "The ones who get kicked out for being gay or trans, or the ones afraid if they slip up they'll get sent into the cold. The ones who do tricks to find a bed. The ones who get HIV and are married to the med regimen before they're legal adults. The ones who do porn because it seems like a ticket out, not because they get off on fucking for cash. The ones who don't leave home but need help because there's no road map for sorting out your gender identity. Who don't know what their rights are. The ones who need help and don't have somebody to jump in front of the bullet for them. The ones right here in the Cities, because I know for a damn fact we're swimming in them."

He felt embarrassed at how Hallmark his speech had gotten, but when he glanced at Ed, he didn't see derision or so much as the hint of an eye roll. If anything, Ed seemed moved. A little excited too, but when he replied, his tone was casual.

"Kid, I'm not buying you a drink. I'm getting your dinner. We have a lot to talk about."

Baz found he was looking forward to it. He exchanged numbers with Ed before they parted ways in the locker room after their session, in addition to setting up a few more therapy times when Ed would also be there. Baz waved his new friend goodbye, feeling not only good but hopeful as he waited for Liz to finish in the locker room.

In the middle of a Fruit Ninja marathon, his phone rang. It was Stephan.

"Hello, Sebastian. Everything going well, I trust?"

"Yeah. Pretty good, actually. What's up?"

"Giselle asked me to give you a five-hour warning. The first announcement comes tonight."

Baz's good feelings cracked and shattered quietly around him. "Thanks for letting me know."

"There's a great deal we'll need you to do. We'll also have a list of things you *shouldn't* do. We'll refresh your media training, evaluate your image. But all that comes later. For now, stand by."

"Okay." Baz hated this already.

"We'll keep in touch," Stephan promised. Then he was gone.

Chapter Seventeen

RIGHT WHEN ELIJAH was about to concede he'd fucked up their friendship before it began, Lewis called and invited Elijah to lunch.

Elijah jumped at the chance. At Lewis's suggestion, they met at a noodle bar in Campustown, and Lewis greeted Elijah with a shy hug. Despite Elijah's protestations, he insisted on buying both their meals. "I wanted to thank you. For helping me in the cafeteria, for the clothes, but mostly for nudging Pastor Schulz in my direction."

Elijah had noticed right off Lewis was wearing almost entirely things he'd bought, tipping harder toward girl than any other time Elijah had seen him. "Does this mean you met with Pastor? Isn't he great? You need to meet his wife too."

"I did. Pastor called me to check up after the beet incident, and somehow I ended up having dinner at his house. I've gone a lot, in fact." The flush of his cheeks consumed his face and part of his neck, and the fingers twirling his noodles onto his fork trembled. "We're...doing counseling. About Lejla. About how I *am* Lejla."

"That's *fantastic*." Elijah paused when Lewis didn't

return his smile. "Or…not?"

Lewis hunched over the noodle bowl. "I'm nervous. I mean—I can't transition fully yet. It's not simple at all, and I'm not talking about people making fun of me in the cafeteria. There are all these stupid legal things, and it's all fucked up because I can't legally change anything until I've gone through a period of living as Lejla even though all my documents and things will still say I'm male. We have to change my registration forms. I'd have to get a single, or live off-campus."

"You'd *have* to?"

"Well—I don't know what the legal angles are exactly, but I'd *need* to, let's put it that way. For me as much as anyone else. But it's going to cost more no matter what I do. So if—" He stopped, drew a breath and continued. "*When* I transition, it all has to happen at once. Which means I can't right now. Except I have to do *something*."

He hunched his shoulders. "It sounds stupid, but the living arrangements are the thing driving me the most crazy. I don't want to live on my own, but I don't see how a roommate I didn't choose would work out right now. I hated having a roommate last year, but being all by myself makes me feel like my skin is crawling. Plus I can't afford a single, even if I could get one. Except I'd rather do that and get a second job or pretty much anything than keep living as a guy, though, with no hope of ever living as who I truly am. This is what talking to Pastor cleared up—how this has hurt me. That and when you bought me all those clothes. I kept all of them. Every morning I went to war with Lejla over wearing them, battles I didn't want to fight anyway."

Elijah winced. "Sorry."

"No. Not sorry. It's not as if they were magical clothes making me suddenly want to live as a woman. It was someone else giving them to me. Somehow those clothes became the point where I couldn't lie to myself anymore, couldn't put it off any longer." His hands shook until he closed them into fists, and his gaze was laser-fixed on his barely touched food. "I don't think I can be out full-time, though. Not on campus. People will be horrible. I know my rights, thanks to Pastor, and how to get help—campus escorts, and so on. But it's going to be awful no matter what."

"We'll help you." *With more than a buddy system.* Elijah itched to send a text, or blurt out the offer he was dying to make about housing, but he had to check with the others first. Because holy crap, would that suck to invite Lejla to live at the White House and then find out it wasn't possible. Except there was a space available, and if people would be willing to shift a little bit...

Lewis glanced up with a shy smile. "I haven't made up my mind yet for sure this is what I'm doing, and I don't know the particulars of how it would shake out, but I know I probably will make this leap soon, because of you. Thank you. I'm sorry I was such a freak-out jerk. I didn't mean to ignore you. I was trying to sort myself out."

"It's a big thing. You get to react however you need to." Elijah twirled a forkful of noodle. "Where do your parents fit into this?"

Lewis looked sick. "I'm telling them next weekend. Whenever I transition, I'm telling them it's coming. Pastor and Liz are helping. We're doing it at their house. Liz is making dinner."

Elijah put his fork down. "Listen—no matter what happens, I'm here. I don't care if they disown you. I'll help. Trust me on this. Okay?"

"They won't disown me. They'll be angry, or scared, or disappointed."

They sat in awkward silence a few seconds until Elijah cleared his throat and nodded at the boxes for leftovers by the soda machine. "What do you say we box this up and walk instead? I'm not really hungry, and you don't seem to be either."

They buttoned up their food and began the walk to campus. They lit up twin cigarettes almost before the door closed behind them.

"I have to give this up if I start hormone-replacement therapy." Lewis grimaced. "It won't be for a while no matter what, because I have to see a psychologist first. Pastor did some research. They're likely going to say I have to do RLE—real-life experience—for at least three months. Which doesn't seem fair. They want me to go bigger, harder, so people can make fun of me for looking like a man but dressing as a woman? Though I guess this means I get to smoke a little longer. Because once I start getting injections, cancer sticks are gone. For good. Right when I'll be the most stressed and wanting a fix. But the risks are crazy huge to smoke and get HRT."

Elijah considered his cigarette a moment before ashing it out. "I'll quit with you, when it's time."

Lewis shoved Elijah lightly. "Get out. That's insane. You will not."

"It's not insane. I should quit anyway. I only re-started last winter when my parents were driving me out of my mind. I have shit to live for now. I'm not going through all this to die of cancer. Besides, it's something I can do to support you."

Lewis bumped him again, a shy shoulder nudge. "You do plenty."

They parted ways at the edge of campus because Lewis had to get ready for a shift and Elijah wanted to buzz back to the White House to engage his plan.

Nobody was there, though. He poked around online, watched his erotic shorts not selling worth a fucking damn, hated himself for ever publishing anything, and surfed Twitter.

His feed was still full of news about the US Attor-ney General resigning, but now he saw a familiar name appearing in those same 140-character news summaries. *Senator Barnett rumored nominee for Attorney General.* Elijah's eyebrows raised as he clicked through and saw yes, it was Baz's uncle. Huh. Boy, that was weird, to have such a short a degree of separation from someone so newsworthy. He figured it had to be a rumor, since Baz never said anything—but then, Baz rarely shared much about his family.

It sure sounded like Barnett was who everyone thought would get the job. The Republicans were all in a lather, though they seemed to be torn between outrage over such a liberal AG and the potential vacancy of an Illinois Senate seat. He wondered how that worked before reading on to learn the governor appointed someone. Like good old Blagojevich and Obama, except hopefully nobody would go to prison for trying to sell the seat this time.

One of the sites, a super-lefty rag, reported Barnett's sister would be appointed to the Senate seat if Barnett got the AG nom. How many sisters did the guy have? No way that could be Baz's mom, right?

Elijah wrote the idea off as nutty and continued down his Google rabbit hole. He quickly exhausted news about Baz's uncle. On a whim, he Googled Baz, nervous about what he'd find, but the results were surprisingly thin. The news was all recent—precious little about the accident when he was sixteen, which made sense. He'd been a minor, and probably they went out of their way to keep things buried.

Most of it was stuff Elijah already knew. He found a few photos of Baz with his mom at charity events, less with his dad. A shot popped up from ICCA quarterfinals where somebody had captured Baz bent over a mic like a rock star. Elijah felt guilty there were no follow-ups of him winning in New York City because the Ambassadors had to scratch when Baz got shot.

Elijah saw a couple articles about the shooting in March, which he told himself he shouldn't read but couldn't seem to stop himself. Some stuff about Baz there, but nothing too deep. Nearly nothing about Elijah, which in hindsight was pretty weird. Why hadn't the reporters hunted him down? Not that he wished they would have, but it was still strange to have escaped unscathed.

Elijah's parents, however, got quite a bit of ink. Lots of commentary about religious extremism, some talk about gun control, but it seemed to degenerate into the same tired argument on both sides. An article about Pastor Schulz talked about how the college intended to take care of its students at a difficult time, how this was an opportunity for Saint Timothy to follow its mission. This dovetailed into the stuff Elijah knew about, including Walter's fund.

He unearthed more articles about the shooting, though—new ones. From a week ago. Two weird right-wing blogs and some Christian newswire thing that seemed right up Elijah's parents' street. They talked about how manipulative Elijah was to deceive his parents and trick them into a year of college education and other financial support. They acknowledged attempted murder was wrong, but they pretty much came out and said it was an understandable impulse, given how twisted in sin Elijah's soul was.

Elijah stared at the articles a long time, rereading them, letting the sentiment they expressed squirm in his belly.

Abruptly, he shut the laptop. After pacing around the house a few minutes, he grabbed a fresh pack of cigarettes and chain-smoked his way to campus, desperate to connect with someone. Anyone. Right now.

He started at the music building, and he hit the jackpot. Mina, Jilly, Aaron, Giles, even Baz—they were all in an empty classroom, strategizing how they were going to run Salvo and Ambassador auditions at the end of August, but Baz stepped into the hall to talk to him.

He gave Elijah a lingering kiss on his cheek along with a not-at-all-subtle grope of his ass. "What's up, hon?" When Baz got a better look at Elijah's face, he sobered. "What's wrong?"

Now that he stood in front of Baz, Elijah felt foolish for letting online garbage get to him. "I'm sorry to bother you. I was all fired up, and I wanted to ask right away." He gave a quick summary about Lejla's potential come-out, and outlined the housing difficulty. "I wanted to know who to talk to about the extra spot in the White House. I know Brian is in the other big room as a single because I'm not in it and Sid is in the actual single, but would they share, do you think? Would the management company rent to Lejla and let her have the single? What kind of application is it? Can we convince them? How much would it cost?"

Baz's expression got hard to read as he rubbed his jaw. Elijah's heart sank, and he got ready to hear *no way in hell they'd rent to her*. Which was why he was so unprepared when Baz said, "You talk to me, the rent is flexible, and she just applied. If she wants the space, it's hers."

Elijah opened and shut his mouth a few times. "How are you in charge of it?"

"Because my family owns the White House. I get to decide everything."

Elijah stared at him. "Shut up."

"Mom likes control. She bought it as soon as I showed interest in moving in." He grimaced. "Sorry."

Elijah stared at him, head spinning as it all clicked into place.

Yes, it *had* been easy to get into the White House, hadn't it? All his friends were there too. Meanwhile, Elijah's fund kept growing and growing, from anonymous donors...

"How much of my Poor Elijah fund is your money?"

Baz looked distinctly awkward. "It's not out of pity. We give to causes all the time. I was glad it was somebody I knew for once." Even with the glasses, there was no hiding his wince. "Don't be mad."

A month ago, Elijah would have been. It made him nervous and unsure right now, though he couldn't say why exactly. Not because he felt like he owed Baz, which surprised him. Being managed wasn't his favorite thing, though at this point he'd grown a callus over that sore point, because *life* with Baz was being managed. It was somewhat creepy, he supposed, that Baz hadn't told him.

Except Elijah knew now why Baz did it. Because he had a thing about keeping people around. Baz directed Elijah's life like a symphony because he cared.

This fact had stopped making Elijah angry, but it sure as fuck still terrified him.

Baz watched Elijah carefully. "Something else is bothering you."

Elijah couldn't very well say he was weirded out that Baz cared about him. He forced a smile. "Nothing worth talking about. But hey, I read your uncle might be the Attorney General? How cool is *that*?"

Apparently not cool at all, as Baz didn't return the smile. In fact, he looked a bit green. "Did it say anything else?"

The article about Senator Barnett's sister flashed in Elijah's memory. *Holy fucking shit, what if that's true too?*

Before he could say anything, though, Giles leaned out the door. "Baz, could you come look at this arrangement and tell us if we're heading in the right direction?"

Baz nodded and brushed Elijah's cheek with his thumb. "We'll talk later. Tell Lejla she's got a spot whenever she wants it. Lewis too. Sid won't care about giving up his single."

Baz disappeared into the room. Elijah stared at the closed door, thoughts rattling around like grenades in his brain.

Then he shook them off, pulled out his phone and sent a text to Lewis. *Give me a call when you're off work. I have a proposition for you.*

WHILE THE REST of the White House hugged a shell-shocked Lewis as Elijah delivered the news of who their newest resident would be, Baz leaned against the kitchen counter and scoured the internet for leaks about his mother.

Mostly the Beltway media circle-jerked over whether or not Paul Barnett would get confirmed, and conservatives trotted out their usual scree about how Paul Barnett was more liberal elite than the Kennedys. Baz dug into a few deeply partisan sites, where he found a lefty blog bragging about inside intel saying Gloria Barnett Acker was on the short list for Senate replacements, and a right-wing one painting his mom as out of touch and snobby and dumber than a box of rocks all in the same breath. That was all, though the teasers on *The Maddow Blog* hinted Rachel was about to spill all the beans. Baz had an email from Giselle too, with five attachment files full of media training PDFs. Pursing his lips, he closed the mail app.

He put his phone away and did his best to engage in the happy moment in front of him. Having come straight over from the cafeteria, their new resident was dressed firmly as Lewis, but Baz didn't want to make assumptions on who it was wiping away happy tears while perched delicately on a kitchen stool. He wasn't the only one wondering, it turned out, and Mina broke the ice by coming out and asking, "Should we call you Lejla or Lewis? How do you want us to refer to you?"

"I don't know. Lewis for now, but not…not for long. I want to be Lejla, but it hurts to be her without *being* her, if it makes sense. I compartmentalize her like a separate self, though that's actually wrong. She *is* me. But I'm still working on accepting that and being comfortable allowing others to address me that way."

"Keep us posted, okay?" This came from Giles, lacing his fingers around Aaron's on the tabletop. "We want you to feel comfortable."

"When will you move in?" Aaron asked.

Lewis blushed and tugged at his ear. "I—I don't know. When can I? I mean—I haven't talked to my parents about rent, and Elijah didn't say how much it was."

"You can move in tonight, if you want," Baz said. "Have your parents talk to me about rent, but it's not going to be an issue."

Lewis began weeping again. Giles and Mina exchanged glances, then began a campaign to haul ass across campus that exact second and move their new resident in immediately. When this idea got some traction, Baz fished out the Tesla keys and tossed them to Aaron.

"Go ahead and get started. The football team should still be at practice, so you've got a clear shot. If you take my car and Giles's both, you might get all of it in one trip. We can move the spare bed from our room." Another news alert flashed on his phone's home screen, and a wave of weariness hit Baz in the gut. He caught Elijah's eye. "Hey, babe, can I talk to you?"

Elijah went still. "Is everything okay?"

"Yeah, I—" He rubbed his jaw and stifled a sigh.

Aaron came to the rescue, herding the others out, leaving the two of them alone. Elijah leaned against the fridge with his arms folded nervously over his chest once they left.

Baz flattened his lips. "Don't look at me like that. I want to tell you something, okay?"

Elijah relaxed, but not much. "Sorry. It's been a weird day."

"Yeah, well." Baz fished his laptop out of a sea of

junk mail on the table and flipped it open to Google News. The article about his uncle for AG was at the top of the feed. "I need to talk to you about this."

Elijah glanced at him. "I take it you knew this was coming?"

Baz nodded. "I've known for a while but wasn't allowed to tell anyone. Not even Marius or Damien, not you."

"It's not so bad, right? It's not like he's President."

Baz pulled up one of the lefty blogs about his mom. "No. But she's about to be a senator. They'll dig into all aspects of her life." He swallowed and spit the rest of it out. "They'll investigate me, and everyone associated with me."

He waited to see how Elijah would react. He wasn't sure what he expected, but what he got was Elijah's face shuttering as he fixated on a dent in the tabletop. "So probably it's not good for you to have controversial people around you right now."

Baz frowned. "No, the controversy will bloom up around me naturally. Why do you say that, though?"

Elijah spun the computer closer to him, typed in his name. After clicking a link, he turned the computer to Baz. "I found this earlier today."

Baz read the bullshit about Elijah being a manipulative evil elf with bile in his throat. His nostrils flared, and he curled his fingers on the table edge. "What a bunch of fuckers. Don't listen to it, Elijah. They're a bag of skinny, withered dicks."

"Yeah, well, there are quite a few bags of dicks repeating this same shit. Like they all got together and decided to paint me as the kind of jerk who deserves to be shot." He hunched into himself, reverting to the sour Elijah Baz had found huddling at the railing at Walter's wedding. "I won't be offended if you have to distance from me while this blows over. I get how it goes."

Baz pulled a chair close and took Elijah's hand. "I don't want to be distant from you. That's not why I brought this up. I wanted you to know, is all. We might have to dodge reporters. I didn't want you to be surprised."

Elijah remained slouched, and if Baz didn't have such a tight hold on his hand, he'd have pulled it away. "Fine."

It wasn't fine, but Baz didn't know how to make it better.

Elijah jerked his head at the door. "We should go get the room ready."

They worked in relative silence, their greatest conversation happening when they maneuvered the spare bed from Baz's room down the stairs, or at least the parts of it Baz could handle. The others helped with the heavy mattress once they were back, and soon the house was full of happy chatter as Jilly and Mina plotted a room makeover and Brian busied himself with connecting Lewis's computer to the house system. Aaron and Giles gave their new guest a tour of the kitchen and other public areas, encouraging Lewis to make himself at home.

Baz and Elijah stood on the fringes, present but absent all the same. It occurred to Baz he should have the conversation with the others he'd had with Elijah, a warning of what might well be coming.

All he wanted, though, was to find the way to wipe the hurt and isolation off Elijah's face. Something he had absolutely no idea how to do.

Chapter Eighteen

FOR THE FIRST few days after Lewis moved in, everything continued as it had been, this time with Lewis decorating the couch and the kitchen table when he wasn't working at food service. He dressed in either male clothing or decidedly ambiguous clothing exclusively, but Elijah noticed his housemates took pains to refrain from using pronouns and stumbled over whether to reference Lewis or Lejla.

Elijah had a hard time balancing Googling himself with the quiet, steady process of Lejla's coming out. He noticed Baz seemed screen-obsessed too, though they never discussed their findings. Baz disappeared several times with a severe-looking blonde woman in a navy suit, and when he returned, he always had a headache. Elijah assumed Baz Googled Elijah as much as Elijah Googled Baz, which meant Baz knew the drumbeat of conservative blogs eager to cast Elijah as some kind of evil gay mastermind was steadily growing, and Elijah knew the neighboring blogosphere was digging deeper and deeper into Gloria Barnett Acker's closet, hoping to find pay dirt.

They never discussed Elijah's offer to fade into the background and take potential heat off Baz and his family, but as the articles about Elijah's machinations grew longer and more intricate in their descriptions of his wickedness, Elijah worried he should bring it up in case Baz was about to do it first.

Then one day they were both distracted from their private worries. At breakfast Elijah paused his obsessive Googling to tell Mina for the millionth time he truly, completely, utterly did not want to be in the Saint Timothy Chorale and had no plans to try out when the door to the kitchen opened...and Lejla walked in.

As much as the first few days in residence had been gender male or gender ambiguous, this person was so clearly *Lejla, female* the vision took Elijah's breath away. She wore a pretty sundress, dainty white ballet flats, a cardigan, and had a bow in her hair—all things he'd bought that day he'd exploded in Target. She lingered in the doorway, a little hunched, a lot unsure, and the rest of the house stilled, waiting.

Eventually she spoke. "I'm Lejla today."

She seemed terrified—defiant, somewhat, but mostly dazed as if she'd announced she was jumping off the top of the chapel bell tower without a bungee cord.

Mina rose first, embracing Lejla and murmuring quiet congratulations. Jilly joined in, and Aaron and Giles, and Brian. Elijah hovered to the side, unsure of how to hug it out until Mina pulled him into the thick of it.

Baz, who remained perched against the sink, slow clapped. "I think this calls for a celebration. How do you want to mark the occasion, Lejla?"

She was free of her hugging housemates now, her

face flushed. "I'm not—this isn't a full thing. I'm trying it out for today, and only in the house. Sorry if that's ungrateful."

"Not at all. But I *meant* something here. For you, and for us to share with you." Baz's smile made Elijah shiver. "I was thinking about pizza, beer, and a Studio Ghibli marathon. Unless you're busy this weekend?"

Lejla grinned. "I'm not. I asked for the weekend off work so I could get ready to tell my parents on Sunday, when they come. I have an appointment with Pastor at his house this morning, and then I'm free."

Baz winked as he pushed off the counter. "I'll make the appropriate preparations."

Elijah hadn't realized how seriously Baz considered *appropriate preparations* until he got roped into assisting. "We need decorations for a movie marathon?" Elijah asked as they pulled up to a party store.

"No, we need decorations for Lejla. Brian's printing out some posters while Aaron and Giles do some creative cutouts, but we're bringing the balloons and streamers and noisemakers. And plates and cups, and a helium tank to blow up the balloons."

"I'm assuming there isn't a section for *congratulations on your gender transition*."

"Like that's going to stop us."

They bought a boatload of decorations, including a few generic movie-themed items. Baz planned to pull a banquet table out of storage and set up a concessions area in the back of the room—he already had a movie-theater-grade popcorn maker. He purchased popcorn boxes, cups, and a few film reel and clapboard props he decreed were within the acceptable boundaries of good taste. They went to the grocery store and stocked up on candy, popcorn, oil, nachos, soda, and beer. He also ordered a stupid number of pies from the east side Pizza Lucé to be delivered later in the evening.

"I had no idea you had this queening-out party-planner side," Elijah said as he aimed the Tesla for home.

"You never heard about my White House parties? I know you never came to them, but surely you heard about them."

"I did, but I wrote it off as more choir insanity."

"Mmm." Baz trailed a finger along Elijah's arm. "So has Mina convinced you to join choir yet?"

Elijah winced. "Not you too."

"I'm just saying, I need a new choir roommate for tours."

"You have me as a roommate right now in the comfort of your own home."

"I suppose I could ask Aaron."

The implication being, of course, he and *Aaron* would fuck. Elijah was unmoved. "Yeah, well, that will make you appreciate me more when you come home because I'd put all my *poor Elijah* money on me being kinkier than he is."

"True." He ran his fingers up Elijah's arm, teasing the hair behind his ear. "It'd be fun to be in choir with you, is all."

Elijah nudged the touch away as he pulled into the driveway. "How about we focus on planning this party."

The others had the living room blacked out when they arrived, and the furniture arranged around the television. Mina and Jilly took over setting up the concessions table, and Aaron and Giles added the decorations and streamers to the pile of anime cutouts. Lejla seemed taken aback by it all at first when she returned from her therapy appointment, but she blushed when everyone clapped and cheered. When she saw the *Welcome Home, Lejla* sign, she began to cry.

"None of that." Baz put an arm around her and led her to the open DVD cupboard. "This is your party. Give me an idea of what you want to watch, and you can get yourself a plate of food and something to drink."

Looking through the cabinet, all her protestations fell away. She shrieked several times—apparently Baz had three or four versions of each movie, always including the Japanese Blu-ray. There were more titles there than Elijah knew existed—if they watched them all, they'd be at it twenty-four/seven well into the next week.

After fifteen minutes of passionate debate, Lejla and Baz decided to start with the English dubs of what they called the "standard canon". First up was *My Neighbor Totoro*, followed by *Princess Mononoke*, *Castle in the Sky*, *Howl's Moving Castle*, and *Spirited Away*. Those were pretty much the movies Elijah had seen, except for *Totoro*, which he'd heard of but couldn't track down. It was good—cute, very Miyazaki, and the music was all Joe Hisaishi, so it was great. The other films were familiar, but it had been a while since he'd seen *Princess*

Mononoke and *Castle in the Sky.*

Howl's Moving Castle naturally resonated in a way it never had before because now Howl was firmly Baz, the handsome, charming boy wizard who didn't want anyone to see how tender-hearted and vulnerable he was. Elijah was Sophie, a self-depreciating young woman enchanted to live as an old woman, where she became oddly much freer. When Sophie released Howl from his curse, Baz's arm around Elijah's shoulder tightened, and when their doppelgängers kissed during the closing credits, Baz made quiet love to Elijah's neck.

Spirited Away got to Elijah the way it always did. They'd had a copy in the homeless shelter where he crashed sometimes, and he'd gotten himself through some dark nights pretending he had a home to go to and all he had to do was get his name back and defeat Yubaba. His own fantasy novel had begun as a kind of fan fiction of the story, except his lead was a young gay man whose parents sold him to the witch. And yeah, the lead had sex with his version of Haku the dragon boy.

The pizza had arrived during *Howl's Moving Castle*, and by the time *Spirited Away* finished, everyone declared themselves stuffed.

"It's only nine." Baz nudged Lejla. "I'll keep watching, if you're game."

Elijah was on a bit of Ghibli overload, but though Jilly, Mina, and Brian bowed out, Elijah, Aaron, and Giles remained. He'd admit he dozed as Baz and Lejla got into some seriously deep cuts—Elijah napped through *Porco Rosso* and *Whisper of the Heart*. He was about to give in and go to bed when Lejla went up with Baz to switch the movie and gasped.

"You have *Black Butler*! Oh my *God*."

Baz grinned at her. "I'm game if you are."

"What's *Black Butler*?" Giles asked before Elijah could. Baz and Lejla regarded Giles with something between exasperation and pity.

"An anime adaptation TV series of a Japanese manga." Baz turned to Lejla. "English dub, or subtitles?"

"Sebastian's English dub is so fucking sexy, but they fuck with the translation too much. Has to be Japanese with subtitles."

Elijah raised an eyebrow. "Sebastian?"

"Yes. The demonic, kick-ass butler is named Sebastian Michaelis." Baz's smile made Elijah want to go upstairs and get naked. "Want to see?"

"Sure," Giles said, arm around a lightly snoring Aaron.

They ended up watching the first episode in both English dub and Japanese with subtitles. Sebastian was sexy evil, and his cultured British voice did nasty things to Elijah's insides and made him yearn to turn off the Blu-ray and go write fan fiction. *That* was the fuck-me guy chewing on his glove in the tailcoat on Baz's shelf. But when they watched the Japanese language version, Elijah noticed the subtitles had nuance the dub didn't, and soon they switched to the Japanese episodes only.

It was a seriously fucked-up show. The premise was a young boy, who'd been about to be sacrificed in some occult ritual, calling out to a demon and entering a pact to surrender his soul if the demon first rescued him then avenged the murder of his parents. When this mission was achieved, the demon could eat his soul. Somehow this meant the boy, Ciel, lost his right eye to some weird pentagram thing and had to wear an eyepatch. The demon, meanwhile, became Sebastian Michaelis, Ciel's butler, and took a ridiculous amount of pride in being fussy British and carrying out Ciel's orders. Usually this involved dismembering people with forks and knives which he stashed in his pockets and whipped out like claws fanning from his fingers.

At first Elijah thought he was writing in his own gay subtext, but pretty quickly he understood he was all but handed the pen and paper to slash Ciel and Sebastian, Sebastian and Grell (a grim reaper who fancied Sebastian) and pretty much anybody else he cared to. The "boy" was technically twelve, but he read as twenty-something. The show writers had a thing for putting him in drag, and during the scene where Sebastian helped Ciel into a corset, it was basically a panel out of yaoi. The lyrics to the opening credits kept talking about kisses and love and moonlight final nights, and they never missed a chance to pose Sebastian as sex on a stick.

When they finally went to bed at three in the morning, Elijah's body was stuffed with junk food and his brain with Japanese movies and television. While Baz took out his contacts, Elijah lay spread-eagled on the bed in pajama pants, staring at the ceiling while soundtracks and images exploded in his mind's eye. They only dimmed a little when Baz leaned over him, eyes naked in the red glow of the room.

Baz trailed fingers down Elijah's neck, and Elijah's dick stirred easily to life. During the movies he'd felt like he couldn't keep up with Baz and Lejla's anime intensity, but now Elijah had a nearly naked Baz in front of him, and mostly he was thinking about sex. He stared at the divot in Baz's clavicle, on the left side, just above an angry red scar. "*Black Butler* is pretty trippy."

"I thought you might enjoy it. I have all the manga, but there's some great art and cosplay online, and fan fiction."

Yeah, Elijah would be finding it directly. For now *his* Sebastian kissed his neck, and Elijah wrapped his body around Baz's, encouraging him to take what he wanted, which became Elijah kneeling and bent over a pillow, gasping out his name as Baz drove into him from behind. They spooned together after, Elijah in front, and Baz whispered in his ear, "Let me know if you want to have a little *Black Butler* role-play."

The comment fueled some steamy, fucked-up dreams where Sebastian Michaelis made love to Howl Pendragon, usually with Elijah in the middle of their sandwich.

He slept in the next morning, and when he came downstairs, he found Lejla and Baz watching *From Up on Poppy Hill*. They put in *Ponyo* when Jilly and Mina wandered in with their breakfast, and *Nausicaä of the Valley of the Wind* after that. Elijah elected to do a few loads of his and Baz's laundry while they watched *The Cat Returns*, but when they resumed their *Black Butler* screening, Elijah sat on the floor between Baz's legs, hiding an erection under his pillow while Baz teased his neck with fingers and occasionally his lips.

In the late afternoon they stopped, as Lejla's parents had arrived.

The Abrahamsens weren't quite as patently awesome as Giles's family, but they weren't Elijah's or Aaron's, either. Lejla had fallen back to not quite Lewis but definitely not the full-on *girl* she'd been all weekend. Her parents didn't seem terribly surprised, but they clearly sensed something was up. Lejla waved over her shoulder as she walked to their car so they could go to Pastor's house.

Everyone mingled in the kitchen for a few minutes, nervous for Lejla but with no real way to help her. Mina declared she and Jilly would take turns with Aaron and Giles, hanging out in the kitchen for when she came home. Elijah was about to put himself on the rotation when Baz led him out of the room, toward the stairs. "I have something to show you in our room."

The *something* was the suit Elijah had worn to Walter and Kelly's wedding, minus shoes, socks, and tie. Three lengths of three-inch-wide black silk lay innocently beside the suit, and unlit candles dotted the room.

Baz came up behind Elijah, wrapping arms around his waist as he nibbled on Elijah's neck. "Would my lord like assistance getting dressed?"

The British accent and silky tone made Elijah instantly hard. He shut his eyes and reached over his shoulder to catch hold of Baz's hair. "Now? You want to play demon and earl *now*?"

Baz kept teasing Elijah's neck, moving his hand to brazenly cup Elijah's erection. "Lejla won't be home for hours. Besides, you were up late. You could use a nap."

Elijah's cock happily filled Baz's hand, but his gaze kept straying to the silk ties. "How kinky is this going to get?"

"As kinky as you want." Baz drew on Elijah's earlobe with his teeth. "Might I suggest, master, you allow me to blindfold you whilst I prepare the chamber?"

Elijah tugged on Baz's hair. "There are three ties. So one is the blindfold? What are the other two for?"

Baz chuckled and nipped Elijah's ear. "Come now, my lord. Surely you have imagination enough to figure that out."

ELIJAH SAT ON the bed, arms spread wide, his wrists tied in loose silk knots against the headboard. Behind the wide, Baz-scented third silk tie, he kept his eyes closed as he listened to Baz putter about the bedroom. In the distance he occasionally heard their housemates, who he hoped to God had no idea Elijah and Baz were playing kinky anime role-play in their room.

Barefoot, his dress shirt half-undone, his dick in a state of permanent semi-arousal inside his trousers, Elijah's world was nothing but darkness and tension as he waited to see what insanity Baz was about to lead them into.

When gloved fingers stroked his cheek, he jumped, but when Baz sat on the edge of the bed, Elijah couldn't help leaning into that touch.

"There, there, young master." Baz still used the sexy British voice, and it made Elijah shiver. "I've dispatched your attackers as requested." He clucked his tongue and ran those gloved fingers across the open vee of Elijah's shirt. "You seem to have become somewhat compromised. I fear you've been given a powerful aphrodisiac and are no longer fit to travel."

Elijah felt ridiculous. He wasn't sure what he was supposed to say—Baz had been vague on a script, which was just as well, as Elijah would have ruined any attempts to follow it. Unwilling to spoil the moment, he held still and waited, until Baz's wandering hands made it clear they would wander near Elijah's crotch but not onto it. Elijah tipped his head back and groaned when his efforts to push into Baz's grip failed. "Stop teasing."

"I'm afraid there's no joke about this, my lord. The drug they gave you is quite powerful. You must ride it out as long as possible—if you give in to your carnal desires too soon, the drug will kill you." Gloved fingers skated over Elijah's nipples. "I cannot allow you to break our contract, so I must guide you through these treacherous waters."

The only thing treacherous was the way Baz kept tormenting Elijah without leading him to so much as the same zip code as relief. Elijah arched as Baz lightly pinched a nipple. "Stop." He tugged at his wrists. "Untie me, Baz."

The pinch came again, along with a slap on his hip. Elijah swallowed a moan. Baz didn't have to say a word for Elijah to know his boyfriend wanted him to stay in character. He felt foolish, though, so he said nothing, hoping if he waited it out, Baz would take them naturally to the next phase of the game.

Three minutes later he broke his whimper to gasp out, "Sebastian. Untie me, Sebastian."

"I'm so sorry, my lord. You're a danger to yourself right now. For your own safety, I must keep you bound. But if you wish, I will remove your blindfold."

"Yes," Elijah said before he could dissect whether or not that was a good idea.

He hissed when the fingers at his nipples ground out even more tantalizing circles. "Remember how you must ask me, young master."

Elijah ground his teeth as he tried not to chase Baz's teasing fingers. In the show, the demon butler always made Ciel give deliberate commands, and Sebastian always responded the same way. Elijah bit back his assigned line in defiance, but he didn't last long against those fingers. "Sebastian, I order you to remove my blindfold."

"Yes, my lord."

As the silk came away, Elijah blinked in disorientation as he adjusted to the soft red glow. His libido kicked up at the sight of the deliciously disheveled Sebastian in front of him. His tux was neatly buttoned up, but he had subtle eyeliner on, white gloves and...

"Holy shit, you dyed your hair black?" Jesus—this was a temporary color, right? Elijah hadn't realized how attached he was to Baz's light brown hair. Then he saw no, it was a wig.

Baz cupped Elijah's cheek, his expression all concern. "Dear me, you're further gone than I thought. Perhaps I should leave you alone to your torment and stand guard so no one sees you in this deplorable state."

Elijah tried to lift his leg to trap Baz with it, but Baz had them pinned with his hip. "Don't you fucking dare."

Baz pouted, his naked eyes even more sensual in the red light. "So many hours remain until you are free of the poison, so much torture you must endure. How kind of you to insist I observe. You know how I delight in your discomfort."

Elijah had never been more pissed off and turned on at the same time in his life. He could barely keep in character, especially when Baz kept touching his chest. "Stop playing around. Fuck me."

"So *vulgar.* So desperate. Alas, much as I would love to see you open for me in such a deliciously carnal way, as I have said, I cannot until the danger has passed."

Elijah wished Baz would come closer so he could bite him. "Enough. No more games. *Fuck me.* Or at least put your hand on my dick."

"But you *love* games, my lord."

Baz put his hand on Elijah's cock—rested it casually over the lump in his trousers, remaining immobile when Elijah thrust into it. When Elijah cried out in frustration, Baz laughed.

"You're so pretty when you're desperate, young master."

Elijah tugged on the silk ties. "Suck my cock, Sebastian. I order you to suck my cock."

"Yes, my lord."

An eternity passed as Baz undid the button and the zipper. He withdrew Elijah's throbbing dick with tender, careful touches, and pressed his hips firmly into the mattress. He glanced up at Elijah with an expression promising mischief as he sucked the barest tip of Elijah's cock into his mouth.

Elijah groaned and fought him, but Baz wouldn't let him thrust, would only hold him in place, technically sucking but mostly licking and teasing. At first Elijah thought the tingle was his own anticipation, but when Baz worked his lips deliberately over the glans, the prickling sensation on his genitals became intense. "What the fuck is that?"

"In anticipation of your requested fellatio, I applied extra lip balm." Baz tongued Elijah's slit, working his lip over the hole until Elijah hissed. "It's possible I used a product with excessive peppermint. I took the liberty as I imagined the sensation would be a pleasant distraction from your unfortunately necessary delayed gratification."

Elijah was willing to bet Baz had slicked peppermint *oil* over his lips.

Baz licked Elijah's cock before withdrawing. Removing a small yellow tube from his pocket, he re-smeared his lips and lowered them to Elijah's balls. Elijah became delirious at this point, and when Baz took off his trousers and pushed Elijah's legs back, he didn't fight, only whimpered as Baz worked his peppermint lips over his taint and hole. When Baz finally kissed his way up Elijah's body, Elijah had tears leaking out and running down the sides of his face. His grip on the role-play was weak—he'd accepted the torture because he'd gotten addicted to the sexy glances and smiles his personal demon kept giving him. His dick, balls, and ass burned with peppermint oil, and when Baz reapplied his lip balm while staring at Elijah's nipples, he gave in to his inner whore and begged for it.

"Please." He watched, dizzy, as Baz bent to take first one, then the other nipple into his mouth.

His cock ached when Baz was finished. He whispered and tried to meet him for a kiss, but Baz pressed still-gloved fingers to his lips and sat up, leaving Elijah bereft.

"May I suggest some refreshment, my lord."

Baz produced a silver tray with a pair of gummy rings on them—they were, Elijah knew, marijuana-laced. Elijah nodded, opening his mouth to receive the treat, groaning when Baz delivered it via his mouth. Baz kissed his neck as Elijah swallowed.

"Only a few more hours, my lord, and I may give you your release."

A few more hours. Elijah opened his mouth to say no, but Baz put the gloved fingers inside as he resumed his lazy nips and licks of Elijah's nipples.

As the drug burned into his system, Elijah became more and more wanton, ordering Baz to suck his nipples, to fondle his cock. Feeling as if he were nothing but one big fucking erection, Elijah rolled over the edge and embraced the kinky game full-on.

"Sebastian, I order you to stick your tongue in my ass."

"Yes, my lord." Baz sucked briefly on the center of Elijah's belly. "Might I suggest some fingering also, and that you allow me to place a large pillow beneath your backside for more complete access."

Elijah drew his knees up until his ass stuck out and his belly quivered. "Just fucking do it."

He watched, buzzing and so horny he hurt, as Baz pushed a doubled-over pillow underneath Elijah before positioning himself at the foot of the bed. He pressed on Elijah's thighs, opening him wider, then withdrew a small bottle from his jacket pocket. When the cap came off, Elijah hissed at the smell. "Fuck you and your peppermint."

"Alas, you will need to wait to be fucked, master." Baz pushed a peppermint-oil-soaked finger against Elijah's hole. "But I will happily torment you sexually to pass the time."

Torment he did, and Elijah watched it all—Baz's finger disappearing inside him, burning even as the thumb of his other hand made Elijah ready to accept Baz's silky tongue. Elijah struggled, gasping and crying out and swearing at Baz as he teased Elijah without giving him any kind of resolution. When Baz brought out proper lube and switched his oral ministrations to Elijah's dick as he pushed two, three fingers inside, Elijah began to punctuate grunts around demands. "Fuck me, Sebastian. Fuck me. Fuck me. Fuck me."

Baz pulled off Elijah's cock with an audible pop as his fingers wormed deeper. "How shall I fuck you, my lord?"

"With your fucking dick."

"But *how*, young master? Do you want it slow and dogged, or fast and rough?"

Elijah kept trying to bear down on those fingers, but Baz kept the rhythm uneven. "Fast. Hard. Rough. Fuck me into the fucking wall. Untie me so I can rake my fingernails over your goddamned back, you fucking bastard."

Baz kissed his way up Elijah's chest and teased the corners of his mouth. "Use the words I prefer, darling."

Elijah wanted to bite him. "I order you to fucking fuck me into the wall with my hands untied so I can claw your skin off."

"Yes, my lord." Baz kissed him hard but quick. "However, I cannot untie your hands. Those I leave bound because you require a reminder."

Elijah watched Baz kneel between his legs, undoing his trousers. "What reminder? *Unf*," he grunted as Baz pressed his cock bluntly at the entrance to Elijah's body.

Baz kept pushing in, tucking Elijah's legs over his shoulders, and he stared at Elijah from beneath his jet-black hair as he buried himself inside. "A reminder that *we* are bound. No matter what you perceive has come between us, I am yours, Elijah." He thrust shallowly, stroking Elijah's cheek. "And you are mine."

For a moment they stared at one another, the game paused.

This was Baz, *his* Sebastian, speaking to Elijah. Telling him, in the middle of kinky role-play, to not ever talk about breaking up because of the political nightmare again. Saying, basically, Baz was prepared to be pretty irrational and insistent about keeping Elijah around. He was staking his claim.

This game, this demon role-play—this was what he feared had been his reality. That Baz was a devil tormenting him, threatening to consume his soul. Without having ever seen the show or read the books, he was convinced he was Ciel Phantomhive in a contract with Black Butler.

Except he knew now Sebastian Acker could wear all the wigs he wanted, could play all the games in the world, but he'd never be dark. He wasn't even Howl with his heart in a demon's belly. He held it aching in his own bare hands, desperate to give it away, terrified to try.

He had, for quite some time now, been passing it to Elijah. Over and over and over.

Elijah melted, broke in half, swallowed hard. He nodded. "Yes. I'm yours."

I'll keep your heart safe, Baz. As best I can, for as long as you'll let me.

Chapter Nineteen

LEJLA RETURNED LATE that evening, looking weary. She disappeared out back to smoke with Elijah, and later in bed, Baz got a rundown.

"She said it was okay. They weren't surprised, but they weren't happy. Her mom cried, her dad worried about how safe she was. But it was a start."

"Does she need anything?"

Elijah shrugged. "Time."

There truly wasn't much else to do except support her, which they did as they'd always done. As August wore on, though, they all, including Lejla, became distracted by the imminent dawn of school resuming.

Giselle and Stephan continued to litter Baz's email with talking points and media guides, which he kept meaning to read but never did. He was too busy helping Liz almost daily now, and he'd had lunch with Ed from therapy twice. For the first time in his life, he talked openly and often about his injury. Not about *getting* injured, but about what a pain in the ass it was to live with chronic pain.

One day in the middle of August someone knocked on the door of the White House. Baz braced himself, ready for it to be reporters, but Damien and Marius stood on his front porch.

Baz opened the door wide, frowning at them as they came into the foyer. "What in the world are you guys doing here?"

Damien gave him a look of incredulity. "Jesus, Baz, what do you think? You don't answer our texts half the time, and you turn down every suggestion we make to get together."

Marius didn't seem pissed half as much as he was concerned. "We saw the articles about your uncle and your mom."

Christ. This was a goddamned intervention. Baz rubbed the back of his head. "Yeah, it's fine. Sorry I've been bad about being in touch."

Damien appeared ready to launch into an angry lecture, but Marius stilled him with a hand on his arm as he glanced around the living room. "Looks great in here. Different, but good."

Baz hadn't thought about the place looking different, but it did. Giles had brought in a new chair. Jilly had brought new curtains. Aaron and Brian had turned some of the posters they'd done for Lejla's coming-out party into living room art, and they hung on the wall by the television. The corner by Fred's practice room was a sea of computer parts.

It was weird to stand there with Damien and Marius, who *didn't* belong in the White House anymore.

Baz turned away from the living room and the conflicting feelings it generated. "You guys eat yet? Care for an early lunch?"

They went to the noodle bar, where they ate and

Baz gave them the story on the new house order, including the addition of Lejla. "Sid's been great about giving up his room, and I think this is the best environment for her." He swished his fork through his noodles. "It's important she know people have her back. I had you guys. Now it's my turn."

Damien shook his head. "We get distracted for six weeks, and you become an adult. Could graduation be next?"

They were teasing, but Baz told them about meeting Ed and possibly volunteering at Halcyon Center. "I haven't been there yet, but I'm already convinced it's going to be exactly the kind of thing I'm looking for. Helping people at Saint Timothy and the White House, except concentrated. And younger. Half the reason I haven't gone to see it yet is I worry if I like it as much as I think I will, I won't want to go back to school at all. I'm pretty sure my parents would flip the fuck out if I went to school for six years and managed to come out with no degree whatsoever."

Damien arched an eyebrow. "Why don't you talk to the dean about getting a degree in liberal arts?"

Baz laughed. "What, major in *nothing*?"

"Not *nothing*. It's nonspecific, yes, but basically it says you went to college and studied broadly. You have to have fulfilled it a billion times over, but you could declare it and do some kind of independent study, make this last semester a kind of capstone course. You might not even need to take any regular classes, only have meetings with an advisor."

Baz's brain was spinning out possibilities of making

his work with Liz and volunteering at Halcyon Center an internship, but when he heard *last semester*, his mental record scratched. "Wait—*what*? You're saying I should graduate in December?"

Damien shrugged. "Why not? By January you could be doing what you want."

Baz balked. "I don't *know* for sure what I want." His first thought was *no more choir rooming with Elijah*, but his second thought was how great it would feel to be a real adult like everyone else his age. His head spun with new possibility, and he tried to anchor it with doubt. "Isn't it failing to drop out of school?"

Damien was a dog with a bone now. "Not drop out, Baz. *Graduate*. And of course you don't know exactly what you want. None of us do." He exchanged a glance with Marius, some kind of somber knowing passing between them. "It's weird, being done. I'm not going to lie. I miss the insulating bubble of college. I get why you keep hanging on. But I'm here to tell you, it's all kinds of fun too. I miss living with you guys, but I'm having a ball setting up house with Stevie. She's nuts with wedding planning right now, but it feels *good*. I'm moving forward. It's scary as hell, but it's good scary."

Marius nodded. "Med school is intense. Crazy intense. But I'm already learning so much, and I just started. Living with Kelly and Walter is good too, and it makes me motivated to not only focus on school. Today, for instance. When I ended up with this odd day off at the beginning of the week, I thought I'd use the time to study or get to know my peers. But then I heard Kelly and Walter fussing over making plans with their friend Rose who just moved to town, and I thought, no. I want to make sure I don't lose the friends I already have." He grimaced. "I'm sorry. I should have been better about reaching out."

Warmth bloomed in Baz's chest. "You were busy with med school."

"It doesn't matter. I told you I'd be there for you, and I wasn't."

Damien sighed. "Same. I'm sorry."

Baz wanted to tease them out of the heavy moment, but he couldn't. It meant a lot to him that they came to see him. "It's okay. I mean, yeah, it sucks not having things the way they always were, and I'm frustrated being the guy time forgot. But that's my bad, not yours. And—well, I'm doing okay."

Marius quirked an eyebrow. "You still with Elijah?"

"Yeah." The smile blooming on Baz's face was one he couldn't stop. "He's a handful, but you know me. Adds to the challenge."

Damien smiled back. "Good. I admit, when he threw down with me at the wedding, I had hope. May things keep going well for the two of you."

Marius's expression became grave. "Talk to us about your mom. Did you know this announcement was coming? Is it affecting you in any way?"

Shrugging, Baz gave them a quick review of his mom's forewarning, her asking for permission, the addition of Giselle and an exponentially increasing number of staff he had to sift through to try and get his actual parent on the phone. To his surprise, instead of nodding and offering their best wishes, Damien and Marius frowned and glanced at each other in silent, sober conference.

Baz frowned too. "What? Why are you looking at me like that?"

Damien rubbed his stubble and grimaced before replying. "She really made you tell her it was okay to drag you through her mud?"

"That's not what…" Baz trailed off, stunned as he realized it *was* what she'd done.

Marius turned his palm face up on the table. "I know she's wanted to run for public office for a while, but it is a bit crass to do it *now*. This wasn't a great time for it to happen to you."

Baz held up his hands. "This is how my family rolls. *Life* is a political opportunity."

"*Their* lives, Baz. Not yours." Damien sighed. "Never mind. This arguing isn't going to help you, and it's not why we're here. We wanted to check on *you*, to hear how things were going with *you*. Tell us everything."

Baz did. It was hours before they drove Baz to the White House, and when they parted, it was after a pile of hugs and vows they would do better at keeping in touch with each other. It had been a wonderful surprise, a great time out with his best friends. But their comment about his family kept ringing in his ears.

Their lives. Not yours.

Baz wandered into the practice room and found Elijah huddled at his computer. He glanced up blearily when Baz entered, but he smiled. He was eating one of

Liz's sugar cookies, drinking coffee Brian had made, writing his fantasy novel, which he'd taken over at the expense of all his erotica, even though he was pretty sure fantasy would sell a billion times worse than the lackluster numbers his erotic shorts were bringing in. He didn't care, he said. He was excited about this one, and he knew what to do with it now. Something about the hero trying to cast an enchanted box of emotions into a demon's furnace. It didn't make a ton of sense to Baz, but Elijah was happy when he wrote the story, and that meant Baz was happy.

This was his life. This was what he wanted. And he *had* it, already, right here in front of him.

If only he could figure out the way to make sure he kept it.

ELIJAH DID HIS best not to let the online articles get to him. He tried not to Google himself, but it felt too much like leaving a door unguarded, so he compromised by doing it only twice a day. The Wednesday before classes restarted, he talked about it with Pastor. Schulz surprised him by suggesting it was time he contact his lawyer.

"Am I in trouble?" The thought made him want to throw up. How could his dad trying to fucking shoot him land *Elijah* in jail?

"No, but you need to keep them informed. Is your dad's trial soon?"

"Not until after the first of the year. They keep pushing it back. I had no idea it took so long."

"Check in with your lawyers. If they don't feel anything needs to be done, fine, but let them know."

Walter wasn't exactly Elijah's lawyer, but the firm he interned at handled Elijah's interests regarding the trial. Walter listened as Elijah detailed the wingnut diatribes, how they were getting worse. He asked Elijah if he could come in the next day for a meeting at the law office where he worked.

"Is this bad?"

"Not bad, I don't think, but I want you to talk with Bob. I'd rather be overly cautious than have this blow up in our face. It would be smart to give you a good PR script in case any of these reporters decide to talk to you."

Elijah rubbed the beginnings of a headache out of his temple. "Great. So I've got the ones hunting Baz on one flank, my own on the other. It might be easier to switch to correspondence courses and hole up in the house."

"Who's hunting Baz?" When Elijah explained about the senator thing, Walter became concerned. "Is there any chance you're free today? Even if we can't snag Bob, I'd like to start working up your talking points."

Elijah ended up going over pretty much immediately. Baz was out at therapy with Liz, so Elijah texted he was taking the Tesla and went into the Cities. He was too unsettled to eat lunch, but Walter made him choke down a doughnut and cup of coffee as he spread out printouts and articles across a conference room table.

Walter had shed his suit jacket and tie, his shirtsleeves rolled up as he sifted through the papers. "Okay, I think I've been through the whole of it, and the good news is this is all smear."

"How the hell is that *good*?"

"Because it's not factual. This is a twisting of minor details, attempting to conflate them into something substantial. The way it's so coordinated makes me think these are Howard's lawyers trying to start a parade on the side street in hopes people don't notice your dad's attempted murder. Premeditated murder. The county prosecutor will flay them alive. They're hoping if they can spin you into enough of a nightmare, the jury will be conflicted. But even if you *were* a monster, there's no way it'd justify trying to gun you down on a public campus—and injuring someone else in the process."

"The thing is, it's not untrue, what they're saying. I *did* trick my parents into a year of college. I *did* fake a conversion."

Walter sat beside Elijah and turned his chair so he could lean forward on his elbows. "You never, ever say those words to anybody else. I'm not telling you to lie—but that's an interpretation, not the facts. As a minor, you were kicked out of your house, and you roamed from state to state aimlessly. You went back to South Dakota because you determined you were choosing between two relative unsafe situations, and it was better to suffer emotional abuse than physical."

"Nobody abused me, not really," Elijah interjected, but Walter held up a hand.

"You've told me you sold yourself so you could eat,

to find shelter from the cold. You were about to be beat up in a back alley for refusing to prostitute yourself when Baz found you. During none of this time were you a legal adult. Did your parents tell you to get out? Did you leave because of threats? Did you recant your orientation and fake a religious conversion because you determined if you didn't, you'd be kicked out again or beaten?"

Elijah's head swam. "Well...yeah, but I did do it to get back at them. I *was* vicious. I wanted to be."

"I understand. And as your friend, I applaud it. As your lawyer-in-training, I'm telling you the court of law isn't the place to throw down. On paper, you're a child of abuse, and when you stood your ground, your father tried to take your life. That's the only story the public gets to hear. Everything else is spin." He took Elijah's hand. "You have nothing to feel guilty over. But whether it's pride or a need to justify your choices, I will tell you all day long, and so will Bob, your father's attempted murder trial isn't the place to work stuff out. That's where we nail him to the fucking wall. *That's* where he pays. For being a shitty father. For *forcing* you to make the choices you did. For nearly killing Baz, and you, and Giles and Aaron, and me, and Kelly. He needs to pay. Don't let the assholes try to make this about you. Don't *you* make this about you. It isn't."

The thought of swallowing all this crap made Elijah nuts. "So what *do* I say if a reporter jumps me? 'No comment'?"

"We'll work up an official statement. I can tell you now, though, it's going to be a terse recitation of the facts. Basically you redirect their attention. Your father wanted to kill you for being yourself. They can spin all they want, but no court in the world will let him off. I doubt there will be a trial. This will play out, and he'll do a plea. And then he's done and gone from your life."

Elijah wanted this over so much he ached. He hugged himself and sank into his chair. It was plush and expensive, and it reminded him of the *other* issue eating at him. "Is this going to be expensive, coming to you for help? I have a lot of the fund left, obviously, but—"

"This is free, hon. Bob's taking it on pro bono. Some of it is because the firm doesn't like the optics of Aaron's dad's involvement in the campus security's failure to stop the shooter. But honestly a lot of it is Bob wants to help make sure your dad doesn't get away with it. His daughter is in high school, and she's lesbian. This hits home."

Elijah didn't know what to say, so he went with, "Okay," and "Thanks."

Walter winked and stood, ready to show him out of the building.

They passed Aaron's dad's office on the way. His door was open, and he sat at his desk, arguing intently into a telephone.

That's the guy who threw Aaron out.

Aaron never talked about his dad if he could help it, and when he did, he tended to make his jaw so tight you could barely understand him. It had to be weird, having such a horrible history between them and trying to move past it.

Elijah wondered how pathetic it made him that after everything they'd done to him, even though he wouldn't take them back for a mountain of apologies and ten billion dollars, sometimes Elijah was sad he'd never see his parents again. Not so much them, but knowing he would never have family again. There wouldn't ever be another awkward holiday meal. There would be nothing. As if they were dead and gone, like Mark. All because they couldn't handle who Elijah wanted to fuck.

Halfway to the White House, he started to feel weird. He tried to push it down, but it wouldn't go, and in the end he gave up. He drove the Tesla straight to Pastor and Liz's house. She took one look at him through the screen door, melted and pulled him into her arms. "Oh, sweetheart. Come inside and let me wrap you in a blanket."

Elijah did.

Chapter Twenty

THE MONDAY BEFORE choir tryouts, Baz ran into his first reporter. It was one news van at the edge of campus on the way to the house, but it was a tabloid, and they had a video camera as well as a still. They peppered Baz with questions about his uncle and his mom. He was walking with Giles and Mina, and they asked Giles if he was Baz's boyfriend. Baz hustled his friends toward the house, speed-dialing Stephan, but before they got out of earshot, it came.

"Sebastian, in 2006 you were brutally attacked in a politically motivated bashing. Do you expect your uncle will make LGBT rights a headline during his tenure as Attorney General? Do you resent that he hasn't done enough as Senator, and do you expect your mother will do more? How much does your assault affect their policy? Would you categorize it as a significant event for either of them, or are they the reason you don't address it in public?"

Mina tripped, and Giles swore under his breath and started moving Mina faster, though he shook while he did it. Baz unlocked the door and whisked them into the house, locking the door behind them, thanking whatever god listening there were no additional reporters on the lawn of the White House.

Yet.

Within an hour Stephan had security talking Baz's housemates through *So You're Being Stalked by Reporters 101*, and while that went down, Baz allowed himself a moment of hating this, wishing he were somebody else. He indulged in a few rolls of nausea as his long-term memory reminded him how exquisitely awful this could get.

Then he called Elijah. "Babe, where are you right now?"

"Walking through the skywalks by the chapel. Why? What's wrong?"

"Reporters have arrived."

"*Shit.* For you or me?"

"Me, but they're hot to find my boyfriend. I'm sending a car to pick you up, and I'll text you the driver's number so you can tell him when you're coming outside. Put the number in your contacts and keep it close. I want you calling it every time you leave school grounds or the house. Tell Lejla it's the same for her. And Lewis." Baz ran a hand through his hair. "Security is here now, and I'm assuming a staffer is already on the way to give everyone in the White House media training. Probably Giselle. I'm calling Stephan next to see if Mom has any direct instructions."

There was a pause. "You're not calling *her*? Or your dad?"

Baz hesitated too. "Um…no, I'll never get through to her personally if things are blowing up this much, and God only knows what Dad's up to. Why?"

"I'd figure going to DEFCON 4 would merit the personal touch."

Baz wanted to point out this was more a level 2, maybe 3, but an edge in Elijah's voice told him to hold this observation back. Threat level wasn't his point. The boy without parents was saying, *Um, where the fuck are your parents?*

It made the conversation with Damien and Marius at the noodle bar echo more loudly in his head. He did his best to shove it off. "Yeah. Well, that's not the Acker or Barnett way."

"Huh. Okay. Well, it's only another half hour until Lejla is off work, and then I'll call for a ride for us both."

"Be safe." Baz wished Elijah could come now, but he really did need to wait for Lejla. God, this crap was a pain in the ass.

"Baz?"

"Yeah, baby?"

"I want you to hear what I said."

Baz opened his mouth to say he'd heard, then realized he hadn't. "Tell me again."

"I will be there. For you. And if you don't phone me every time you bump your ass on DEFCON's second cousin, I will be very pissed off."

The cold, hard knot in Baz's chest warmed and unfurled. "Message received."

THE REPORTERS LINGERING on the fringes of his

existence weren't horribly disruptive to Baz, but he could tell they bothered his housemates a lot. Once Mina was late for a meeting because she couldn't get through the crush. Aaron got jumped in line at the noodle bar. Everyone had to call the security team before they so much as walked out with a bag of garbage. Lejla and Elijah switched from smoking on the patio to climbing onto the fire escape in Baz and Elijah's bedroom, which Elijah complained was a real pain in the ass. Lejla used it as an excuse to curtail her cigarette use earlier than planned, but Elijah was stress-smoking. When people couldn't find him, they usually discovered him leaning against the iron rail, huddled in the open-topped canvas tarp structure Brian had rigged for him in an attempt at maintaining privacy.

They couldn't go out easily either. Lejla was a con-firmed homebody in every available moment, and Brian also was content to hole up in the White House whether or not there were reporters on the lawn, but Jilly, Mina, Aaron, Giles, and Elijah were clearly feeling the strain. Baz didn't like it, but he didn't know what to do about it.

One night he was sitting with Aaron and Giles at the kitchen table going over an Ambassador routine when the distinct sound of a bass beat filtered from somewhere in the house. They frowned at each other as they tried to figure out what was going on.

Giles jerked his head at the door to the kitchen. "It's not coming from Lejla's room. She doesn't have a stereo. But it's not the living room either." On their way to investigate, they ran into Sid and Brian coming in from the other direction, equally puzzled expressions on their faces. Standing together in the living room, however, it was clear where the sound was coming from: the ballroom.

The White House had been the centerpiece of a rather splashy country estate one hundred and thirty years ago, and as the lady of the house had fancied herself a high-society hostess, she'd had a small but not insignificantly sized ballroom built behind the carriage house. A set of narrow stairs led from there into the kitchen on one side and the ballroom on the other, but there were also a set of now-somewhat-rustic French doors leading from the far corner of the living room into the party area. A sound system had been installed in the west wall, and auditory evidence made it clear it was currently in use. Playing, Baz noted as they came closer, RuPaul. At full volume.

"What's going on?" Aaron shouted over the beat.

Baz opened the doors. The bass throbbed in his chest as he peered into the murky semidarkness of the room. The lights near the stage were on, but that was it. Elijah and the girls danced with abandon beneath the spotlight. When Elijah saw Baz, he grinned and stumbled over, laughing as he tripped on the air.

Elijah reeked of alcohol, weed, and cigarettes, and the rakish smile told Baz a full Xanax had been consumed as well. "Hey, sexy. Want to dance?"

Mina cast an apologetic glance at Baz. "He stumbled up our stairs drunk, high, and teetering on the edge of a panic attack. I can't explain how it led to this exactly, but it seems to be working, so we're going with it."

Elijah looped his arms around Baz's neck and blinked up at him. "I partied without you. Sorry." He ran a fingernail down Baz's nose, staring at the trail as if it were the most mesmerizing thing he'd ever seen.

Baz scanned Elijah's face carefully. "What drugs did you take, honey? How much?"

Elijah bit his lip and frowned, as if engaging in difficult thought. "I ate your pot brownie. The whole thing. Took a whole Xanax. And one of your oxycodone." He hiccupped and giggled before tracing a clumsy circle around Baz's lips. "Actually, I had two. Washed them down with Oban. Then I wasn't nervous anymore. Wanted to dance." He cupped Baz's crotch with a lascivious grin. "Dance with me, lover."

Aaron glanced worriedly at Baz. "Is he going to be okay?"

"We're pouring water into him." Lejla produced a bottle and passed it to Elijah, nudging it to his lips. "We figured the dancing would help too. Sweat it out."

Baz was aware of a distant wave of guilt, knowing exactly how much of this episode had come from *his* bullshit. Now wasn't the time for that, though. Right now he wanted to chase the last of the shadows out of Elijah's eyes. Smiling, he ran fingers through Elijah's hair. "I'll always dance with you, baby."

They did—for hours. All of them. Awkwardly at first, everyone worried about Elijah, but as it became clear he was okay, especially if they kept moving, they gave in to the beat and helped their housemate dance out his demons. Elijah led them without flagging—he was an Elijah Baz hadn't seen before. Laughing. Wicked. Uninhibited. More relaxed than the night they'd been high in Chicago. Light, almost carefree, if you could ignore the way sometimes you could see him climbing on top of his fears. His drug cocktail led him onto the stage, into the arms of everyone in the room, and over and over again in front of a cold mic so he could lip sync to his favorite songs.

Sometimes Aaron or Mina would sing along, but while they were actually making noise, Elijah never let a single note pass his lips. He kept striking poses and demanding Brian play "Sissy That Walk". As the party wore on, people let go. They danced like they were the center of a throbbing crowd. They whooped and pumped their fists as Elijah took center stage, peeling off his restrictive layers until he unleashed the unrestrained version of Elijah Baz had a difficult time dragging to the surface.

"You need to let go." Elijah slipped his hands into the back of Baz's jeans. "Don't worry what other people think of you."

"I don't worry," Baz told him, but Elijah shook his head.

"You keep trying to do what you think you should. With your internship. With your mom. You keep trying to find the right life to grow up and live." He squeezed Baz's ass. "Stop it. Just be you. Sebastian Percival Acker. He's the best guy in the world, and don't you be ashamed of him. Tell anybody who doesn't like him to fuck themselves. Do what you want. Do what feels right."

Baz took a fistful of Elijah's shirt, right over his ass. "Right now it feels right to dance with you."

Elijah grinned and pressed their groins together. "Then let's dance."

They did, until the wee hours of the morning. Baz forced one last bottle of water into Elijah before rinsing him off in the shower and pouring him into bed. Unfortunately this didn't stop the inevitable groan of misery at five in the morning, right before Elijah hurled into the bucket Mina had placed by his side of the bed. He vomited again at the toilet, where Baz camped out with him for a full half hour.

Elijah whimpered as he rested his forehead on the side of the tank. "I'm going to die. I'm seriously going to die."

Baz rubbed his back. "Too many drugs, baby. Next time find me, and I'll walk you through a better cocktail."

"Couldn't stop freaking out. Didn't want to bother you. Hate bothering people."

"I hate it when people I care about don't bother me when they're in trouble." Baz swatted him lightly on the ass. "You find me from now on when you get this low. Got it?"

Elijah nodded, then moaned in the way that told Baz he needed to drag his boyfriend's head over the bowl again. Eventually they were able to make it to bed, where Baz held Elijah tight as he shivered.

"If it's any consolation, you were glorious." Baz stroked Elijah's hair, smiling. "I wish you could find this part of you without substance abuse."

"Sometimes I think I maybe could, when I'm with you."

Baz stilled. Something shifted deep in his heart, and he ran a hand down Elijah's back. "Oh yeah?"

Elijah didn't reply because he'd fallen asleep.

Baz held him close, letting the confession ring in his heart, taking him into his dreams.

Chapter Twenty-One

T WO DAYS BEFORE classes began, Giselle came to
the White House to school everyone on how to
behave with the press. Elijah hated her on sight.

"It's very important you never engage with any
press we haven't vetted." She said *very important* with
the clear implication it wasn't possible they could
understand the sheer depth the situation presented. She
looked like she came from a paper-doll set of Washington Power Women, Liberal Edition.

She brought in a reporter one day who did a web
video about Baz, making him sound like some prepack-
aged weirdo. They didn't interview anyone else in the
house and wouldn't let any of them eavesdrop on the
taping. Elijah watched it once it was published. He
could tell they weren't Baz's answers. The only authentic part was when they'd asked him about Elijah, if they
were dating. He blinked, like he hadn't expected that,
but then he relaxed and said yes, they were. The
reporter wanted to know if it had anything to do with
his rescuing Elijah, but Baz laughed and told her no, it
was the other way around.

It made Elijah smile. Except then he remembered
Giselle scolding Baz for going off-message after the

interview had ended.

Elijah resented Giselle not only because she was an ice bitch who didn't hide her distaste for him, but also because they had other things to do than dodge her bullshit. Serious things—like how everybody kept ignoring Elijah's insistence he sucked at singing because they loved the idea of him in the chorale. Eventually he caved, saying he'd try out, knowing he wouldn't make it. Except immediately Aaron and Giles hustled him into the White House practice room, perched him beside Fred and queened out in unison as they fussed over what song they were going to have him sing.

"He's a pretty solid second tenor." Aaron, seated at the bench, leaned over his shoulder to look at Giles. "But he needs something that will do the work for him."

Giles thumbed through a folder full of sheet music. "What about Bieber? He could pull off 'Baby'."

Enough of this shit. "How about CeeLo? I could sing 'Fuck You' right now."

Aaron looked thoughtful. "That's not a bad suggestion. He'd have to use the 'Forget You' version, obviously, but it could work nicely."

That was what they ended up doing. Elijah had it on everyone's authority he basically had to stay on key eighty percent of the time and he was in, but they wanted him to *bring it* because they had fantasies of the whole house, or as much as possible, being in Salvo and Ambassadors together. Elijah ignored this, knowing he didn't have a chance in hell, and even if he did, he didn't want it.

Lejla, however, was another story.

She wanted to be in Salvo the way fish wanted water, but she wouldn't so much as try out for choir. She only wanted to do it as Lejla, but she was registered as Lewis. Worse, if she tried out as Lewis, she'd be placed as a tenor. Aaron assured her she was a countertenor as a male, which was basically the same as an alto for range. But she'd have to perform in a tux, or come out. She wasn't ready to do that yet, so she wasn't trying out.

"It makes me feel like I'm taking her place." Elijah confessed this one day while he and Baz drove around town to get away from the house. "This is the thing she wants. I should sit out with her."

"She can try out again at semester. Or next year. And you'll be there to help her through."

"I guess."

"Speaking of semester." Baz took Elijah's hand. "I was going to tell you. I'm thinking…it's not for sure, but I'm kicking around the idea of graduating in December. I'd still live in the White House, but…well, it seems like it might be time."

Wow. Elijah laced their fingers together. "If it feels right, I say do it."

Baz kissed their joined hands. "Thanks."

The buzz from the kiss made Elijah's insides dance. "I meant to ask. You volunteered yesterday at the place where the guy from therapy works, right?"

"Yeah. It was great. Mostly kids—well, young adults. They're focusing on an LGBT homeless program, working in concert with Avenues for Homeless

Youth. I'm not sure what exactly I'll do there, but Ed swears he can find use for me, and Pastor is helping me set up an internship for credit."

Elijah got an out-of-body sensation. "What's the name of this place? I don't think you ever said."

"Halcyon Center. In Saint Paul."

Elijah let the Tesla slow as he drew a centering breath. "That's where I stayed, Baz. When I ran away. It closed a lot for overnights, but I went to Halcyon Center to eat and shower and feel semi-sane. I would have lived there if I could have. If they'd had more money to stay open as a shelter."

Baz took his hand, squeezed it. Once they were back at the house, they went up to their room. They didn't speak, just spooned together on the bed, soaking everything in.

"I'm telling Mom Halcyon goes on the top-tier list of our charities."

Elijah turned in Baz's arms and kissed him. Hard.

WHEN CLASSES FINALLY started, Elijah relaxed gladly into routine, but Baz couldn't say he joined his boyfriend on that one. It felt odd to be on campus, especially with all the students back. He'd always been a little too old for college, first starting when he was almost twenty, but now he felt *old*. He was glad he'd taken Damien's and Marius's advice and done an internship and independent study, not regular classes. Knowing he'd be graduating in December had become a balm, not a cause for concern.

He made regular treks into Minneapolis to visit Marius and Damien, especially Marius. This meant he saw a lot of Kelly and Walter too, sometimes more than he saw the man he'd actually schlepped into town to see.

"I always heard med school was tough, but I never realized how much of an understatement that was." Marius sank into his end of the couch, staring blank-eyed at the ceiling. "I think I average twenty hours of sleep a week. Kelly keeps slipping meal bars into my bag because they got called once when I passed out because I hadn't eaten since the night before." Marius sighed and shut his eyes. "I don't think I'd make it if I hadn't moved in here. I will owe those two for the rest of my life." He put a hand briefly on Baz's ankle. "Thank you for hooking me up."

"I'm glad it's going well."

"Totally. The only problem is they keep insisting I could bring girls home, and I can't figure out how to explain there is nothing further from my mind than sex right now."

This didn't surprise Baz, since Marius hadn't ever been much of a player, but the defeat and flatness in the way he wrote off sex at twenty-two gave Baz pause. "We should book a night to get you laid, though. There's fasting, and there's starving."

"I'd only embarrass myself. Every now and again if they're going at it loud enough, I can manage a half-assed solo act, but usually I pass out so hard I have to set three alarms to wake me up." He stifled a yawn on the last part and shifted to sit more upright. He also raised a sleepy eyebrow at Baz. "You and Elijah are still doing okay, I hope?"

"Yeah." Baz wasn't sure how else to qualify that, so he pulled at a loose thread on the couch, as if fraying the cushion might unleash the way to confess to his best friend *how much* he felt for Elijah. How he kept feeling like he should say it, but he didn't know how.

When Baz finally glanced up, ready to fumble out a preamble, Marius was fast asleep.

Baz did his best to shutter his disappointment. They'd had a whole twenty minutes together, and Baz had known all along Marius would have been napping if not for Baz's visit. But it made Baz feel like shit. He was in the middle of calling up an Uber ride when keys rattled in the lock, and Kelly came in. Marius's roommate smiled, opening his mouth on a greeting, swallowing it and waving with his keys instead as he spied sleeping Marius. "Hi."

Baz rose, holding up his phone. "About to call a ride and get out of your way."

Kelly frowned and motioned for him to come into the kitchen. "Don't be silly." He dropped his backpack on the counter. "Unless you have to get home? Because Walter just texted to say he'd be late *again*, and even if Marius is awake, he always says he should study. I'd love someone to go to pizza with."

"Only if you let me pay."

Kelly held up his hands. "Not stopping you."

The restaurant was pretty busy, meaning they had to wait a few minutes before they got a table, but there wasn't anything unpleasant about passing the time while chatting with Kelly. He was so damn *happy*. It should have annoyed Baz, but he found Kelly refreshing, almost healing.

"So what's up with you?" Kelly leaned back in the booth and nudged Baz's foot with his own. "Are the paparazzi still stalking you?"

"Not paparazzi. Reporters, and they seem to have mellowed out. They've done a little bit of background info on me, but we're not the full focus yet. The whole drama is if my uncle will get confirmed right now." He smiled wryly. "If you were worried, no, nobody's going to photograph us going to dinner and blast you on TMZ for being my piece on the side."

Kelly wrinkled his nose and bit his lip. "Damn. That would have made Walter all jealous." He rolled his eyes at himself. "God, sorry. I'm so rude. Elijah would be jealous too, wouldn't he?"

Baz turned his butter knife over and over. "I don't know. He's hard to read sometimes."

"But you guys are dating, right? And it's going well? You seem good together. Connected."

Baz shrugged. "We're okay."

Kelly folded his arms on the table and regarded Baz with gentle concern. "Something's wrong?"

"I don't know. I can't tell how much of it is my own paranoia." He let go of the butter knife and pushed fingers under his glasses to rub the bridge of his nose. *I want to tell him I love him, but I don't know if it will fuck it up or not.* Yeah, no way he was saying that. "Seriously, you don't want to hear this. It's fine."

"I know I'm not Marius, but...well, I don't mind

listening."

"I'll keep my laundry to myself, but thanks. Tell me about your classes or something."

"Boring, but okay. Business classes won't light the world on fire for excitement, but I'm doing well, and I know I can go get a good job when I'm done. I'm never going to have a flashy career like Walter. But I'm getting good at the nuts and bolts of how organizations and businesses work from underneath." Kelly wrinkled his nose. "I can't say I wouldn't mind if people got breathless over *manager* the way they do *lawyer*. My dad keeps telling me it shouldn't be about how exciting your title sounds. The world is full of silent soldiers. Your work is your reward, if you do it right."

Baz's lips quirked. "Spoken like a Minnesotan."

"How about you? What are you thinking of doing when you're finished with school?"

"I like the volunteering, but it's not an actual job. And I am, for all practical purposes, disabled. I'd also never pass any drug test because I use pot for pain, and I don't qualify under Minnesota medical marijuana law. I couldn't handle a desk job, and I have eyestrain difficulty. I'm getting through college with a lot of exceptions and greasing of palms by my family. That will never work in the real world." He thought about Ed, who had an arrangement with Halcyon, but he doubted they'd give *two* special jobs.

"Well, first of all, that sucks. But I don't think you should write yourself off so completely. If you were anybody else, I'd say you could apply for disability, but you don't *need* money. You'd probably prefer to earn your own way, and I'm not saying you couldn't. Except you don't seem to strike me as someone determined to pave his own road. Which means you're in a perfect position. You can pretty much do what you want."

"This is my problem. I don't know what I want to do."

"You said exactly what you wanted just now. You want to help people, but you don't need to be paid to do it, or not much. You need somewhere that won't be ableist and has either a flexible schedule or a liberal policy about when and how you turn work in, but if you're not expecting to make a million dollars, or even a hundred thousand dollars, that opens up a lot of doors."

Baz pursed his lips. "*What* doors? Seriously, I can't so much as come up with a career track to dream about."

"You need somewhere with people. Lots and lots of people who need you." Kelly tapped on his phone screen a few times, then passed it over, revealing a web page. "Rose is doing an internship at a social center for immigrants, and she loves it. They're always teetering on the edge of closure, but they do great work. I bet they'd take another volunteer."

"So what, you're saying I should be a professional volunteer?"

"I think the word is philanthropist. And yeah. I totally think that's what you should do."

Hope flickered, and Baz quickly batted it down. "I can't waltz into places and start throwing money around. And I'd have to clear it with my parents, my uncle."

"I'm not talking about using your family's money. You could be a public face for these places. Shake hands. Rub shoulders. In either role, you'd be an asset. But mostly I'm saying you can go volunteer because you don't *have* to work."

Their pizzas arrived, and Baz rubbed his jaw thoughtfully as the waiter put out the industrial-sized cans to stand their pizzas on. A busboy helped set them out. After urging Baz and Kelly to let him know if they needed anything else, the waiter left, but his assistant lingered.

He was young, likely not even eighteen. "Um—are you…Sebastian Acker?" Before Baz could answer, the boy pulled a pen and order pad from his pocket with shaking hands. "Can—can I have your autograph?"

Baz blinked. "Autograph?"

The kid's face was blotchy, and not just from blushing. He was lanky, skinny, and underwhelming in the skin-care department. He had a hard time making eye contact, and when he spoke, his voice wobbled. "If it's okay. I…read about you. Online. And I saw the video interview on your mom's website." Now the red was all blush, and he glanced briefly at Kelly before frowning. "Are—are you still with Elijah?"

"Yes, he is." Kelly smiled a very manager kind of smile. "I'm Kelly Davidson, Sebastian's friend. He's keeping me company while my husband is at work. What's your name?"

"Chris." He stared at the pad, crushing pages as he worried the edge.

Kelly's expression was something of a cattle prod. Baz cleared his throat and reached for the paper and pen. "Sure, I'll give you my autograph. If you give me yours."

Chris ducked, rubbed his ear. "Oh—okay."

Feeling weird, Baz scrawled out an official-looking *Sebastian Acker*, then realized he'd fucked up. He needed to sign it *to* the guy. Trying not to make it seem crowded, he added, *To Chris, my pizza hero.* He passed the pad over, pulling off the sheet he'd scribbled on, revealing a new page. "Your turn."

Chris put the pad on the table, clearly writing more than his name. When he handed Baz his paper, he folded it in half. "Thanks."

Gathering his autograph and pad, Chris took off. Baz opened the paper. When he'd read it, he placed the note on the table so Kelly could see it too.

Every day at school kids tease me, but reading about you standing up for your boyfriend and overcoming your disability made me feel brave. I'm trying to get a scholarship to go to Saint Timothy when I graduate. Thanks for being my hero. Love, Chris.

"Wow," Kelly said.

Baz felt queasy. "I'm such an idiot. I signed it *to my pizza hero.*"

"That's cute. He'll probably put it in a frame."

"It's stupid. Pizza hero, when he wrote *that*? What am I supposed to do with this?"

"Be *his* hero. Be the reason he doesn't let the turkeys get him down. Be the guy who let him express how much you being an example means to him."

Christ. "And you're saying you want me to do *this* for a living?"

Kelly leaned back in his chair, smiling. "I want you to keep doing what you're doing. Being you, being out there, letting people see you. Being the little thing getting people through their day."

It sounded wonderful. And terrifying. And destined to fail. "That's a lot of fucking pressure."

Kelly winked as he pulled a piece of pizza onto his plate. "I think you can handle it."

Chapter Twenty-Two

THE EVENING BEFORE upperclassmen choir tryouts, Elijah was a wreck. Part of it was he couldn't smoke, since Aaron and Giles and Mina had all pointed out smoke and vocal cords weren't the best of friends. He told himself he didn't give a fuck, but now that they had him all worked up about it, he *did* want to get in to choir. Not in to Ambassadors, no matter how they bugged him. But the chorale, yeah. He kind of wanted it.

"I wish you were trying out," he told Lejla as they sat together in her room.

She drew her knees to her chest with a sigh. "I know. Me too."

"You still could."

She shook her head.

The first few days of classes had been rough. She wasn't out as trans beyond the White House, and apparently being Lejla at home made being Lewis to the world much harder. She'd resumed her genderfuck wardrobe, unisex clothes with added female adornments, and when she wasn't getting an out-and-out hazing, she at least got funny looks.

She went with him to his audition, though he told

her she should stay home. "I want to be there for you." Since Aaron and Giles were deep in the music clique, they managed to sneak her into his audition.

Elijah had what Aaron called a part voice, perfectly fine for a group but not appropriate for a heavy solo. He did his best to project the way they told him to, but he was nervous. Baz, who was on the student selection committee, had to treat Elijah like anybody else, but he did smile and tip his glasses down for a quick wink as Elijah left.

"I think I sucked," he said as they exited out the back door of the choir room.

Lejla hugged his arm. "You were fine."

They took the skywalks to the coffee shop outside the library, where they planned to hunker down until Giles texted it was time to come see the results. Most students had tried out during freshmen orientation, but Elijah was part of the few returning students auditioning. Once the last prospectives were through, the committee would meet, and the results would be posted. That would be in about an hour.

"It's no big deal if I don't get in." Elijah spoke this lie into his coffee.

"It is a big deal, and you'll get in." Lejla tugged at the hair in the center of his forehead. "You were great."

"I sound all wheezy." He wrapped his hands around the mug. "*You* sound great. I've heard you singing to yourself in your room. It should have been you."

"It will be me. Later."

She sipped her drink, and Elijah studied her. She was in Lewis clothes, but he could always see her now, even if she left the femme at home. Today she wore a hint of eyeliner and lip gloss, which went nicely with her *My Little Pony* Fluttershy tee. Aaron had taken her to some fancy stylist friend of Walter's in downtown Minneapolis, giving her a flirty androgynous cut which reminded Elijah of the *Black Butler*, all angles and blunt edges and asymmetrical swoops.

"How are your classes?" Elijah asked. "Are you doing okay, going as Lewis?"

She shrugged. "I feel like people treat me differently, but it might be in my head. I can butch up, and they still whisper and give me side eye. Which sometimes I think, fuck, I'll whip Lejla out and be done with it, but I always get cold feet."

Giles texted to call them back because results were going up, and as Elijah watched his friend walk to the music building, he thought he might have some insight on why everyone was able to see through Lewis in a way they hadn't been able to before. The feminine movements Lejla had let herself indulge in at the White House had crept into her on-campus persona. The way she walked, the way she moved, the way she, well, *was*. It wasn't like the deliberate Lolita stuff that had brought on the beets. He would bet money none of this was intentional. This was Lejla's new version of subconscious takeover. The more she let herself be authentic, the harder it was to stop.

As Elijah moved with her through the herd of hopeful choir auditioners to get a peek at the printout on the wall outside the practice room, he realized he was having the same problem. She was right. It *was* a big deal for him to get into choir. He wanted it, and it would hurt if it didn't happen. He wanted a lot of things now, and the hope that he might actually get them was a cancer he couldn't eradicate. It twisted his gut as he moved toward the announcement sheets. It burned his heart, promising pain if hope turned out to be a lie. Which it would. He knew *better* than this, why had he—

He stopped, the burning in his heart pinching before blooming as he stared at the listing of tenors. Specifically at the sixth name down.

Elijah Prince.

That was his name. On the choir sheet. He was in the Saint Timothy Chorale.

He was in.

As Lejla hugged him tight, more hands fell on him. Mina, Giles, Aaron—they were all around him, beaming.

"I'm in the choir," he whispered, still staring at the paper.

The thought kept ringing as they led him away, congratulating him. This time it was *Elijah* waltzing across the skywalk out of the music building surrounded by the cool kids. He was one of the cool kids. Hope hadn't let him down. It was a moment of victory, of joy, of normality, of rightness, a world where good people were rewarded and good things did come to those who wait and people did live happily ever after. The joy inside Elijah practically vibrated, ready to explode like a goddamned rainbow over his life.

As they rounded the corner by the student union

lounge, someone called out, "*Freak.*"

Elijah could almost hear the record scratch. The call was little more than a murmur rising above a din, but it shafted their happy moment, a sharp edge leaching out the air. Giles tripped. Aaron hunched his shoulders, moving closer to Lejla. Lejla herself seemed the least affected—her smile dimmed, her head dipped, but she soldiered on. She put a hand on Giles's shoulder, and Elijah could hear her whisper, "It's all right."

It wasn't. It wasn't fucking all right.

The rest of them kept walking, but Elijah stuttered to a stop. The football assholes were across the lounge, and the beet-dumping fucker looked smug. Elijah admitted he couldn't know the comment had been directed at Lejla, or any of them. And yet in his bones he knew they addressed her—or at the least, they *could* be addressing her. They *would* be. He'd been too absorbed in freaking out over singing in front of people to notice in line for auditions, but Lejla had probably fielded some glances. She would absolutely get some more.

It wasn't like Elijah hadn't gotten the well-placed accidental elbow in the hall, either, or hate glances from the Bible group he'd attended as cover last year until he gave up his charade of *gay converted.* Through the window of the lounge, Elijah could see the street where he'd stood with members of the choir, where Howard Prince had tried to gun down his own son, would have succeeded if Baz didn't have a hero complex as part of his luggage. Somewhere at the edge of campus, or possibly *on* campus, reporters scoured Sebastian Acker's backstory, hunting for dirt. They might be trying to tie the umbilical cord of that story to Elijah's family scandal. At any second they could leap out of the bushes, figuratively or literally, to make his life a circus.

Laughter trilled in the distance as Elijah remained frozen in place. He felt cracked open and vulnerable.

Giles pulled him close while he whispered, "Don't make a mountain out of this. Lejla is fine. She's not letting it wreck her day. Don't you, either."

Elijah wanted to say it was so much more than a *freak* comment, that he was barely holding it together on his best day, but he nodded instead. He pushed his panic aside as best he could, papered over it with a fake smile and did his best to be happy.

But the bad feelings didn't go away. He was starting to think they never would.

BAZ THOUGHT A lot about what Kelly had said as September wore on. He started his internship September fifteenth, Walter's birthday, and he went with Elijah afterward to Pizza Lucé to celebrate with the gang—everyone from the White House, Walter, Kelly, Marius, Damien, Rose. While Elijah and Lejla talked about how much they loved their English classes, Damien talked about his first days on his job as a music therapist with Giles, and Marius and Walter gave grisly tales of graduate school, Baz shared stories about some of the kids he'd worked with on the first day at Halcyon Center. He felt like he'd begun to find his place. Maybe he didn't have all the answers, maybe he still had things to figure out, but for the first time he believed he *could* figure it out.

At the end of the month, he got a text from Giselle saying a car would take him the next afternoon to the Saint Paul Hotel, where his mother would be waiting for him.

It annoyed Baz, this royal summons, because it meant he had to call Ed and apologize for bailing at the last minute on a presentation. He was pretty sure he'd miss therapy too, and choir practice. He went to the meeting, though, because his mom never called him unless it was important. He missed seeing her, and found he looked forward to it despite the hassle.

When he got to the hotel, he found out how important it was. His dad was there.

Baz did a double take in the doorway when he saw the two of them seated together on the couch, and he stumbled when he saw they were holding hands. When Gloria saw Baz, she let go of Sean and rushed to embrace him. Hugged him, not exactly hard, but like he'd come home from war.

That's when the flashbulbs started going off.

"The taping got bumped up at the last minute. So sorry to spring this on you," she whispered in Baz's ear. When she pulled back, she had her political smile on as she touched his face with exaggerated gestures. "Good to see you, sweetheart. Thanks for making the time to come by." She kept a hand on his shoulder as she turned to the room. "Stephan? Can you find someone to put Baz in makeup?"

Makeup? *Taping?* Baz opened his mouth to protest,

but Stephan had already grabbed his elbow and pulled him into an adjoining room of the suite.

"We have a few suits picked out for you, but I can tell you now you should choose the gray. It'll go best with what your parents are wearing." Stephan gestured to a young blonde woman hovering by the wall. "Giselle's assistant Bess will take you through the layout. I have to go finish seeing what I can get out of the interviewer."

Baz grabbed Stephan's arm before he could escape. "*What interviewer?* I thought I was coming here to talk to my mom, not sit down with a reporter. What the fuck is going on?"

"Bess will take you through it," Stephan repeated. He cast a cold glare at the assistant. "You have to get him ready, in every way, in fifteen minutes tops. Understand?"

Bess nodded, and Stephan left.

The assistant smiled at Baz and gestured to a small stool before a makeshift makeup counter. She was no Erika, whom Baz couldn't help notice was nowhere in sight. "If you wouldn't mind, I'll give you a bit of color and powder for the lights."

Baz wanted to shake her and demand answers, not sit patiently and let her remove the shine from his forehead, but he sat anyway. "Please tell me what's going on because I honestly have no clue."

"They've been trying to get airtime for a week, and today out of the blue they find out Rachel Maddow is doing some special tour in the Cities. Stephan got the word an hour ago that they were interested in an exclusive. So the rest of the day is run-throughs, a few local spots, and at six we go to the theater."

They were going on *Rachel Fucking Maddow*? Tonight? After other interviews? Baz felt dizzy, and it wasn't from all the powder Bess was making him inhale. "Why am I going on *Rachel Maddow*?"

"Because your mom's approval rating isn't great. The focus group determined she needs to increase her family appeal, so your dad is doing lots of events with her now. They'd originally planned the photo shoot this afternoon and the interview with the *Star Tribune* and the *Chicago Tribune* and Hill reporters we brought with us, but now it's all gone crazy. You're a draw for Maddow because...well, you know."

Because we're both gay. Christ, Baz already had a headache. "Nobody told me I was getting interviewed. Or photographed. I thought I was having lunch and a lecture."

He got both those things, but not with his parents. Some new person, a slick advisor who appeared to have been peeled from Uncle Paul's campaign, gave Baz a sandwich and a PowerPoint presentation.

"We need to work on your backstory." The advisor pushed a button for a new slide. "We're assuming Rachel will ask you about your past, about the attack on you when you were sixteen. We'd like you to draw attention to the fact it happened as an attack on your uncle. The focus groups have responded positively to the martyr angle."

"The fuck I'm saying that."

The advisor pursed his lips. "I have it all written

out on these slides. We can have someone coach you through it. It's okay if you don't get it verbatim, and if you stammer a little, we think it will go over especially well."

Baz had skimmed enough of the canned crap in front of him to know he'd offer his ass to the football team before he'd give so much as a summary of that shit. "I need to talk to my mom. Right now."

His mom had gone off for an interview, the advisor said, but she'd return in time for the photo shoot and the *Chicago Tribune* reporter. So Baz spent the three hours refusing over and over again to memorize shit about his tragic past, and eventually they gave up and moved on to the next talking point.

They wanted him to downplay Elijah.

Baz clenched his hands at his sides and forced himself to speak as calmly as possible. "I'm sorry. I don't think I heard you right."

The advisor pointed to the infernal PowerPoint. "We're not telling you to say you're single. But if asked about your relationship with Mr. Prince, deflect to your mother. The young man isn't exactly on trial, I know, but that business with his father is grisly and not the kind of image we're after. Project a more, shall we say, *carefree* image and maybe make a joke about how you're not ready to settle down. Because *you* track wonderfully as an eligible bachelor. We might be able to get you a spread in *Out* or *The Advocate*."

Behind the safety of his glasses, Baz shut his eyes as he drew a breath. Looking the man squarely in the eye, he smiled and shut the laptop. "Go. Fuck. Yourself."

He rose from the sofa, grabbed his jacket from the closet and beat it the hell out of the suite.

They chased him, of course. The aides, advisors, Stephan—there were a few lower-grade reporters lurking in the lobby of the hotel too, and when they saw Gloria Barnett Acker's son fleeing the hotel with the potential senator's entourage chasing him, the press descended like locusts. "*Mr. Acker, Sebastian—where are you going?*"

He had no idea. He had absolutely no fucking idea.

He thumbed through his phone with a shaking hand, but it was the middle of a Thursday afternoon, and nobody was around. Elijah was in class, same with the rest of the White House residents. Even if they weren't, he couldn't subject them to this.

His phone buzzed with calls and texts—Stephan, his mom, his *dad*. Baz turned it off, stuffed it into his pocket and hailed a cab, all but jumping in front of it. It felt like a movie chase as he shut the door and the mob following him threatened to swallow the car.

"What the hell?" the cabbie said, as faces pressed to all the windows, most of them angry, all of them hungry.

Baz ignored them and thrust a hundred-dollar bill at the front seat. "Just drive. Please. Go. *Please.*"

The man did. Slowly at first, but as the people on the car moved away, the driver sped up, until they were clear of the hotel and the crush.

"You some kind of celebrity?"

Baz's head hurt. His hip killed him from running. He wanted to go home, but they'd look for him there.

He wanted to punch somebody, and cry, and curl in a ball in the back of a closet. All at once.

He wanted Elijah—who his mom's advisors wanted him to disavow.

"You okay, kid? Where do you want me to take you?"

He couldn't bring this circus to the White House. He could go to Pastor, or Liz. He almost gave the cabbie those directions. But as they passed a billboard, a new idea hit him. He *did* have somewhere else to go, somewhere nobody would ever find him.

Staring at the smiling children on the billboard, he said, "Take me to Halcyon Center."

Chapter Twenty-Three

B AZ FOUND ED in the weight room. When he saw
Baz's face, Ed paused long enough to tell the kids
to remember to spot each other and pulled Baz into an
office. "What's wrong? What happened? Did something happen to you? Do I need to call the police? Take
you to a hospital?"

Baz's laugh cracked in the middle, and he reached
under his glasses to pinch the bridge of his nose. This
was so fucked up. So fucking, *fucking* fucked up.

It took him five minutes, but he was able to spew
out the overall gist. It was hard because Ed had absolutely zero context. He hadn't known Baz's mother was
the possible senate candidate he'd vaguely heard about
on the news. He knew his family was well off, but no,
Ed hadn't realized Baz was part of *those* Barnetts. Baz
fumbled most trying to explain the summons and what
they'd asked of him.

Ed was furious. "So you're telling me they demanded you show up in the middle of the school day, didn't
give you any advance warning what it was about, tossed
you to a bunch of handlers, and told you how to spin
one of the most personal, painful events of your life? To
add insult to injury, they told you your boyfriend

didn't fit their tidy profile so you should pretend he didn't exist? Jesus. I can't believe you didn't deck them."

"Escape seemed the better part of valor. I'm pissed at my parents, but I don't want to tank Mom's campaign."

"I'm sorry, kid, but *fuck* your mom's campaign." Perching on the edge of a desk, Ed wiped a grimace away. "Christ, is it true, about you getting attacked, your boyfriend killed because of your uncle's stance on LGBT issues?"

Baz nodded, gaze on the floor. "The attacker was fringe, but yeah."

"That's all kinds of awful. What a fucking shit deal, going out on your damn birthday and getting disabled for life because your uncle took a stand. But it's *your* shit deal, man. *You* get to decide if and when and how you talk about it. Not some slimy political advisor. And as for Elijah—I haven't met him yet, but you seem pretty serious about him."

"I love him. I haven't told him, but I do." Baz hunched forward in the chair, elbows on his knees. "My attack is one thing. My reluctance to address it is mostly pride and not wanting to go to a bad place. But Elijah's the only reason I made it through this summer alive. He's *everything*, Ed. I would give up every other thing in my life to keep him. And they wanted me to toss him aside."

Baz shut his eyes as the fury and sick sensation that request inspired rolled through him again. "Fuck, what if he finds out about this? There's all this crap with his dad's trial, a bunch of right-wing fuckheads writing blogs about how Elijah is a manipulative asshole who essentially deserved to be shot. He doesn't ever come out and say it, but sometimes I know he *believes* that shit. Then my fucking mother's Storm-the-Senate team basically says they want me to join in." He pushed his fingers into his hair and tugged. "Fucking *hell*, I want to scream. My head hurts, and my shoulder and hip are on fire—and I have no meds, no TENS unit, nothing. I don't know where I'm supposed to go now. They'll be all over the house. I should go, help diffuse it—"

"Hey. Slow down. Relax. You're going to be okay. We're going to figure out who needs to be called, and I'm calling them, and you're coming to my place and resting until you're calm and don't hurt so badly."

"I can't, they—"

"They can fuck off. I'll get word to your friends, but if any of your parents' handlers try to come over and muscle you home, I'm calling for backup. A line of semipro football players ought to do the trick." He rubbed gentle circles between Baz's shoulder blades. "Come on. We've got to walk over to the studio to get my car and tell Laurie what's up, and then it's a big fat narcotic, a sedative if I can scare one up, an ice pack, and some measured electrical pulses. Because I bet you and I have the same set of painkillers, or close enough to count, and my TENS unit is in fighting shape. I'll toss in a couple Jucy Lucys if you're feeling like molten cheeseburgers, and beer if that doesn't fuck you up while you're on narcotics."

Baz should have protested, but he was so sore, so

exhausted, and so lost it was too hard to fight Ed. He let Ed escort him across the street to a small building of painted white brick. Inside kids laughed as they followed the instructions of a male dancer slightly older than Ed, doing ballet at the front of the room before a row of mirrors. When the instructor saw Ed, he smiled, told the class to take a five-minute break, and came over to kiss Ed on the lips.

"Hey, hon." Ed gestured to Baz. "This is the kid for the internship I've been telling you about. Baz, this is Laurie. Laurie, this is Baz."

"Pleased to meet you." Laurie shook Baz's hand. He got a better look at Baz and added, "Is everything okay?"

"He needs to borrow some of my stash and sit in the dark for a bit. I'm stealing the car. You okay to take a cab home, or should I come and get you later?"

"Oh, I'll find my own ride." Laurie smiled kindly at Baz. "I hope you feel better."

Ed packed Baz into a car, drove him to a loft apartment not far from the studio. Herded him into a bed smelling like Ed and his husband. Brought Baz some Vicodin and ibuprofen, a Benadryl, and a TENS unit. Once Baz had those in his system, Ed sat beside the bed on a chair, notebook and pen in hand.

"Tell me who I'm calling. Names, phone numbers. If you can pick a few who can call the others, do."

"Elijah for sure. But don't make him call anyone. Have…Damien be the other contact. He knows all the numbers to call. Marius would be better, but he's probably still in school." Baz stared at the ceiling through his sunglasses—the bedside lamp was on while Ed took notes. "I should check my phone. I turned it off before because it was blowing up."

"Nope. You don't get it back until you've rested and eaten. If there's someone else you want me to call for you, tell me now, but otherwise let them take care of it. You were a mess when you walked into my weight room. You're only marginally better now. You're letting me handle this, got it?"

Nothing in Ed's voice hinted he'd allow discussion on this point, so Baz gave the numbers, took off his glasses, and went to sleep. He didn't think he was tired, but one second he was thinking how he'd never sleep, and the next Ed shook him gently, saying he had dinner waiting for him.

Laurie puttered in the kitchen, smiling and waving as Ed put takeout on plates and Baz collapsed on a barstool by the counter. "Doing any better?"

Baz nodded carefully. His head still pounded a little, but he didn't feel so frayed around the edges. He shifted the TENS pads from his hip to his neck. "Did I hear something about a beer?"

They moved to TV trays in the living room area, ate greasy cheese-stuffed burgers and chatted. Laurie asked how Baz liked his internship, which got them talking about volunteering and philanthropy, and eventually they discovered they had a mutual acquaintance—Oliver Thompson was one of Baz's mother's oldest friends, and he was Laurie's godfather.

"If you're serious about pursuing a career in Twin Cities philanthropy, I *have* to hook the two of you up.

Oliver has his fingers in every pie, and he could set you up like *that*." Laurie snapped his fingers in emphasis. "You let me know when you want to meet."

"I will." Mentioning his mother, though, brought Baz back to reality. "Did you get ahold of Damien? Elijah?"

"Damien, yes, Elijah not yet."

Baz had been ready to camp out on Ed's sofa for the night, but the thought of Elijah made him itch to get to Saint Timothy. When he glanced at the clock on the microwave, though, he thought of another question. "Did my mom call?"

Ed pulled out Baz's phone. He didn't pass it over, turning it on and scrolling through Baz's missed calls himself.

Shaking his head, he put the phone down with a grimace.

Baz sat quietly, letting that sink in. That when the chips were down, when he flipped out and bolted into the unknown, his mom would carry through with the political opportunity. Baz could wait.

Except Baz was done waiting. Utterly, completely done.

ELIJAH WAS IN the middle of Intro to British Literature when his phone started buzzing.

The first time he ignored it, but after the third buzz on his ass, he pulled his phone out to see who was trying so hard to reach him. He didn't know the number, but whoever it was kept calling. He shut his phone off and did his best to focus on his class. Once it was done, he ducked into a quiet hallway and turned his phone on to check his voicemails.

He had thirteen, and four times as many texts. All of the messages said the same thing. *Baz is missing. Do you know where he is?*

Giles's phone went to voicemail, but Aaron picked up. "Hey. We've been trying to get ahold of you."

No shit. "What's wrong with Baz? What do they mean, he's missing? He went into Saint Paul to see his mom. Did he not make it?" *Is he okay? Is he hurt?*

"I don't know. I think so, but something happened, and now they're looking for him."

Elijah slumped against the wall, dizzy and sick. "Have they called the police? Where are his parents, at the White House?"

"I honestly don't know anything, only that this guy named Stephan keeps calling me, and the suits who usually escort us all took off at once."

"What are we supposed to do?"

"Do you have any more classes?"

"No. Just choir." Which he was so skipping, and fuck the attendance policy. Where was Baz?

"Good. Come over and be in the student lounge with us, and we'll brainstorm this. Do you want me to come get you? Where are you?"

It was on the tip of Elijah's tongue to refuse the offer, but he really did feel sick and slightly crazed. "If you don't mind. I'm in the humanities wing of Fletcher Hall. Back hallway by the stairs leading to the auditorium."

"Be there in five."

When they hung up, Elijah went through the rest of his texts, desperate to find one from Baz, but there was only the note he'd sent earlier about going to see his mom. Elijah jotted out a quick *Where are you? Please call me*, considered adding more before squelching the idea and scanned through the rest. There were several unknown numbers, though, and after one voicemail and two reporter texts, Elijah deleted everything unread.

Soon after that, Aaron appeared on the stairs, and Elijah about burst out of his skin in his eagerness to get the fuck out of there. "We have to go look for him. I don't know where to look, but I have to do *something*. I know I'll miss choir, but I don't care."

"Nussy won't mind—there seems to be a special rule for Baz. Can I go with you?"

Elijah had sudden images of the entire White House turning the Tesla into a clown car. "Yes, but only if it's *just* you."

"Come on. We can go the back way to the White House."

They crossed the street like thieves escaping a jewel heist. Nobody was in sight, no press, no security goons, nobody at all. Elijah was starting to feel ridiculous about how *Mission: Impossible* they were being—and then they rounded the corner to the White House.

The driveway was full of cars—the Tesla and Giles's car were completely blocked in. The suits who usually escorted them silently around campus huddled in groups, looking grim.

Aaron glanced sidelong at Elijah. "Um. This is intense. What do you want to do?"

Elijah wanted to get to Baz. "Maybe we can use a side street and call a cab, or Uber. Or Walter."

"Something tells me anyone who knows Baz is getting this same insanity right now. I think we should stick to a cab."

They slipped into the alley, but before they could escape, one of the suits saw them, called out "*Hey!*" and it was over.

Aaron hadn't been kidding about intense. The suits grilled them about why they were taking off. When Aaron said they were looking for Baz, the suits told them they were handling the search and asked them repeatedly if they'd had any contact with Baz or anyone he was with.

"I think we should go to choir rehearsal," Aaron suggested when they were finally able to escape the suits. "We're clearly not going to get away to the Cities—these guys are going to follow us. We might as well go sing it out."

Elijah didn't want to sing it out, but with no other real recourse, that's exactly what he did. Virtually all their songs had a religious bent, which drove Aaron crazy but Elijah secretly enjoyed. They were working on a song for the homecoming concert, "What Wondrous Love Is This?" with eight-part harmony, totally a cappella. It wasn't all fancy and jazzy like the Ambassadors or Salvo, but Elijah loved it. It reminded him of going to church with Pastor Schulz, or the services when he was young, when his brother was alive and his parents had been merely gruff and stern.

Today he pushed his heart into the song, willing the music to bleed off some of his crazy. *When I was sinking down, sinking down*—that was now, holy fuck. The idea of Baz being in trouble, being out of his reach—yes, he would take divine intervention from *anybody* to get him home. The last verse made him choke.

And when from death I'm free. He told himself not to get overly dramatic, Baz wasn't in any danger of dying, but he was all hyped up now, and the minor key and swelling harmony of the choir got to him.

Come back to me, Baz. I need you. So much. I don't want to, but I do. More than I can say, more than I know how to manage. Please come make everything okay again. Like you always do.

They waited in the lounge for Giles and Mina to get out of orchestra, and Aaron and Elijah gave Lejla, Sid, and Jilly the update. Sotto voce, as their escorts lingered in the hallway, watching them with stony expressions.

"This is creepy." Lejla huddled into herself and glanced at the door. "Are we under house arrest or something?"

Aaron glared at the security guys. "I'm not liking this. At all. I know Baz says his parents are fine, just a little offbeat, but this is too much. I called Pastor and told him. He already knew, because he got the same locust attack we did, and he's not happy. I don't care if Mrs. Acker is getting appointed to be President. This is out of line. Way out of line."

When Giles and Mina joined them, they agreed with Aaron. Giles took point beside his boyfriend. "We're going to the house, and we're getting some goddamned answers. Also some dinner. Jesus, I'm starving."

They walked home together in a small mob, actively ignoring the suits walking beside them, though a few times Elijah thought Giles was going to tell them to fuck off. When they got to the house, things were crazier than before. Giselle standing stonily beside him, Stephan paced up and down their living room rug, barking out orders. Until he saw the residents arriving, and then he started barking at *them*.

"We're going to have a few words about your failure to return my calls, but first you're telling me everything you know about where Baz is. I know something is up, and I'm not playing any games."

"I don't know what's going on," Sid said, his patience clearly wearing thin, "but you guys need to back the fuck off. If Baz knew what was going on here, he'd be all kinds of pissed."

"Well, Baz *isn't* here, is he?" Giselle's perfectly pink lips pressed into a neatly outlined seam. "Nobody can find him. His parents are worried sick."

"Where *are* his parents?" This came from Aaron. "Why haven't we received any phone calls from them?"

"Because Ms. Barnett Acker and her husband are busy people." Giselle's lip curled in a baby sneer. "Do you have any sense how much this disappearing act has upset their schedule? Do you have any comprehension of how much work went into getting them these interviews?"

Mina got into her face. "Baz is a person, not some political pawn you can whip out of your ass."

Elijah closed his eyes and stifled a wince, slipping into trick head as Giselle's demands for them to tell what they knew became pointed and too intense for him to deal with. Then Stephan was in front of him, bellowing and vibrating with rage.

"I know he told *you*. There's no way he didn't let you know where he went. Tell me *right now*, or so help me God, I will make you pay."

The flashback to being yelled at by his dad hit Elijah so hard and fast he stumbled. Lejla steadied him, and Mina and Giles and Sid started yelling at the same time, but Giselle zeroed in on Elijah like a dog who had found the bone.

"This isn't a game, Mr. Prince. You have no idea how influential the Barnetts are. They want to find their son. Just because you're setting up house with him doesn't mean you get to dictate terms. You're on thin ice as it is, with the drag you have from your father's trial—and this is saying nothing of how much the Barnett-Ackers have single-handedly pulled your ass out of the damn gutter—"

"*Shut the fuck up.*" Aaron had shoved his way to the front, fists clenched at his sides, body vibrating with rage. "You arrogant pieces of shit—shut the *fuck* up. You don't talk to *anybody* in this house that way, but you sure as hell don't talk to Elijah with disrespect. And fuck your delusions about who's helping who around here. We've *all* put into Elijah's fund. You're full of shit, with your threats—and if by some insanity you manage to follow through on them, *we* are going to make *you* pay."

While everyone else shouted, Lejla pulled Elijah aside and hustled him up the stairs. She led Elijah into his room, and when Stephan shouted after them, she locked the door and dragged the dresser in front of it.

Elijah collapsed onto the edge of the bed. He felt dizzy and fucked up and terrified. It was like a bad dream. Or more to the point, a bad memory. In his mind Stephan kept morphing into his dad, looming over him, shouting, calling him names, making it clear every horrible thing that ever happened to the world was because of Elijah.

Lejla sat next to him, gently putting an arm around him. "Hey. It's okay."

Elijah shut his eyes and wrapped his arms over his stomach. "I just need a minute."

"That guy is crazy. The woman too. This whole thing is insane."

Each time Lejla spoke, Elijah felt more and more like he was going to throw up. He could feel the panic attack coming, and his whole mission in life became to have it by himself. "I need to be alone for a few minutes."

He croaked out the words, and at first he wasn't sure Lejla was going to leave, but whatever she saw in his face convinced her to stand. She touched his hair lightly, stroking in a hesitant, stuttering gesture. "I'm going to wait outside. You'll holler if you need me?"

Elijah managed a wooden nod, though it was a lie

because he wasn't hollering anything. He wanted to crawl under the bed. He wanted to take enough drugs to turn him into a zombie so he wouldn't see his dad looming over him anymore. He wanted to erase what Stephan had said from his brain because the words kept echoing, burning deeper and deeper into his soul, letting loose so many things he'd worked his fingers to the bone trying to forget.

He hesitated over Baz's dresser top full of drugs, but the memory of how badly he'd fucked himself up the last time made him turn away. What he was supposed to do instead of drowning in chemicals, however, wasn't immediately clear. All he knew was the panic kept rising inside him, threatening to blow out the top of his head.

He didn't consciously plan on climbing out the window. It simply happened. Stuffing cigarettes and his wallet into a backpack, he slung it over his shoulder and climbed down the rusty fire escape as silently as he could.

Except he didn't know where to go. He couldn't make his legs work right. His feet were so heavy he couldn't get farther than the garage. He crawled behind a hedge and tucked his legs against his body, shivering in the cold as the shouts from the house punctuated the night.

Though he'd brought his cigarettes, he didn't smoke. He only sat there, rigid, curled in a ball, vacillating between rage and hatred and fear—because he didn't understand what had happened, why he'd melted down, or what was supposed to happen next.

This isn't a game, kid. You have no idea how influential the Barnetts are.

Howard Prince can be forgiven his rage when it's learned what a manipulative, soulless fiend drove him to his crime.

You disgust me. You aren't the man your brother was. You'll never be. You should have died instead of him. You should crawl through the dirt in gratitude and pray the world never finds out how full of evil you are.

Elijah shut his eyes tight, digging his fingernails into his jeans. "What wondrous love is this," he whispered, repeating the song under his breath in a vain attempt to drown out the bilious echoes of his memory.

BAZ WAS PREPARED for a small circus at the White House, but the sheer volume of suits and muscle milling around his driveway pretty much blew his mind as Ed drove them close enough to get a full view.

Laurie leaned forward in the passenger seat with an expression of alarm. "This is because you skipped out on an interview?"

Ed parked the car a discreet distance from the house, but the goons in the yard were already eyeballing them. Ed looked pretty pissed. "I'm starting to regret not asking the guys to come along. This is a bit fucked up, Baz."

It was. "I'll get it sorted out." *As soon as my mother is done being interviewed.* God, that was going to sting all night long.

"We'll be coming with you." Laurie exited the car

with grace and poise. "I believe your mother's people have overstepped themselves. Let's go remind them of a thing or two."

Ed frowned at the security detail. "I really think we should call the guys."

Laurie waved this idea away. "This isn't a moment for muscle. But feel free to appear menacing, if you like."

At the house they were immediately besieged by pretty much every part of the Barnett detail on the lawn. A few reporters who had smelled a story lingered at the edge of the drive, but when the security guys attempted to block them, Laurie kept his smile in place as he leaned over to whisper to Baz.

"Pick out one you like and invite them inside."

Baz blinked, and despite how sick he felt, laughed. "Laurie, you're an evil genius."

"This ain't my first time at the rodeo," he replied, letting go of Baz to warmly welcome the confused but excited press junket forming around them, asking their names and where they were from.

Baz chose the young but aggressive-looking Asian woman who had on a power suit for a stakeout. Her name was Susan Meeks, and she turned out to be a senior journalism student from the *Minnesota Daily*. Since he was still a bit shell-shocked, he murmured his choice to Laurie, who told her she was entirely welcome to bring a cameraman inside.

The security guys balked, and several suits came over with hands extended, as if to push them back, but Susan had her crew aim the cameras at them, and

Laurie simply smiled serenely as Ed moved in front of them to become their personal bulldozer. Soon they were at the front door, where an angry Stephan and Giselle stood ready for battle.

"Where in the world have you—?" Stephan went white as he spied the camera aimed on him. "Turn that off. Turn that *off.*"

Laurie stepped around a bristling Ed and extended his hand to Stephan. "Laurie Parker. I'm sure you've heard of my parents, Albert and Caroline, and their foundation. My godfather, Oliver Thompson, has had so many good things to say about Gloria."

Stephan paused before composing himself warily. "Sebastian, it's wonderful to have you back. Is there some reason you saw fit to bring the press?"

Baz ignored him as he scanned the room. He saw most of his housemates huddled around the couch, looking pissed off and concerned, but not his boyfriend. "Where's Elijah?"

"He's in your room." This came from Lejla on the stairs. "He's pretty upset."

Baz pushed through the wall of aides, and when they tried to detain him, Ed came to his side. "I'm sure he's fine," he assured Baz as they hustled up the stairs.

But nobody answered when they knocked on the door, or when Baz pounded on it and pleaded with Elijah to open up.

"Relax," Ed urged when Baz started to lose his shit. "Do you have a key for this?"

Baz was pretty sure he had a universal skeleton key—in his room. Along with all kinds of substances to abuse. "We need to break it."

Brian appeared behind them. "What about the fire escape?"

Baz pretty much leapt down the stairs, wanting to punch Stephan in the face on the way by, but he was on the other side of the room, getting his ass politely handed to him by Laurie, on camera. Baz barreled out the door to the patio, hoping to hell he'd find Elijah, but there were just more security goons keeping a watchful eye on who the hell knew what. He wanted to climb the fire escape, but Lejla wouldn't let him. She had Ed hoist her up to the drop ladder, and she scurried up the iron stairs to the window. "The light's on—oh, the window is open." She leaned into the room, called out, then shook her head at the contingency on the ground. "He's not in here. I think he came out this way, though."

All the house residents were home now, and a great deal of the security—Ed barked out orders for everyone to start looking for Elijah. They spanned through the yard and into the street, calling his name, pulling out their phones to call and text him.

Baz did his best to think like Elijah and attempt a guess as to where and why he might have gone. Mostly his brain cycled through a manic urge to bring him home.

Aaron took his arm. "It's okay. We'll find him."

Baz gripped his own leg. Fuck his hip, he wasn't sitting this out, even if he had to limp to Canada. "What happened? Why would he take off?"

Mina, who had been calling into the yard, answered

with steel in her gaze. "Those fuckheads reamed him out, basically threatened him if he didn't tell where you were. We got up in their grill, but Elijah went upstairs. We thought he was checking out to avoid this bullshit." Her face fell. "I'm so sorry, we should have done better."

"How long ago did he go upstairs? What did he take?" *How many drugs?* God, Baz was flushing all of them down the fucking toilet.

Lejla climbed into the room, poked around, and reemerged. "Looks like his backpack, maybe a sweatshirt. His phone's on the dresser."

"Is there somewhere he would go?" Ed asked.

"Pastor Schulz, maybe." Baz didn't know. He swayed on his feet and swallowed more panic.

Someone made a call to Pastor, which was a dead end, so they resumed their search. Giselle came out and approached Baz, but the others held her back, and he let them. He had to find Elijah. Had to tell him. Had to make sure he was okay.

But he was nowhere. Baz knew he should follow the others into the streets, but he couldn't make himself go, and Ed kept urging him in a gentle voice to stay close, to be home base. *We'll find him,* everyone kept saying.

But no one did.

Baz leaned against a tree behind the garage. "This is all my fault."

Ed rubbed his back. "It isn't."

"It's my stupid family. I should have come home earlier. I shouldn't have stayed away."

"We're going to find him. Laurie's making some calls."

"I want him to come home," Baz whispered. "I need him, Ed. I can't function without him. I don't *want* to." He tightened his fingers into his hair, tugged. "I feel sick that I let fucking Stephan and Giselle drive him away. I want to fucking *kill them*."

"We'll deal with them next. Come inside with me a minute and rest. Have a drink of water. Take some deep breaths."

"I'm staying here." Baz clung to the tree. "He's not in the house. He went this way. I'm staying here until somebody finds him or he comes back."

"Fair enough. But I'm going inside to get you a chair and a bottle of water, okay?" Ed glanced around, frowning. "Damn it, they've all gone. It's only us here."

"I'm fine." Baz wasn't, but he was fine enough to stand there for five minutes. "I'm not leaving."

Ed squeezed Baz's biceps. "I'll be right back."

Baz watched him go, scanning the darkness in the vain hope Elijah would pop up once it was just the two of them. "Elijah, please." He clung to the tree, feeling like his guts were spilling out at his feet. "Whatever they said, it's bullshit. Come back so I can fix it. *Please.*"

Silence, except for car doors and calls for Elijah in the distance. It sounded as if more press had arrived on the lawn. Baz shut his eyes.

"Elijah Prince, come home. I need you. You need me. Don't make me go through this again. I don't want to lose you. Not even for an hour." He let out a ragged breath. "I love you, dammit. I love you more than anything or anyone else I've ever known."

There was, of course, no reply. Despondent, defeated, Baz sank to the ground, to his knees. His soul hollowing out, he stared dully into the bushes behind the garage.

Stared at something in the bushes behind the garage.

Pulling off his glasses, Baz crawled forward, blinking at the play of lights on his vision, focusing like hell on the shadows. He didn't know what to hope for, what to think, so he didn't—he only kept moving, until his vision adjusted and he came close enough to confirm, yes, there was a person sitting in the patch of mud behind the shrubbery. A small, dark-haired person with his knees drawn to his chest, staring at Baz with shame and fear.

Elijah wasn't crying, which was somehow worse. It was Baz's blender freakout magnified a thousand times. A panic attack. A bad one. An emotional retreat he couldn't quite maneuver his way through. Drug-free from the look of him, which meant everything was dialed to eleven.

But he was here. He wasn't bleeding, and he was *here*. Baz could help him.

When Ed came around the corner of the house, Baz shot out a hand, stilling him. "Ed, I need you to bring my car around to the alley." He fished in his pocket for his key fob and tossed it on the ground between them. "The Tesla. Put your foot on the brake to start it. Bring it around without anyone else coming, please. No press.

No goons. Nobody else from the house. Tell Laurie what's going on, and Giles and the others, but they have to stay inside. Everybody needs to give us space."

"Okay." Ed sounded unsure. "Baz, have you—is he there?"

"Yes. But I need you to get us away from here for a bit," Baz replied, still staring right at Elijah. "You and me and him. Absolutely nobody else. I'd do it myself, if I could drive."

Ed relaxed. "Okay." He came close enough to pick up the keys, glancing toward the bushes, but there was no way he'd see anything from where he was. "It might be a few minutes."

"That's fine. We're in no rush."

When Ed left, Baz put his glasses on and moved closer. Elijah stayed where he was, but he didn't look away.

Baz didn't either. "Let me take you for a drive. Let me get you somewhere safe."

Elijah's eyes filled with tears, and some spilled down his cheek.

Baz climbed in enough to put a hand where Elijah could grab it. "Either you come out and let me take you away from here, or I come in to you. Your call."

More tears escaped. Elijah blinked, let the rest fall. Then he took Baz's hand, helped pull himself out of the bushes. Out of the darkness and into the safety of Baz's arms.

Chapter Twenty-Four

I T TOOK ED almost fifteen minutes to get the Tesla into the alley. No one else came but Ed, which was good because Baz understood there was no way in hell Elijah could take any additional people right now.

Elijah allowed himself to be removed from his hiding place and ushered into the Tesla, but he was wooden-limbed and jumpy, even once they were ensconced together in the backseat. Baz wrapped his body around his boyfriend and met Ed's gaze in the rearview mirror.

"Head east on Tenth Street." He leaned between the seats to punch at the display. "I'll find it on Google Maps and let it navigate you there."

He set up the coordinates for the lake, then pulled out his phone, turned it on, and used the Tesla app to run the stereo. When he settled into the seat, drawing Elijah in close once more, the opening theme of *Howl's Moving Castle* soundtrack played softly through the speakers.

Tentative fingers closed over Baz's sleeve, tensing and releasing a few times before settling on his forearm.

Baz kissed Elijah's hairline. When this made Elijah shudder a sigh, Baz held his lips gently in place, as if he could draw the stress out through the contact. It almost seemed to work. Some of the tension leached out of Elijah, his body less rigid, his breathing more normal.

Once they were at the lake, Ed dropped the key fob on the seat and left the car, closing the door quietly behind him.

Only when they were alone did Elijah finally speak. "I think I'm crazy like my mom and dad."

"Not even close, baby."

"I *feel* crazy." His voice shook. His hands tightened into fists that he drew to his body as he curled tighter into a ball on Baz's lap. "It's all too loud. Everything is too much. I want to run. Go. I don't know where. I want to walk to California. Swim to China. *Go.*" His laugh was brief and bitter. "I got as far as the garage. I'm a mess. All fucked up."

"You're not fucked up."

"I am the goddamned *definition* of fucked up. I melted down in a goddamned hedge, and I don't know *why*." He threw up his hands, but though his eyes glistened, no more tears fell. "It was all a fucking waste. All the planning with Walter's firm, everybody standing up for me, you getting—" He covered his mouth with his hand, shutting his eyes as tears fell. Baz tried to touch his arm, but Elijah shook him off, eyes open and glaring as the escaped tears sank into his skin. "What the hell was it *for*? I'm too fucked up. My parents were right—"

"Don't. Don't you fucking dare finish that sentence."

"*I am fucked up.* Are you not listening? I fought for

years to get free of them, to *win*, and I'm king of a goddamned *trash pile*."

"You're no king, you're a Prince."

The quip should have at least taken some of the wind out of his sails, but Elijah was so worked up he made his own weather now. "*Of what?*"

Baz took off his glasses and put them in the back window. Catching Elijah's cheek with trembling fingers, Baz looked Elijah in the eye. "You're the Prince of my heart."

Elijah stared at him. His angry expression melted, but not into romantic goo. More melted wax, the face of an ugly cry without the tears.

"Why?" Elijah asked at last, in a rough whisper. "I'm so fucked up. Why would you *want me?*"

Baz nodded at the lake glistening in the moonlight. "You know how many times friends have dragged me out to somewhere so I could vomit out a remix of everything you just said?"

"You aren't vomiting anything now." Elijah pulled a sarcastic smile. "Are you telling me *it gets better?*"

"No. Wounds are wounds. Shit that happened remains shit that happened. *You* get better, though. Maybe you're forever decamped on the Island of Misfit Toys, but you're better." He stroked Elijah's hair. "I'm saying I'm better with you. I should probably be noble and tell you I'll let you go if it's what you want, but I'm a spoiled, selfish brat. I'll follow you, beg you, bribe you to stay. Because you're the first one to make it to my island. I don't want to let you leave."

Elijah melted out of the ugly and into…Elijah.

"You have too many metaphors going. First we were *Sid and Nancy*, then we were *Howl's Moving Castle*, and now we're *Rudolph the Red-Nosed Reindeer*."

"How about we be Baz and Elijah, together forever?"

Elijah moved closer, into the circle of Baz's arms. "Prince of your heart, huh?"

"Yeah."

Elijah rested his head on Baz's shoulder, settling in. "You really don't care that I'm a mess?"

Shutting his eyes, Baz rubbed his cheek on Elijah's temple. "Sometimes I think it's my favorite part."

"I still want to run away. I can't, but I want to."

"I'd take you. Anywhere you want to go. Anytime you want to leave."

Elijah punched him lightly in the shoulder he wasn't leaning on. "You would not."

"I would. In a hot second. For you."

"But they'd be pissed."

"Too fucking bad. They've been on my ass for just shy of a decade to find a purpose for my life. They have to put up with whatever I decide that is. Whenever I fucking find it."

"So *I'm* your purpose?"

Baz glanced away. "You don't have to sound so incredulous."

Elijah pulled Baz's face back. His gaze might as well have been a laser peel. "You were serious? Because if you're fucking with me—"

Baz sat up too, taking Elijah's face in his hands. "I would *never* fuck with you. Why do you think that?

Why do you always think that?"

"Because *people go out of their way to tell me you will.* You've done it to everyone else, over and over."

"Yeah, well, everyone else isn't *you.*" Baz let his hands fall to Elijah's shoulders. "What you said about feeling like people saved you only to be disappointed you were broken—I've felt that since I was sixteen. I started calling myself Baz instead of Sebastian because Sebastian Acker was a snotty prick who thought his family's wealth and network would take care of him. Baz knows all the money and connection in the world can't replace some things. He will never be as strong as he wants, or as stable. This is the way survival is, for him." He pressed his cheek to Elijah's hair. "All I know is for me, being with you, taking care of you, fills up my holes. I don't want to stop."

Elijah's hands had moved to Baz's back, and they tensed. "I—I like you. A lot. But sometimes it makes me nervous, and I don't know if I can—"

Baz lifted his head enough to still Elijah's lips with a kiss. It lingered longer than he'd originally intended, and when he drew back, he nuzzled Elijah's nose. "We have different curses. We have to undo our own spells."

"It makes me feel shitty and alone. I don't want to be alone." He sagged. "But I think maybe I have to be. Even in a crowd of people, my heart will always ache."

The statement resonated in the furthest hollows of Baz's soul. "Then we'll be lonely hearts together."

Elijah shuddered and caressed Baz's neck. "I don't want to feel anymore. Not today. I'm tired of feelings."

"Let me take you somewhere so you can rest. Ed

will drive us anywhere. Tell me where you want to go, and we're there."

"Home." Elijah's voice was small, exhausted. "I want to go home. To the White House. With you."

Baz kissed his hair. "Then that's what we'll do."

ELIJAH REGRETTED HIS request to go to the White House as soon as they arrived. The driveway was clogged with cars and news vans and those bright lights reporters stood under.

Ed sighed and gestured at the house. They'd stopped far enough away nobody had seen them yet. "What now, guys?"

"Pull around to the back again." Baz stroked Elijah's hair. "Turn down this side street, and they might not see us."

Nobody did. There was a security guy near the garage, but he only nodded gruffly at Baz as the three of them approached. When they headed toward the door, though, Elijah withdrew.

"I can't. Not with everybody there."

He'd hoped Baz would say they could go up the fire escape, but he only put his arm around Elijah and drew him forward. "We'll walk straight to the stairs. No passing go."

"I locked the door."

"We'll send someone to open it."

He wanted to fight more, but he didn't have it in him. He couldn't put up walls, couldn't fight, couldn't snark.

You're the Prince of my heart.

I love you more than anything or anyone else I've ever known.

All eyes were on them as they came into the living room, but before they got far, Baz took something out of his jacket and pressed it into Elijah's hand. His spare glasses. The reddish-brown ones, which were his outside-in-daytime ones. Elijah slipped them on, grateful. He stumbled, because damn, those things were practically blackout-strength. But they hid his eyes, became his mask as Baz navigated them through the room. Their housemates tried to approach, but they kept their distance when Baz gestured them back. The reporters and the political operatives were a different story entirely.

"I need everyone to leave." Baz held Elijah close, standing at the foot of the stairs. "Anyone associated with my mom's campaign, with the press. I'll do interviews with anyone who wants one, but not until tomorrow, and *not* if you camp out in my yard."

Stephan looked ready to blow several gaskets. "Sebastian, I cannot allow—"

Baz's whole body tensed. "Get out. You especially, you and Giselle, *get out*, or I don't care how much it fucks up my body, I will *throw* you out."

"I'll help," Ed offered from the other side of the room.

Giles, Aaron, Lejla, Mina, Jilly, Sid, and Brian voiced their heartfelt agreement.

Baz led Elijah up the stairs.

Someone had already unlocked the door, but Baz

turned the latch once they were safely inside. After dimming the lights, he shut the window, the blinds, then took off his glasses and undressed Elijah.

Elijah shivered, mostly from overstimulation, but he didn't fight. "You haven't turned on the red lights yet. Put your glasses back on."

"You like me better without them."

"I like you without a migraine."

He snorted. "Six hours too late."

Elijah opened his mouth to protest, but he stopped when Baz removed his sunglasses. Now they were both naked.

In the faded brown light of the bedroom, Baz's face shone with gentleness. Elijah got a rush acknowledging nobody else ever saw this face. The eyes were a treat, yes, but in everyday wear, Baz's expression was a mask of cool or wry humor. Tonight, as was so many times they were alone together, Elijah realized, Baz's face was tender.

Being with you, taking care of you, fills up my holes. I don't want to stop.

Baz's words echoed in Elijah as Baz finished undressing him and kept him close as he stripped out of his own clothes. He lowered them to the bed together and tucked them into the comforter, pulling it over their heads. In the rapidly heating cocoon, they wrapped around one another, their bodies close, their noses nearly touching.

"I feel kind of dumb," Elijah said at last. "I've never freaked out so much."

Baz kissed him lightly, stroking his hair. "Funny. I

was about to say the same thing."

Elijah lifted his head. "What happened?"

Baz kept petting Elijah, but his expression became heavy. "I thought I was going to see my mom. Talk with her. It was inconvenient, but I felt like I knew what my job was, so I sucked it up and shifted my schedule. Except it wasn't to see her. It was to be a prop. They had this slideshow of talking points. They'd rewritten the attack when I was sixteen to make me sound as if I should be wearing a bandage over my eye and an arm in a sling as I wept into a golden bowl before it could be blessed by a gay-rights deity. That pissed me off, but—" He stopped, then plowed on, his expression hard. "They wanted me to pretend I was single because it polled better. So I took off."

That hurt, and combined with the earlier shit from Stephan, Elijah admitted it cut pretty well. "You didn't have to do that for me."

"Elijah—you're what I care about. You're everything to me." His hands slipped to Elijah's shoulders. "They crossed my biggest line. You said at the lake you were worried I was going to abandon you. If you told me to get lost, I'd probably keep trying to take care of you. I'd do my best to not be creepy and stay out of your way, but let's just say if your sidewalk magically cleans itself, you know who to blame."

Elijah nestled into the crook of Baz's shoulder, turning his face to inhale deep scents of Baz. "I'm not going to tell you to get lost."

"Even though my family is fucked up and will probably continue in the same vein?"

"Sorry, I have no experience in that department. No point of reference whatsoever."

Baz chuckled and pulled him closer.

As he snuggled deeper into the delicious cocoon of their bed, Elijah made himself acknowledge how hard Baz had pursued him not only tonight but also every other time Elijah had tried to withdraw. Tonight he'd found Elijah when everyone else kept walking right past him—Baz seemed to zero in, as if he'd known exactly where to look. He with the shit vision. Baz had found him, swept him away in his moving castle and talked him into sanity. Confessed that he loved Elijah, loved taking care of him. Baz wasn't a little bit of affection. He wasn't a flame like Aaron or Giles or Mina or Lejla. He was a goddamned lighthouse calling Elijah's moth-eaten soul home.

Elijah shut his eyes, giving in to the beacon before him. "I love you."

Baz stilled, lips brushing Elijah's hairline. One hand tightened on his shoulder, and the other gripped Elijah's hip, slightly desperate.

Say it again.

Elijah did. "I...love you. I'm scared and I don't want to, not anybody, but I do. Love you. And I don't think I can stop."

Hot breath exhaled on his cheek as Baz sighed, then nuzzled his temple. "I love you too."

Chapter Twenty-Five

B AZ WANTED TO stay curled up in bed with Elijah, fall asleep and pretend the world didn't exist. A few weeks ago, Baz would have given in to the temptation. Tonight, once Elijah fell asleep, he climbed carefully out of bed and into his clothes.

Everyone was in the kitchen—his housemates, Ed and Laurie, Damien, and Walter. Stephan, Giselle, and their crew were nowhere in sight. No reporters, not in the house, not on the lawn or in the driveway. His friends' expressions made it clear, though, there would still be an interrogation.

"Elijah's okay." Baz deposited himself wearily into the chair Damien indicated, giving in and letting his head fall sideways onto his friend's shoulder. "He's sleeping now."

Damien didn't dislodge Baz from his shoulder, but he did poke him in the leg. "You scared the shit out of us, you know. Marius kept trying to leave class. The only way we got him to stay home was to promise we'd bring back a report."

Baz reached under his glasses to pinch the bridge of his nose. "Can somebody switch the lights for me? Then I'll tell you whatever you want to know."

Giles got up to switch the lighting scheme from energy-saving fluorescent to incandescent red, but he didn't sit. "We know what happened. We want to know if *you're* okay. How we can help."

I'm fine. But as Baz removed his glasses and stared at them with his own eyes, he realized the lie would be pretty obvious. He sighed and stared at the tabletop instead. "I don't know what there is to do. At some point I have to call my mom, but I don't know what to tell her. I need to chase these reporters permanently off our damn lawn, but I don't know how to do that either."

He expected some coos and reassurances, but instead they exchanged irritated glances. Ed and Laurie were the exception. They watched the others, almost as if they were the parents at a family meeting, quietly, lovingly urging the kids to sort out their own shit.

Aaron broke the silence. "Baz, you need to tell your parents to fuck off. No more reporters. No more campaign. No more using you as a prop or doing focus groups on you."

They weren't simply united. They were a god-damned wall of resistance. Baz fought a new wave of tired as he scrambled to explain. "Look, I know I need to make them ease up, but a full-scale fuck you isn't appropriate—"

"Baz." Damien went full-on mama bear. "Everyone here at this table had their lives thrown into chaos because your parents pushed you too far."

Shame and sorrow hit Baz in the middle of the chest. "I'm so sorry. You guys didn't have to—"

Giles looked about as pissed as Damien. "You don't get it, Baz. We're not saying it's your fault. We're saying your mom's campaign is taking over your life so much when you try to resist, it consumes ours. It's bad for you. It's bad for your life and everyone you love." His cheeks stained as he added, "A lot of people love you, Baz."

Mina leaned in. "You took a bullet for all of us. Now we're forming a wall around you. You're letting us protect you. It's not up for discussion."

The table erupted in nods and murmured variations on *yes*. On Baz's other side, Lejla found his hand and squeezed. He turned to meet her gaze and found himself staring at unvarnished strength—and loyalty. Baz searched for another argument, a way to make them understand why it wasn't going to work the way they wanted it to—but to be honest, he wasn't sure how to convince himself of that any longer. He sagged in his chair and held up his hands in surrender. "Okay—but I still don't know what to do."

Walter leaned around Damien and grinned. "No worries, Acker. We already came up with a plan."

Their plan was weird, to Baz's mind, because it began with them sending Baz to bed. When he protested he really had to call his mom, Damien replied *he* was fielding that call. Baz wanted to ask what his friend was going to say, but he was afraid to find out. So he hugged everyone, passed over the keys to the Tesla when Damien asked for them, and went to bed.

He woke tangled in Elijah. An orgasm for Baz was utterly off the table, but when he tried to give one to

Elijah, he only shook his head and burrowed in closer. "I just want to hold you."

They kissed a lot, though. In bed, in the shower they took together, in the hall before going down the stairs hand in hand. Everyone else was already awake, and to his surprise, Baz found Damien having coffee and chatting quietly with Aaron.

"What are you doing here?" he asked after bussing the top of Damien's head. "Did you sleep on the couch or something?"

"Nope. Drove home and back in your fabulous car. Which I'm going to find more excuses to drive in the near future, by the way."

Mina handed Baz a cup of coffee and kissed him on the cheek, while Lejla gave the same treatment to Elijah. They sat, and their friends explained their day to them.

"Elijah, you have class at ten fifteen, right?" Aaron tapped a notebook as he spoke. "Lejla's your escort there, but Jilly's picking you up and taking you to lunch and your afternoon classes. Brian will bring you over to the music building, at which point Giles and I own your ass until after choir."

Elijah raised an eyebrow and glanced at Baz. Baz shrugged. "Don't look at me. I'm not driving this bus."

Damien clapped a hand on Baz's shoulder. "I, meanwhile, will enjoy a moment of silence in the chapel while you have your morning session with Pastor, and after, we're heading into the Cities to have lunch with Marius. Hopefully we convince him to stay on campus for the afternoon, but I'm pretty sure he'll be coming with us to the showdown with your parents. As soon as the brief meeting with your mother is done, you're resuming your regularly scheduled life. I'll escort you to your internship, get you home in time for choir. By the time you're done, I'll be at the White House with Marius, Walter, and Kelly. We'll all have a nice dinner, drink a bit of wine, and chill the fuck out."

Baz blinked at them all. They were as resolute as the night before. "Damien, it's Friday. You have work today."

"Took the day off."

Baz winced, scrambling for another excuse. "I told the reporters I'd give them interviews."

"You'll give a statement. Walter wrote it for you before he left." Giles pushed the paper across the table. "The press is meeting you outside the chapel—Pastor set it up. You go to your independent study meeting with him right after."

Baz scanned the paper in front of him. The statement was short and very lawyer, mostly saying while Baz supported his mother's political aspirations, he wasn't running for office and he was focusing on finishing school. It was pretty good, actually. He wondered if it would work.

An hour and a half later, he discovered that it did. Damien stood at his elbow as he read the statement verbatim and took four follow-up questions. Walter had a series of stock redirects for everything political, and Baz used them. The last question, though, he answered directly. It came from Susan Meeks.

"Is it true you're still involved with Elijah Prince,

the young man whose life you saved in March, and would you consider it a serious relationship?"

"Yes and yes," Baz replied, and they were done. The reporters shouted more at them as they disappeared inside the chapel, but campus security was there in force, and they informed the press they needed to leave campus now.

Pastor gave Baz a hug before leading him up the stairs to his office. "You look like things are going a bit better than what I understand was your experience yesterday."

Baz grimaced, realizing Pastor had been dragged into this as much as everyone else in his life. "I'm sorry for any trouble it caused you."

Schulz waved this apology away. "I've fielded worse crises during my tenure as campus pastor."

They actually didn't talk about the whole thing with his mom long. Pastor seemed to have been at the same meeting as everyone else, either that or what people kept saying was so obvious Baz was the only one who couldn't see it. Pastor listened, letting him vent about the chaos and confusion. He encouraged him to talk at length about Elijah and praised Baz for how he'd taken care of his boyfriend and himself. He nodded in approval at Damien's plan for Baz to tell his mother he was done with politics.

Then Pastor asked about his assignment for his independent study, the twenty-page paper he was due to present in draft by homecoming, in full by his graduation in December.

By the time Damien got him to Marius, Baz had

the feel for this dance, and he was starting to like it. When Marius bear-hugged him and babbled worry and demanded Baz never let this happen again, Baz promised he was done with his family's political dynasty. The more he said it, the better he felt.

They stopped off for coffee at the law school with Walter, who showed Baz some online articles based on the statement he'd drafted and congratulated Baz on a job well done. Then he coached him through a remixed version for his parents.

"I know you probably have an impulse to really get into it and explain yourself, but I'd encourage you to steer away from that at this point," Walter said. "Your goal is to disengage, and theirs is to keep you engaged. Therefore any engagement beyond your stated intention to remove yourself works in *their* favor, not yours. While I understand your desire to smooth things out with your family, you need to be realistic about it probably not happening right now. Later you can have a goal of mediation and resolution, but right now the prize is getting out of current and future involvement in the campaign. My goal is to help you achieve that with a few sturdy roadblocks you can tear down later. No bridges will be burned in this if we play our cards right."

Baz stared at Walter as if he'd never seen him before. "When the hell did you get so smart, Lucas?"

"When I became a Davidson." Walter winked and sipped at his coffee. "Marriage suits me. A lot."

No shit. Baz reread Walter's talking points, but he found himself distracted by thoughts of Elijah. He was pretty sure Elijah worked the same kind of magic on him.

Marriage would suit me too.

Elijah wasn't on Walter's talking-points memo outside of a bullet point about how important Baz's relationship with him was, but when Baz waltzed into the Saint Paul Hotel flanked by Marius and Damien, the thought of being with Elijah, clearing this snarl so nothing threatened them anymore, gave him a center and a passion to succeed.

The suite was full to bursting with people, and though the whole room zeroed in on Baz as he entered, his mother and father sitting on the couch together were the whole of *his* focus. He took the chair cleared for him, drew a breath, and before his mother could take hold of the conversation, he said what he'd come to say.

"Mom, I love you and I wish you the best on your career. But it's not my career, and I'm not having any part of it any longer."

He wanted to blurt out the rest, but as Walter had advised, he waited, let his mother blink and frown and rebut. "Darling—no one ever said you had to be a part of it. You're blowing this entirely out of proportion. It was only a couple of interviews, and all your statements were prepared—"

Baz couldn't help going off message. "I hope to God you didn't have any idea *what* they told me to say. Because if you did, I'm walking out of here right now."

Gloria blinked at him and glanced at Stephan. "What's he talking about?"

Your goal is to get out of this, he reminded himself, and returned to his script. "Your campaign has invaded my life. Yesterday the lives of everyone I care about were thrown into chaos because no one told me I was walking into an ambush, not a casual lunch with my mother. My boyfriend was insulted and attacked in every way possible, and we spent the evening pulling him out of a panic attack. I'm done. I'm seriously done. My life is finally going in the right direction, and I'm not derailing it. I love you, but if you don't leave me out of this, especially after the bullshit of the past few weeks, I don't know if I can keep saying that much longer."

This comment hadn't been in Walter's prepared remarks either. But the truth of the words rang in his heart all the same.

His parents stared at him in shock. His father looked mostly uncomfortable, as he did whenever emotions were involved, but his mother looked…stricken. Hurt. As the pregnant moment expanded, her expression didn't change.

"All right, darling. If you feel that strongly about it, I'll see to it none of this bothers you any longer."

As Marius and Damien escorted him out of the suite, hugging him and murmuring *good job*, Baz realized, a little dizzily, he'd achieved his goal.

He was still slightly out-of-body as he arrived at Halcyon Center. Laurie loitered in Ed's office as Baz reported for duty, and it was clear Ed's husband had come along chiefly to hear the news of how things had gone. Still not entirely sure how to trust it had happened, Baz told them. He accepted their hugs, their praise. Then everyone but Ed left to go back to their lives, and Baz went with Ed to go over their lesson plan for the after-school classes.

In short, he got on with his life.

ELIJAH TRIED TO withdraw from his circle of friends, still feeling awkward about his meltdown, but they ignored all his barbs and attempts to dissuade them and carried on herding him through his day anyway. They babysat his ass all damn day long.

To be honest, he was grateful for it. It wasn't because they dodged stray clumps of press every now and again either. It was because panic this intense took more than a night's sleep to recede, and he felt it clamoring to reclaim him all day. When he admitted as much in the spare hour before choir, Mina dragged him practically by the ear over to student services, where the doctor said he'd give Elijah some chill pills, but only if he added an antidepressant.

"It might well be a short-term thing," the doctor said when Elijah balked. "But given the chaos of your year, and the admission you're managing it with substance abuse, I can't in good conscience add any more fuel to the fire. All these pills and drugs you're using are surface fixes. An antidepressant works from the chemical base up. And while some take work to get on and off, they don't require rehab."

There was no way in hell Elijah was taking an antidepressant. They'd tried after the attack with no real luck, and when he'd read about what they could do to creativity, he'd sworn them off for life. "There has to be some other way to get a handle on myself."

"Of course there is. Limit stress. Remove all illegal and harmful substances from your diet. Switch to a whole-foods regimen of largely fruit and vegetables, and consider going either vegan or paleo. Practice mindful meditation and deep breathing. Take up yoga. And I'm talking the Hindu, Vedic style, about your mind and spirituality, not the gym-bunny, trendy stuff."

Elijah was about as far from gym bunny as you could get. "Fine. I'll do it."

The doctor raised an eyebrow. "You understand these are *lifestyle* changes. Big ones. Making expensive fruit smoothies in a high-powered blender every morning. *No* substance abuse. Not even caffeine. You should consider limiting refined sugar too."

There'd be no blenders, but Elijah didn't figure he needed to get into that story with the doctor. "I get it, yes. It sounds like a bitch on wheels, but of course, this has been the story of my life."

"It's more than simply a diet. Don't expect to eat healthy for a week and your panic attacks will vanish. This is basically purifying your body so you can focus on strengthening your mind. It's possible most of the benefit comes from you deciding to do this. Sending the signal to your anxious thoughts that you're actively addressing them. Also know this will take *work*. Years. You have to sit with the pain. Process it. Though I'll tell you, even on antidepressants the greatest success rates come with this mindset."

"You're saying if I make these changes, I might be able to handle the bullshit. So, yeah. Give me the pamphlet, the web address, the hipster hat, and I'm in."

The doctor ended up handing Elijah a stack of books from his own library.

Out of the office, Elijah lost a little of his verve, especially when he reached for a cigarette before grudgingly handing them over to Mina to dispose of instead. The bustle of his circle of friends was more noise than comfort. But choir practice worked its usual magic. This time when he sang "What Wondrous Love Is This?" he didn't feel bittersweet. He felt hopeful. Like he could see the first fingers of a new dawn.

Baz arrived in time for choir, and on the way to the house afterward they held hands and shared the experiences of their day. Baz was all for Elijah's proposed lifestyle changes and promised to join him as much as possible.

"I don't know if I can cut out all the drugs—definitely not most of them—but I can cut the weed to medicinal, not recreational, for sure. They've been after me to try this kind of a diet for years, but it always seemed like a kick in the teeth. If it works the way they say it should, though, if I can feel better and be nicer to my liver, yeah. I'm down for health-nut shit."

I love you, Elijah thought. And then told him so.

The Twin Cities gang joined them for dinner—it had been meant to be pizza, but when word got out about Elijah and Baz's health quest, it got rerouted to a burgeoning salad bar. Kelly directed that ship, showing them how they could have a satisfying meal without dairy and processed junk, promising to bring his mom up some weekend for a crash course in cooking healthy.

The salad was good, even if Elijah was pretty sure he'd be hungry in an hour. When he'd said as much, Mina suggested he make another one if that's what happened.

It was three hours before he got peckish, but by then he was neck-deep in a homework assignment from Walter. His almost-lawyer had parked him in front of his laptop and an open document and told him it was time to tell his story.

"Maybe you publish this somewhere, on a personal blog or someone else's—or you don't show anyone at all. I think you need to write it, though. What happened to you. How you got through it. How it hurt, how you healed yourself."

Elijah's stomach curdled thinking about it. "I'm not healed. Not by a long shot."

Walter sat on the edge of the desk. "You're a writer. You process the world through story. I'm not saying this needs to be some kind of soul-baring confessional. I'm saying *choose your narrative.* It's not about countering the right-wing bloggers or throwing down with Baz's family. It's about telling *yourself* you're okay. Not perfect. *Okay.* That you're managing. That you have your life under control. Maybe getting a better visual on where your missing pieces are."

It all sounded so fucking Oprah Elijah wanted to gag, but after his vow to the student health doctor, he couldn't see how he could get out of it. Because this was pretty Zen, or something spiritual and centering.

Processing my pain. "I'll try it."

"Good." Walter hopped off the desk and nudged the laptop. "Go ahead and start right now."

Elijah did. The first hour was nothing but crap, and he kept deleting, but by the time Mina brought him coffee, he was starting to get into it. He decided to embrace the Disney and let it go. Wrote everything, no matter how pulpy or cute or gag-worthy emotive, and after a while, he didn't judge it anymore. He lost himself to the flow, pausing only long enough to piss and inhale the second helping of salad somebody brought him. By the time he staggered to bed at three in the morning, he had eight thousand words of complete and utter garbage.

It felt good though. Really good.

He let it sit for a day, but by Sunday night he had it open again. For a week he rewrote it obsessively. Unpacked the schmaltz and honed it into…something.

He understood, slowly, what Walter meant. Because the more he worked on the essay, the more he realized he could spin it any way he wanted. He could paint himself as the victim. The devil. The hero. The noble martyr. A regular college-aged adult struggling to find his place in the world amidst some unusual odds.

He steered the piece into that last option, because it felt the most comfortable. Hero seemed weird. Victim and martyr weren't great places to hang out and involved the kind of gaggy stuff that drove Elijah nuts. But average guy—he'd never known he could be one of those. The more he wrote, the more he believed that's exactly who he was.

The end of the first week in October, he showed the essay to Baz. By then it was twenty thousand words. Elijah had ideas on how he could tone it down to something a little more sane, but he wanted Baz to see the whole thing. Unadulterated and raw. Elijah Prince, no filter.

When Elijah began to fidget as he read, Baz plunked him in front of *Howl's Moving Castle* and disappeared into the practice room to digest it properly, as he put it. Lejla drifted in almost immediately to watch with him, snuggling into the other end of the sofa.

"He really is your Howl, you know," she said as they finished the scene where Howl rescued Sophie by teaching her how to walk on air. "He's better with you, and you've found your true strengths by being with him. You bloom together."

Elijah squirmed under Lejla's microscope. "My parents are the Witch of the Waste, I suppose?"

"Maybe. Except we're always our own villains in the end. Which makes them easy to defeat, once we're ready to admit we were the only ones in our own way."

There was nothing to say to that, so they enjoyed the movie in companionable silence. It distracted Elijah from the fact that Baz was taking forever, that they were all the way to the moving spell part of the movie before he emerged from the practice room. It was one of Elijah's favorite parts because he loved watching the castle transform, how Sophie briefly lost her spell as Howl gave her the special room with the flower fields. Baz perched on the edge of the couch through that part, his fingers sneaking into Elijah's hair as Sophie transformed at the water's edge and confessed she felt at home. When she stopped believing in herself and reverted to an old woman as the warships passed overhead, Baz tugged Elijah's hand and led him up the stairs to their room. Once the door was closed, he switched the lights, took off his glasses, and held Elijah's face in his hands.

"I love your story. It made me cry twice. I read it three times and then sat with my eyes closed, swimming in it, before I could come out and tell you."

Elijah wanted to fidget under this attention too, but he couldn't get away from Baz, with or without his glasses. "It's too long. I have to cut it down."

"Why? I think you should keep going. I think you should make it a whole book."

Now Elijah did try to draw back. "Are you nuts? I can't write a memoir at twenty."

"Why not? You've lived more life than most sixty-year-olds. Your story will mean more to most people too." He led Elijah to the bed and sat beside him, still holding his hand. "The other day I was at lunch with Kelly, and the busboy asked for my autograph. Because he knew about our story, about the shooting, and followed the stuff that dribbled out about us during Mom's campaign. I felt weird about it, but Kelly pointed out it wasn't about me. It was about the kid feeling my story—*our* story—helped him find his way. That was him responding to some sound bites. Can you imagine if he had a story like yours to find? I know it's not your fantasy story, and I'm not dismissing it.

But this is important too. I know Walter said you could make it whatever you want, but I know my Elijah. You want to clean up. And this is one hell of a mop and bucket."

It was true. The thought of writing something which could make a difference for other kids with shitty parents, or in any kind of crap circumstance, really, was a heady prospect. The idea that he, Elijah Prince, was good enough to be such spokesperson, though, gave him serious pause. "It's not good enough for that yet."

"It's an excellent start, and there's no rush." He kissed Elijah sweetly on the mouth, nuzzled his nose. "Just remember Sophie has more powerful magic than Howl. She breaks her spell by using it. She breaks everybody's spell. And lives happily ever after."

It was a mushy, sappy, *Disney* moment. And God help him, Elijah waded right in. "Sophie has Howl with her, though. In her ever after."

"So do you, baby. So do you."

Chapter Twenty-Six

A S OCTOBER ROLLED on, Baz's relationship with his mother was chilly. Money still rolled anywhere he wanted it just for asking, but the cozy feeling of being united with his mother against the world had ended. This state of affairs only further served to draw attention to the people he *did* feel connected to, and that number had somehow become legion. His posse formed an honor guard around him whenever he felt vulnerable. They made the switch to healthy living with him and Elijah, and now it was pretty standard for them to start the mornings with yoga in the living room, some private prayer or meditation, and then a breakfast of oatmeal, fruit and veggie smoothies, and green tea.

They ran the blender while Baz took his shower.

He couldn't stop hoping for a reconciliation with his mother, but as absorbed in her campaign as she was, there was no way this could happen unless he dove back into her crazy—an invitation she kept extending, subtly, then overtly.

When these efforts failed, she politicked him.

In mid-October when he was on the way to rehearsal, the choir director pulled Baz aside. "We've had a request come in to the department." Nussy put his hands in his pockets and gave Baz a solemn look. "A local gala event wants Salvo and the Ambassadors to perform for a function mid-November. They're offering a rather handsome fee to the department, and the request is coming in from one of our biggest patrons. But it's my understanding this situation might be awkward for you, and I want you to know, if you ask me to decline, I'll do it."

Baz sighed. "Let me guess. It's my mother."

Nussy nodded. "Technically it's not a campaign event, or we'd have to say no because of college policy. It's a charity function."

But it was probably the result of some kind of focus group, something to improve her image. "It's here in the Cities, not in Illinois?"

"Yes, at a community center in Burnsville. The money raised will go to local efforts to combat LGBT youth homelessness."

Baz set his teeth. *Well played, Mom.* "Hard to say no, isn't it?"

Nussy held up his hands. "I leave it entirely up to you."

Yes, because who wants to be the one who says we can't sing and dance to keep kids off the streets? Baz forced a smile. "Sounds great."

Smiling, Nussy clamped a hand on his shoulder. "Excellent. I trust you'll come up with something special to dazzle them. Maybe a joint number, I thought."

Baz passed the news on to the others as they returned to the White House, and everyone was pretty much as pissed as he expected, which in a weird way was comforting. Elijah surprised him, however, by saying he should have declined.

"But *how*?" They were lying in bed together, red lights on, staring at the ceiling. "How could I look him in the eye and say, *Sure, fuck the homeless gay kids anyway?*"

"First of all, let's get one thing straight. While it's true Halcyon Center and other local organizations might get some funding, this event is largely to make your mom and local politicians look good. If they really wanted to help homeless kids, they'd skip the place plates and expensive napkins and maximize the money donated, not the quality of attendees. God, I hope they leave the actual recipients out of it. If a ragged set of L and G and B and T stand on the stage like sad sacks holding up a giant check, I'll punch somebody in the face."

Well now Baz felt worse. "You think I should tell Nussy to cancel?"

Elijah sighed. "No. But God, I wish you could find a way to sandbag her with this."

"Sabotage it? How will that help anything?"

"Not *it*. Sabotage *her*." Elijah smiled evilly in the red glow. "Make her sorry. Show her she can't fuck with you."

Baz had no idea how to do this, though, and Elijah admitted he didn't either. So Aaron and Giles started drafting options for joint numbers, and Baz did his best not to think about it.

Then one day as Baz crossed the U of M campus, leaving coffee with Walter to have lunch with Marius before cabbing over to Halcyon, he ran into Susan Meeks.

She didn't have on a power suit today, but she wore it on the inside because when she approached Baz and shook his hand, asking him how he was doing, he could practically *see* the metaphorical camera and microphone. Which meant he was honest in his reply, but careful.

"I'm okay. Getting crazy close to graduating, something I was starting to think I'd never do. I'm in love with my boyfriend. Surrounded by friends. So all in all, pretty good."

Susan tucked a strand of hair behind her ear. "I know you said you're not interested in a full interview right now, but if you ever change your mind, I'd love to do a feature on you for the paper. I mean, I'll be honest, I'd love to do a full-on documentary for my senior project, but mostly I want to get your story out there. Not your mom's. Yours. You're an incredible inspiration."

"If you're looking for inspiration, you need to catch my boyfriend's act." He was saying *boyfriend* too much, but he kind of wanted to tattoo the word across his shoulders right now. "I might be the flashy one, but he's the meat and potatoes. Plus he's writing a book, so he'll need the publicity."

"Okay, I'll bear it in mind. I didn't realize he was on the menu—he seemed so uninterested in the spotlight. But I'm down, totally. You'll put him in touch with me when he's ready?" She passed over a business card. "I'd do something on the two of you, you know. I've been tracking your story and his for most of this year, and it's completely gripping. You really found out who you are, the two of you together. It's more than overcoming. It's that you're real. Your compasses are *on point*. You don't let people make you do anything you don't want to do, and when you do something, you own it. *That's* the article I want to write." She smiled, and the internal power suit bloomed. "Unless I can talk you into a documentary."

Laughing, Baz held up his hands in surrender. "We'll see."

Her comments rang with him all day. He realized she was right. When he wanted to reach for it, his compass *was* on point. But as it came time for him to leave the White House for the special Salvo-Ambassadors practice, getting ready for his mother's event, he got annoyed. He hoped Susan didn't see this because this *wasn't* his compass driving him. He didn't own it.

"You'll be fine," Elijah assured him when he voiced this frustration out loud. "You'll figure out how to own it. To make her squirm and the charity shine." He picked up the remote and waved Baz gently at the door. "Now, not to be rude, but we can discuss this later. Lejla and I have a date with the queen." He settled into the couch and his happy place as *RuPaul's Drag Race* came on.

Baz stared at the TV, and as he watched the drag queen own the airwaves, the shard of a crazy idea formed in his mind. He went to his room to call Damien because he figured if anyone would tell him he was nuts, it was him.

"It's not nuts." Damien laughed, a delicious, vindictive chuckle. "It's genius. *Evil* genius."

"Seriously? You don't think it would be inappropriate?"

"How could it be? It's an LGBT event. And yet it would be the last thing your mom's focus groups would want to see."

"Would it reflect badly on the Ambassadors or Salvo, though? Because in my head, I'm going hard. If there aren't gasps and shocked whispers, we're doing it wrong."

"It'll look like kids having fun, which is exactly what it'll be. But if you're worried, have that guy you work with help you. And his dancer husband."

Christ, Baz could only imagine the fun Ed and Laurie would have with this. "So you think I should go for it? Tell Aaron and Giles and Mina, and line it up?"

"Yes, but only on one condition."

"And that is?"

"You let Marius and I come along to do the number."

Baz grinned, the whole thing laying out beautifully in his mind's eye. "I'm pretty sure it can be arranged."

ELIJAH DIDN'T KNOW what in the hell his housemates were doing for the charity concert, only that everyone seemed to be in on the act except him. They were always having meetings in the practice room, usually punctuated by laughter and frantic, giggled protestations to *shh*. It also involved all of them—except Elijah—hauling ass into Saint Paul to some studio near Halcyon Center. They would tell Elijah exactly nothing, except *you'll see*. Every single Ambassador was involved, and Salvo, as well as Marius and Damien for some reason no one would explain. Giles and Aaron had arranged the music, so of course they were both neck-deep. Lejla was in it too, somehow, which didn't seem remotely fair. When Elijah found out even Brian was in on the gig though, he got pissed.

"Don't take it that way," Brian urged him. "I only got involved because they need me for lights and tech. Baz wants to go without his glasses, which means a few precautions. I played with some different filters, and if he uses heavily tinted contacts and we make sure nothing's too bright, he should be okay. I should be able to make it work."

"Make *what* work? Why won't anybody tell me?"

"Because Baz wants to surprise you."

That's what they all kept telling him. *Baz wants to surprise you.*

It was the only thing Elijah was looking forward to at the event. It was the same kind of fancy-pantsy deal as the horrible house party, except bigger and in a community center, not a house. The meal was fifty dollars a plate, choice of salmon, steak, gluten free, or vegan option. The theme was *rainbow with some more rainbow*—tastefully done, each table a subtle shift in gradient, the decorations running the rainbow spectrum with a display of flowers. Elijah couldn't help comparing it to Walter and Kelly's actually gay wedding, which while cheesy at least had some personality.

During dessert, there would be the presentation of a big cardboard check to the center directors. Salvo and the Ambassadors would perform to conclude the evening. No homeless LGBT kids would be in attendance, but Elijah wondered how many would be huddled against city Dumpsters that night, no meal option of any kind in sight.

There were no place cards at this dinner, and he was able to sit with Kelly and Walter at a table near one of the reserved rounds at the front. To his relief, they didn't know what the performance would be either.

"All I know is it's epic," Kelly said. "Marius falls into bed every night. And keeps complaining about his calves."

"I've got my camera ready to video." Walter patted his suit-coat pocket.

There were plenty of cameras in the room, local press and a few national. Elijah was surprised, though, to see Susan, the U of M reporter Baz had introduced him to the other day. She waved at him when they made eye contact, then went back to setting up her team's gear.

Gloria presented the check, beaming as the spotlight made the silver sequins on her gown glitter. Once the ceremony was over, she milled around the room shaking hands and smiling while they waited for the show to start. She looked pleased, triumphant. Elijah thought he recognized a face here and there, which

meant some of these people had come all the way from
Chicago.

Elijah hated how she was getting political capital
from the backs of people who had so little. He hated
that she had maneuvered Baz into performing for her.
He knew they had some scheme, that the performance
was supposed to put her in her place or something, but
as he watched Gloria beam, Elijah didn't have a lot of
confidence.

He did his best to make peace with it. His life was
with Baz, which meant his life would include at least a
little Gloria Barnett Acker. He told himself he could
bide his time, get the lay of the land, and figure out
how to be a thorn in her side. Because she might have
won this battle, but when the prize was Baz, there was
no way he'd let her win the war.

The lights went down, a hush fell over the room,
and Elijah turned toward the stage with the others,
ready to see what the fuss had been about.

When the lights came up, they were subtle. The
stage glowed more than it shone, and it was dotted with
shadowed figures. Trench coats with the collars up and
fedoras for the guys, and one of the girls—who in Salvo
was that tall?—in full-on fuck-me heels and sex-kitten
sequins in the center. All of them had their backs to the
audience, and the lights cast them in shadow.

Then the girl in the middle cocked a hip, shot an
arm in the air—and Baz's voice called out over the
sound system, "*You. Better. Work.*"

The lights went up the rest of the way, the trench
coats fell. Everyone on stage turned around, and

Elijah's jaw fell into his lap.

Baz. It was Baz in the fuck-me heels and dress.

He was in full fucking drag, and the guys who'd shed the trench coats weren't guys at all. They were the members of Salvo. As the girls beat-boxed, the rest of the Ambassadors sashayed onto the stage, looking like refugees from *RuPaul's Drag Race*. Which was appropriate, because they were performing "Sissy That Walk".

Actually, it was a full-on mashup of RuPaul. The girls began in the sidelines, but when "Dance With U" started up, several of them stepped forward to merge with the Ambassadors, playing gallant gentlemen to the Ambassador's sexy ladies. There were two extra Ambassadors, Elijah realized, and one spare Salvo member—Marius and Damien and Lejla. Marius, who'd been growing a beard, was working some serious Conchita Wurst. Damien had his glasses off and looked pretty damn fly. Lejla was very Victor-Victoria.

Through it all, though, Baz was center stage. No glasses—the contacts *were* weird, and he'd have looked freakish in everyday wear, but in drag they worked pretty well. He wore a waist-length strawberry-blonde wig of artfully arranged curls, more eye makeup than he had eyes to put it on, and one hell of a rack. Because Elijah watched him the most, he noticed Baz was a little bit Cher, letting everyone else dance while he did subdued variations and largely belted out the melody line. The only time he didn't was when he ground with Damien, Aaron, or Marius, and when Lejla dirty danced in front of him during "Champion".

It was, to put it mildly, a fucking fabulous performance. It was fun and felt edgy without being controversial at all for an LGBT event. College kids in drag, grinding on each other and singing RuPaul. Who cared? A bit of harmless, topical fun.

And *yet*.

Not everyone in the audience felt that way. Yes, the room was full of liberals, but they were older, rich liberals, and only a handful were LGBT themselves. This wasn't the polite, polished, *poor little gay homeless kids* sanitized rainbow they'd signed up for. Certainly no one had ordered up Damien and Marius making an obscene drag-queen sandwich out of Baz as he fanned himself in faux-overstimulation. Nobody asked for Marius to fluff his breasts proudly as he bellowed the bass line.

The best part, though, was the way Baz sang right to his mother during "Sissy That Walk". Delivering the line about only caring about the opinions of people who pay your bills—which, technically, was Gloria. Baz sang the line right at her, as if to say, *Go ahead. Cut me off and see if I care.*

When he sang the line about his pussy being on fire—using the word, not muffling it or bleeping it out—he looked Gloria in the eye, grabbed his crotch and told her to kiss the flame.

Elijah laughed. And clapped, and whooped, and catcalled his heart out.

As the last note rang, the stage full of performers struck a pose, lifted their chins, and basked in their applause. It was decidedly choppy—some tables, like

Elijah's, whistled and shouted their approval. Some clapped more quietly, and a few individuals looked decidedly strained. Gloria Barnett Acker was one of them.

Baz took the microphone, out of breath and smiling.

"We're so proud to be here tonight, raising money for the LGBT youth of the Twin Cities. Saint Timothy was given a stipend to bring us here, but we wanted you to know every penny is going directly to Avenues for Homeless Youth and the Halcyon Center, and after passing a hat around the music building, we'll be adding a not entirely insignificant additional donation of our own."

He paused for applause. Two figures moved out front to stand at the edge of the stage and watch: Ed and Laurie. When Baz spoke next, his smile had faded, his expression serious.

"The truth is, ladies and gentlemen, tonight in this very metropolitan area, possibly in the alley behind this building, young men and women not yet old enough to vote, maybe not even drive a car, are homeless and alone. Some were kicked out of their homes because they're gay. Some left because it was too dangerous to stay. Some will find help at the community organizations you're supporting tonight. Some won't, because there are sadly more LGBT homeless youth than there are people willing to help. Some aren't homeless but living in a different, equally awful kind of hell."

He indicated the line of Salvo and Ambassador members behind him. "We're asking you to do more than write a check. Volunteer at your local centers. Give your time as well as your money. If you have space in your home, become a host home for Avenues and foster some of these youth, to show them love and acceptance in person. If you're a member of a faith organization, ask them if they're doing as much for the homeless youth of Minnesota and Illinois and Wisconsin and Iowa as they are for people hungry in faraway lands."

His gaze flashed like the flicker of a candle toward Elijah. "A lot of us know firsthand how difficult it is to grow up gay, lesbian, bisexual, and transgender. We know what it's like to fear simply being yourself, to know that can be not only scary but dangerous. Life can be hard, and lonely, and cruel. But what we've learned by singing together, by being together, is when we face adversity *together*, we can overcome almost anything. You don't have to put on drag and sing and dance to make a difference. You only have to open your hearts."

Replacing the mic, Baz stepped back into the line of performers. He hadn't given them a clear indication he was done, and before they could fumble around to applause, the soft note of a pitch pipe cut through the silence. Damien, standing next to Baz, counted out quietly, "One, two, three, four."

The tenors and altos began to sing a chord, the goofy *deh, deh, deh, deh* they used to make background notes. Aaron riffed over the top of it, a lot of *yeahs* and *hey-ey* noises before launching into the first verse. Elijah recognized it right away because it was the only song of

Baz's favorite artist, Maino, that Elijah liked: "All the Above". It was kind of a half rap, half R&B, with a guy singing falsetto between Maino rapping about surviving. How he'd been through pain and sorrow, how he'd experienced loss, been covered with scars, but he made it. He gave thanks for his struggles because they defined him.

The song as it was recorded on the album had always given Elijah a slight thrill and a shiver of hope, but when he sat in the front of a rainbow room watching his boyfriend rap in drag about how no matter what happened to him, he would keep going, he would survive—Elijah was moved to his soul.

It was more than an emotional moment. It was a *connection*. It was the song of anyone who had made it, who had been through hell and out the other side again. It was *Elijah*. And Baz, and Aaron, and Giles, and Lejla…it was everyone.

I'm not outside. I'm inside. I'm included in that "all the above". I don't have to be on that stage singing with them. I am with them. I am them.

I belong.

I'm home.

Elijah cried silently, wiping his tears away as discreetly as he could so he could keep watching. So he could see his boyfriend singing to him. Looking right at him, belting out that song for Elijah. For anyone who had survived, who was still working on getting through to the other side.

When they finished, this time the room erupted. Walter and Kelly rose to their feet, whooping and calling out, and Elijah joined the chorus of joy. When Baz led the performers off the stage and into the audience, Elijah went into his lover's embrace with his heart glowing hot and full inside him.

He laughed when Baz pressed Elijah's face into his cleavage.

Walter and Kelly joined them, and Walter grabbed Baz's head and kissed the side of his wig roughly. "One hell of a speech, Acker. Out of the fucking park."

Baz wrapped his arms around Elijah's waist and swayed lightly as dance music began to filter through the speakers. "It started as me trying to get back at my mom. To show her up." He glanced at the room, his expression serious again. "Then I realized she didn't matter. Because all I could think was someone else's Elijah is out on the streets tonight. Someone's Aaron. Somewhere someone is getting smashed with a bat and they won't have a rich uncle to find them super surgeons. All I cared about was driving the point home." He glanced at Elijah, eyes naked and squinting, his emotions bared for the world in the dim ballroom light. "I hope I did okay."

Elijah held Baz's face in his hands, stared into those beautiful, fragile brown eyes. Saw the heart shining through them—Baz's huge, beautiful, perfect heart. "You were wonderful. You're always wonderful."

Baz smiled at him, a bright, boyish beam firing straight into Elijah's soul. Out of the corner of his eye he could see reporters coming their way, and Gloria's staff, and half the goddamned event. Ignoring them all, Baz kissed Elijah. Right there in the middle of the charity ballroom, in full drag, while flashes popped around them.

Focus group that, bitches, Elijah thought, and kissed him back with everything he had.

Epilogue

SEBASTIAN PERCIVAL ACKER graduated in a small mid-year ceremony on the sixteenth of December. It didn't have the full pomp and circumstance of a May graduation, but that was okay with him. His friends were there, and Damien's fiancée, who was graduating too. His favorite professors were all in attendance, as well as Ed and Laurie.

His family came too. His mom and dad were there in the front row, cheering and clapping, and afterward they hugged him, told him they were proud. Then his mom pulled him aside and dropped a bombshell.

"I told the governor to remove my name from consideration for your uncle's senate seat."

Baz did a double take. "You—*what*? Mom, *why*?" He took a good look at her face and got a bad feeling. "Do not say it's because of me. I know you were mad about the Burnsville event—"

She held up a hand to stop him as she shook her head. "It's true, at first I was annoyed with you for the drag stunt. It wasn't part of my plan or my vision, and I was sure you'd done it to get back at me. And then I started getting phone calls. Lots and lots of phone calls, and emails. People from all over the country, the *world*, saying they saw the viral video that university reporter posted of your performance and your speech. Telling me how they were taking action in their cities and states and countries. I can't go anywhere now without someone telling me what a good job I did, what a wonderful cause I've championed." She clasped his hands in hers, and her eyes got damp behind her eighty-dollar mascara. "But it wasn't me who made that happen. That was you. You and your friends, but mostly you, Sebastian. You and your great big heart."

His great big heart swelled in his chest. "But why in the world is it making you quit?"

"Because while I did care about the charities the event served, I was mostly thinking of myself. I wasn't appointed to anything yet, and this was how my career was beginning. I'd told myself all these grand stories of how I'd be a better politician than my brother, than anyone else in Washington—and I failed before I arrived." She wiped at her eyes with a handkerchief Baz's dad passed her. "It made me open my eyes and reexamine everything, including admitting how much I'd already become part of the machine. I was never going to make the kind of difference I wanted. I was going to be exactly what the right-wing blogs said: a pawn to my brother and the party. That's not the career I want. I'm making the announcement tomorrow I'm withdrawing my name to focus on my family."

Baz rolled his eyes. "They're going to think you got caught having an affair."

Gloria pursed her lips. "It's true. I've been focused on my own ambitions and my drive to live up to the

Barnett name. I need to shift my priorities."

Baz would believe his mother would stay home and bake cookies and rub his dad's feet after a long day of work when hell froze over. Though his parents were in the same room, touching each other without a camera aimed on them. Would they be June and Ward Cleaver? No. Could they be something else, though?

He had found happily ever after. Who knows. Maybe they could too.

Sean Acker squeezed Baz's good shoulder. "We're going to stay in town for Christmas at the Barrington Hills house. Will you come?"

"No Christmas parties," his mom said. "I promise. So you can bring Elijah."

Baz ran a hand through his hair nervously. *Still politicking me. Yep, this is my family all right.* "We'll come, sure. But I'll be bringing a fiancé, not a boy-friend."

He'd hoped they'd be excited for him, but it was still a relief to watch their faces light up, to hear his mother squeal, a splashy society wedding exploding in her imagination. "That's *wonderful*. Have you already asked him? How did you do it? Please tell me someone took video."

"I haven't asked yet, no, and it's not going to be videotaped. I was going to take him out to the lake sometime. He wouldn't want anything big and flashy for a proposal, and no audience. We've talked about it, though—not in so many words, but we've made it clear we're permanent, and pretty much our friends are tired of waiting for an announcement." Everyone except

Aaron and Giles, who grumbled about why were people in such a damn rush to get married.

"All right. But I expect the two of you to do karaoke at our New Year's gala."

He laughed and kissed her cheek. "Sure thing."

She kissed him back and told him to call her the moment the engagement was official. And she promised *she* would be answering her phone, not an assistant.

They went home to Chicago, and Baz launched himself into his last days with his Ambassador brothers. He understood now they wouldn't be the last moments at all—the last *official* moments, yes, but he'd be jamming with Ambassadors past and present for the rest of his life. He wasn't moving out of the White House, though he would continue to have a daily commute into Saint Paul to volunteer at Halcyon. He'd met with Oliver Thompson, who had also heard about Baz's gala speech, and was impressed. There were good odds Baz would have a legitimate position at Thompson's charitable foundation before the summer.

The Christmas with Timothy concerts, which came after graduation, were rough. The last one on Sunday was mostly him choking his way through the notes.

It was okay, though. It was bittersweet, but it was still sweet. One part of his life was ending, and another part beginning. As he squeezed Elijah's hand before disappearing with the Ambassadors to sing "Goodbye Cruel World" and receive his sending home, he reminded himself he wouldn't be facing this next chapter alone.

He was still wiped as fuck when he trekked home

with Elijah to the White House. Somehow they ended up trudging through the snow just the two of them. It felt right to finish it with only Elijah by his side. If he weren't so tired, he'd suggest they go out to the lake so he could relieve himself of the ring he kept carrying around in his pocket.

"You doing okay?" Elijah asked as they rounded the corner to their street.

Baz nodded, pulling him closer. "Yeah. Endings are hard, but important. You have to have an end, so you can have another beginning."

"You should put that on a pillow."

Baz tweaked his nose. "I'll go on CafePress and put it on a mug. With me grinning at you beside it. You can drink out of it while you finish your memoir." Fuck, he was totally doing that and rushing it for Christmas.

Elijah punched him lightly in the stomach, but when they stepped onto the porch of the darkened house, Elijah gave Baz a grin, making him look like a cat with a canary in his claws. "You know, I figured something out the other day."

Baz was down for some nails in his back. "What's that?"

"I always make fun of Kelly and Walter for their sappy Mickey Mouse-company moments." Elijah opened the door to the house, pausing with his hand on the light. "Then I realized. Studio Ghibli is based in Japan, but in the United States it's distributed by Disney."

He flipped on the light and revealed a living room

full of Salvo, Ambassadors, Walter, Kelly, Marius, Damien, Brian—basically everybody.

Damien hummed a note, and they started to sing.

Soft and slow, and after a few bars, Baz recognized the tune as "Paradise" by Coldplay. Even Walter and Kelly sang. In the corner, Susan Meeks had her camera rolling, and she was nothing but grin.

As Elijah led Baz to a chair and took off his glasses, Brian flipped the lights to a muted version of the one they'd used for the LGBT event and the singers hit the first verse. The opening had been rewritten to something similar but notably different than what Coldplay sang.

"When you were just a boy, you lost hold of your joy."

The rest of the verse was the same, mostly—they sang at Baz how he couldn't reach happiness, so he'd dreamed of it instead. The second verse, though, departed from the original entirely.

"Then you met another boy, who also lost hold of his joy. But he didn't know how to dream, so he hid away in the streets. He had no paradise."

Baz's breath caught, and he blinked as Elijah stood in front of him, looking a little nervous. He hadn't sung with them yet, but after the series of *la-la-la*s, he sang along with the others, exchanging their "him" for "me".

"You showed me how to escape the lonely nights. You say, 'Hold on, hold on, I know together we will rise.'"

Baz gave up, letting the tears well up as Elijah sang to him—words Baz knew his boyfriend had rewritten. Lyrics cheesy as *hell*. So fucking perfect, zinging right into Baz's heart.

"You taught me paradise."

By the time the song finished, Baz was weeping like an idiot.

Elijah had got on his knees. With a ring, and as the last note rang away, he popped the question. "Sebastian Percival Acker, will you marry me?"

"*Yes*, you jerk. I was *going* to ask you tomorrow at the lake," he said, his voice breaking, partly on a sob, partly on a laugh.

"I know, but it wouldn't have been right for *you*. You want a little bit of show. And yeah, maybe I like it quieter, but when you're part of the performance, I don't mind the stage." Elijah kissed away his tears. "I know where you keep your heart, Sebastian."

Baz dragged Elijah off his knees and onto his lap. "Yes." He pressed the flat of his hand over the fluttering organ inside Elijah's chest. "It's right here."

About the Author

Heidi Cullinan has always enjoyed a good love story, provided it has a happy ending. Proud to be from the first Midwestern state with full marriage equality, Heidi is a vocal advocate for LGBT rights. She writes positive-outcome romances for LGBT characters struggling against insurmountable odds because she believes there's no such thing as too much happy ever after. When Heidi isn't writing, she enjoys cooking, reading, playing with her cats, and watching anime, with or without her family. Find out more about Heidi at heidicullinan.com.

Did you enjoy this book?

If you did, please consider leaving a review online or recommending it to a friend. There's absolutely nothing that helps an author more than a reader's enthusiasm. Your word of mouth is greatly appreciated and helps me sell more books, which helps me write more books.

MORE BOOKS IN THE LOVE LESSONS SERIES

Love Lessons (also available in audio and German)

When Kelly arrives at Hope University, he realizes finding his Prince Charming isn't easy. Worst of all, he's landed the charming, handsome, gay campus Casanova as a roommate, whose bed might as well be equipped with a revolving door. Walter thinks everyone is better off having as much fun as possible…except his shy, sad little roommate is seriously screwing up his worldview. As Walter lures Kelly out of his shell, he discovers love is a crash course. To make the grade, he'll have to overcome his own private fear that love was never meant to last.

Frozen Heart

Walter Lucas knows his boyfriend has been looking forward to the newest Walt Disney movie, *Frozen*, but he isn't prepared for the reality that is the front row seat of Kelly Davidson's cartoon obsession. However, there's more going on in November than just the movie—a certain question Walter has been waiting quite some time to ask.

Fever Pitch (also available in audio and German)

Aaron Seavers isn't excited about going to college until he meets (and makes out with) Giles Mulder at a graduation party. But Giles isn't so happy when Aaron turns up at his college, bringing dark memories of their hometown with him. Just when they begin to successfully navigate an undergraduate relationship, Aaron's parents and a campus tragedy threaten to bring their bright crescendo to a shattering end.

Short Stay

Baz and Elijah, looking to escape a pressure-filled New Year's Eve party in Chicago, run away with Walter and Kelly to Las Vegas. But they accidentally packed their troubles in the Tesla, and it's clear what happens in Vegas isn't going to stay there. With the help of new friends and old, Baz and Elijah face—and confess—their fears together...and have a whole new set of adventures.

Rebel Heart (coming 2017)

Other books by Heidi Cullinan

There's a lot happening with my books right now! Sign up for my **release-announcement-only newsletter** on my website to be sure you don't miss a single release or rerelease.

www.heidicullinan.com/newssignup

Want the inside scoop on upcoming releases, automatic delivery of all my titles in your preferred format, with option for signed paperbacks shipped worldwide? Consider joining my Patreon. You can learn more about it on my website.

www.patreon.com/heidicullinan

THE ROOSEVELT SERIES
Carry the Ocean
Shelter the Sea
Unleash the Earth (coming soon)
Shatter the Sky (coming soon)

THE DANCING SERIES
Dance With Me *(also available in French, Italian coming soon)*
Enjoy the Dance
Burn the Floor (coming soon)

MINNESOTA CHRISTMAS SERIES
Let It Snow
Sleigh Ride
Winter Wonderland
Santa Baby
More adventures in Logan, Minnesota, coming soon

CLOCKWORK LOVE SERIES
Clockwork Heart
Clockwork Pirate (coming soon)
Clockwork Princess (coming soon)

SPECIAL DELIVERY SERIES
Special Delivery (also available in German)
Hooch and Cake (coming soon)
Double Blind (also available in German)
The Twelve Days of Randy (coming soon)
Tough Love

TUCKER SPRINGS SERIES
Second Hand (written with Marie Sexton) (available in French)
Dirty Laundry (available in French)
(more titles in this series by other authors)

SINGLE TITLES

Antisocial (coming June 2017)
Nowhere Ranch (available in Italian)
Family Man (written with Marie Sexton)
A Private Gentleman
The Devil Will Do
Hero
Miles and the Magic Flute

NONFICTION

Your A Game: Winning Promo for Genre Fiction
(written with Damon Suede)

Many titles are also available in audio and more are in production. Check the listings wherever you purchase audiobooks to see which titles are available.